CONTRACTUALLY YOURS

NADIA LEE

To Mom. Thank you for teaching me how to be a strong woman.

1

LUCIENNE

NOBODY SHOULD FEEL like murder when they're listening to "Il est né le divin enfant." Especially when it's coming from a TV above a fireplace full of merrily dancing orange flames in an opulent five-bedroom suite in the middle of Paris.

And yet...

"What do you think?"

I stare at the string of akoya pearls around my half-sister Vonnie's neck. Rage beats in my chest like an imprisoned falcon. The luster on the pearls is amazing, and the size is also good at eight millimeters each.

Those are *my* pearls, the ones my mom gave me last week. She was sorry she missed my ballet recital because Vonnie cut her finger—probably on purpose—and Dad insisted Mom stay home to help deal with the injury. And of course Mom can never say no to Dad.

"At least I sent Matthias," she said as she presented me with the pearls. Like sending the butler made everything better.

Matthias seems to live his life on Mom's behalf. He dutifully filmed my part of the recital and gave me a bouquet of red carnations. Mom said my Sugar Plum Fairy from *The Nutcracker* was fabulous—of course, I actually danced *Swan Lake*.

"Give it back," I say to Vonnie. "That necklace is mine."

"So? Don't be such a greedy bitch, Lucienne. Didn't Daddy tell you to share?" Vonnie sneers, her dark eyes flashing with envy and entitlement, then taps her fraternal twin Karl on the back of the neck, which is covered with brown, shaggy hair.

He doesn't look up from his phone. "What Vonnie said."

She gives me a smug smile. Even when Karl thinks he has better things to do—like texting with his friends—he'll always be on Team Vonnie. Every time Mom and Dad want to know why Vonnie and I are fighting, Karl always says something to paint me as the bad guy. Even when his lies are nonsensical and idiotic, they buy them.

And it has emboldened Vonnie.

There's nothing of mine she doesn't covet. If she could, she'd filch my clothes. But even though I'm only fourteen, I'm already taller than her. Nothing of mine would fit.

"It's stealing if you take what's not yours without permission," I point out. I'm tired of having to fight Vonnie and Karl for what's mine. Although Karl doesn't steal my jewelry, he's taken four hundred bucks right out of my wallet. And when I brought it up with Dad, he looked at me like I was the villain.

"It isn't that much money," he said with a heavy sigh and a frown of sheer disapproval and disappointment. It never fails to make me feel like an outsider in my own family. "I don't know why you have to make a fuss."

Vonnie's sneer grows uglier and more superior. "It's not stealing! Daddy said it was fine!"

"Daddy isn't the one who gave it to me! My mom did!" I shoot back. "Give it back!"

"Bitch." Vonnie pulls the pearls to her mouth and licks them, making sure to cover them with her saliva.

"Ew, that's gross!"

"You said you wanted them back, but you didn't say I couldn't lick them!"

I've had enough! I march toward the upper level, where the bedrooms are. The double doors to my parents' room are slightly ajar, and I lift my hands to push them open. But voices coming from inside stop me in my tracks. One belongs to Dad, but the other one isn't Mom's. It's Gwen's.

What's that skank doing in the master bedroom?

My father's secretary is the worst kind of human being in the world. Her duties apparently include getting naked with him. *So disgusting*—I caught them at it three years ago. The saddest thing is that nobody believed me. Mom said I shouldn't confuse dreams with reality and talk about my nightmares like they were real, because I could hurt people. It never seemed to occur to her that I wasn't making up anything or that, as an eleven-year-old, I was too young to have disgusting dreams about Dad and Gwen rolling around bare-assed in bed.

"Why do you want to teach Lucienne how to share?" comes Gwen's voice. "Just buy Karl and Vonnie what they want and be done with it. It isn't like you're poor."

"This isn't about the kids fighting. It's about what happens after Olivia's gone. Wilhelm doesn't consider Karl or Vonnie his own," Dad says like it's the most unfair thing in the world.

But why *would* Grandpa? Karl and Vonnie are from Dad's previous marriage.

"When Lucienne was born," Dad says, "the old man officially made her a Peery, so as to show everyone *she* was his heir, but not Karl or Vonnie. Only a Peery is worthy of the Peery Diamonds fortune in that man's eyes." Dad's voice seethes with resentment. "Which means if *Olivia* isn't around, I'll have to get the money through *Lucienne*. If I don't teach her to be nicer, how am I going to get her to cough up anything?"

"But the laws of Nesovia are on your side. You're her father."

"Yes, and thank God for that."

I bite my lip, not really following the conversation. Peery Diamonds is incorporated in Nesovia, I know that much, but I never spent much time there. I was born in L.A. during one of Mom's vacations in SoCal, and mostly raised there.

"But things would be better if she'd never been born. Then Wilhelm wouldn't have anybody to leave his money to other than Karl and Vonnie."

I take an unsteady step back as a combination of shock and pain reverberates through me. I've always known that Dad likes Karl and Vonnie more. He was always nicer to them, more indulgent. He said I was too willful and toxic. Too tall, too wild, too...everything. Just too much.

But to learn that he wishes I'd *never been born*? It's like I'm not even his child.

"Heard enough?" Vonnie's whisper into my ear might as well be a crow cawing in victory.

I turn my head slowly to stare at her. I didn't realize she followed me upstairs. Her dark eyes flash with glee. Tossing her long chocolate-colored hair, she gives me a smile.

"Nobody wants you here, Lucienne," Vonnie says. "Why do you think not even Olivia wants to bother with you these days?"

The barb hits home. The recital wasn't the only thing Mom couldn't bother with. There's been a string of disappointments, all because Dad, Karl or Vonnie needed her. Mom doesn't seem to care that I'm her child and need her, too.

"Things would be so much better without you." Vonnie smirks, running her finger along the pearl necklace still around her neck.

I want to launch myself at her and rip her face off. But I know from experience that if I do, I'll be blamed and punished. And there's no point in calling for Mom. She isn't somebody I can count on.

But I can't stay in the suite with these...assholes, either. I storm out, slamming the door behind me. If Mom hears me, she doesn't come out. Probably has more important things to do. Like... I don't know. Literally anything in the world.

I take the elevator to the lobby. Nobody stops me—it's like they know I should be on my way out, since I'm not wanted here.

Tears spring to my eyes as my sneakered feet slap the wintry streets of Paris, but I blink them away. The wind slips cold fingers into my sweater and runs them along my skin, leaving goosebumps. Snow falls soundlessly, muffling the sounds of the city. Lights are everywhere, turning the crystal flakes red and green in the Christmas festivities. Somewhere a group of kids is singing carols.

Those kids all belong somewhere. They're all wanted somewhere.

I don't fit. The realization slides into me like a rusty nail. Mom had me because that's what Grandfather wanted. He needed an heir he could leave Peery Diamonds to because he thinks Mom is too flighty and weak-willed to run a big corporation. He's disappointed I'm a girl—I can see it in his gaze every time he looks at me, because girls are soft and sentimental and unfit to take on the family legacy, the all-important company. Dad and his other kids—the ones he treats like his own—only tolerate me.

I wish Bianca were here, but she's spending Christmas with her family in the States. My best friend's family loves her, unlike mine. They hug her, ask about the details of her life and feed her like she's been through a famine.

I'd do anything to trade places, but... I shake myself mentally. It would be cruel and unusual punishment to make my bestie to go through what I'm going through.

I walk aimlessly along the streets, shoulders raised high. I wish I'd grabbed a coat before leaving the hotel, but I'd rather jump off a bridge than go back for one now.

Is there anyone who gives a damn about me? If I freeze to death tonight...will anyone care?

I picture Mom's face crumbling with shock and sorrow, but then I shake off the imagery. It's pointless, wishful thinking on my part. She'll just get distracted as usual because Karl or Vonnie needs her. She doesn't care that they're only nice to her because she's an heiress. If she hears them calling her a sucker behind her back, she doesn't show it.

Time passes. I stop when I can't feel my face anymore. I look around. The streetlamps are blurred like starbursts and my breath turns white in the air.

A guy says something in French near me, but I don't even turn to look. He's probably out here in this beautiful city with somebody who likes him. Bet he has a welcoming home to go to. A family that adores him.

Okay, no more self-pity. If people could read my mind, they'd call me entitled and spoiled. I should be grateful for what I have—the wealth of Peery Diamonds, what it represents. I have nice, expensive things most people can't even dream of owning.

A light tap on my shoulder. "*Est-ce que tu vas bien?*"

I turn around and see a tall, dark-haired man standing behind me. He's gorgeous—slightly slanted dark eyebrows over brilliant eyes, a straight nose and surprisingly full mouth that looks like it should be reciting some romantic French poem. *Maybe he's a model*, I think, taking in his presence, his black cashmere coat. He most definitely has somewhere to go, people who are waiting for him.

Suddenly, I feel shabby and small. And I don't want his pity or sympathy. I want to cling to what little pride I have left, since I don't have anything else.

"I don't speak French," I lie. I try to say it in my most unfriendly, leave-me-alone tone, but I can't hide the shakiness or the chattering of my teeth now that I've opened my mouth. I clench my jaw shut.

"Are you American?" he says in perfect English, his voice a low baritone that reminds me of caramel.

"Yeah. So?"

"Where are your parents?" He looks around.

I don't want to think about my parents. Another gust of wind cuts through me. Uncontrollable shivers rack my body.

"You're freezing." He shrugs out of his coat and wraps it around my shoulders. The heat from the cashmere is like a warm bath, sending little shocks through my system as my body begins to thaw. The garment is long enough to shield me from neck to ankles, and I realize how harshly the winter wind has been clawing at me. "I don't need your coat." As soon as the words slip out, I wince at how bratty I sound.

"Your teeth disagree." A corner of his lips quirks a little.

Okay, so he heard my teeth chatter. I should probably shrug his coat off, but my shoulders refuse to move. My whole body is reveling in its warmth and its soft, clean smell of soap and pine. "Aren't you cold?"

He shrugs his broad shoulders. He's wearing a dark sweater and slacks, probably made of wool. The wind ruffles his hair, and he runs his fingers through it, easily putting it back in place.

If I were just a normal kid, I might be overcome with gratitude. But people are never nice to me just because. Maybe he's a model who needs work. Or maybe he expects some money from my family for helping me. He wouldn't be the first.

"Do you know who I am?" I ask stiffly.

He looks amused. "No. Should I?"

"Why are you being so nice to me, then?"

"Because you're obviously cold."

"So you've decided to give up your coat and be cold instead?"

"I'm warm enough." He smiles charmingly.

It doesn't make me feel better. It only reminds me of how easily Dad charms Mom, making her swoon and call him her "prince."

So gross.

It's wrong to be upset with this stranger for being nice, but the bitterness that's been accumulating in my heart won't shut up. "That makes you stupid, not charming," I spit out, expecting a fight.

He laughs. "Well. I guess I'll be stupid, then."

Suddenly, all my resentment and anger drain away, replaced by shame. I'm just being bitchy when he's been nothing but sweet. "I'm sorry," I say. "I'm not having a good day, but I shouldn't be rude to you."

"Apology accepted," he says lightly. "So... You lost? Need help finding your parents or something?"

He wants to take me back to my parents, like a responsible adult. But I don't want to go back. Not right now. Maybe not ever. "I'm just out for a walk."

"A walk, huh?" A skeptical eyebrow jumps up.

Of course, nobody goes out for a walk in nothing but a light shirt, jeans and sneakers in the snow. But I'm not going to explain.

There's a pause while we stand there in the snowfall. Finally he says, "Okay, well... Are you done with your walk?"

"Actually, I just want something warm to drink." That's better than admitting I have no place to go back to. Or at least no place that'll welcome me.

"Fine."

I expect him to take his coat and go on his way, but he puts a hand on my back and escorts me down the street like a gentleman. When we start to approach a brightly lit hotel, I slow down.

"Um..." I say, suddenly unsure about following him. All sorts of awful crime headlines flash through my mind.

"What?" He laughs softly. "You said you wanted something warm to drink. The hotel will have something. There's a bar and café in the lobby."

Sure enough, the hotel's huge first-floor windows show people inside, waving their drinks around and laughing. Even in the cold, my cheeks start to heat with embarrassment.

We step inside, and he takes me to a booth in a quiet corner of the lobby away from the boisterous crowd. He speaks to a uniformed clerk in French and returns to me. "They'll bring out some hot chocolate. That's okay, right?"

"Yeah."

The hot chocolate quickly appears, along with a glass of some amber liquid for him. The waitress gives Mr. Coat a flirty smile, but his smile back just seems to be polite. He seems really at ease with everything and everyone around him.

In the brighter light, I can see his eyes are an odd mixture of gold and green. Something about him reminds me of a satisfied lion after a successful hunt. I saw it on a nature special once. It's weird that he's being kind without expecting anything in return. People are always nice to me because they think it might get them something. My grandfather can be a generous man, and he's *really* generous when it involves his flesh and blood.

But maybe this man really is being good to me just because. I don't know what to make of it.

I take a small sip of the chocolate. The steaming, bittersweet flavor is amazing after the chill outside, and I shiver as the heat seeps through me. "You're pretty nice for an old guy."

He almost chokes on his drink. "I'm twenty-three."

"Like I said."

"Oh yeah? How old are you?"

"Fourteen."

He smirks. "Just a kid."

I open my mouth to say I'm not just a kid, but...I am. "Yeah. A dumb kid."

Sympathy softens his tone. "You don't seem dumb to me. If you were, you wouldn't be wearing my coat. Or getting me to buy you a drink."

I laugh a little at his attempt to cheer me up. "If I were smart, I wouldn't have been out there. If I were smart... Well, people might take me more seriously. They might love—care about me more."

He frowns. "You break up with your boyfriend or something?"

Maybe it's because his voice is soft and without judgment that the dam in my heart cracks. Or maybe it's because we don't know each other, and the anonymity lets me vent. "My dad only cares about me because of money, and my grandfather is disappointed I'm not a boy."

"How about your mother?"

"Mom's too busy with everything and everyone else but me."

"Ah. So you got upset and ran."

"Yeah." Now I feel stupid about everything. "It's like, maybe they'll be happier without me."

"Is that what you want?"

"What do you mean?"

"Do you want to just run away from everything, so they'll be happy?"

Run away from everything... I blink. What does that even mean? "Everything" would include Mom, who doesn't love me enough to put me first, but who's the only parent who seems to care about me at all... and my inheritance and my position as the sole heiress to the Peery Diamonds fortune...

Dad, Karl and Vonnie would love it if I vanished. They'd start drooling, dreaming up ways to divvy up all the stuff I leave behind.

It's gross. I'd rather set everything on fire than let them have anything of mine. They aren't worthy.

The man says, "You're scowling. I guess that's your answer."

"Yeah. But they just want to use me and hurt me." I look down at the steaming chocolate. "They just want my money."

"More reason to stay and fight for what's yours. If you leave, you're surrendering. Instead, even the scales."

"How?"

"Take away what they want the most from you. You said they want your money, so make sure they never get a penny. You're young, so they'll push back when you try. But keep on fighting until you win, no matter what it takes, or how long it takes. Don't give them an inch."

I give him a long look, wondering if he's just saying things. "Is that what you would do? I mean, for real?"

He leans forward, glancing around like a spy. "Want to know a secret? I'm doing it right now."

"No way! Somebody wants your money?" He doesn't seem poor or anything, and he's dressed in designer clothes, but...

He laughs. "My situation is a little more complicated."

"Are you winning?"

"I'm getting there." He smiles. "But I'll win in the end."

His eyes gleam with confidence. And why wouldn't he radiate self-assurance? He's good looking and seems smart and well off.

Meanwhile, I can't even make my own mother believe me.

"Well, that's great for you," I say. "But like you said, you aren't in my situation."

"Don't be so down on yourself. Look, if you don't respect yourself enough to fight for what's yours, everyone'll just walk all over you. The first time asserting yourself is the hardest. But it gets easier."

I think about that while finishing my hot chocolate. *Maybe I didn't fight that hard.* Even though I was boiling over with anger, I have to admit that I'm still concerned with fitting in. With having Mom look at me like she loves me.

He doesn't say anything else. Instead, he nurses his drink. When I'm done, I stand up. "Thanks for the hot chocolate. I think I need to get back." I start to shrug off the coat, but he puts a hand on my shoulder.

"Keep it. Let me walk to your place."

"I know how to get there. And it's freezing out. I don't want you to catch cold or something."

He nods and gestures at a uniformed concierge who's walking by. He instructs him to bring a car. "The hotel will drive you home. I can't let a kid like you wander around Paris at night, especially when you don't even speak the language."

I feel a little guilty for lying about my French. "Maybe you should take a car to your place too," I say.

"I'm actually here to see a friend, so..."

"Oh."

The concierge returns, saying the car's ready.

"Thank you," I say to the man, extending a hand.

He shakes it, his palm shockingly hot against mine, then frowns. "Your hand's icy."

"It'll warm up after a hot shower. Anyway, since I'm taking the car..." I try again to give the coat back, but he waves me off.

"You're still cold. You need it more than me."

"But—"

He's already walking away to the elevator bank.

The concierge clears his throat. "Mademoiselle?"

I sigh, then let him lead me to the car. I tell the driver where to go, and he navigates the slushy road expertly. I should send the coat back, I tell myself, but then I realize I have no idea what the man's name is. I shake my head. I can't believe I didn't introduce myself, either. He probably thinks I'm a complete brat. *Ugh.*

It's too late to turn back now because I wouldn't even know what to say. I ask the driver if he saw the man who waved me goodbye in the lobby, but no luck.

Soon I'm back in front of the hotel Mom picked out for the trip. I walk inside. The staff don't stop me, like they know I'm a guest who has every right to be here.

I take the elevator to the top floor, where our suite is. I tighten the coat around myself like armor and keep my chin high as I step into the suite.

"What the hell is the meaning of this? You can't even watch a child?" comes my grandfather's irate voice from the living room. *Oh, that's right...* He's joining us for Christmas in Paris today. "And you kids! You just let her walk out?"

"We didn't know. She snuck out behind our backs," Vonnie says.

I walk inside, the thick carpet muffling my steps. Dad, Karl and Vonnie are standing on one side, with Mom and Grandfather on the other. Mom isn't standing next to Grandfather to render support, but to calm him down so he doesn't yell at Dad too much.

There isn't even a hint of concern for my wellbeing on Dad's face. The only thing that he's worried about is that Grandfather is upset. Dad knows it's Grandfather who controls the money in the family, not Mom.

Then Dad notices me. "Lucie! Where have you been? You had everyone worried sick!" he says, instantly jumping into blame-Lucienne mode. He knows Grandfather won't yell at me the way he does at others because I'm the youngest and I'm legally a Peery.

I look at the man who basically donated sperm to make me. He has no qualms about using me to shield himself. I don't know why I ever thought he was my dad.

"I didn't know you were so worried, *Roderick.*"

He flinches in shock, his olive complexion paling a little. This is the first time I've ever called him by his first name.

I almost laugh. I don't know why he's acting so stunned. He should've known he couldn't stomp all over me forever. I turn to Grandfather. "I'm sorry, but I needed to take a long walk to blow off some steam after Vonnie took my pearls and refused to give them back," I say calmly, trying not to be whiny or pleading. Grandfather hates both equally.

His blue eyes, cool under thick platinum eyebrows, then swing to Vonnie.

Tears instantly fall down her cheeks. "I'm sorry, Grandfather. I didn't realize Lucienne would be that upset. I just wanted to try them on because they looked so pretty."

"I told you not to touch my things," I tell her with forced gentleness before Grandfather can respond.

"You should've told me you wanted pearls too, Vonnie. I would've bought some for you." Mom walks over and runs her hand down Vonnie's dark hair, trying to ease the tension in the room.

But is that attempt for me or for everyone else?

I look around slowly. Mom wants me to give in and bring peace. Roderick wants me to be an obedient little girl and "share" what's mine with him and his other children. Karl is an opportunistic jerk who treats me like shit because he can, while enjoying what being my half-brother brings him. Vonnie wants anything that's mine.

Take away what they want the most from you. Mr. Cashmere Coat's voice rings in my head.

"Give them back," I say to Vonnie, palm out.

Her lips tremble. God, I'm so sick of her theatrics. Poor, poor Vonnie. So persecuted by her mean little half-sister.

Grandfather watches, his expression unreadable. Mom is wringing her hands, anxiety flickering in her pale blue gaze. Roderick stays back, observing the scene, probably trying to decide how he should behave next, and Karl glowers at me like I'm being a bitch.

"Well?" I prompt when Vonnie doesn't move.

Her gaze darts around. When nobody comes to her defense, she reluctantly undoes the clasp and hands the necklace to me.

I take it by the end—the part she didn't run her tongue all over.

If I want to follow Mr. Coat's advice, I need an ally. I slide my gaze to Grandfather, study his granite Nordic features—the platinum hair, arctic-blue eyes and hard mouth. What would he do if he were me?

He thinks I'm not fit for Peery Diamonds because I'm a girl—too weak and too soft. And he might be right. If somebody messed with him, he would never walk away like I did. There's a reason Mr. Coat told me I need to stay and fight if I want to keep what's mine—that I need to respect myself enough to fight for what's mine.

Vonnie screwed with me, and I need to show Grandfather I'm not some soft little girl. Not if I want him to see me as his true heir, somebody he can leave the Peery fortune to. I need to act like the way a man would—a man who's furious that somebody touched what's his, even if the item in question isn't that sentimental.

I throw the string of pearls into the flames of the fireplace.

Mom gasps. Vonnie shouts, "What the hell?" while Roderick and Karl stare at Grandfather, waiting for the most powerful man in the room to explode first before they join the fireworks.

"Those were nice pearls," Grandfather says, his voice hard.

"I know," I say, keeping my gaze steady as I look up at him. "But the necklace could be infected. Since *some*body licked it all over like an animal." My eyes slide over to Vonnie, who's flushing. "Why should I keep something she grossified?"

"You could've let her have it," Grandfather says, his tone still the same, although his eyes are gleaming with a hint of approval.

"I don't want her to have it. Not after she disrespected me. If she wanted it that bad, she could've just asked nicely."

"Lucienne." Mom's whine is full of embarrassment.

Roderick *tsks*. "It's no big deal if your sister wants to put it on for a bit. We've been trying so hard to teach you to share."

I shoot him a look filled with contempt. It's impossible to hide how much I despise him.

"Why should she share?" Grandfather says.

There's a sudden silence in the room. "Wha-what?" Roderick stammers.

"Why should Lucienne have to share anything if she doesn't wish to?" Grandfather turns his attention to me. "You may go and get yourself warm," he says, as though he hasn't noticed a man's coat on me.

I nod, go into my room and lock the door behind me. My heart starts racing, a delayed reaction to the scene I just took part in. The air in my lungs shudders out. If it weren't for Mr. Coat's encouragement, I would've apologized for inconveniencing everyone. Then I would've put up with all sorts of sly put-downs from Karl and Vonnie, all the while pretending I was fine, even as fury and resentment built up like acid.

It felt *so good* to lash out! And show Vonnie that nothing she takes from me is valuable enough that I'll just accept it back with relieved gratitude. Besides, the pearls were a reminder of just how little I matter to Mom. I don't need a present like that.

Mr. Coat was right. If I don't respect myself, I'll be left with nothing.

I walk to the bed, my legs still a little shaky. I shrug the coat off and hug it, burying my nose in the soft fabric, inhaling the spicy, woodsy scent. As I tighten my hold, something crinkles. I reach into the inside pocket and pull out a yellow paper. It's a credit card slip with a name at the end: Sebastian Lasker.

So that's who he is. I smile a little, then unplug my phone from the charger and look him up.

My smile falters when Google tells me he's in line to inherit Sebastian Jewelry, Peery Diamonds's rival. And when the search engine shows me photos of him with other women in short dresses, something cold and lumpy settles in my heart. Which is stupid. It's not like he's my boyfriend or anything.

I toss the phone on the pillow and hug the coat again. *Who cares?* None of those women got his coat, I think, sinking my fingers into the soft fabric.

2

LUCIENNE

—ELEVEN YEARS later

THEFT in and of itself is awful enough. But by your own family? That should come with some public flogging.

As my limo slogs through the streets of Barcelona, I glare at the video that just popped up on my social media feed. It stars Karl, flashing his standard dick smile. The background indicates he's in a casino, living the life of a high-roller.

His physical resemblance to Roderick wasn't really obvious when he was a teenager, but now he looks like a replica. The brown hair, the Roman nose that's a bit too large for his slightly narrow face. His jaw is somewhat narrow, and if his chin receded just a tad more it'd be considered weak. But he has an irritatingly excellent pair of wide-set brown eyes that make up for the other subpar features. Mom often told me she fell in love with Roderick when she looked into his eyes, like that could excuse years of neglect.

I wish Karl had beady, bloodshot eyes that reflected what a horrible human being he is.

"The key to a great poker game—to *winning* that game—is having a heart of steel and a face that betrays nothing." He winks.

Yeah, sure. He can't bluff to save his life. I've seen two-year-olds who lie better. In addition, the casinos know he gets wild and unpredictable after a few whiskeys, which is why they ply him with alcohol the second he steps inside. He loses heavily, but he continues to push his nonexistent luck because he's convinced that the great win is waiting for him just around the corner.

Karl waves a hand around, a cigar between his fingers, and holds forth about his gambling strategies. Is that a Cohiba Behike? I squint at the screen. Oh yes, it is.

Fury slashes at me. There's no way he can afford cigars that cost hundreds of dollars with his own money. He doesn't make enough as a junior marketing executive.

Wanting him to do something useful, Grandfather gave him a position at Peery Diamonds. Karl managed to climb the ladder, although I'm certain nepotism had a lot to do with his glowing evals and promotions.

Regardless, he did what he could because he thought he might be able to suck up to Grandfather and get a portion of the Peery fortune. He even pretended that he wasn't furious when Grandfather capped his annual salary at two hundred thousand dollars, although it's two hundred thousand too high, if you ask me. Karl quit showing up for work since Grandfather passed away a little over a year ago. Karl got nothing in the will, and he's done hiding how he really feels about having to work.

I wish I could fire him, but I can't exert my full influence at Peery Diamonds yet, even though I'm the CEO. I'm *female*, in addition to being "still too young" and "unmarried."

That godawful Gwen was right. The laws of Nesovia are on Roderick's side on every level. Until I turn thirty or get married, I'm not allowed to run Peery Diamonds unencumbered or freely use the trust fund Mom left me when she lost control of her Jet Ski.

Currently, Roderick's acting as my trustee, which is laughable because he's about as trustworthy as Judas. Roderick votes as my proxy at every shareholders' meeting, and he's been doing everything to screw with me and reward his allies within the company. He even made himself a "consultant" at Peery Diamonds. I have no idea what he "consults" on, since he knows nothing about the jewelry business. In addition, his self-directed generosity knows no bounds, and he's taking advantage, spending my money lavishly on himself and his twins.

He calls it "sharing." I call it "theft." The laws of Nesovia say he's in the right because he has a penis and happens to be my biological father.

Damn Roderick. And most importantly, damn Nesovia.

Roman Wellendorff, the deputy minister of finance from Nesovia, is in Barcelona. I was supposed to meet him, but he canceled last minute, which is why I'm heading back to my hotel with nothing to show for it. But then, he probably didn't want to face me for what was bound to be an unpleasant interaction. I've never hidden how I feel about the archaic laws and customs of the country. I even donate heavily out of the private fund I've hidden in the United States to his party to ensure they do something about it.

But so far, nothing. The latest measure to repeal the inheritance law failed. *Again.* The overwhelming majority voted against it. Those men think that their fancy suits and fancier cars can hide the fact that they're nothing but medieval, unenlightened Neanderthals.

Wellendorff had the nerve to leave me a voicemail, telling me in that condescending, paternalistic voice, "It's for the best. For your own good, really. Women are to be protected and taken care of."

Of course. I feel *sooooo* protected and taken care of right now, fuck you very much.

I exhale, trying to shake off the frustrating image of my so-called family living a luxurious life they don't deserve. I need to calm down and focus on my countermeasures.

Men like my dad and Wellendorff think women are helpless, docile little creatures. I'll show them how mistaken they are.

Because I'm about to get engaged and married, quickly and efficiently, to a man neither my father nor the laws of Nesovia can affect. Once that's done, I'm moving the company's headquarters to the United States and will prove to the board of directors that I'm worthy of continuing as CEO by starting a successful joint venture in a new market.

My phone pings, pulling me out of my stewing.

—Preston: It's all right, I guess. But diamonds are like dicks. All else being equal, bigger is better.

That's his response to the picture of the engagement ring I picked out for our photoshoot later today? "All else" is never equal when it comes to diamonds or dicks. I know because I'm the heiress to Peery Diamonds *and* I'm a woman.

—Preston: We can do better than this.

Did he not see that the stone is an exceptionally deep blue, princess-cut, ten-point-two-carat beauty? Even on a phone screen, he should be able to tell based on the proportion of the stone to the gorgeous platinum band studded with clear round-cut diamonds. There aren't that many natural blue diamonds of this level of saturation, not at this size. I had to pore through our absolute top-tier inventory before I could find one that looked suitably impressive.

—Preston: Leave it up to me. I have just the thing.

—Me: Fine.

I wait for him to send me a picture, but he doesn't. *Whatever.* I mentally wave off my crabby mood. The ring isn't worth an argument. Given that he's a member of the Comtois family—part of the Sebastian Jewelry dynasty—I assume he has good enough taste to select a suitable ring. Obviously, he wants an enormous stone on his fiancée's hand, something more than a mere ten-point-two-carat blue diamond, estimated at over a quarter of a million dollars. Something monumental.

This isn't just a marriage—it's a business deal. Every detail needs to be assessed based on whether or not it can create the maximum publicity and buzz. After Preston and I marry, our companies are going to launch a Sebastian Peery collaboration in Korea to sell jewelry for weddings and romantic occasions. Koreans spend an ungodly amount on jewelry for their weddings, and it's going to be a lucrative market to pursue.

In addition, I will also finally get something I've been dying for: the ability to chart my own destiny. Although I can't control my own money or the company until I'm thirty, there's a loophole. If I get married, control of both goes to my husband. And if he decides to let me take the reins, voilà! I'm in charge.

The contract between me and the Comtoises has a specific clause on that point. As soon as the wedding's completed, Preston's going to sign a legal document my lawyers drafted, giving me full autonomy over my assets.

And for that alone, I can indulge Preston's need to put something *he* likes on my finger.

The traffic back to the hotel is congested. I check the details that my best friend Bianca, who's also now my assistant, sent for the day.

Photographers—booked and ready.

Florists—done.

Hair and makeup crew—check.

All Preston and I have to do is play-act a romantic engagement with lots of happy smiles...and without revealing that we had never even spoken to each other until two months ago.

But then he wasn't my first choice of husband. I wanted Sebastian Lasker.

He probably doesn't remember the teenager he was kind to, but I've followed him—and his career. He's become quite accomplished—a man worthy of admiration. He's grown Sebastian Jewelry, not just in size but in profitability. Clever marketing campaigns he's spearheaded have made it one of the top luxury brands in the world. And even though he's appeared in public with many beautiful women, there's never been a whisper of scandal about him. Either he's very careful or his PR team has done an amazing job.

I've sighed over Sebastian's photos like a high school girl having a secret crush, but I didn't have the courage to do anything about it until I approached the Comtois family and asked for Sebastian as my husband.

Coco Comtois refused. Apparently, he's too "special" to be wasted like this.

What the matriarch meant is he's too good for a girl like me, one with a billion scandals attached to her name. From her perspective, I'm a pig trying to get her precious pearl. Her assessment stings, but I'm not explaining my past to her. Trying to make other people understand has never done me any good.

Besides, I haven't forgotten the lesson Sebastian taught me. It's never steered me wrong. And Preston is good enough for what I need to do.

Almost an hour later, I'm in a gorgeously appointed corridor, striding toward the penthouse suite I booked for myself and Preston. I hold my phone screen over the security panel on the door at the end of the hall. The light turns green, and I open the door and walk in, the thick carpet muffling my stilettos.

The living room opens up to a gorgeous Spanish vista of white buildings, narrow streets and cloudless cerulean sky. The suite comes with an ivory Steinway baby grand and four vases of fresh cream and pink roses. The photoshoot is going to take place during sunset, when the light's at its best. The florists are sending even more flowers later, and the makeup and hair people will show up, too.

An ice bucket sweats on a silver tray on the table, but the Dom's already uncorked. A flute that has clearly been used already and another clean one sit beside it.

I let out a small, resigned sigh. Preston isn't known for delaying gratification. When he saw the champagne, he probably couldn't control himself.

Where is he? I look around the living room area or the fully stocked bar. Did he feel jet-lagged and decide to nap? Or is he taking advantage of the Jacuzzi?

Then I hear something. *A moan.* If it were lower-pitched, I might assume my ersatz fiancé was jerking off, but the sound is too thin. Unless he has some hormonal dysfunction I don't know about, he shouldn't sound like that under any circumstances.

The frustration that's been building up reaches my eyeballs. I struggle to suck in air through sudden fury.

When Preston and I discussed our expectations for this marriage, I told him I'd appreciate some faithfulness and discretion, and he agreed. Screwing a woman a couple of hours before we're supposed to take photos as a newly engaged couple in the suite *I* booked and paid for is anything but being faithful and discreet.

The desire to grab one of the vases and crack it over his head is nearly overwhelming, but I stop and put a hand to my forehead. I can't just call this off. *Focus on the goal: to be free—to be my own person.* I'll have to find a way to deal with Preston after my lawyers successfully expatriate Peery Diamonds from Nesovia to the States.

But the fact that I'm stuck in this awful situation is like cement being forced down my throat. Desperately ignoring the rage pounding through me, I stride to the bedroom and shove the double doors open with a crash. I glare at the giant bed, where Preston's on top of some woman I can't see. His ass stops in midair.

"What the fuck?" he yells, craning his neck. "Who the—"

Our eyes meet. All color leaves his face. His Adam's apple bobs; his mouth opens and stays that way, making him look like a particularly dim-witted chicken.

Can we still proceed with the wedding if I cut his balls off? It isn't like we'll need them. *I* certainly won't. His filthy, indiscreet, cheating penis isn't getting anywhere near me.

"Oh, shit," he whispers.

"What's wrong, baby? Just tell them to go away," the woman beneath him says in an annoying, nasal whine.

My blood roars. This better not be who I think it is.

The woman shifts to look at me. And it's *exactly* who I think it is —Vonnie.

"Oh, it's just you," she says.

I should've brought a vase in here—to crack it over *her* head.

"Why are you acting so mad? I'm more his type anyway," she adds.

Despite the fact that we have the same father, we look nothing alike. She took after her mother—dark eyes, dark hair and a petite build that brings out the protectiveness in men. Unlike Karl, her nose is correctly proportioned, and her features are delicately carved.

I took after my grandfather—who gave me platinum-blond hair and pale blue eyes that some gossip sites call "hard and unfeeling," and a tall, statuesque frame, which is often referred to as "intimidating" and "domineering."

"You're fucking my *sister*?" I demand to Preston, rage thundering in my veins.

"I can explain!" He puts a hand out. He doesn't bother to glance at Vonnie.

But I do, and I notice something else that triples my blood pressure. "Are those *my shoes?*"

"It isn't like you were wearing them," Vonnie says, sitting up and defiantly tossing her hair over a shoulder. She doesn't bother to hide her nakedness.

"They're brand new Guccis I picked up in Milan!" Last week, as a matter of fact, for today's photoshoot. What an idiot I've been. The realization that I've wasted so much of my time and energy renews my fury.

"So?"

"So take them off before I cut off your feet!"

"Oh my God, you're going to wear the shoes I wore while fucking your fiancé?" Vonnie throws the stilettos on the spot near me, since she doesn't have the balls to throw them *at* me. She doesn't want to provoke me too much. She never forgot about the burnt pearls—and some other things I've done since.

"No, I'm going to fantasize they're your face while I pour acid on them." I grab a pillow, strip it of its case and shove the shoes inside. Then I straighten and regard the anxious Preston, ready to give him the tongue lashing he so richly deserves.

"I was doing this for you," he says quickly.

"*What?* In what crazy universe is any of this for *me?*"

He stretches his arms out beseechingly. "This was a dress rehearsal for the photoshoot. I was getting nervous about it, you know, because we have to show everyone how much we're in love with each other, so I asked Vonnie to help me."

"Help you *what?*"

"You know. Practice."

Holy mother of God. Horror starts to mix into my rage. I'm engaged to an idiot. Actually, calling him an idiot is an insult to all the idiots of the world. There has to be some other term reserved just for this, this...

Vonnie smirks and lifts her left hand. A pink, fifteen-carat, heart-shaped diamond winks on her ring finger.

I stare at the hideous monstrosity. *That's* what he chose over my blue diamond? What am I? Five? I hate pink and I hate hearts. If Preston had bothered to check my preferences, he would've known.

"And your penis just happened to fall into her vagina when you slid that ring onto her finger?" It occurs to me that the Guccis inside the pillowcase would make a pretty good weapon. Would beating him bloody be a crime in Spain, given the circumstances?

"I kind of slipped," Preston says.

They're Latin. They'll understand.

"He was sleeping with me before you took him from me!" Vonnie yells, throwing gasoline onto the fire. "I had him first!"

"Vonnie!" he hisses.

"Then why did he agree to be *my* fiancé?" I say, not bothering to hide the disgust coloring my voice.

She merely glares. Typical. She always does that when she has nothing to say. Then she smirks. "He might've agreed to be your fiancé for money or whatever. But it's me he *wants*."

Humiliation burns my face. Men generally prefer Vonnie over me. They call her nicer and sweeter. I'm an impossible bitch because I won't tolerate crap from anybody, including my so-called family. She's gotten worse since Grandfather's death because he left her nothing. She thought she'd be able to get something for all the sucking up she'd done over the years.

"I just want you to know, it's you I want to marry, Lucienne," Preston says quickly.

"Fuck off. You're fired!" I start to walk away. I've seen enough, and my brain feels like it's full of nuclear toxic waste. If he'd cheated on me with some anonymous hooker, I might've overlooked it—because I'm just that desperate at this point—but *Vonnie*?

No. I just can't. I'll have to find a new husband.

"Wait, what? You can't do that! I'm your fiancé!" The bed creaks as he hops off to follow me.

"Uh-huh. And who just had his penis in my half-sister's vagina?" I continue my march to the door.

"Lucienne, please. I only got to thrust, like, twice. I didn't even get to come!" Like that excuses what I had to witness. "What about my money? The company I'm supposed to get?"

"Take it up with your grandparents."

"Wait!" He wraps his hand around my wrist. "But the ring! It's really pretty. Don't you want it on your finger? It's *huge*! Fifteen-point-one carats!"

Okay, so stupid *and* blind. No one with any taste would think that ring was pretty or deserved to grace my hand. "What was it you said, Preston?" I give him my most sugary voice. "Dicks are like diamonds." My gaze flickers down, then rises back to his face, and I smile. "I've seen bigger and better."

His face turns dull red.

Dropping the fake smile, I break his hold and start to walk out.

"*You bitch!* Who the hell's gonna marry *you?*"

"Oh, I'll think of someone." I don't turn back, and the door closes behind me.

3

SEBASTIAN

EVERY EMPLOYEE at Sebastian Jewelry is gathered in the giant auditorium in our L.A. headquarters. Those who are in our HQ1 in McLean, Virginia are teleconferencing.

There's nothing more thrilling than announcing that the company has not only hit every target, but exceeded it. Every department performed above expectations.

With each slide and announcement of our achievements, our people clap and whistle. Hell, I cheer, too. Sebastian Jewelry has always been a great company with an excellent reputation, its financials solid. But it wasn't until I took over that it became the household name it is now. The company's revenue quadrupled, and margins are higher than ever before. We've expanded overseas as well, although there are more markets to reach, especially in Asia. That's one place we haven't fully cracked yet.

One step at a time. This isn't the time to think of strategies to enter a new market. Right now, we celebrate our wins. I'm proud at what we've achieved at Sebastian Jewelry, especially after Preston's latest screwup. Everyone had to work extra to compensate, but we did it.

Hell yeah.

"It goes without saying that the company couldn't have accomplished all this"—I gesture at the final slide behind me— "without *you*. Therefore, we're announcing special bonuses for everyone."

The cheering and clapping grow louder. I smile at the employees' happiness. I believe in rewarding people for a job well done. And they definitely deserve this.

Even the janitors are applauding, since the bonus will go to them, too. Everyone at Sebastian Jewelry gets a slice of the pie.

I step off the podium, and the people start to disperse to grab the snacks HR prepared. My phone pings.

–Grandfather: An excellent job.

He must've watched the presentation. Grandmother and Mom would've watched it, too, if it weren't for their annual mother-daughter trip to Europe. Unless I'm mistaken, they should be in Paris today.

Thinking about the city reminds me of the girl I met eleven years ago. Most people don't leave much of an impression, but she did. She looked so lost and alone. And based on what she said—and left unsaid —I could piece together her situation. I despise adults who take advantage of children to validate their life choices. My own father did that, and to a certain extent Mom is the same way. But unlike that girl, I have my brothers.

Still, there was a fire in her, although it was so weak, it was ready to be extinguished. I hope she didn't let it die. My advice and encouragement wouldn't have been enough unless she really wanted to do something about her situation. And I've followed my own advice, like we're on a team working toward the same goal of evening the scales —as if that would keep the fire in her burning. Unrealistic, of course, but sometimes the most irrational things motivate me.

Christoph hurries over. It's difficult to miss his flaming red hair in the crowd, especially when he's six-two. He started working as my assistant two years ago after graduating from college. Although his wide brown eyes make him look a little like a stunned child, he's quick and understands office politics. On top of that, I appreciate all the gossip he brings me. Some executives believe employee gossip is stupid. Not me. Gossip reveals a lot about what's in my people's heads.

Christoph's in a neat dress shirt, jacket and dark slacks. He tries to emulate my dress code, but that's beyond his budget. I'm in a three-piece bespoke suit from Paris, with Sebastian Jewelry cuff links and a tie pin. A timepiece from our newly launched luxury watch division is on my wrist. The market response has been stellar.

"Why don't you go grab something?" I say, tilting my chin in the direction of the food table. Christoph's rail thin and always hungry.

"I will, but later. Your mother is here."

"She is?" *Why?* There's no reason for her to cut the trip short, unless there's an emergency she and Grandmother's highly trained and experienced assistants can't handle—and I can't think of anything that could be so dire. Money and influence can fix almost anything.

Is Grandmother sick?

I check my phone, but there's no message about that. Besides, if she were sick, Mom would've asked me to go to a hospital instead of visiting me here.

I don't bother to ask Christoph for details. If it's something too complicated for Mom's assistants to take care of, they wouldn't tell mine.

"I moved your next meeting, so you have about an hour. She's in the grand reception room."

"Thanks." This kind of quick action is why I hired him.

His gaze flicks toward Penny from finance. She's standing around the dessert table, eyeing the spread like she can't decide. His expression says he'd love to help her make up her mind. Or better yet, become her dessert himself.

I hide my smile at his reaction. He thinks he's subtle, but he's crazy about her. "Go take a break, Christoph. I'll text if I need you."

"Okay, thanks." He smiles, then ambles off toward her.

The grand reception room is one of our best conference rooms. It overlooks the city—all the buildings, cars and energy, along with the San Gabriel mountains in the background when the smog isn't too bad —but the view isn't the only attraction.

Ivory leather seats, silver animal figurines with glittering crystal accents. A glass-top coffee table and elegant contemporary chandeliers in circular shapes. Glass cases with some of our most prized jewelry.

The air has a whiff of our signature scent, which smells like buttery opulence and exclusivity without being cloying. I commissioned it when I took over the company, and now every Sebastian Jewelry location smells like luxury.

The room isn't for holding meetings about boring business issues, but for welcoming people to Sebastian Jewelry and making them feel special. We reserve it for business partners and exceptionally important clients.

I enter the room and close the door firmly so nobody can overhear us. Mom is in an armchair, leaning against the back of the seat with a practiced casualness. Her elbows are propped on the armrests, and she hasn't touched the steaming jasmine tea in front of her.

My mother is a carbon copy of Grandmother—the same hazel eyes, light brown hair and straight patrician nose. But unlike Grandmother, who favors pastel shades, Mom prefers to make a bolder statement. And today is no different. She's in a scarlet dress I've never seen before, and it is, as usual, fashionable.

She's crossed her legs, left over right. Her feet are in gold stilettos with heels so thin and high that they could serve as nails in a pinch, and her left foot bobs steadily.

To any casual observer, she looks calm, without a care in the world. But I know her too well. Mom always sits this way when she's confronted with a problem she can't handle on her own.

Shit.

But even if she weren't flashing her tell, all the elation from the earlier town hall would've vanished, leaving nothing but cold dread. A long necklace made with three strings of brilliant-cut diamonds glitters around Mom's throat, an heirloom piece she received from Grandmother after she had me. She always wears it when she wants to remind me of who and what I am—Sebastian Lasker, the dutiful son and heir apparent to Sebastian Jewelry. And she usually reminds me of that when she needs me to fix a mess my half-brother Preston made.

What the hell did he do now?

He's never made it a secret that he resents me for kicking him out of the company after his third screwup. He can't accept that keeping his incompetent ass on the payroll would be nothing but gross nepotism.

He claimed I was being a greedy jerk who was jealous of him. Ludicrous, since it's impossible to be jealous of somebody that inferior. He's pissed he isn't going to get the company, or the fortune attached to it. And without the gravy train from Sebastian Jewelry, he might actually have to get a real job—*the horror!*

He must've created a monumental fuck-up for Grandmother and Mom to cut their trip short. So. What did he do? Or did they have something to do with it? And to what purpose? They know he's inept, even though they don't want to acknowledge it.

I take the seat opposite Mom and put on a calm mask of my own. "What's going on?" My voice is so steady, she'll never know that what I really want to say is, "I'm going to murder Preston."

"Oh, nothing. France became boring." She smiles. "You know how it is."

"Mom," I say mildly. "I have a meeting soon."

"All right." She huffs a little. "There's been a small incident." Her eyes flick in my direction, then quickly drop to the tea in front of her.

"How small, exactly?"

No answer.

I force myself to be as still as possible, so I don't betray the impatience and annoyance scraping at my nerves, while telling myself, *I don't yell at Mom. I don't yell at Mom. I don't yell at Mom...*

She pulls her lips in briefly, and uncrosses then recrosses her legs.

I try not to sigh. "Well?"

"Darling, you know I love you—"

"Mom."

She looks like a woman about to face a firing squad. "You'll need to marry Lucienne Peery."

"*What?*" I couldn't be more stunned or outraged if she told me I needed to fornicate with a three-legged pig on national TV.

Lucienne Peery is the female version of my father, Ted Lasker, who apparently hasn't ever heard of a scandal he didn't want to emulate. The only difference is she's from a jewelry family and he's a movie producer. Also, she's young and hasn't had a chance to create seven children with seven different partners. But just give her time.

Her exploits are legendary. Men. Drugs. Parties. I don't follow social gossip, and even I've heard about her numerous improprieties. I'm still not sure how she's managed to avoid getting arrested for some of the stuff she's done. On the other hand, she's wealthy—the heiress to the Peery Diamonds fortune—so I suppose she has good professional and legal help. The reality is undoubtedly much worse than the gossip.

It's vaguely disappointing. She seemed like a nice girl when I met her at her mother's funeral seven years ago.

"It isn't that bad. She's a very pretty young woman. Prettier than when you last saw her," Mom adds.

"She could be the goddess of beauty herself and I'd still say no."

"Don't be difficult, sweetie. You don't have to actually *do* anything. Just marrying her will suffice."

"Oh. Well. I feel so much better." I look at the woman I love dearly. All these years, I've been quietly relieved over the fact that my mother isn't insane like some of my brothers', but now I see I have the gold medalist in crazy on my hands. "I'm seeing somebody right now."

"That model?"

Her dismissive tone loosens my grip on my control. She can't just show up here unannounced, demand I marry some lunatic heiress, then act like I'm being unreasonable for saying no! "Her name is Gabriella Ricci. Yes, she's a model. And a very nice woman."

Mom looks skeptical. "Nice enough for you to propose?"

Damn it. She knows me too well. Gabriella's nice, but not marriage nice. Fine, I didn't want to bring this up, but I have no choice. "Grandmother wants me to have grandchildren, and I can't have children with a woman like Lucienne Peery." There. Mom hates to cross Grandmother.

"Oh, sweetie." Her tone says, *Don't hate me, I'm just a messenger.* "Your grandmother has agreed to this. Actually, everyone in the family did."

What the fuck? "You mean everyone but *me*."

"Besides, I don't think you're contractually obligated to create babies with Lucienne, although you should check that and make sure, just in case."

"*Contractually obligated—?*" It's all I can do to not scream at my own mother. "What have you done behind my back, *Mother*?"

She winces a little. I only call her that when I'm really upset with her. "It's going to help Sebastian Jewelry." She gives me a *don't you trust me, sweetie?* smile.

Bullshit. If that were the case, she wouldn't be here with that necklace around her throat. "Then you'll have no problem telling me all about it."

"It's just a little contract," she says, after a moment to gather herself. "You know we would *never* leave you without legal protection."

"Is it a prenup?" They can't sign one of those behind my back and expect me to honor it. Fuck it. I'm litigating this whole damn mess. Nobody corners me into doing things. There's a reason I've made sure to have my own damn money, funds that have nothing to do with Sebastian Jewelry or my father.

"Oh, it's far more ironclad than some silly prenup," Mom says with a little laugh. "Jeremiah Huxley handled it herself, and you know how she is."

Of course I do. Jeremiah is my brother Huxley's mom. She's a senior partner at Huxley & Webber, and a complete sociopath when it comes to protecting her clients. She went to Harvard for both her undergraduate and JD and is known in legal circles as "the H-bomb." "Was she *our* lawyer?"

"Well, no, but..."

God save me from my family. "Then we're fuck—screwed."

"No! We had our lawyers review it, of course. Lucienne will be handing over ten percent of the voting shares she holds at Sebastian Jewelry to her husband over a two-year period, which is to start as soon as vows are exchanged. This will cement our control over the company further, which you know we've always wanted."

The muscles in my jaw tighten. Nobody asked *me* if *I* wanted to sell myself for ten percent of what she has. The ten percent *is* sort of a big deal, but it isn't worth being tied to somebody like Lucienne Peery. If it's that important, I could probably just buy the shares with my own damn money.

"She's also giving her husband five percent of the *voting* shares at Peery Diamonds, which we'd love as a family."

And nobody bothered to ask me if *I'd* love that, either.

"In addition, her husband will get a seat on the board of directors at Peery Diamonds." Mom smiles like she's expecting lavish praise. But why the hell does she think I'd want a seat on the board of Lucienne's company? I'm already busy running Sebastian Jewelry, and I don't give a damn about Peery Diamonds.

Mom's smile fades as she realizes I'm not liking anything she's said. Her tone grows desperate, her words more hurried. "The best part is, we and Peery Diamonds are going to start a highly profitable venture in Korea, and she's handing us a fifty-five percent stake, while Peery Diamonds gets the rest. I know you've been trying to expand our footprint in Asia."

"Mother, *I* am the CEO, not you, and I don't need you, Grandmother or anyone else meddling and signing contracts behind my back," I tell her in my coldest voice. I've never used this particular tone with her before, and she flinches.

"But we don't have to provide any capital for the extra five percent stake!"

"Because she just wants me as her husband on top of our money." Lucienne can keep all the profit from the fucking venture if she'll just leave me alone.

"Don't take it so personally, sweetie." Mom leans forward. If she were sitting closer, she'd pat my hand. "She didn't really want *you*."

The tension in my gut eases a little. "Well then. Why didn't you say so? Give her Preston."

"Yes, about that..." She bites her lip. "We tried."

"And she turned him down?" How ridiculous for her to think she can do better than Preston. Ha! She should be grateful anybody would agree to marry her scandal-laden ass at all! "Never mind. I'll convince her he's the one for her."

He's worthless when it comes to running the family business, so this is the least he can do. And I don't care if he sits on the Peery Diamonds board. It's Lucienne's company, not mine, and she can deal with whatever screwups he creates. I'll even tell her we can split the profit from the venture fifty-fifty. That'll ramp up Preston's desirability.

"That would be difficult. There was a, um, hiccup with the arrangements."

"A hiccup."

Mom expels a small sigh. "She caught him with another woman on the day they were supposed to get engaged."

"Okay, so the timing was bad. But sex with another woman? That's actually relatively tame." There's nothing he could've done that would be worse than her damn scandals.

"The other woman was her half-sister. Vonnie."

Murder is too good for Preston. I'm going to rip his balls off and shove them down his throat, *then* kill him. "All right, he messed up. But that doesn't mean I need to marry his former fiancée. I barely even know her!"

"Oh, that's all right. Preston didn't know her either when he agreed to do this seven or eight weeks ago."

If he has no feelings for her, he must be getting something from the deal. He's too self-centered to take one for the family without a proper reward. And I want to know what side deals they made with him. "Why did he agree to do it?" And why couldn't he keep his dick in his pants so I wouldn't be forced to fix this ridiculous business deal my family agreed to behind my back?

Mom presses her lips together, then finally picks up her tea and sips it. She makes a face. She doesn't like lukewarm tea, and it's gotta be tepid by now. Her index finger taps the rim of the cup. Her left foot bobs in an agitated rhythm.

And my own irritation and apprehension mount.

"He was getting Sebastian Jewelry for marrying Lucienne." She speaks super-fast, like that's going to make me miss the import of what she's saying.

"What? Says *who*?"

"Well...all of us, more or less. We felt like he needed to be recognized for his sacrifice."

"*Sacrifice?* How is that a sacrifice?" I didn't pour my all into Sebastian Jewelry, only to have it yanked from me by my own damn family and that scheming heiress bitch! "He was getting a sugar mama, which is the best he can aspire to in life, since he's too incompetent and lazy for anything else! And you know as well as I do it won't take him a year to bankrupt Sebastian Jewelry!"

"Of course! Which is why he was going to *own* Sebastian Jewelry, but not *run* it," Mom explains soothingly.

What the fuck? "Who was supposed to run it, then?"

"You."

"*Me?*" I shout. I'm too pissed to care that I'm speaking to my mother.

"Well, yes. Everyone knows you're the best CEO we've ever had."

"You want me to work like a dog *for Preston*? For one, that idiot's ego wouldn't be able to handle it. And two, I wouldn't be able to handle it because I just know he'd question everything I did and try to micromanage me, just to make himself feel superior."

Mom raises a placating hand. "He's not *that* bad, sweetie. And really, he has nothing. You're already rich from all the investments you've made with your brothers."

"Because I'm not stupid like him! I told him he was welcome to throw some money in with me, but he turned me down, saying he had 'better opportunities.' And every single one of them lost money— which, by the way, was no surprise!"

"Calm down, sweetie. You wouldn't be this upset if we gave Sebastian Jewelry to one of your Lasker brothers." Her tone says I'm being unfair to Preston.

"Because they aren't morons! I'd *prefer* it if they got the company instead of Preston. They wouldn't ruin it or consider it a cherry on top of their ego sundae."

"Well, they aren't part of the Comtoises." She huffs. "It was fairer this way."

"Fairer for who?" My throat hurts from my effort not to raise my already loud voice. "It certainly doesn't seem fair to me!"

"It would be so sad to see him with nothing," Mom pleads, her tone saying that'd be the worst possible outcome. "We just don't want him to be destitute. And you're so capable, Sebastian. You'd be fine without the company, but we know how much you love Sebastian Jewelry, so we didn't want to take it from you completely."

I'm so angry, I can't speak. Mom refuses to understand that this isn't about money or ego. It's about *legacy*, what the company represents.

She's too fond of Preston to see anything from my perspective.

Apparently, he's lovable—as long as you don't have to clean up his messes, so I would never understand his charm. And I'm not the most likable person in the family, since I've always had to make the difficult decisions. Running a company the size of Sebastian Jewelry demands it.

My family's assessment of me and Preston is biased. However, I've accepted it as something I can't do anything about. The deal they engineered with Lucienne Peery, on the other hand... That's a fucking betrayal, not something I ever thought I'd experience from my own damn flesh and blood.

Part of me wants to say, "Fuck it," and walk away. Mom's right. I already have more money than I can spend in ten lifetimes.

But Sebastian Jewelry is my baby. *Mine.* Given how Mom feels about Preston, if I refuse to marry Lucienne Peery, the family will simply give the company to him, with or without a connection to Lucienne. This whole contract thing is a pretext. Otherwise, the family would've told me everything before now.

Sebastian Jewelry doesn't exist in a vacuum, but in a huge economic and social ecosystem. My position as its CEO isn't about status. Ensuring that the company does well gives me a sense of pride and accomplishment. The responsibility I feel isn't limited to my family, but extends to our suppliers and employees and their families.

Preston will never understand it. He doesn't care what happens to our people as long as his ego gets stroked.

I'm going to have to figure out a way to punish my family for their duplicity.

"If you don't go through with it, we don't know what else we can do. If we can't honor the contract, we're obligated to give her thirty percent of the shares in Sebastian Jewelry," Mom adds in a small voice. "All you have to do is just suck it up and marry her, and the company will be yours. That's the condition your grandparents set."

I want to flip the damn coffee table over. That thirty percent means the family will lose control over the company to our damned rival. Fucking Preston. Fucking backstabbing family. Fucking Lucienne Peery.

"You need to go, Mother," I manage, even though my breathing is too uneven to hide my rage.

"Sweetie—" She stretches her hand out.

I jerk away. "Now. *Please.* I can't look at you right now."

I need to find a way to undo this ridiculous contract. I'll be damned if I'm forced into marrying anyone, much less Lucienne Peery.

4

SEBASTIAN

Two weeks pass, and Lucienne Peery doesn't try to get in touch with me to discuss the indentured servitude contract. I drum my fingers on the desk in my office, trying to figure the angles. Is she waiting for our lawyer to tell her she's getting the shares rather than a husband?

However, I had a chance to get a copy of the contract and read it over. My lawyer—the one *I* ultimately ended up hiring—sent me succinct summary of the deal as well.

Upon marriage, Lucienne Peery's husband will receive ten percent of Sebastian Jewelry shares from her, plus five percent voting share of Peery Diamonds, in addition to a seat on Peery Diamonds's BOD. This is contingent on the husband signing the legal document prepared by Lucienne's legal team in Nesovia, giving her the full control over her finances. Refer to Exhibit A.

I already read the exhibit. It's beyond ridiculous. Like I want or care about her money.

The husband can file for a divorce after five years of marriage. Lucienne can divorce him at any time.

Completely unfair, but my family's idiot lawyer never questioned it. And it's too late to undo it.

There will be no commingling of assets after marriage. Any assets acquired post-marriage are to be divided fifty/fifty upon divorce. Joint custody should there be any children.

There's no way I'm bringing a child into this unholy mix.

If the Comtoises breach the deal, they'll hand over thirty percent of voting shares of Sebastian Jewelry to Lucienne Peery. If Lucienne Peery breaches the deal, she'll hand over thirty percent of the voting shares of Peery Diamonds to the Comtoises.

Just what was my family smoking? And why the hell didn't their lawyer stop them?

The Sebastian Peery collaboration in Korea requires capital investment, split fifty/fifty between Sebastian Jewelry and Peery Diamonds, but the profit is split fifty-five/forty-five in Sebastian Jewelry's favor. Lucienne Peery will be spearheading it.

The family not putting Preston in charge of the collaboration is the only sensible thing they've done in this deal. I make a mental note to look into this collaboration arrangement more closely. Knowing what I know about Lucienne, she'll be dropping balls left and right—assuming there are any left to drop—and I'll have to clean up the mess.

More texts from my brothers arrive.

–Huxley: Why don't you try John Highsmith from Highsmith, Dickson and Associates? He's good.

–Me: Already did.

–Emmett: How about Ken Hayashi? He works for Barron and Justin Sterling, and you know they don't hire idiots.

–Me: Tried him too. There's no way out of this contract without handing over thirty percent of Sebastian Jewelry.

I'm bitter as I send the text to my brothers. I've consulted one high-priced lawyer after another. And I have nothing to show for it.

–Huxley: I'm sorry.

He feels bad because his mom represented Lucienne in this deal, which explains the lack of loopholes. But it isn't his fault his mom's so good at her job. It's my family's fault for agreeing to this infernal deal in the first place.

–Noah: You gonna hand over the shares?

–Griffin: You don't need Sebastian Jewelry or the money from it. Fuck them.

–Nicholas: I still can't believe your family screwed you over. What the hell happened to family loyalty? You certainly deserve it after what you've done for them.

–Grant: It's gotta be criminal. You gotta show them they can't fuck you over like this and get away with it.

My brothers are just as outraged as I am about the situation. We only have each other, and we always watch our backs. An attack against one of us is an attack against all of us.

It was the only way we could cope with and survive our childhood as Ted Lasker's seven sons. He never wanted children or a family. He got stuck because his vasectomy failed and he managed to impregnate seven women before he discovered that fact. We were born within four months of each other, and since he's never given a damn about us, he named us after our moms and shipped us off to European boarding schools when we were old enough to walk.

Actually, I can't even claim I was named after my mom, Marie Comtois. Dad named me after our family business. He probably didn't even get Mom's name before…the deed. *Ugh.* I need to quit thinking about that. Otherwise, I'm going to puke in my office, and our janitors shouldn't have to suffer because my dad is a shitty human being. These days, only thing Dad wants from us is to make him look good. It confuses him that we aren't interested. In his world, everyone wants what he wants.

–Me: I'm pissed off too, but I'm not giving Lucienne that much control over the company. It's outrageous. Peery is our rival.

For all I know, she approached my family with these seemingly too-good-to-be-true terms purely with the intent to get the shares. After all, she didn't even want anybody specific. Agreeing to take Preston is setting the bar low, and that should've set off my family's collective alarm *hard*.

—Nicholas: Which dumbass reviewed the contract for your family? So I can avoid using them.

—Me: You won't be able to use them even if you want to because I already filed complaints. I'm going to have the motherfucker disbarred!

—Grant: Good plan. Let me know if I can help.

Grant is eager. His motto in life is "Nobody fucks me over and gets away with it." He almost lost his wife Aspen because of that, but he still kept the rule. Apparently, she's the only exception.

To be honest, most of us are kind of control freaks. And more than a little vindictive. We've worked hard to ensure we have our own money and success, so nobody can run our lives. Having Ted as our father did a number on us. It doesn't help that some of our mothers are also self-absorbed, although nothing compared to Ted.

—Me: Thanks, I will.

I looked Lucienne Peery up after Mom left to get a more complete picture of who she is. Calling her history "colorful" is like calling Leonardo da Vinci "a decent artist." She beats my dad hollow in the Scandal Olympics. She even kicked a dog a few years ago, according to one grainy video I found online. What kind of heartless psycho does that? Not even my dad's ever done that—although it wouldn't shock me if he did.

When he noticed I was morose about all the crap I'd unearthed about Lucienne, Noah mentioned that gossip sites never tell the full truth. I appreciated the gesture, but of course I already knew. Dad's scandals are always *much* worse than what's reported. Lucienne probably kicks kittens as well.

—Noah: Do you think it's possible she just wants a husband to have a baby? Like, her biological clock's ticking? Because if that's the case, you could just donate some sperm and be done with it.

—Me: No. The contract has almost nothing on children, just details on the division of assets in case the marriage doesn't work out after five years.

—Huxley: Why five?

—Me: I don't know, but she wants us to be married for at least that long. Unless she wants to end it early.

—Nicholas: She could just want the semblance of a family for five years for some reason.

—Griffin: No "for some reason" about it. She probably wants to have a husband for the same reason Dad wants a grandkid.

—Huxley: So she can out-brag Josh Singer?

—Me: Don't be idiots.

I close my eyes briefly. Dad's nonsensical rivalry has been going on for years, although the only people who seem to be aware of it are him and his assistant Joey.

It's possible Lucienne wants something similar—because there's some rivalry only she knows about. But why would she want to marry somebody from the Sebastian Jewelry fortune? Why not a handsome guy who'd be ecstatic to marry a meal ticket? She's only twenty-five. Doesn't she want somebody closer to her age? Someone whose hobbies include clubbing and snorting coke? I'm a thirty-four-year-old CEO who's set in his ways. The only exciting thing I do these days is play tennis, because polo matches take too long. And she probably doesn't even know how to hold a racket.

Assuming she doesn't have some nefarious intent to screw my family out of the shares, she's making me suffer over some passing fancy.

Damn her.

I hate her for it. I want to punish her. *Nobody* corners me, tries to control me like some soulless puppet and gets away with it.

I'm going to find out what's truly important to her and rip it from her in a way that doesn't damage Sebastian Jewelry. That's the only way to even the scales.

But there's no time to stew over how to strike back. My phone pings, reminding me that I have a meeting with the Comtoises.

This won't be pretty. But it's necessary.

I'm a fair man, after all. Lucienne won't be the only one to suffer.

Christoph's voice comes over the intercom. "Your family's here. I put them in the Topaz Room."

"Thank you," I say.

"Your mother really wanted some tea, though..." he adds hesitantly.

"And...?"

"I told her we were out." *Like you ordered me to.* I can hear the silent addition. His low throat clearing betrays his discomfort with the lie.

"Good." Mom should know this is no friendly conference.

I put on my jacket and head out of my office, carrying an accordion folder stuffed with documents my lawyer has drafted.

The Topaz Room is one of our most basic conference rooms. It has a view of the city, but nothing else. A long oak table and seven executive chairs, upholstered in black faux leather.

This is where I fired Preston.

There are no refreshments. Displeasure and tension stretch in the air like violin strings pulled too tight.

On one side of the table are my grandparents. Grandmother is in a jumpsuit that flows over her petite frame perfectly. The fabric's satiny, and it's in the exact shade of pastel blue from Sebastian Jewelry's logo. If she thinks that'll soften me into accepting my "duties" stoically, she's mistaken.

She must not be feeling too confident. Although she's smiling serenely, one corner of her mouth is higher than the other—a sign that she's uncomfortable. A fifteen-millimeter South Sea pearl of exceptional luster glows on her finger, a gift from Grandfather on their thirtieth anniversary.

He's holding that hand, running the pad of his thumb over the stone. He says it helps him feel more connected to her, but it's really a supportive gesture because he can tell she's unhappy. His silver hair is slicked back, revealing his high forehead. There's nothing but open friendliness in his deep brown eyes.

But I know better than to be fooled. He's one of the best poker players in the family.

On the opposite side sit Mom and her husband Travis. She's decked out, more so than last time, in a bright scarlet suit and smoky eye makeup that say, "Nobody messes with me." The same diamonds are around her throat again, and she has a matching bracelet on her wrist as well, which Dad gave her because she asked on a whim. I hope that

42

isn't a hint that I should do the same and give her whatever she wants, because Dad and I are polar opposites. He thrives on scandals and being obnoxious. I like my life orderly and calm.

Mom is probably under the delusion that she needs to come down on me stronger than last time because I haven't given her an answer to the outlandish proposal. She'll never understand I'm not interested in taking responsibility for Preston's unfortunate failure to master the art of keeping his dick where it belongs.

Travis is your typical dark-haired, dark-eyed pretty boy with the square jaw Mom loves so much. Now that I think about it, he kind of looks like Dad. But unlike Dad, Travis is quiet and unassuming. Or at least he tries to give that impression. But you don't get to marry—and keep—somebody like my mother by being meek and timid. He has a few sneaky moves up his sleeve.

"If there's no hot tea, could we at least have some ice water?" Mom says. "Your assistant just left without asking. It's so rude. I thought we taught you better."

My grandparents and Travis nod. *You've been a bad boy, Sebastian.*

"There's no water either, Mother," I say as I take the seat at the head of the table.

Uncertainty slackens her jaw. Wariness settles over my family. They know I don't call her "Mother" unless I'm out of patience, and they were probably hoping the intervening two weeks had replenished my tolerance.

"I find it hard to believe there's nothing to drink in the break room," Grandmother says smoothly.

"I don't offer refreshment to my enemies," I respond.

Travis lets out a soft laugh meant to break the tension. "Come on, now. We're hardly your enemies."

My eyes slide to him. Whatever he sees there makes him shut up instantly.

"This is irregular. If you have something to say, you should've come to McLean," Mom tries again, referring to the family estate that overlooks the Potomac in Virginia. "It's very inconvenient for all of us to travel out here."

"And have this fight on your turf?" I say. "I don't think so."

"Sebastian, what's gotten into you? We aren't your enemies." Grandfather puts a warm and conciliatory spin on the words.

"Really. So what do you call somebody who gives you a choice between marrying a nightmare of a woman or losing what's rightfully yours?"

His smile freezes for a second. He wasn't expecting me to be so blunt, since I'm generally circumspect around my elders. But the good humor returns to his face just as quickly as it dissolved. "It's called making a sacrifice for the good of the family."

The other three nod like puppets.

"I see. Then you won't mind if I ask you to share in the sacrifice," I say.

Mom blinks. "What do you mean? We can't all marry Lucienne."

I pull out some copies from the folder and pass them around. My family dutifully takes one each. "It's a contract. Read it and sign it."

They begin to take a look. Mom's the first to react, but she's a fast reader. "This is preposterous!"

Grandfather lifts his head. "Is this a joke?" The open friendliness is gone now.

Their complaints feel like pebbles tossed by a toddler in a snit. "What's so unjust about it? I'm getting tied to a woman I don't want to marry. This is the least you can do."

"But giving you full control over our trust funds?" Mom's gone shrill. "And we can't even leave our trusts to whomever we want without your permission?"

"Correct. I wouldn't want you bequeathing money to somebody I don't like. Preston, for instance." He doesn't have his own trust fund anymore. It was something Mom had to agree to take away when I was forced to clean up after him for the third time.

"So you can keep all our money for yourself?" Travis looks stunned. He's never seen me in even-the-scales mode.

I laugh. "Why would I want that petty cash?"

"Then why are you doing this?" Grandmother sounds like she's about to have a heart attack.

"I'm taking away control over what's important to you—money." My family never shows how much money means to them, but they adore it. The luxurious trips. The ability to indulge every whim. The gorgeous clothes, jewelry, homes and cars.

They're too scared to trust that I won't strip them of their money.

"We aren't signing this," Grandfather announces.

"Well then." I shrug. "I'm not marrying Lucienne Peery."

"But the family can't afford to give her thirty percent of the company!" Mom wails.

"I know." I smile, happy that I won't have to waste my breath explaining the situation to her. "You've backed yourselves into a corner quite nicely."

"Sebastian!" Mom says, trying for some maternal authority.

I shrug. "You shouldn't have signed the contract behind my back."

"But it benefits you! You're getting Sebastian Jewelry!" she says.

"I should have—and would have—gotten it anyway. You know it and I know it. I'd never have run it if it wasn't mine." I pin each of them with a hard stare. "Let's be clear here. I don't need the company's money. I only run it because I love to, but I can always find a few new hobbies to occupy my time." It's a half-bluff.

Grandmother is clutching Grandfather's wrist, her hand vibrating with tension. Unspoken words are stuck in her throat. She wants to complain—maybe even plead. My grandparents have too much pride to protest about giving up control over their money to me—but they are dying little by little as I remain resolute.

"But we'll be destitute!" Travis says finally.

Well, well, well. Go, Travis. He just earned a lot of Brownie points with my family. "Don't be so melodramatic. All I'm asking for is insurance."

"For what?" Grandfather is bewildered.

"For what? Are you serious? For something to ensure you all don't betray me again."

There are knocks on the meeting room door, and the person I've been waiting for comes in. A deeply tanned man with sun-bleached hair in a cheap suit. If a teenage Californian surfer was forced to grow into a middle-aged office worker, this is what he'd look like.

"There you are. Just in time." I gesture him in with a smile, then direct him to an empty seat next to Travis.

"Who is this?" Mom asks.

"A notary public. My lawyer said I should have one for this."

"We need our lawyers to review this," Grandmother says.

"Feel free, but I'm not changing a word of it. It's a take-it-or-leave-it deal."

Mom opens her well-lipsticked mouth. "But—"

"You won't find any loopholes, Mother. John Highsmith drafted it himself."

Shock settles over them. John Highsmith is a legal shark, as lethal and vicious as Jeremiah Huxley. Seeing my family's reaction is worth every penny I paid for his services.

Mom is the first to give in. She picks up a pen and signs. "There. Happy now?"

"Do I look happy to you?" I respond with a sarcasm I can't hide anymore.

"Sebastian, this is just so...unseemly." Grandmother stretches her hand out in a plea.

"I'm not doing it to be seemly." I hold a lingering eye contact with her. Then I shift to Mother. "I'm doing this for satisfaction." Then Travis. "*All* of you need to sign, or the deal's off." Grandfather. "Your choice."

5

SEBASTIAN

IT'S ALMOST funny how quickly my family folds.

But fold they do, and now I control their finances. One wrong step, I'm cutting them off. I've been too soft with them, obviously, for them to think they could "sell" me like some painting or something.

On my way back to my office, I hand the signed and notarized documents to Christoph. "Send these to John Highsmith."

He nods and makes a note.

Once back in the office, I roll my shoulders. I'd prefer not to have to marry Lucienne Peery and take over everyone's finances. But we all have to do things we don't like. At least I didn't have to look at Preston's face. Lucky for him, since I wouldn't have been able to hold myself back. A kick in the balls is the least he deserves.

Wait a minute...

Speaking of people I hate to see—I pull out my phone and start texting.

–Me: I'm getting married. Wanna attend the wedding?

I don't have to wait for long.

–Dad: Is this a prank?

I let out a short laugh. Dad doesn't read or answer his texts. That's a job for his assistant, Joey the Toady. And Joey is wary. He thinks I'm fucking with him and doesn't want to get into trouble with Dad.

It's not surprising. Three of my brothers are married, and Dad did his best to crash all three weddings. He failed, of course, the last time having to flee in a helicopter that Grant assaulted with fireworks, mainly because my brothers wanted ceremonies that were romantic and dignified. You bring Dad into something, it's going to be all about *him*. The great Ted Lasker, Hollywood legend, producer of blockbusters, God's gift to the world, the man who never produced a flop in his long and storied career. No one knows how many celebrities owe him their stardom, and countless wannabe actors and models fawn over him, praying he'll turn them into stars. He now honestly believes that he shits rainbows and pisses eau de toilette.

Exactly the kind of guest I want at this farce of a wedding.

–Me: Nope. 100% legit.

–Dad: I didn't know you were engaged.

Is Joey demanding to be convinced?

–Me: Well, I am. You wanna come or not?

–Dad: Of course! When and where?

–Me: I'll let you know.

–Dad: You want cash or presents?

–Me: Your presence will be present enough.

For me.

Hopefully, Dad will bring his A-game and set a new record for packing embarrassment into the moment. When he first met Grant's wife Aspen, he told her he'd cast her in a movie with lots of sex scenes with the actors of her choice. I'm counting on Dad to outdo himself with Lucienne.

That done, I pull up the new marketing plan on my laptop and shift gears. I scroll down the document, reading quickly. So far, so good, although...

I make a short comment within the document for Otto from marketing to address later in the day.

The intercom on my desk beeps.

"Sebastian, your fiancée is here." Christoph's voice is less certain than usual.

"My *what?*"

"Fiancée...?" A slight pause, then an uncomfortable throat clearing. "Lucienne Peery."

Guess she finally deigned to crawl out of her coke cave. "Don't I have a meeting soon?" *Say yes, Christoph!*

"There's, um, half an hour before the next one."

I swallow a sigh. Sometimes he's too honest. "Tell her I'm busy and she has to make an appointment to see me."

"So next Tuesday? You're free at eleven."

"No. I'm not free on Tuesday. I'm not free on Wednesday, Thursday, Friday, Saturday or Sunday. Or Monday. As a matter of fact, I'm never, ever going to be free. *Not for her.*"

"I can hear you," comes a slightly amused female voice, smooth as aged whiskey. And like aged whiskey, it sends heat through my chest. "He put you on speaker."

The heat is just anger pulsing under my ribcage. It's doubly annoying that she sounds nothing like the shrill, grating harpy I imagined. She sounds sensual—slightly smoky, edged with cool confidence. I hate her for it, just like I'm irritated with myself for noticing.

"I don't have an hour to waste," I say flatly.

"It won't take more than half an hour."

"Fine." I check my watch. She's not getting a single second more.

I look at the office door and wait for a petulant, spoiled woman-child to flounce in. Hopefully she doesn't get naked and try to attack me. In a bid to get himself a grandchild, my father sent a hooker to my place a few months back. The experience was more than a little traumatic.

The door opens. Christoph's holding the handle meekly, and Lucienne walks in, head held high.

She seems even taller than she was at her mother's funeral, with shapely legs that go on for miles. Most women that tall feel self-conscious and wear flats or stoop a little to make themselves appear smaller. Not Lucienne. Her feet are in sleek teal high heels, her spine erect, her shoulders straight. There's a stubborn set to her chin that says she knows she's not only in control but will be victorious. Like a Valkyrie before a battle.

Desire tugs at me, and my blood starts to run hot. The fact that I find anything about her sexy is exasperating, but I refuse to lie to myself because that's the surest road to bad decisions. I can't afford to make a mistake with her. She's sneakier than the viper that tricked Eve into taking a bite of the apple.

Her ice-blue eyes, framed by lashes two shades darker than her golden hair, are guarded as she scrutinizes me. So. She's not a completely self-absorbed narcissist; obviously she's capable of gathering that I'm not thrilled with the situation she forced me into. My esteem for her goes up, but not by much. There's still a lot I'm furious with her about. Her not being a blind fool isn't going to be enough to redeem her.

The golden off-shoulder dress reaches an inch above her knees. How conservative. I thought she might show up in a "dress" that barely covered her tits and ass. Although the outfit isn't outrageous, it does show off the smooth, creamy skin and full breasts that are just big enough to fit my palms. My spine prickles a little, but I force myself to keep my battle face on. She's not getting the upper hand in my office.

"Mind if I sit down?" she says when I don't offer a seat.

"I didn't realize you were waiting for an invitation. I thought you did whatever you wanted, Valkyrie, consequences be damned."

"You can call me Luce," she says, like she hasn't noticed my sarcasm. "That sounds more intimate than Lucienne." She takes an armchair opposite my desk and crosses her legs carelessly. Her skirt rides up, revealing more thigh. She isn't exposing much, but somehow it feels erotic.

What the fuck? What's the matter with me? I've seen a lot more skin than this and remained unaffected. "Noted. *Valkyrie.*"

A soft sigh. "What are you upset about?"

"What *wouldn't* I be upset about?"

Lucienne arches an eyebrow. "I thought your mother spoke to you and you understood the situation." *How could you not see everything from my perspective?* I can just hear the unspoken, chiding question.

Fabulous. She really is a female version of my father. "You thought wrong."

She exhales softly in another sigh. "I need reassurance that I can only get from your family."

"Reassurance for what?"

"That I won't be backstabbed."

"Backstabbed," I repeat conversationally, while fantasizing about strangling her and everyone on the Comtois side of my family. "What an odd choice of words coming from you, when you've forced that exact experience on me."

Confusion fleets through her eyes. "Did they not tell you what you'd be getting out of this marriage?"

"Some lousy shares and a seat on the board? *Ha!*"

"And Sebastian Jewelry, too."

Rage digs its claw into my gut. She should've never tried to bargain with the ownership of Sebastian Jewelry, the company I've nurtured and grown over the years. If I only saw it as a source of income or amusement, I would've walked away. But it's my baby, no matter how much I pretended I didn't care in front of my family. "I never needed you to get Sebastian Jewelry, Valkyrie." Underneath my soft tone is an edge sharp enough to draw blood. "You've disrupted my plans with your little scheme."

"I thought the offer was fair."

"I'll be the judge of what's fair, not my family."

She studies me, her eyes shuttered. Her full lips are set in a flat line that gives nothing away. She doesn't squirm. She maintains a posture so perfect, even my grandmother would approve.

The fact that Lucienne's so calm makes me want to shatter her composure. Maybe even make her cry. She doesn't get to upend my life, then stroll into my office and play "I didn't do anything."

She wants to marry me because she doesn't want to get backstabbed? Fine. I'll give her the backstabbing of her life.

Starting with the wedding ceremony. A girl like her is bound to want a lavish event with everyone watching. She probably wants to stream it on some social media site, so everyone can see her—a glowing bride in a priceless dress, covered in gemstones—and burn with envy. Well, *fuck that.*

"Since you're here, I'm going to lay down a few terms of my own.

We'll have a civil ceremony with no guests, except a witness, who I'll provide. No photographers or flowers. No music."

As I spit out the conditions, I watch for signs of an oncoming temper tantrum. But there's nothing. She almost seems...relieved.

What the hell?

I shake myself mentally. I must've seen it wrong. Or she's doing an awfully good job of faking it, damn her.

"You also won't be moving into my place. I don't let just *anybody* come into my home," I add.

She nods. "Particular—and private—about where you live, are you?"

"Yes. Very."

"Aren't you at the Aylster Residence?" Her tone says, *It's just a hotel, not a real home.*

The fact that she knows where I live further stokes my annoyance. The Aylster Residence comprises the residential penthouse units at the Aylster Hotel. I like it because it has its own entrance, comes fully furnished, and the hotel provides housekeeping. I can also use their room service twenty-four seven, which is convenient, since I don't cook. "I am, and I don't want you invading my space. You've done enough already." I look at her, then flick my gaze around the office.

I wait for her to pout, complain, whine—something to indicate she's unhappy with my terms.

"We can live at my place, then. It's plenty big enough," she says calmly, like a normal, well-adjusted adult.

I don't trust that façade. Not even a little. "I don't like orgy pads."

"Oh, no orgies lately. These days it's just a drug den." She shrugs with a small smile.

"Like that's *better*?"

She laughs. "I'm joking. Loosen up."

Did that little witch just tell me to "loosen up"? "I *was* loose. And happy, and pleased with my life. Until you showed up with your ridiculous contract."

"I don't really—"

"You know why they call it a 'contract'? Because that's what it makes your sphincter do. *Contract.*"

"Look, I'll let you have all the private space you need, including your own bedroom. But I can't just disregard the contract, so we'll have to deal."

We'll have to deal, my ass. It's me who has to deal with this bullshit. "You don't have objections to anything I said about the wedding or the living arrangements?"

"If us having a quiet civil ceremony is what's going to make you happy, I don't want to argue about it. And it isn't important to me where we live, as long as it's comfortable and reasonably large."

Huh. Reluctant respect ripples through me. This woman is willing to forgo some minor things to get what she really wants. It's too bad she has her sights set on me for some reason. If it weren't for that, we might've been inoffensive acquaintances.

But she's decided to screw with my life behind my back, so we'll never be anything but enemies now. She might think I'll be a husband who won't backstab her, but I'm not going to let it go.

Let's see if there are some other buttons to push. "What about sex? You didn't put specifics into the contract." But the second the words leave my mouth, I regret them. She's probably fucked a donkey for the hell of it by now. She won't bat an eye discussing sex with her would-be husband.

Her mouth parts for a moment. She drops her gaze to my lips, then abruptly lifts it back up, like she's just realized what she's done.

Aha. A first crack in her composure.

"We'll do it if we feel like it. We're both adults." Her tone is like over-buffed marble.

A corner of my mouth quirks up. "Babies?"

"No."

"I'm glad we're in agreement," I say, enjoying her reaction and wondering what she's thinking. Is she flustered? Does she think she's too young to have a child? Or does she have more traitorous plans for my life, and kids would get in the way? "I've always wanted to have a girl, but I don't know if that's a good outcome, considering."

She frowns briefly, then smooths her expression. "Right."

Next step. "And if I'm already in love with someone else?"

The little crack that cut through her composure before is bigger and more noticeable now. She stares at me like I just asked her to build a dirty bomb.

She's stunned—and there's something else I can't put my finger on. But why is she acting like this? She can't possibly think I'd never fall in love. Or...did she honestly believe that I would fall for her? After what she's pulled?

A lot of people consider me one of the most eligible bachelors in the country. I'm young enough and—more importantly—wealthy and well connected. Lots of women have wanted to be Mrs. Sebastian Lasker, and none of them worked out. I have plans for my married life—or did. Meet a nice, scandal-free woman who shares the same values I do. She can't be stupid or lazy or boring. And we'll have a peaceful and dignified life together.

Lucienne Peery does *not* fit the bill.

Suddenly, she lets out a soft laugh. "*Love?* Surely you don't believe in such a thing, Sebastian."

Something hot grips me by my dick at the way my name rolled off her tongue, and I hate my body's reaction to her. Okay, so she's pretty. That doesn't mean I want to fuck her.

My penis disagrees.

Fine, I want to fuck her, but that doesn't mean anything. Jesus, I'm a man. Of course I want to fuck a pretty woman.

Not all of them. You didn't want to fuck Shawnie, my brain reminds me.

Shawnie and I had no chemistry. That's why. And I don't want the names of all the pretty young things who have left me cold.

"You're too practical for something as sentimental as love," Lucienne adds with a smile that appears strangely self-deprecating. Her quiet, resigned response doesn't make sense, but I ignore the slight unease in my gut. "By the way, if it makes you feel better, you were my first choice. Your grandparents thought Preston might be better because we're closer in age."

It's a ridiculous lie. Mom already told me I wasn't her first choice, and nothing Lucienne says is going to lessen my anger over how close I came to losing Sebastian Jewelry. "I'm seeing somebody right now, you know."

Uncertainty ripples over her face, but when she blinks, it's gone. "Is she the one you fell in love with?" she asks softly.

"Yes." A lie for a lie.

She bites her lip, her eyes flicking away briefly. If I didn't know better, I'd think she was feeling guilty, even hurt. But why would she be affected by my lie? She and I don't know each other.

Suddenly, she puts on a bright smile. "I'm sorry, but there's nothing I can do about the arrangements. However, I'll do what I can to make up for it."

"I don't know what you can possibly do to compensate, but..." How the hell does she think she can make up for something like that?

"Anyway, I don't care what people say about our marriage, but will it bother you if people gossip that there's something off about us?" Lucienne asks.

The smooth mask is back on her face, and the sight of it both relieves and frustrates me. I don't want to see her be vulnerable, but I also don't want her to hide her reactions. It makes it difficult to gauge how to deliver damage.

"Gossip?" I say it dismissively, although I'm not looking forward to the whispers to come. I hate being the topic of idiotic speculation, and Lucienne's pushing me onto center stage. "Not to put too fine a point on it, but everything is off about us."

"Fine, then. Why don't we do a couple of 'dates'?"

I shoot her a sardonic smile. "So everyone knows you moved on as soon as you caught my half-brother in bed with your sister?"

"*Half*-sister," she says. "Somebody I wish wasn't related to me, truth to be told. I don't suppose you approve of Preston?"

"No."

"Well. We have that in common, at least." She gives me a smile that's trying a little too hard.

Her oscillating between uncertainty and calmness betrays her nerves and anxiety. The fact that she's standing her ground despite my overt hostility is commendable. Most men can't, and women usually just break down into tears.

"Anyway, about the dating—"

"I don't have time to waste on this silly charade. Unlike you, I actually run my company."

If the jab hits the mark, she doesn't show it. "Surely you need to eat."

"I eat at my desk," I say, trying my best to sound like an asshole. It's another lie. I try to have a normal lunch break when possible. I work to live, not live to work. Enjoying a good meal is part of the deal.

She smiles like she hasn't heard a word I said. "I'll make a reservation and pick out flowers. You know, so you can look like a considerate boyfriend. All you have to do is show up."

6

SEBASTIAN

LUCIENNE ACTS like she's doing me a big favor by arranging our "date." She doesn't realize I have a lot to clear off my plate before this marriage can proceed, and "dating" doesn't even rank.

I hit the intercom. "Christoph, make a reservation for tonight at a suitable restaurant for me and Gabriella. Pick out a black pearl necklace as well. Akoya."

He doesn't comment, although he knows as well as everyone who follows society gossip that I give black akoya pearls when I want an amicable breakup.

So at seven thirty sharp, I'm at the French bistro where Gabriella and I had our first date. It's near her agency and her favorite.

Not surprisingly, I arrive first. Gabriella is always five minutes late, no matter what. Even if Christoph tells her we're to meet five minutes earlier than we're supposed to, she still manages to be five minutes late.

I order a glass of Sauvignon Blanc and wait for Gabriella's entrance. Bizet's "Habanera" fills the restaurant, Anna Caterina Antonacci's voice soaring effortlessly. It's a pleasant enough interlude.

Exactly five minutes later, Gabriella walks in, all smiles. Her olive skin is glowing—she probably did something to her face, since she spends half of her life in one spa or another—and anticipation twinkles in her dark eyes. I'm not sure what's gotten her so excited. Christoph knows better than to hint what this dinner is about to anybody, especially to her.

She tosses her high ponytail as she sits down. The V of her white sleeveless shirt plunges so low, it's obvious she isn't wearing a bra. As she leans over, I can see the outlines of her nipples.

Oddly enough, I'm unmoved by the sight. I'm thinking of another set of breasts instead—ones encased in golden fabric that didn't show any nipple outline but made my blood run hot. What the fuck? Annoyed, I take a sip of my Sauvignon Blanc. The wine's color makes me think of Lucienne's hair.

Damn it.

Gabriella isn't stupid, and she notices my disinterested irritation. "What's wrong?" She usually speaks with a faux Italian accent, but when she's agitated it goes away. And right now, that accent's nonexistent, her Bronx roots subtly coming out.

"Here." I place a gold and pastel-blue jewelry box on the table.

An uncertain smile curves her full lips. "Well. What's the occasion?" She opens the box. The light in her eyes dims. "What's this?"

"Black pearls. They're from Sebastian Jewelry's premium collection."

"That isn't what I mean." She closes the lid. "I thought we were getting along great."

We were, although things have been getting a bit stale recently. We've both been busy, and I was starting to get restless. A relationship is past due when I'm looking forward to a tennis match with Grant or Huxley more than rolling around in bed with the woman. "I'm getting married, Gabriella."

She sits back in her chair, all her earlier lean-in body language completely gone. "Since when were you engaged?"

Her demanding tone grates on my nerves. I don't need this after the crap I've been putting up from my family and Lucienne's unannounced visit. "Since twenty-four hours ago." It comes out more tersely than I'd prefer. "I want an amicable breakup. I thought you'd agree that's better, given our professional arrangement."

"You mean with me being the main model for your current marketing campaign."

"Yes. And I hope you'll continue."

Her throat tightens. An angry shade of red suffuses the face pretty enough to grace countless fashion magazines all over the world. "You've been seeing somebody behind my back?" Her voice quavers.

"No. Seeing multiple women at the same time is my dad's thing. I don't do that."

"Then?"

"It's complicated, but I thought it best that you found out from me before it's officially announced."

"Are you in love with her?" Her tone says she can't believe any man could fall in love with another woman when he could have her.

No is on the tip of my tongue, but I swallow it. My family has a vested interest in making this marriage look good. Gabriella doesn't.

Her expression twists like I just threw a bowl of chowder in her face. Finally, she blinks a few times and shakes her head. "Well. Fine. I suppose we can be friends."

"I'm glad you understand."

"But you'll still buy me a last dinner as a couple?" she says with an unnaturally bright smile.

Something sharp flashes in her eyes, but I'm too tired to analyze it. She's probably just upset and shocked by the abrupt end to our relationship. "Of course."

"And we'll be friends? This won't impact my deal with Sebastian Jewelry?" she asks, like she needs to reassure herself.

"Yes to the first and no to the second," I say, since I feel just the tiniest bit guilty about how abrupt I've been with her.

Her smile grows relaxed. "Well then." She lifts her glass of water. "To your marriage."

7

LUCIENNE

Two days after I meet Sebastian in his office, my chauffeur James drives me to Gion Shiyaki for our lunch date. Bianca is sitting next to me and unloading all her concerns.

"You sure you're going to be okay?" Her dark eyes dart back and forth between me and the windshield. On her ears are the diamonds I gave her for her last birthday.

I smile to reassure her. "I'll be fine."

She raises an eyebrow and makes a vaguely skeptical noise. She knows me, probably better than I know myself. We grew up together, ever since her dad started working for Mom as a chauffeur when we were babies. Went to the same schools all the way up through college. My mom and grandfather paid for her private tuition because they wanted me to have a friend I could count on.

Bianca's been that and so much more. I don't know how I would've managed everything that's been going on with Roderick and Peery Diamonds without her. She even got into an *I'm going to scratch your eyeballs out* fight with Vonnie when we were in high school because she tried to sleep with my boyfriend.

Bianca slides an impeccably manicured hand along her black chignon. It's something she does when she's unhappy about a situation.

She was shaking mad when I told her what I discovered when I walked into the suite in Barcelona. If I hadn't told her I needed somebody to hold me, she might've driven to Preston's place and run him over with her car.

Which would've been a shame. She just bought her dream car—a pretty silver Mercedes coupe—and getting blood all over it would have been terrible.

"I don't like any of this," she says finally. "Sebastian Lasker is a capital-J jerk."

"He doesn't want to marry me. So his attitude is understandable."

"But ignoring my request for an appointment for over a week, then treating you like that in front of his assistant?"

"He didn't know he was on speaker. I'm sure he was chagrined about that." But he clearly doesn't care about my feelings. He couldn't have made it more obvious that he hates me and this arrangement.

"And he was seen with his girlfriend immediately after you went to see him! You know he did that on purpose!" Bianca rages, her hands clenched.

"I know, I know." Google Alert sent me links to the photos of the two. They looked amazing together. Gabriella Ricci is a stunning woman, gorgeous enough to grace Sebastian's arm. She pressed her breasts against his arm with a sexy smile, and he dipped his head and whispered something in her ear, the picture of a loving boyfriend.

She must be the woman he loves, the one he has to give up to marry me. The thought lances me with an abrupt force that leaves me breathless for a moment.

"Based on how obnoxious and rude he's been, he's going to stand you up and do everything he can to humiliate you," Bianca adds.

"He won't," I say, although I'm not so sure. I texted him the lunch date details, but he never responded. In case he thought my messages were spam, I told him it was me, but still nothing. I know he read them. Maybe he wants to be difficult and contrary, just like he was when I visited him.

If he stands me up, he stands me up, I tell myself, even as dismay wriggles its way to my heart at the possibility. I'm not going to let it bother me too much as long as he shows up for the wedding. He wouldn't be the first person to humiliate me. Lots of people have, and I've stopped expecting anything better, even though a part of me is extra-disappointed at the thought of *him* doing it.

He was so nice to me in Paris. Showed me what I needed to do to fight.

And I *am* going to fight. Once I get Roderick out of the way, I'm going to pour all my energy into getting the Sebastian Peery collaboration launched. I need something to show the board at the next shareholders' meeting that I have what it takes to keep my position as CEO. Some of the board members, especially those from Nesovia, are going to be nervous that Roderick will no longer "manage" me. They might even try to replace me with somebody else—someone with a penis, of course.

"Even if he does come, he's still too old for you," Bianca grouses.

"He's only nine years older."

"Nine years more insulting."

"He's just busy."

"So busy that he had you buy your own flowers?" She snorts. "I can't believe I spent five hundred dollars of *your* money on a bouquet. A bouquet that's only going to make *him* look good. So annoying. He should pay for his own PR."

I pat her hand. "You know what's at stake." Bianca can be hotheaded, and I don't want her to be overly antagonistic toward Sebastian, since both of them will be in my life.

"He's getting Sebastian Jewelry for marrying you." The subtext is clearly *he should be grateful to you.*

"And I'm getting my life back." I smile and lay a hand on her forearm. "Look, I know what I'm doing. I promise."

"If you're sure. But I swear, he's not the guy I would've wanted for you. I was relieved when Preston was willing and able." Suddenly she sighs. "Sorry. I'm totally *not* defending that cheating asshole. I'm just a crappy judge of character."

"Hey, I was fooled too." He was slick the few times we met. All smiles and charm.

"I hope his dick falls off."

I laugh.

"Both their dicks, actually." She's still fuming over Sebastian.

"And I'll be stuck with...what?" I'm still laughing.

"I'll buy you all the toys you need. Silicone Dream has this new line."

Before Bianca can tell me about the cool adult toys she found, the Cullinan comes to a stop in front of Gion Shiyaki. James opens the door, extending a hand. I take it and step out. Bianca has errands to run, so he's going to drop her off at a nearby store and return.

The waiting area past the front entrance of Gion is a gorgeous stone garden. A thin stream of water pours down into a hole in a bamboo tube, which flips, hitting the wet black rock underneath with a dull thunk as it empties the water into the garden pond. I saw one in Kyoto a few years ago—the tour guide called it a "souzu" and said the sound it makes as it slaps the rock scares wild animals away.

A lithe Asian woman in an ivory kimono with colorful butterflies on her skirt comes over with a smile. "Welcome to Gion Shiyaki. Do you have a reservation?"

"Sebastian Lasker? Party of two?"

"Oh yes. He's here," she says.

I let out a breath and relax a bit.

"This way." She gestures to my right. Another lady in a pale blue kimono leads me through an elegant wooden corridor with off-white walls and wooden carvings and partitions. Many of them are decorated with bold Japanese calligraphy. The soothing sounds of Asian string instruments being plucked comes from the speakers.

Gion Shiyaki is a Japanese restaurant that opened not too long ago and is always booked. It's considered one of the chicest places to dine in the city.

Gion doesn't have a menu you can read and order off. It only has *omakase*, which leaves the meal up to the discretion of the chef. He serves whatever his inspiration leads him, adjusting for allergies and food intolerances. You can't dine here if you're concerned about price or have a fear of trying something new.

When I spot Sebastian seated at a dark lacquer-wood table, I put a hand on the hostess's arm. She turns to me, eyes curious, but I shake my head and study him for a moment.

My fiancé. Something hot and cold skitters along my spine, gathering in my chest until it's difficult to breathe. Those two words aren't something I'd ever thought to associate with Sebastian Lasker. Not because I don't care for him, but because I never thought it would be possible. Paris wasn't the only time I saw him. He came to my mother's funeral seven years ago.

I was able to hold back my tears, but when he said, "I'm sorry for your loss," I started to silently cry. Instead of acting awkward or annoyed, he wiped my tears away. I could tell from the way he looked at me that he didn't remember that night in Paris. He was simply being nice to a young woman who'd just lost her mother in a Jet Ski accident.

When Roderick tried to apologize to him for my "inappropriate" behavior, he coldly said, "There's nothing wrong with a daughter mourning her mother."

That made more tears fall, as it seemed okay to be sad that Mom was gone—even though she'd never really been there for me—because she was the only one who showed she cared at all. But Roderick considered my grief a nuisance—though he never said so publicly—and Grandfather thought I was being overly emotional.

"You can't wear your heart on your sleeve, Lucie," Grandfather said with a frown. "Not if you want to lead a company like Peery Diamonds." To this day, I wonder if my tears at Mom's funeral factored into his ultimate decision that I needed a man to direct me. As medieval as Nesovia is, there are ways to get around its rules, if you're willing to expend the energy and resources.

It's too bad there's no way for Grandfather to come back from the dead to change his will. I didn't shed a single tear when we buried him.

Sebastian has changed quite a bit since Mom's funeral. His muscles are thicker underneath the bespoke suit. And he's still taller than I am—somehow, when we're in the same space, I don't feel like an awkward giant. He gazes at the world with a casual languor that hides the sharp edge of his personality. It hurt when he was being so mean in his office. It was all I could do to smile and act like nothing could touch me. I've read articles about him, and they all say he's highly capable and intelligent. Some of the gossipier pieces praise his sense of fashion and generous nature.

But I'm certain that isn't all. The media is all about cultivating an image. They can only report on whatever persona he's decided to show the world.

Sebastian's large hand cradles his phone, and he's studying the screen with a frown that leaves small lines between his slanted eyebrows. No groom-to-be's happy anticipation. He might be meeting an IRS auditor for all the excitement he's displaying, which is disappointing. But of course I shouldn't be depressed. He never wanted this. His family didn't want this for him. They made themselves clear when they said he was too good for the likes of me. And his attitude two days ago only proved that he agrees with them.

When he lifted his cool gaze and regarded me like a poisoned apple, I couldn't bring myself to tell him I was the girl he was so kind to in Paris eleven years ago. Or that I only want his help for a few years to make my family pay. Maybe I was scared he would mock me for thinking any of what happened back then meant anything to him, when it meant so much to me.

Would he like me a little if I'd managed to maintain a better reputation? People look at me with lurid curiosity because they've all heard about me. But I don't know how to have a good-girl rep. Everything I do is judged harshly, and I've given up on explaining myself. The more I try, the worse it becomes.

A cup of green tea is in front of him, and he brought the bouquet of pink-orange dahlias I had Bianca order this morning.

Time to play my role.

I paste on my most carefree smile and infuse all the excitement I can muster into my step.

"Sebastian!" I say with a broad smile.

He looks up. "Lucienne." He stands, then places a hand on my shoulder. I air-kiss him, and he gives me the bouquet. "For you."

"How pretty! I love dahlias! How did you know?" I gush.

His expression grows guarded. "A little birdie told me."

He pulls out a chair for me, all solicitous. Our waiter brings out hot tea and water. I ask for lemonade, and he leaves.

The small amount of warmth on Sebastian's face disappears. He probably doesn't want to make an effort when it's just the two of us. But at least he isn't as overtly hostile as he was the last time.

"Next time, let me handle the props," he says. "That bouquet you ordered was embarrassing."

"By all means." I look down at the gorgeous flowers. "But what was wrong with the flowers?"

"Too shabby. Nobody gives flowers like that, unless they're trying to be insulting. I had my assistant buy a different bouquet." His jaw muscles flex.

There's no way five hundred dollars gets you something that awful. "I thought you wanted to be insulting and difficult about our marriage." Making a joke of the situation seems the best way to go. I don't want to fight him over some dahlias.

"My personal feelings about our union aren't for public consumption. Furthermore, giving you crappy flowers would make me look like an asshole, which I'm not. In public, at least, we'll play a civil couple. You might enjoy the attention of paparazzi and gossip rags, but I don't."

The tight muscles around my shoulders loosen over the fact that he's going to make an effort in public. He could've vowed to say all sorts of horrible things about me, and everyone would believe him. No matter what happens, I'm the bad guy. I can't even sneeze without someone attributing it to some awful intent. "Thank you."

He stares at me for so long, his expression inscrutable, that I wonder if I have something stuck between my teeth. My smile falters, and his eyebrows tighten.

Our server brings our first course of sashimi and cold tofu simmered in some kind of light brown sauce on delicate white and blue plates. I take a bite of bright red maguro.

"How's your day been so far?" Sebastian asks abruptly. "Done anything productive?" His tone says he expects the answer to be no.

I let myself smile a little. "Very. I went over our financials, and I was finalizing the distribution agreement with the Hae Min Group for the joint venture between Peery Diamonds and Sebastian Jewelry."

His eyes narrow slightly. "You really care about Peery Diamonds."

"Of course." I didn't at first, but then I realized it was a means to ensure Roderick, Karl and Vonnie got nothing. And the more I learned the business and worked at the company, the more I loved it. "It's my legacy. It means everything to me." I'd rather die than let Roderick and his awful children take a piece of it.

"You know, it *is* possible for companies to do joint ventures without marriage. Contracts are binding and enforceable regardless of our marital status," he says to me like I'm a misled child. "Your lawyer should've advised you of that."

"Jeremiah's great. It's not her, it's the laws of Nesovia. That's where the company's incorporated, if you didn't know. I can't control Peery Diamonds fully without getting married."

He tilts his head. "Even if you're the sole heiress?"

"Nope. Roderick controls the company on my behalf by voting my shares in a special trust." I can't keep my face completely impassive. The top of my head feels tight with rage, especially since the company isn't the only thing he controls. I can't audit how my own trust fund is being used because I'm not in charge yet.

"Like a regent for an underage queen in the old days," Sebastian says.

"Yes. And that's not what I want. I'm old enough to vote, drink and get married. I should be considered old enough to manage Peery Diamonds without Roderick—or anyone else—exerting undue influence."

It makes my blood boil that he would touch anything at Peery Diamonds. He's unworthy. He only married Mom for her money and couldn't even bring himself to stay faithful to her for giving him the lavish lifestyle he so desperately dreamed of. He's been trying to find me a spineless husband he can control so he can leech off me for the rest of his life. He's still pissed that Darren and I broke things off because he considers the CFO of Peery Diamonds eminently manipulatable. But Darren couldn't keep his penis to himself either.

I squint a little. Are Mom and I both cursed with cheating men?

"Barbaric," Sebastian mutters.

"Yes. Precisely. Anyway, there are a lot of things I want to do once I'm in charge. There are multiple projects on hold because I'm not able to spearhead them properly." I lean forward as excitement builds over all the possibilities. "I know we can grow so much bigger. Peery Diamonds can become more than just a jewelry company. I want our employees to feel proud to work there. When people hear our name, they'll think of beautiful things that can make them feel inspired and special."

Grudging respect flickers in his gaze as he listens. "When do you find the time to do all that and party?"

"I don't party. Not nearly as much as the gossip sites make it sound like."

He grunts. "Must not. Or maybe you have the vision, but not the will to work through it."

I pull back. "What's the point of having a vision if you don't work to make it happen?"

He shrugs. "Some people think it's enough to just have the vision."

"An 'idea guy'? Yeah, I'm not one of them. You'll see."

"I look forward to it." A corner of his mouth quirks up in amusement. The shutter in his eyes disappears, revealing a glimpse of warmth.

My heart starts to pound. Although the restaurant is cool, my cheeks grow heated.

"By the way, if you don't mind, I'd like to have our civil ceremony in San Francisco," I say.

He looks slightly suspicious. "Why there?"

"Because that's where Mom and I had our last mother-daughter trip. It's sentimental." We went a few months before she died, just the two of us. She was nice to me, like she wanted to make up for being neglectful. Although it was too late, I appreciated the gesture. And we had a good time without Roderick, Karl and Vonnie around to create issues.

His expression softens. "That's fine."

"Thank you." Thank God he gave in without a fight. "And can we have a party and invite people after our elopement to celebrate our wedding? And a couple of photographers, too?"

Quick annoyance replaces the sympathy. "Is that going to be in San Francisco as well?" He probably thinks I'm trying to circumvent his edict about a boring civil ceremony.

"No, L.A. It'll be good for publicity before launching our Korean collaboration. You should've received a preliminary report on the venture."

"I didn't." He taps the table with a small frown. "Explain it to me."

Did he really not get it? Bianca told me she sent everything Sebastian needed for the collaboration. Or...this could be some kind of test to see if I can pitch the idea without fumbling. He might have doubts about my capacity as an executive. Guess I'll have to reassure him, just like everyone else who doubts my abilities.

I start as soon as our waiter finishes serving our second course: fish and vegetable tempura. "The Sebastian Peery venture will target couples. Korea is a small but lucrative market. Their per-cap expenditure on luxury goods is the highest in the world, over three hundred dollars according to Morgan Stanley. It went up twenty-four percent last year, and many experts expect the trend to continue. In addition, they spend more on wedding jewelry than many other countries."

"It's just a couple of rings," he says dismissively.

He either really hasn't read the report or he's being difficult. My money's on the latter. He's too good an executive. "Actually, it's not. The bride receives a set of diamonds and a set of pearls, each consisting of a ring, necklace and earrings, in addition to the wedding band and a watch. The groom in return is given a ring, watch, tie pin and cuff links, possibly a bracelet as well. The bride's mother is gifted with a pearl set or a high-end purse. The groom's mother gets a high-end purse. We can create special pendants and loops for those bags."

His eyebrows pinch in surprise. "You've done a lot of research."

"Of course. I wouldn't have approached Sebastian Jewelry without solid market data. Just so you know, not all couples follow this custom, since it's expensive to buy all of that on top of paying for the ceremony and honeymoon. But many do, and they love to splurge."

His eyes defocus slightly. "I can see possibilities."

"Plus, we can also add what Koreans call 'couple rings' to our offerings."

"'Couple rings'?"

"The locals buy a set of matching rings to wear as a couple while dating. Just imagine the double-dipping we can do as we sell them their 'couple rings' and then the wedding sets. Anyway, since these are the kind of products we're launching, I want to make sure we have the proper publicity lined up. You're a handsome man. You'll look fabulous in photos."

He cocks an eyebrow. "And you?"

I shrug, trying to hide my discomfort. I'm not particularly pretty or feminine. I'm too tall, and I give off too cold an image. Some people even say I look downright bitchy. I doubt makeup would be able to soften me up much. "I'll do my best to be presentable."

He regards me like he's trying to peel back layers. "These ceremonies and parties are really about the bride. You should shine."

I give him a small smile to hide the uncomfortable, squirmy feeling in my stomach. He seems sincere, but I rarely "shine," even when the event is about me. For whatever reason, something always goes wrong, and I'm thrust into the center of some controversy or scandal. I hope that having Sebastian by my side changes my luck. I just can't picture anything going wrong when he's around. The confidence he exudes says everything happens the way he wants.

"Anyway," Sebastian says finally. "We can have your party."

"Thank you. I'll send you a few possible dates."

"A week or so after our ceremony should be good."

"Okay." I make a mental note. "And since you're being so agreeable, I'll let you ask me for a favor later."

"I didn't agree to get a favor out of you." He sounds mildly annoyed —even insulted.

"I know, but I want to be fair. I know this has been an imposition."

He opens his mouth as though he wants to say something, then waves his hand dismissively. "I'm never calling it in, so don't think this is how you can placate me."

It's a little sad that he can't accept what I'm offering at face value. On the other hand, nothing about what's happening between us is normal. "All right, but if you change your mind..." I shrug. "Just ask."

We finish our lunch. He picks up the leather folio our server brings.

"Here." I slide my credit card toward him. "For lunch. I figure I should take care of it, especially since you didn't want to come."

"Don't be ridiculous. I wouldn't let my fiancée pay for lunch." He pushes my card back and sticks his card into the folio instead.

I curl my hands around the hot green tea the server brought out with our bill, warming my fingers. I try not to put any meaning behind him calling me "my fiancée" even though my stomach is fluttering. He might *call* me his fiancée, but his attitude says he'd do anything to change that.

However, he plays the part, escorting me like a gentleman through the restaurant as we exit, his hand at the small of my back. The warmth from the touch seeps through the thin silk of my dress. Little electric *frissons* rush down my spine. His presence wraps around me like a shield, like his coat did in Paris. I feel warm and protected for some inexplicable reason, even though it can't be real.

I spot a sandy head following us in my peripheral vision. It's a paparazzo who's been after me ever since I graduated from college. I call him That Stalker because he's everywhere. And when he shows up, others do too, like sharks scenting blood.

"I'm sorry, but the paparazzi are ready to snap some photos." I lean toward Sebastian and whisper it with a small smile for the benefit of any onlookers.

He curses under his breath, but he doesn't give away his annoyance. "How many?" he says, tilting his head in my direction.

"Too many to evade. It happens."

"*It happens?* You put up with them?" Disapproval and disbelief crackle in his voice.

"What can you do? These days they all have those superpowered lenses and can get a shot no matter how far away they are. I prefer to know when I'm being watched." I paste on a warm smile, since I have no idea how many of them are busy snapping away. "Why? Do you want to give them something to post?"

His eyes narrow. "Maybe we should."

I tilt my head up. It's nice—and kind of novel. I'm too tall to look up at most men. Even Preston complained about my height, saying I should only wear flats. Apparently, it isn't "cool" for a woman to be so tall. Probably because he's half an inch shorter than me in heels.

Sebastian tightens his arm around my waist, pulling me closer and making me gasp. Little fireworks go off along my back where he's touching, and his mouth slants over mine.

His tongue pushes in between my lips, strokes mine. He plunders me like he has the right—like I'm his property. I should be alarmed, even offended, at the blatant display of ownership, but the hot rush from the kiss makes it seem unimportant. Every inch of my body heats and shivers with a potent thrill. I grip his shoulder, feeling like the ground is shifting.

He flexes his long fingers along my side, digging in a little, like he wants more than a kiss.

Yes, yes...

A loud honk pierces the sensual fog clouding my head. I jerk back, breathing hard. My lips throb, and his mouth is red and wet. Absurdly enough, I want to kiss him again.

Get a grip, I tell myself, forcing some emotional distance between us.

A glimmer of something that's halfway between disappointment and greed surfaces in his darkened gaze, then disappears.

Disquieting need digs deeper into my belly, but I shake it off. This isn't real, I remind myself. But it doesn't feel like a show.

8

LUCIENNE

"I'm so sorry." Bianca rushes over as I step out of the elevator in Peery Diamonds' North American headquarters the next morning. "I don't understand how they can twist a picture between you and Sebastian kissing into you stealing him from Gabriella Ricci."

"I would've been shocked if they hadn't. There's nothing to be done about it, so don't worry."

"They're saying that she's 'too heartbroken' to make an official statement about the incident. It sounds like you put her in the hospital or something!"

"Pfft. Let it go." I try for blithe unconcern, like I always do when stuff like this happens. It's better than showing how much it hurts.

To bolster myself for the day, I picked out one of my best outfits—a gorgeous teal Versace suit that never fails to make me feel untouchable—and extra-tall high heels in sunflower yellow. On my throat and ears are diamonds—because when a girl's feeling down, nothing cheers her up like some impeccably cut stones. "This isn't my first rodeo, Bianca."

"Yeah, but he's your *fiancé*. It's so unfair what people are saying about you."

"As opposed to when?" "Bitch" is among the kinder words strangers fling at me online.

Bianca purses her lips. "We should announce your engagement soon."

"Why don't you contact Sebastian's people and see how they'd like to proceed?"

We walk together toward my office. My eyes narrow when I spot Roderick walking toward us from the opposite end of the hall.

He hasn't changed much over the years—just some silver at the temples and extra lines around his eyes and mouth. For a jerk, he's aged pretty well. He should've acquired some scars or something to reflect what an awful human being he is inside.

I study his Brioni shirt and slacks, the A. Lange & Söhne on his wrist and the huge yellow diamond on his finger. His face is radiant—he probably had a facial in the last couple of days.

Familiar resentment stirs again. How much of my money has he spent on himself? What else is he doing with it behind my back? He doesn't limit himself to extravagant shopping sprees. He also uses my funds against me: hiring people to look for a spineless husband he can pair me up with, retaining lawyers to foil my attempts to audit my own finances. Donating to Nesovian politicians who openly state women shouldn't have the same property rights as men.

It's appalling, but my hands are tied until I'm married and can audit everything to see what he's done. Nesovian laws are lenient toward trustees—so long as they aren't caught. The politicians are sexist enough to keep the laws the way they are, but image-conscious enough that they don't want scandals arising from the improprieties of male trustees.

Roderick probably thinks he has enough time to find me a husband he can manipulate. I can't wait to see his face when he realizes he's wrong.

"What are you doing here, Roderick?" I say as I enter my office.

"What am I *doing*?" He follows me in, leaving the door open. "I'm entitled to be here." He doesn't try to force me to address him as "Daddy" or "Dad" because he's finally accepted that I'm never going to.

Bianca hovers. So does her assistant Julio, who's trotted over. The former is worried, and the latter is half concerned, half anticipatory. The fact that Roderick and I don't get along is no secret.

I put my purse on the desk and turn to face Roderick. What wouldn't I give to wipe that smug look off his face. "You don't hold any position at Peery Diamonds."

"Sure I do. I'm a consultant, remember?"

"A 'consultant' with nothing useful to contribute."

"Plus, I'm your father and proxy, so I have a say here." He shoots me a superior smirk.

Asshole. I can't *wait* to reincorporate the company in the States.

"And I have an appointment with Darren," he adds.

"About what?" I say, wary at the mention of the CFO and my former fiancé. *What are they plotting behind my back?*

"About you. How long are you going to hold a minor indiscretion against him?"

"It was neither minor nor 'indiscreet.' He was screwing his assistant in his office. You *do* remember that, right? You're not that old."

"So? You did that model... What was his name again?" He snaps his fingers. "Filip Novak?"

"Filip and I went to a gala together once. That's it." And it was after I caught Darren with his assistant. It's hardly the same thing, but somehow it's turned into a "Lucienne's fucking a model behind her fiancé's back" scandal. I was frustrated but resigned because things like that happen to me all the time, and Bianca was furious. Darren practically sagged with relief that he didn't look like a complete asshole. "But good old Roderick. You've never been interested in the truth, just what's most convenient for you."

"And you've been nothing but shameful," Roderick says with a harrumph. "Filip, and now Sebastian Lasker? At least Filip wasn't taken. Do you have to go stealing men from other women, too? Gabriella Ricci doesn't deserve this."

Wow. "When did you become so concerned about Gabriella Ricci?" Assuming he even knows her well enough to feel anything one way or the other.

I shouldn't be let down that he hasn't said a single kind word about me, but a tight knot is lodged in my chest anyway. The only comfort is that it's grown smaller over the years. "Instead of wasting your breath on me, you should have your 'thou shalt not steal other women's men' lecture with your precious Vonnie."

He blinks in confusion. "Why?"

"I found her in bed with a man who isn't hers, *like a little slut.*" I infuse my words with all the contempt I have for him and his children. I want him to lose control and strike me, right here in front of two witnesses. Nesovia might be stuck in the Dark Ages in so many ways, but if Roderick hits me, it'll strip him of the right to oversee my finances. The country takes physical abuse seriously—probably so it can pretend it's civilized. Too bad it doesn't care about emotional or mental abuse.

On top of that, I'd love to see him thrown in jail for assault.

Roderick's face colors. If he were a cat, all the hair on his back would be stiffening with outrage. I wonder if he's ever been upset on my behalf? Or if he's even capable?

He points a finger. "You can't talk about your sister like that!"

"She's not my sister, not in any way that matters." I let my gaze rake over him. "She *is*, however, *your* daughter. As for Darren and his 'minor indiscretion,' it was a dealbreaker. Grandfather sided with me on this matter because, unlike you, he cared about basic human decency." I try not to be bitter about the fact that Grandfather's care for human decency didn't extend to firing Darren.

A vein on Roderick's forehead throbs.

"You're the only one who thinks fucking an assistant isn't a big deal." I tap my chin theatrically with my index finger. "But then, that's understandable. You did the same thing while Mom was alive. So keep your morality lectures to yourself."

"You can't talk to me like that! I'm your father!"

"A father who only sees me as a human ATM." He's never loved me or cared for me. It's tragically comical how he focuses on our blood relation when it suits him. "So no, you're not. Donating sperm doesn't make a man a father," I sneer, praying I finally push him over the edge. "And you're barely a man at that."

He breathes roughly, his eyes dark as he glowers at me. He clenches his hands into shaking fists, but doesn't come at me.

How disappointing.

My phone pings. I glance at the screen, dismissing Roderick, since he isn't going to get violent anytime soon.

–Jason: Sure, I can officiate the ceremony for you.

I smile a little. Jason Choi is a judge in San Francisco and one of my closest friends. I asked him if he could facilitate my romantic elopement in the Bay Area. Jason doesn't know who the groom is yet—I told him it was a surprise.

–Jason: Tomorrow at around 5:30 p.m. good? Or is that too early? You sounded like you couldn't wait. But my schedule's pretty flexible, so up to you.

Hmm. I haven't been able to decide how soon to get married— Sebastian and I haven't even announced our engagement. But hurrying things along seems like a great idea. I don't want to take my time and give Vonnie a chance to try to work her way into his bed. Sebastian seems like a man of good judgment, but you never know.

I can't afford to have anything derail this engagement. I've put up with so much already. Besides, won't it be oh so satisfying when Roderick finds out I married a man he will never be able to manipulate?

–Me: I'll speak with my fiancé and get back to you. And thank you! I definitely owe you one. Can you also be a witness to a contract signing afterward?

–Jason: Shouldn't you sign the prenup before the ceremony?

–Me: Not a prenup. And we can't sign it until you complete the ceremony.

It's the document Sebastian has to sign to hand over full control over myself to *me*. My legal team in Nesovia is going to file it with the proper authorities and work with Huxley & Webber to start moving Peery Diamonds. Just thinking about it makes me shiver with a sense of liberation.

"Are you ignoring me?" Roderick sounds a little pissed off.

"Um. What are you still doing here? Don't you have to talk to Darren?" Then I start singing, "Birds of a feather, flock together..."

Roderick turns redder. Finally, he storms out, and Bianca and Julio return to their desks.

I turn my attention back to my phone.

–Jason: That should be fine.

–Me: You're amazing. Love you!

–Jason: LOL. Love you back.

I pull out my laptop and boot it. There are three knocks on the doorframe. I lift my head and see Bianca. Her face is white, except for the red, blotchy spots on her cheeks. Tears are falling from her red-rimmed eyes.

What the hell? "What's wrong?" She's too tough to crumble like this.

"It's my uncle."

Oh no. She's close to him. I rise from my seat.

"He was in Budapest with my aunt," she continues, her voice teary. "For their anniversary. And there was an...an accident, and I... I..." She sniffles.

I hug her, hating that she's devastated and there's nothing I can do to help.

She cries harder. "I need to go to... They're trying to find his body, and..."

"Then go. Take all the time you need." I reach into my purse and pull out my black AmEx. "Take this with you."

"I can't—"

"Just in case. Otherwise, I'll be worried sick." I can't give her the private jet because Karl—*of course*—is using it. That bastard. As soon as Sebastian and I are married, my parasitical family's going to get completely cut off. "Fly first class," I tell her. "And do whatever you need to do, okay?"

"But... You need me here, too."

"Not as much as your aunt, Bianca." I pluck Kleenex for her, then pat her shoulder. "I can handle things with Julio. Trust me."

9

SEBASTIAN

As I walk into the office after my brunch meeting with our regional retail manager, Otto gives me a sympathetic look in the elevator. Penny glances at me like she doesn't know what to say as I step out.

And Christoph clears his throat as he follows me into my office. "I'm not sure if you saw the news articles..."

"Is that what we're calling groundless gossip these days?"

"Er..." His eyes shift like he can't figure out how he should respond. "No...?"

It isn't his fault he's nervous. I've never been the subject of lurid gossip before, and he probably has no clue how to react. "I saw them," I say.

It was impossible not to, even though I don't do social media or read gossip-rag junk. Noah's addicted to every social media app there is, and he reads every word like the salvation of his soul depends on it. When he sees something about the brothers or somebody we know, he group-texts so we can be in the know as well.

This morning I woke up to over thirty texts from my brothers, all of whom were acting like a bunch of high school girls. On the other hand, maybe they were worried because it's my first time in this particular type of spotlight.

—Noah: Whoa, I didn't know you were dating Gabriella Ricci.

—Emmett: You broke up with her, right?

—Griffin: Of course he did. Seb wouldn't be seen with Lucienne if he were still dating Gabriella.

—Emmett: Just making sure.

—Noah: What does she think she's going to get by claiming Lucienne stole Seb from her?

—Nicholas: She never said that. The writer just implied it.

—Grant: That's a good shot to go with the story. Look at Gabriella crying.

—Huxley: That's not a recent picture.

—Griffin: How do you know?

—Noah: Fewer wrinkles.

—Huxley: That's a shot from an ad campaign she did with us a couple years ago. I don't know how it got leaked. We don't share unpublished campaign material with anybody.

Huxley owns an ad agency, and he remembers all the details about every campaign his agency has done. His family disapproves of his refusal to use his judicial chops at their legal dynasty of Huxley & Webber. He only attended Harvard Law to placate his grandmother, then went into advertising.

—Emmett: Could've been your client. Regardless, this story's nasty.

—Noah: Yeah, it makes Lucienne look like a bitch who stole Sebastian.

—Nicholas: Gabriella's pretty and popular, so she's going to get a lot of sympathy. The public's going to tear Lucienne down. Maybe Seb, too.

I read the first two links Noah sent. Nicholas is correct. The comments are full of hate directed at Lucienne. *Jezebel,* from the religious nuts. *Jumped-up side-piece. Home-wrecker.* Ludicrous, since Gabriella and I weren't serious enough to move in together. A few call me an asshole. I've heard worse.

Gabriella texted me, too.

—Gabriella: FYI the media stuff has nothing to do with me. I never gave a statement.

Oh, I know. It's the damn paparazzi and their asshole writers. They had two shots of me and Lucienne outside Gion, and that only seems to fan the flames.

–Gabriella: But if you want me to, I can say something to set the record straight. But I left you, not the other way around. You can do that much for me, right?

Figures. Her pride can't handle anything else, and not even black pearls can sooth those ruffled feathers.

–Me: Spin it however you like.

My grandparents and mother tried to call. I ignored them. Preston has sent me whiny texts, as usual.

–Preston: I didn't know you were dating Gabriella Ricci! Damn, she's hot.

–Preston: Anyway, be careful with Lucienne. She's desperate to get married. But she's a bitch! A heartless ho!

He's apparently forgotten what he did—shoving his dick into her sister's pussy. But then, he has the brain of an amoeba. An amoeba with amnesia.

Oddly enough, the one person who should've demanded to talk to me is silent. Nothing from Lucienne—not a single text or call. Either she hasn't seen the trash, or she doesn't think I'm the person she should reach out to draft a statement to set the record straight.

I'm skeptical about the former and irritated about the latter. My mood is darker than it should be because I can't pinpoint exactly why the second possibility is so grating.

I shrug out of my suit jacket. Christoph takes it and hangs it up.

"Any calls?" I ask as I take a seat at my desk.

"Your mother—twice—to see if you were in. Your grandmother called, too. Three times. I told them to try you directly, but they said you weren't answering your phone. Do you need me to charge it?"

I hold my phone up to show him the charged battery. "No. I'm not answering calls from my family right now." They don't get to judge me or give me shit about what the tabloids published. "Did anybody else call about the gossip?" Maybe Lucienne called the office for some reason, although she has my number.

"No."

"Okay. Make a lunch reservation for me and Lucienne and text her with the details."

"And if she has another appointment?" Christoph asks.

"Tell her surely she needs to eat."

LUCIENNE DOESN'T SAY no to lunch. She shows up at Nieve, an elegant bistro inside the Aylster Hotel, on time. Christoph did well to pick this venue because the ambiance is romantic, almost bridal, with its ivory color scheme. A lot of couples have dates here.

On the other hand, it isn't the best place because it's on the first floor and two of the walls are floor-to-ceiling glass. Anyone can peer inside if they want, and the disastrous articles are still trending. There's nothing more exciting than a love affair gone wrong, especially when it involves famous people writhing with jealousy and love-hate. Of course, there's none of that in reality, but then, reality isn't important. People don't stay glued to their screens for the truth, but for entertainment. The messier the better. If they could, they'd bring out a pool of mud for us to dive into.

Lucienne walks in, a huge pair of sunglasses covering most of her face. But that doesn't mean the other patrons don't recognize her. You can't miss the striking height and regal bearing as she struts into the restaurant. She takes off her sunglasses and drops them into her Birkin purse. A two-piece skirt suit in dark blue-green flows over her curves, ending around mid-thigh. She's in a pair of strappy heels, and a diamond anklet winks with each confident step.

As she reaches me, her eyes flick to the other customers. They're pretending to eat, but you can't miss their gazes darting in our direction.

I rise to greet her. She hugs me, dispensing air kisses. Her breasts press against my chest, and her soft floral scent washes over me. Lust stirs in my gut, and her smile is overbright. I wonder if she knows the effect she has on men. On me.

Yes, I decide as a mischievous gleam sparkles in her eyes. It's annoying that my body responds to her at all, especially after Gabriella's little display did nothing. Lucienne's suit covers everything.

"For me?" she says when she sees the bouquet of tiger lilies.

"Yes. I figured I should provide my own prop, since I'm the one who called for this date."

She brightens in what seems to be genuine pleasure, looking at the lilies like it's been forever since anybody bought her flowers. It's disturbing because she shouldn't react like this—and I shouldn't be feeling like a caveman who just single-handedly killed a mammoth and brought it home for his woman. Lucienne must've received hundreds of flowers, thousands of gifts. Or maybe she's only been around coke snorters who squander all their money on drugs.

A wing of golden hair slides forward as she buries her nose in the lilies. She straightens and casually flicks it back with one hand, a huge Toi et Moi diamond and sapphire ring sparkling on her fourth finger. The stones are set in a simple platinum band, which emphasizes the extraordinary cut and size of each one—at least seven carats for the diamond, and a lot more for the sapphire because they appear smaller at the same carat size as a diamond.

She notices me looking. "Like it?"

"It's pretty." I go along with her for now, since she doesn't seem interested in talking about the tabloid crap. "You have good taste."

Toi et Moi rings used to be fairly popular. Some even have historical value. The one Napoleon gave to Joséphine de Beauharnaise sold for about seven hundred and thirty thousand Euros at an auction some ten years ago. Grandmother was upset she couldn't win it, but she was down with pneumonia. Grandfather wasn't going to leave her side to bid on a ring, even one that famous, and Mother wasn't going to cut her vacation short, since she doesn't care for jewelry auctions. She's an art collector.

"Thank you. And I'm glad you like it. What I'm thinking is, it's the engagement ring you gave me yesterday when you proposed at Gion." She gives me a comically broad wink. "I would've put it on sooner, but had to get it resized."

"Why are we doing this?"

"So that the scandal rag writers won't have anything that sounds off to pick at when we get married."

I think it through. "Makes sense. We got engaged at the restaurant, which no one saw because of the partitions. But you weren't wearing a ring when we kissed outside Gion, and this story explains that little anomaly."

"Exactly." She leans closer. "Sound plausible?"

"Plausible enough. Except I would have never brought you a ring that didn't fit." Part of me is irked with myself for not thinking of the ring sooner. The most important prop in an engagement or wedding— no matter how fake—is the ring.

She shrugs. "If it makes you feel better, you can tell everyone my finger was too thick."

"Don't be ridiculous." The casual way she puts herself down scrapes my nerves. "If anyone asks, we'll just say it was my error."

She opens her mouth to say something, but the waiter interrupts our conversation. I ask for the lunch special, and she orders French toast with two strips of bacon on the side, explaining, "I love breakfast, especially French toast. Nieve has some of the best in the city."

I wait for our server to leave. "Where are your PR people?"

"Taking a lunch break, I suppose. Why?"

She's either stupid or deliberately obtuse. My money's on the latter. "Didn't they see what happened?"

"Oh, the articles?" She blinks like she's shocked I'm bringing them up. "Do they bother you?"

"Bother *me*? I'm not the one people are calling names. Well, mostly."

"I know." Her tone says she doesn't understand what the problem is.

"Don't you want to explain things? Set the record straight?"

"My policy is never explain, never complain. Just makes things worse." Her lips are curved into a perfect smile, and she tilts her head in that playful don't-you-agree? way. But a glimmer of resignation and bitterness fleets across her face like a rain cloud. It isn't that she doesn't want to explain herself—she's convinced nobody will believe her. And she's going to cope by pretending she isn't affected, no matter how many people point fingers and judge her.

Without thinking, I reach over and take her hand in mine, the two stones on her Toi et Moi pricking my palm. Her mouth sags slightly as she stares at me.

Shit. I didn't mean to do that, but when she's trying to be brave in the face of unjust criticism, I just...

I just don't like people getting screwed for something they didn't do, I tell myself. I still haven't forgiven her for forcing me into this untenable marriage.

"No fiancée of mine will put up with bullshit," I say.

Her face colors. "It'll blow over." She clears her throat. "But are you and Gabriella okay?"

The unguarded concern throws me off for a second. "We're fine." Although stuff like this irritates me, whether she admits it or not, Gabriella loves the attention. To her, the worst thing that can happen is nobody talking about her.

Relief eases the set of Lucienne's shoulders. Her consideration is surprising. It also makes me wonder if she's really as terrible as the stories make her out to be. My dad wouldn't have given a damn. The idea that I could've judged her too harshly is disquieting. "You seem unwilling to have your PR team earn their salary, so I'll take care of it."

She looks at me like she doesn't know what to make of the offer.

"What? It's not a trap," I say, annoyed at her wariness.

"I... That isn't..." She sighs. "Right now, they're after me. If you try to get in the way, they might go after you, too. It isn't worth it."

I hold her gaze, oscillating between being touched and insulted. "I'm a big boy. And I can shield you from those wolves."

She shifts. "All right, then. I'll leave it up to you." She straightens her shoulders. "But you may not have to do anything. It might be easier to quash the gossip if we just go ahead and elope as soon as possible."

"Elope?"

"You wanted a very basic civil ceremony without any guests, and an impulsive elopement fits the bill perfectly."

True...

"A friend of mine is a judge in San Francisco, and he agreed to officiate the ceremony for us. Tomorrow at five thirty, if that's something you can manage. It's Thursday, so the timing might be a little tight, especially with us having to be back for work on Friday. But we can pick another date if you want. I'm sure he can be flexible."

The rushed timing is surprising—I didn't think she was the type to act so fast. The contract between my family and her specifies that we get married before the year's over, but there's no point in delaying things. I don't need a chore I can't escape hanging over me for the rest of the year. It'll just sap my mental energy. "Tomorrow's fine."

"Excellent." She beams. "And thank you for being so agreeable. I'll have our rings ready."

10

LUCIENNE

"THIS ENTIRE VENTURE is doomed to fail."

Mental fatigue. That's what this negative voice is generating. I smooth my expression and gaze at Darren. He always appears in my office after our afternoon meetings to tell me I'm wrong. Ever since I caught him with his assistant, he's dedicated his life to informing me how wrong I am on every metric.

What he really wants to say is I was wrong not to go ahead with our marriage.

He firmly believes that men occasionally make mistakes, and it's "a woman's lot in life" to let those mistakes go. As he stands opposite my desk and stares down at me, he looks awfully like one of those humorless old-time Jesuits—minus the somber piety, fiery intellect and thick beard. But he has the scowl down pat.

Even if he hadn't cheated on me, our marriage would've been a spectacular failure.

"We can agree to disagree." I give him a we-can-agree-you're-wrong smile.

"You don't even have the distribution sorted out."

I lean back in my executive chair and cross my legs. "But I do. The Hae Min Group."

"Have you signed a contract?" He sneers almost immediately. "No, of course not."

"We're in negotiation. But even if it doesn't work out, there are other chaebols and their luxury department stores. You should consider broadening your horizons." Thinking of horizons makes me think of horizontal, which brings back the memory of him screwing his assistant on his desk. She sure was horizontal then. *Ugh.* I need to stop thinking about that. It's gross *and* counterproductive.

His gaze drops to my cleavage—*creep!*—then climbs back to my face. "I can't allow you to spend money on frivolous new designs."

I prop my elbows on the desk and let a couple of beats pass. "'Allow'?"

"You know what I mean."

"No, I don't. Please, explain exactly how you won't 'allow' me."

A feverish attempt to come up with something clever is going through his head. I hope it doesn't break the gears in his little brain... Nah, who am I kidding? I hope it does.

Finally, he slashes the air with a stiff hand. "You're just being difficult because you're bitter over our breakup. I know you still love me."

"They say hope springs eternal. I guess delusion does, too. Whatever affection I might've felt for you died when I saw you with Frankie."

"She doesn't work for me anymore!" Like that makes everything okay.

"Only because Grandfather said it was going to be you or her—and you chose to throw her under the bus. Selfish, but typical. He should've fired both of you."

Frustrated anger twists his face. The sight of it gives me a small, bittersweet pleasure, even as a slightly insecure voice inside my head wonders what Frankie gave him that I couldn't. Whatever it was must have been greater than all the benefits of being my husband.

"But he didn't," Darren says finally. "I don't give a damn what you say, but I'm opposing this collaboration. Your father's on my side, too!"

"Of course he is. He's never met an invertebrate he didn't like."

"God, you're such a bitch!"

"Would you care to say that for the record, in front of HR?" I give him my most soulless smile.

He storms out, although his rapid pace ruins the effect. He's probably scared I'm going to call HR for real. But I won't. The pleasure of firing him face to face when I finally have control of the company is too great to pass up.

I'll never know what Grandfather ever saw in him when he decided to pair me up with that godawful excuse for a man. I thought Grandfather would pick somebody who would at least be faithful. But Darren simply isn't capable, and our engagement ended six months before Grandfather's death.

In retrospect, I think Grandfather felt bad, although he had too much pride to admit he was wrong to hand-pick Darren. I wish he'd felt bad enough to allow me to run Peery Diamonds with free rein.

But no. He just couldn't trust me to run it because I happen to be missing a penis.

So unfair.

Karen Jackson, COO and my right-hand woman, knocks. She's in her early fifties and has been with Peery Diamonds all her life. She's also probably the only woman my grandfather respected. She has sharp gunslinger eyes and an attitude to match. She doesn't play games, and she doesn't believe in wasting time or energy on things that don't add value. The only makeup on her pale narrow face is mascara and red lipstick, and she's always in a black pantsuit with a white top. She's barely five-five, but doesn't bother with heels. Black ballet flats only.

Next to her, I'm a giant.

She comes into my office, closes the door and sits down, facing me squarely with her feet on the floor and legs uncrossed. "We're having issues getting buy-ins from everyone on the Sebastian Peery collaboration."

"I know." Like Darren.

"You need to find a way to get rid of Roderick. He's toxic, and he doesn't care about the company, just whatever money he can get out of it. He's been submitting dodgy expense reports." A deep frown lines her face. But then, Karen rarely smiles. She takes her job seriously.

"I know." I sigh heavily. "But accounting didn't pay him, so..."

Amazingly, her frown gets even deeper. "They *did* pay him last pay cycle. Darren asked them to."

"What?" That bastard! Actually, make that *bastards*! "Claw it back."

"That's just a bandage solution. He's creating operational issues. Darren is claiming Roderick needs to be paid for the 'work' he's done," Karen says.

"I'm going to get rid of Roderick permanently soon." I don't say more. I don't want to jinx anything. Look how things with Preston turned out, and I only told seven people about him.

Although Karen is loyal, I want to be extra careful.

"I'll hold you to that," she says.

He'll be gone before the next shareholders' meeting, I vow to myself.

We discuss some of the labor shortage issues in some of our stores in the bigger European cities. Karen says she's coordinating with the local teams to sort them out. If they can be resolved in the next two weeks, it won't be a big deal. If it takes longer, we'll need a contingency plan.

After the meeting, I wrap up a few urgent items on my agenda and shut down my laptop. Have to hurry to make my flight.

As I walk through the lobby and into my waiting Cullinan in front of our headquarters, I have the feeling that something is missing...but can't put my finger on what. I have everything, including an overnight bag that Matthias packed and sent to my office after lunch.

As the car glides smoothly through the L.A. traffic, it hits me. *That Stalker wasn't around when I came out of the building.* Normally, he's always hovering, ready to follow me everywhere, even when I change my schedule abruptly. But not today.

And the other paparazzi weren't around, either. The tension in my shoulders dissipates, and I let out a soft sigh as my whole body relaxes. It's nice to know that I can move at least somewhat freely, without somebody watching all the time, ready to capture an innocent moment and turn it into an opportunity to judge me.

Still, when I arrive at the airport, I don my armor—spine straight, shoulders pushed back and head held high, with a cool expression that says nothing can touch me. But there's no sign of the paparazzi anywhere. And it's the same when I land in San Francisco and my hired car takes me to the hotel near city hall.

Weird... But I'm not going to complain about the reprieve. Maybe the universe feels sorry for the current outlandish scandal and is proffering an olive branch.

Well, universe, I hope you keep on being nice to me, because you have a lot to make up for. Over a decade's worth of sheer crap.

I check into my suite, shower and change into an ivory dress with a modest bateau neckline. It's made of silk and lace with little pearls sewn in. It fits me like a glove until it flares out below my hips, with layers of lace and chiffon adding volume. It's long enough that it hides the matching stilettos I'm wearing. Although it's an arranged marriage that my husband-to-be doesn't want and there won't be a photographer or anything special, I want to look pretty. I put on some makeup, braid a portion of my hair, then twist everything into a nice updo. A few flower-and-butterfly pins made with lavender alexandrite in my hair add the final touch.

Pretty enough, I decide as I study my reflection in the full-length mirror, then scan the opulent suite, which is as silent as a tomb. Mom and I stayed in this same hotel, although not this particular suite. What would she say if she knew what I was doing? Would she tell me to be kinder to Roderick? He was everything to her, only because he somehow conned her into believing he was the only one who could give her the kind of love she sought.

I wish Bianca were here. She'd give me a pep talk and cheer me up. But she has a more pressing issue, and I don't want to be selfish. I make a mental note to send her aunt some flowers.

On my way out, I instruct the concierge to overnight my suitcase to my place in L.A. and check out so I can head to the city hall.

The structure is enormous—taking up two full city blocks. It's taller than the U.S. Capitol, with a trace of baroque architecture. The dome reminds me of an old European church, not a modest one you might see in a village of farmers, but one the Vatican spared no expense on. I step inside.

Our ceremony is going to take place on the balcony rather than the rotunda. Jason told me there's a two-hour window when we can do it.

I walk across the marble floor and up the steps until I reach the balcony, which overlooks the grand staircase. My pulse throbs unevenly, for inexplicable reasons. I've been content with the arrangements from the beginning when I approached the Comtoises to hammer them out. At first, I was disappointed that they didn't want to match me with Sebastian. He was so sweet to me—twice—and if I had to have a fake husband, I wanted one who'd be kind. After all, I'm trying to get rid of the jerks in my life, not just replace them with different jerks.

However, meeting Preston allayed my anxiety because he seemed like perfect husband material—nice looking enough that nobody would doubt I'd fallen in love with him at first sight, and smart enough that he wouldn't let himself be swayed by Roderick, although I didn't factor Vonnie into my calculations.

But this marriage with Sebastian? He can't hide how much he hates me. Although he's been polite and considerate in public, I have no clue what he's going to be like in private, when it's just the two of us sharing the same home. He told me to even the scales back in Paris, and I imagine he will do exactly that with me for messing up his relationship with Gabriella and forcing him into marriage. The only question is how.

I feel shaky, like I'm stepping onto a frozen lake. It's murky under the ice, and I don't know how thin that ice is going to be. But it's too late to stop now. I have to keep on walking.

My stomach lurches, nerves fraying.

Lucienne Elise Brigitte Peery, get a grip. Within the next hour, I'm going to be my own person. Turning back now isn't an option, no matter how unnerved I am all of a sudden.

Footsteps ring from behind me. I turn and see Jason approaching. He hasn't changed much since our time in high school and college. He was one of the few guys in school who was actually a little taller than me. A black suit fits his lean frame well, and his rectangular wire-rimmed glasses give him an air of scholarly sophistication. He smiles broadly, his arms spread wide. "Lucie!"

"Jason." I step toward him with a smile of my own.

His arms wrap around me tightly. I hug him back, closing my eyes with relieved happiness. It's so *good* to see an openly friendly face. I realize I really needed to feel like somebody was on my side today.

"You look good," he says finally, pulling back a little, his hands still on my arms.

"Thanks! So do you. How long has it been?" The hair on the back of my neck bristles abruptly. Goosebumps break out, sending hot and cold shivers through my belly. The paparazzi, finally?

I glance around for That Stalker, but I don't see the familiar sandy head. Instead, my eyes collide with seething green and gold.

"Sebastian," I whisper. He approaches like an avenging angel in an impeccably tailored black Brioni suit, an elegant ruby and platinum tie pin the only splash of color. His self-reassured presence looms large, much bigger than Jason. Just staring up at him sends an electric chill racing along my spine, which I straighten further to hide my reaction. The hard set of his jaw says he doesn't want to be here and everything about the situation is infuriating.

The ice underneath my feet grows more brittle.

My smile turns polished and practiced. "Hi, Sebastian."

He wraps an arm around my waist, pulling me away from Jason and drawing me close until my side is flush against his. At this distance I can smell his pine scent and soap—something minty and refreshing. His body radiates so much heat that I start to tingle. I make a surreptitious attempt to put a little space between us, but his arm just tightens.

"Who is this?" he asks, his voice entirely too sweet for me to trust.

"Jason Choi. The friend I told you about." I gesture. "Jason, this is Sebastian Lasker."

"Nice to meet you," Jason says with a neutral smile.

"Likewise." Sebastian's mouth is curved into a beautiful line, but his eyes are hard. "*My fiancée* said you were doing us a favor."

Why did he put that strong emphasis on "my fiancée"?

"Well, it's not much of a favor. Anything for Lucie."

"*Lucie*." Sebastian repeats the name like it's a curse. "I didn't realize you two were so familiar."

"Yeah, we've known each other since high school. Actually dated our senior year." Jason laughs. "Prom king and queen."

"How lovely." Sebastian's tone is like broken glass. "*Luce* must've been stunning."

I start, stunned that he'd use my nickname. It's like he's having some weird competition with Jason, except he has no reason to engage in such a silly contest.

"The most beautiful girl in the world." Jason's eyes take on a dreamy look.

What? He's never behaved like this when we've talked about our time in high school. And it's a little alarming, because hostility is now starting to openly pour from Sebastian.

Jason's phone rings, and he checks the screen. "Oh, damn. Sorry, but I *have* to take this. I may be a few minutes. Excuse me." He adds the last part more for me than Sebastian, then walks away, head bent to his phone.

"Well, well, well." Sebastian's eyes are dark with disapproval. "You never told me about your history with *Jason*."

"Because it's not relevant." What is he getting at, anyway? If I didn't know better, I'd say he was jealous, but why? He couldn't have made it clearer that he would've never agreed to marry me if it weren't for the contract between me and his family. And he's in love with Gabriella.

"You could've told me an ex-boyfriend was marrying us," he says.

"I could have, but I don't see how it matters."

"You don't? Especially after that spectacle?" He points where Jason was just moments ago.

"What 'spectacle'?" What did the gossip sites publish now?

"You were all over him." His eyebrows pinch together in harsh judgment.

"Don't be absurd! We gave each other a friendly hug!"

"A *friendly hug*? More like a friendly dry hump."

Is he serious? Outrage bursts in my chest. "For God's sake, we didn't do anything of the sort. You should get your eyes checked, just in case you're going blind in your old age."

Sebastian's jaw flexes.

"What?" I hiss.

"I don't like the way you said 'we.'"

Oh my God. I'd rather face the paparazzi. "There's nothing wrong with the way I said 'we.'"

His eyes burn. Instinct says I should back down, but pride won't let me. Besides, I can't let him boss me around just because he gets out of sorts. It'll set the tone for our marriage.

I jut my chin out, my eyebrows raised. Sebastian glares like he wants to wring my neck. My heart races, tendrils of fear and something luridly exciting spiraling up inside, like I'm facing an unrestrained tiger. His gaze drops to my neck, and my heart pounds faster.

"Finally!" comes a booming voice from my left, shattering our standoff. "My apologies, kids. The traffic in this town!"

A tall man is approaching. He and Sebastian share a striking resemblance. The man looks to be in his late fifties—maybe early sixties —his hair still dark, without a hint of silver. He's overdressed in a cream-colored tux and a pale blue bow tie, but he's fit and the clothes look good on him. A Rolex glints on his thick wrist as he waves. This must be Ted Lasker, Sebastian's father. I've never met the man, but who hasn't heard of one of the most successful movie producers of all time?

A pale man with an exceptionally huge forehead and over-gelled orange hair follows him in. Mr. Orange Head is in a white dress shirt and black slacks, no jacket or tie. However, he's carrying an absolutely enormous bouquet of at least a hundred red roses.

"For the happy bride!" the producer says, coming straight for me.

The pale guy starts to extend the bouquet toward me, but Sebastian blocks his path. "Back off, Joey."

The guy bounces backward, and I glance at Sebastian. What did this Joey do to deserve this treatment?

"I'm so thrilled to be here." Seemingly oblivious, Ted Lasker puts theatrical hands over the center of his chest, and his neatly shaped eyebrows scrunch like he's overcome with emotion. Then he stretches out his arms and pulls me in for a tight hug. "You're the most beautiful bride I've ever seen."

I have to laugh. I can't think of a time somebody was this exuberantly happy to meet me. Most are too worried about all the rumors. "*Thank* you."

"This is my father, Ted," Sebastian says between clenched teeth. "He's here to be our witness for the wedding."

"And I'll be helping," Joey says with a wide smile.

Sebastian doesn't respond, but I'm close enough to catch a quiet snort.

"What's your name, love?" Ted asks. "Sebastian never told me."

"Because you never remember," Sebastian mutters.

My God, Sebastian is in the worst mood. He doesn't have to be so overtly unhappy about our marriage. However, pointing that out would probably just upset him more, so I do my best to smooth the situation over. "Lucienne. But you can call me Lucie."

Ted spreads his hands. "Like *I Love Lucy*!"

"Just like that." I smile.

"It's perfect! You know, if we were to reboot that show, you could star in it"—he makes a noise of satisfaction deep in his throat—"even if you're not Sebastian's type." He looks me up and down. "He likes them buxom and Mediterranean, like Gabriella."

The mention of Sebastian's ex is a little deflating. I guess Ted has seen the embarrassing "articles."

"Not that she matters. When a woman bitches about another woman taking her man, it just means the first woman wasn't hot enough to hang on to him. You're so much better than her anyway. Nordic beauties are like diamonds—perfect the way they are. Not all women are created equal, you see. Some look better when covered in clothes, but not you. I can just tell. I've seen millions of women."

Sebastian makes a choking noise, but Ted ignores him. I keep listening in mute fascination. I've never been around a person with such an unpredictable bulldozer of a mouth before. It's amazing how he can say things that are simultaneously complimentary and offensive.

Ted continues, "Lovely proportions. Very rare. But if you ever feel the urge to augment yourself—and every woman does—you come to me first. I know the best surgeons in Beverly Hills. Their work not only looks real, it *feels* real." He puts his hands out and makes a kneading motion. "Hand feel is critical. I mean, what's the point if they're like plastic? Am I right? Am I right?" He looks around.

"Totally right," Joey says.

"Damn right I'm right. And since you're so pretty and I absolutely adore this wedding, I'll pay for everything. Actually...you know what? I'll pay for anything you want. You just call Papa Ted, all right?"

I can barely process all the things pouring from his mouth, but I say, "Yeah, I'll do that," anyway.

Sebastian looks like he's in pain. "*I* will provide you with whatever you need."

"You don't know plastic surgeons the way I do!" Ted gestures at his assistant. "Joey, give her my most private number."

"Yes, sir." Joey hands me a card. "His direct number. Only three people in the world have it."

"You're such a liar," Sebastian says.

I take the card with murmured thanks and do my best to pretend I'm not affected by Sebastian's crappy mood. If he's going to be this upset around his father, why did he invite him?

"If Sebastian had told me earlier, I would've redone my mansion and had you get married there. It's an impressive place, and Joey here can turn anything into a perfect venue instantly."

Joey beams.

"Welcome to the family, my beauty. You're just..." Ted puts his hands over his chest again. "You inspire me to be a better man. I'm already getting ideas for my next movie. It's going to be amazing."

I smile a little. He's chaotic and all over the place, but he seems well-meaning. Not much of a filter, either, but then, he's a highly successful movie producer, so maybe that's to be expected.

Most important, I like it that he doesn't try to play power games or demand something from me. His offer to pay for plastic surgery—if I ever feel the need—is a bit off the wall, but endearing in an odd way. Roderick never offered anything to me. It was sweet of Ted to say he'd have opened up his mansion for our wedding if he'd had more notice. And I adore how he referred to himself as Papa Ted.

Jason reappears. "Really sorry about that."

Ted turns to him. "Who's this?"

"The judge who's going to marry us," I say. "Everything okay, Jason?"

"Yes. It was just some..." Jason gestures dismissively. "Anyway, it's been taken care of." He looks around. "Do we have everyone?"

"Looks like it." Sebastian couldn't sound more pained if he were being flayed alive.

Jason gives him an odd look, then smiles at me. "Okay then! Let's get started."

11

SEBASTIAN

THIS CEREMONY WAS A MISTAKE.

I was in a better state of mind when I landed in San Francisco and made my way to the city hall. The wedding bands Lucienne sent to my office after lunch sat in my pocket. Her taste is flawless, assuming she selected them herself. The matching platinum bands are set off with three brilliant-cut diamonds of exceptional clarity. The bezel setting makes the rings perfect for everyday jewelry, discreet and classy. In addition, hers won't compete with her engagement ring for attention.

A good sensibility is an absolute must in our line of business. Nothing's sadder than ruining good stones and metal because somebody has the discernment of a three-year-old. Worse yet is when a customer pays good money for some hideous item.

So based on that, I presumed Lucienne—no, no, no, I'll be damned if I call her Lucienne like a stranger when that ex-boyfriend of hers is *Lucie-ing* her like they still have something going on—*Luce* wouldn't be as awful as Dad, even though everything out there suggests she's the female version of Ted Lasker. Dad's taste in jewelry runs gaudy and gaudier.

My cautiously optimistic mood was still intact when I reached the balcony and saw her standing there with her aloof, expressionless mask on. It made me think for a moment.

Wasn't she getting exactly what she wanted by forcing me into marriage? Or was she annoyed that she'd been deprived of her first choice?

Would she have dropped the mask if it were Preston she was marrying? The notion of her pining over my worthless half-brother was annoying, but I wanted to know what she'd look like without the mask. I tried to imagine it...

Then suddenly, she smiled. I always thought she had a pretty smile, but this was nothing like what I'd seen before. It changed her entire countenance. All her defenses came down, and her eyes sparkled more brilliantly than our finest diamonds. She revealed a vulnerable side, glowing like the full moon in a midnight sky.

It pinned me to the spot, and I stared, unable to breathe. My heart knocked against my chest.

Her smile grew wider, and I started to move toward her. She spread her arms—and I picked up the pace. But then, eyes closed in bliss, she hugged this asshole like *he* was her damn fiancé.

What the fuck?

The aching euphoria was shattered, replaced instantly by hot ire pouring through my veins. Even when they broke the hug, the jerk kept his hands on her arms.

And she didn't shake him off. When she noticed me, she gave me a smile, but it was nothing like the one she gave the other guy. It was the smooth, practiced one she hands out from behind her wall.

She's never given me a true smile. And she's never hugged me like I meant anything, even though *I'm her fiancé.*

I don't know why the situation infuriated me so much. But it did.

Jason's eyes glinted with a cool male challenge, and it was all I could do to not kick him down the stairs.

I should've never suggested a civil ceremony. I certainly shouldn't have decided to have Dad attend. Or allowed Luce to select the venue.

I should've dictated a lavish wedding, away from San Francisco. Preferably away from Dad and Joey as well.

Most importantly, we should've never had some snotty Bay Area judge officiate. I could've asked the mayor of Los Angeles, and he would've been more than thrilled.

There's no bridal bouquet, and that monstrosity Dad brought isn't going to work. So Lucienne doesn't have anything to hold in front of her. Then Dad had to suggest that we hold hands, because wouldn't that be romantic?

And I agreed to it before he made any *really* outlandish suggestions, like having Joey lick rose petals and stick them onto our clasped hands to "seal our love." You never know with my father.

So Luce and I end up holding hands through the short wedding. Her bare skin against my palm is warm and soft.

I tighten my hold, shooting Jason a hard stare. You can call her Lucie all you want, but at the end of the day, she's my fiancée, soon to be my wife.

Her fingers will be gliding up my arms, my shoulders—my body. They'll wrap around my neck for a kiss while our tongues tangle.

Jason drones on, and my senses are hyperaware—like a million needle tips are touching my skin, not enough to hurt but enough to make their presence known. Although my eyes are trained ahead, my focus is entirely on her. Every inhalation, every tiny movement of her pink lips...

Jason has said something and is looking at me expectantly. So I give the obligatory "I do."

The bastard turns to Lucienne, his expression brighter. I didn't like him when I first laid eyes on him, and I like him even less now. Her *friend*, indeed.

Luce takes her vows and becomes the newly minted Mrs. Sebastian Lasker. Jason smiles beatifically, like a respectable pillar of our judicial system, but I know the pervert is stripping her out of her modest white dress in his head.

The dress really is stunning, making her look tall and regal. It shows off the lovely lines of her straight shoulders, long, elegant arms and perfect breasts. The dip of her waist and the firm curve of her ass. The dress covers her from the neck down, its long sleeves reaching below her wrists to hide half the backs of her hands. She looks like the most beautiful gift, and as her husband, I'm the one—the *only* one—who gets to unwrap her.

I take out the rings and slide one onto her finger. The sight of the wedding band against her skin sends something satisfying unfurling in my gut. The weight of Jason's gaze rests on me, and I shoot him a hard smile.

Look all you want. She's mine now.

"You may now kiss," Jason says.

I cradle her cheek, turning her toward me. Her skin is warm and smooth against my palm. My pulse accelerates. Our eyes meet, and her lips part. Her lashes flutter—not in a calculated move to seduce but in a nervous gesture. I can't decide how I feel about her anxiety. I want her to suffer, but at the same time, I want to shield her. The contradictory desires are annoying.

Whatever. I dip my head and claim her mouth in our first kiss as husband and wife. My tongue slips between her lips, delving into the sweet heat. Although there's a ring on her finger, the need to stamp her as mine rears its head, and—

"Way to go, son! I'm so proud of you!"

I flinch. Luce turns away, breaking the contact.

God damn it. I give my father a glare scorching enough to melt metal, but he just grins like some cocaine-addled idiot.

And Luce still hasn't given me the smile she did Jason, even as I sign the document declaring her in charge of her own finances and legal affairs, as specified in the contract between our families. When she finally beams, it's at herself, for her newly won freedom.

I might as well have been an inanimate prop.

Still, I'm happy that I've helped her achieve true independence. You can't fully exercise your agency if somebody else controls your money. And I have a particular distaste for a system that's set up to restrict people based on an immutable characteristic like gender.

We go to a steakhouse because Dad insists that we have dinner together.

"It's the least I can do for you and your lovely new wife. Lucy." He looks at her like she's his next Oscar-winning masterpiece. *And she nods,* as if she'd like nothing better than to spend more time with him.

I'm going to throw up.

Jason is at the table, too, because Luce's decided he deserved to be here for officiating, even though I told him rather pointedly that we'd hate to take more of his time.

Obtuse bastard.

I nurse my whiskey. She laughs at every godawful story pouring out of my dad's mouth. Maybe he should start a new career as a standup comic. Meanwhile, Jason is ultra-attentive, pulling the bread basket closer to her, pouring her more wine. She thanks him and smiles at him too.

Fucking former prom king and queen.

Let's grade her smiles like a diamond's clarity. The ones she gives Jason are Flawless, while the ones she directs at Dad are Internally Flawless, mainly because he says things that are outright embarrassing. But the one she shoots me every time our gazes happen to meet?

Her face freezes for a fraction of a second before she pulls the corners of her mouth up. I can't even rate that kind of rictus an I3, which is given to the shittiest gems. Actually, what she gives me isn't even a diamond. It's a pebble. Some worthless, random bit of stone you can find anywhere.

I knock back my sixth whiskey. Just look at her giggling at whatever it was that Jason said, her cheeks flushed. Her eyes skitter past me, and suddenly I've had enough of this bullshit. I'm her husband.

"We need to get going," I say.

"No, we don't," Dad says.

"'We' doesn't include *you*. Luce and me. Us. *We* have a flight to catch." I turn to Luce. "Don't we, *wife?*"

Jason's smile dims, and Luce gives me an uncertain look. "Right now?"

"Uh-huh. Did you forget?"

"Nonsense," Dad says, oblivious to anyone's needs except his own. "I brought my own jet. We can fly together."

I'd rather cut off my arms and swim across a shark-infested ocean. "So did I. And unlike you, I have work tomorrow and a routine that I stick to."

"My God, live a little." Dad picks up his wine glass. "You talk like you're in your sixties."

Being around him is what's aging me, but I keep that to myself. I don't want to have a pointless argument he's going to refuse to admit he lost.

Since Dad is the one who insisted on this dinner, I let him handle the bill while I take Luce's hand. "Good night, everyone," I say. *Hope to never see any of you ever again.*

Luce and I climb into the limo waiting outside. The partition between us and the chauffeur is up for privacy.

She lets out a satisfied sigh and looks out at the sky. "It was a great ceremony, don't you think?" she says, finally turning her focus on me.

"Fantastic."

"It was really good to see Jason again."

There she goes. Confirming what I already know. Did she fuck him? Well, obviously she did in high school. Bet he sucked. She didn't ask *him* to marry her, did she? Couldn't have, because there's no way he would've turned her down.

Don't be so smug. You aren't that much better. She wanted to marry Preston, remember?

The thought makes me want to kick Preston's ass.

"And to meet your father," she adds. "He seems so *nice*. I like him."

This is starting to feel like something out of Kafka. None of my brothers' wives like Dad. Aspen actually left a restaurant before her meal was served because she couldn't stand him.

"Why are you looking at me like that?" Luce says.

"Like what?"

"Like I just told you I have syphilis."

"Do you?" *Should've checked before I married her.* Given her wild history, who knows what she's carrying?

"No!" She huffs. "It was a figure of speech. Not a very good one, obviously, but I'm a little worn out after all the excitement. And why are you so grouchy? Everything went well."

"I'm not grouchy. I'm thinking." I'll be damned if I tell her how much her interaction with Jason bothered me.

Besides, this marriage isn't about me not being her first choice or her blatant smile discrimination. It can't be. It's about her cornering me into a position I never wanted. Frankly, if she hadn't forced me, I wouldn't be plagued with this uncomfortable feeling—like the burning sensation you get in the gut after eating a bunch of raw jalapeños.

Low-grade resentment starts to simmer.

"Okay, then," she says skeptically. "Do you want to move in tonight?"

I shrug. "Why not?"

"I'll have Matthias ready the second suite, then. I'll set up a home office for you as well, since you're keen on having your own space."

Matthias? "Who's that?" Her live-in pool boy? Some rent-a-gigolo?

"My butler." Her guard is fully up. "You can bring someone, too, if you want, but Matthias stays. He's been with me since I was a kid."

"I don't have anybody to bring," I say. "I'm at the Aylster Residence, remember?"

Her mouth forms an O.

Guess she forgot in her excitement over seeing Jason and my dad. I stretch my legs out, wishing I could kick both of them. "How airtight is your NDA?"

"What do you mean?"

"You don't want your butler telling everyone we have separate bedrooms."

"Don't worry, he's discreet. And yes, he signed an NDA." She shifts until she's sitting with her back straight with her hands folded in her lap, like a proper lady.

It's cute. And oddly sexy—it makes me want to muss her up until she's no longer seated so respectably.

Her skirt pushed up to her waist, her legs spread and her hair messy and falling around her lust-flushed face. That's how I want her.

"And if he wants to know why we're using separate bedrooms," she continues, "we'll just tell him you snore."

I bark out a laugh. "I do not snore."

She pulls her lips in for a second, then finally sighs. "Fine. *I'll* be the one who snores, if it'll spare your dignity."

"Are you loud? Or do you sound like a little puppy?" I ask, hoping to crack her composure.

"Neither. I don't snore," she responds primly.

Then I recall how she reacted when I asked about sex. "What if you need to scratch the itch? Are you going to sneak into my room at night? Or ask me to sneak into yours?"

"No sneaking around will be required." Her pose couldn't grow more rigid. "I'll deal with my itches my own way."

Images of the men she's been involved with flash by in a maddening slideshow. Even if only half the sex scandals are true, she's slept with most of the male population of L.A., all of whom would undoubtedly want to do it again. "My wife will not turn to other men."

Her mouth tightens. "I said *I'll* deal with it. These days there are plenty of mechanical options. Your services will not be required."

"And what if *I* need to scratch the itch?"

Her gaze makes a quick circuit, roaming over me from eyes to mouth to crotch and back. In the dim light, I can see her throat move. "You're free to do whatever you please, so long as you're discreet." Her tone is tart, almost dismissive.

Would she have said that if Jason were sitting here?

The unbidden question slices through my head, bringing the unpleasant burning feeling back to my gut. "If you got on your knees, I might not turn to other women."

She laughs, the sound a little resigned. "Sebastian, I don't expect anything more than what you've already done." Her tone says expecting more would be an exercise in futility.

She expects me to cheat on her.

And not just cheat on her, but not even be a minimally decent husband. All she wanted from me was that damned "I do" and a signature on the document she needs to send to Nesovia.

The realization is insulting and infuriating. I hate her for sitting next to me like a princess while she expects me to behave like some lowlife. She's acting like I'm the one who forced this union on her, when in fact it's exactly the opposite.

An abrupt need to shatter her composure surges inside me. If I can't get a Flawless smile, I'll get the next best thing. "I take my wedding vows seriously. And I won't be going to other women when I can have you."

Before she can respond, I crash my mouth down on hers, claiming her in an openly carnal kiss. She lets out a muffled gasp, but I don't care as my tongue glides in. I devour her, ravishing her mouth like I own it.

Her breathing goes erratic. She slides her hand up, along my arm and shoulder. Then her fingers are plunging into my hair, holding me close.

Yes.

I run my hand along the lush lines of the body I've been dying to possess since I saw her on the balcony. Her fingers dig into my shoulders, hard enough that there will be marks tomorrow. The minor pain only fuels my excitement.

I can't find the zipper on this damn dress. I grab the material to rip it, but she lays a hand over mine and pulls back.

"Wait. I have nothing else to wear," she says hurriedly, her voice raw but thready.

No other man gets to see what's mine.

I retake her mouth, my hand on her breast. It's soft and warm, even through the silky dress, and she whimpers, her head thrown back. I shower kisses on her neck, feeling her pulse beneath my lips. She smells so good, all aroused female. I nip her neck, and she lets out a moan, her body shaking.

Her legs move restlessly. I pull her onto my lap, pushing her dress up until it's bunched around her waist, and touch her between her thighs. She's shockingly hot; what little blood I have left in my head drains to my already turgid cock.

I watch the pleasure I'm giving her slowly twist her face. She doesn't seem like a lady anymore, but a corrupt goddess of desire. I run my other palm along her smooth, soft thigh and cup her ass. She grinds against me through our clothes. It's a kind of torture, but I don't give her what she needs even as I push her closer to the edge.

"Please," she whimpers finally.

"Tell me what you want from your husband," I say, "wife."

Her breath catches in her throat. Her eyes glitter with need, but she seems torn for some reason.

I trace the V-shaped crease between her belly and thighs, up above her pubic bones, back down over her thin panties. Air shudders in her lungs.

"Do you want to fly wet and horny like this all the way to L.A. until you can grab one of your vibrators?"

"I..."

I pull her close until her chest is flush against mine. I can feel her heart pounding. "Or I can finger-fuck you," I whisper into her ear, then feel another wave of tremors rack her body. I slide my index finger back between her legs, over the damp fabric of her underwear. Her pelvis moves—she's desperate for more.

"Please. Finger me," she begs, her hot breath tickling my cheek.

Dark satisfaction settles over me. "Good choice, wife."

I pull the thin fabric out of the way and touch her directly. Her flesh is searing hot and slick with need. I gently thumb her clit while my other fingers tease her further down. Her arms tighten, and she grinds against me, chasing her climax.

"I need more," she whispers. When I continue to tease without entering, she says, "Put your fingers inside me."

"Like this?" I slide two in effortlessly.

"Yes!" she hisses, moving her hips along my fingers.

I grip her hair and angle her face for a kiss. Then I let her ride my fingers until she climaxes over and over again, her pussy convulsing around me.

My cock is impossibly hard now. The need to drive into her is overwhelming, but I don't have a condom on me, and I doubt she does, either.

Impatience mounting, I use my free hand to undo my belt, rip at my pants and underwear and pull out my aching cock. Still moving against my palm and fingers, she reaches down and wraps her hand around the shaft. *Jesus.* The firm grip makes my cock tingle, igniting electric sparks along my back. She pumps her fist gently.

I claim her mouth again, thrusting inside with my tongue, and move my pelvis against her. My penis is happy to be imprisoned in the tight sheath of her hand.

I'm thirty-four, for God's sake. But her touch, the warm female scent of her and the shaky sound of her breathing are all driving me insane.

She lets out a soft sound as she shudders one more time, and I let go and come into her hand. The pressure that's been plaguing me since I walked into the city hall eases, and normally I would regain my composure, but no. *I want more.* I want to push into her, feel her convulse around me as her arms are looped around my neck, clinging, as her legs clasp me, taut and quivering, as my name falls from her lips in an endless scream.

My sane side tells me to get a grip. Going all the way right now would mean a possible pregnancy, *and that can't happen.*

Luce rests her head on my shoulder as her breathing settles. The limo has been stopped for a while now, but the chauffeur waits in silence.

"Time to go," I say.

She nods. I grab a fistful of Kleenex and dry her tenderly, although part of me wonders what the point is, since her underwear is soaked. But I want to clean her up. She's my wife, and I don't want her out in public in a disheveled state. I wipe the cum off her hand, then her dress and my shirt and tie. There's a lot of mess, and I tidy both of us as much as possible, then signal the chauffeur that we're ready.

He opens the door. I exit and extend a hand, which Luce grasps as she steps out. Searing satisfaction burns through me at her unsteady walk. Her cheeks are rosy, her artic-blue eyes glazed with the orgasms I gave her. Her lips are swollen and red, and everyone can see what we've been up to.

Except I don't want anybody to see her pleasure-softened expression. That's reserved only for me—her husband. Several men look at her covetously, like dogs would a piece of meat.

I put my arm under her knees and scoop her up, positioning her so her head rests against my shoulder. She buries her face, and her fingers squirm against my chest, betraying her unease.

But what could she possibly be anxious about? She has what she wants. If she's embarrassed about what we did in the limo...well, it's too late now.

I carry her through the terminal. The one reserved for private jets isn't as crowded as the main one, but SFO is still a busy airport.

"Aren't I too heavy?" she asks, the words tentative and muffled.

That was what was making her nervous? I seriously wish I could peer inside her head. "Valkyrie, you could quadruple in size and you still wouldn't be too heavy."

She doesn't respond. But her fingers stop moving. If she says anything, I don't hear her over the voices of the crew wanting to confirm the flight's final details. As more people move around us, Luce grows tense in my arms.

The irritating, frustrating wall is back in place. Part of me wants to smash it right now, but the cool air out in the hangar wipes away the whiskey haze in my head. *I've already given in to impulse with her.*

I look down at the woman in my arms—my wife. The need to coddle her and the need to even our scales wage a battle.

Neither comes out a clear winner even after we arrive back in L.A.

12

LUCIENNE

I didn't give enough thought to the marriage, I decide as I lie in my bed alone, in the dark.

For me, marriage has always been just a means to an end—a way to claim my independence. That outcome consumed me until all I could do was keep my eye on the prize.

What I didn't consider was what the marriage *entails.*

I shouldn't have talked about separate bedrooms, sex toys or Sebastian being discreet so blithely. On the other hand, I've never had any expectations about a perfect marriage—not for myself, anyway. I've never sighed over a wedding dress, or daydreamed about what it'd be like to have a loving spouse and family, because none of that felt attainable. After all, I grew up watching Mom and Roderick.

But something's bugging me, and I can't fall asleep. It's like there's a small lump underneath the mattress that I can't get rid of.

Then I finally figure it out. Sebastian wants my body, even though he's in love with another woman.

Gabriella Ricci. The woman even his own father says is exactly his type. Somebody I could never emulate.

I've been feeling guilty, but now something else is eating at me. A particular mélange of self-recrimination and shame that maybe I'm a horrific combination of Gwen and Mom—the body that Roderick couldn't ignore, and the money he couldn't give up.

It's a relief to know that Sebastian won't be cheating on me, but I hate it that the relief is there at all. Even though I'm legally his wife, I feel like the other woman.

I punch the pillow and turn, pulling sheets closer. This marriage will be a massive success if Sebastian doesn't do anything to embarrass or humiliate me.

Even the scales.

His motto was simple eleven years ago, and I don't think it's changed since.

Well, it is what it is. Focus on the positive. I conjure up all the things he's getting from this union. The company he loves. A brand-new market for Sebastian Jewelry.

And later, once I'm done expatriating everything out of Nesovia, I'll give Sebastian whatever he wants, including a divorce if he wants to be free to be with Gabriella.

You always have to make sacrifices. Nobody gets everything they want.

I just wish it didn't sound so self-serving in my head.

13

SEBASTIAN

When I open my eyes the next morning, it's barely a quarter past five. I sit up and roll my neck. It's my strict workday routine to be up before six. My head is a bit foggy from the lack of sleep. I can't blame the unfamiliar bed, since there's nothing wrong with it, just like there's nothing wrong with the huge, sprawling mansion. It's the laundry detergent. It smells unfamiliar. And it reminds me of Luce.

Which still is no reason to not sleep like a baby, especially after I jerked off to see if that'd help, but there you go. Shit happens.

After grabbing a quick shower, I pull some workout clothes from the suitcase the Aylster concierge sent last night and step out into the long, quiet hall. Luce's suite is on the opposite end, past the winding staircase.

Having separate bedrooms isn't something I ever thought I'd put up with in a marriage, but this isn't an ordinary situation. Luce makes me feel things that I've never felt before, none of them logical or orderly. Thinking about it now, I shouldn't have expected her to look at me the way she did Jason, and I certainly shouldn't have lost my cool or made my point in the limo, even if it did feel perfect.

Even now, as I recall how she melted and sighed, and my dick swells. But I'll be damned if I sneak into her bed for a repeat.

Not a repeat. You have condoms now.

Ah, yes. The ever-efficient concierge stuck a box into the suitcase. I should be pleased at the considerate gesture, but right now everything exasperates me.

Luce's home is a massive two-story structure with a basement. She took me around the entire place. Seven bedrooms, ten baths, a five-car garage for everyday use, an enormous twenty-five-car garage that can be converted into a ballroom for entertaining, a living room that overlooks the garden. She said one of the bedrooms is being converted into a home office for me—another considerate gesture I hadn't anticipated. To be honest, nothing is really what I expected.

There are two kitchens, both of which would make any chef weep with envy, and two fully stocked pantries. A well-equipped home gym and a theater in the basement. And she told me I was welcome to make use of anything as I saw fit, except for the garage-cum-ballroom, because she doesn't like to have a lot of people over without notice.

There isn't a hint of orgies or any sort of carnal excess. Every surface is spotless, the air fresh and clean. The paintings on the wall are classy modern pieces that I might've hung in my own home.

A miniature bronze by François occupies a nook in the living room near some floating shelves. Luce gazed at it fondly when she showed me around. "Isn't it just gorgeous? My favorite. I wish I had more of his work."

She must be a super fan to own a piece at all. François offers almost all his works to Catherine Davis, chief art collector for the billionaire Barron Sterling. Most people never get a chance to own a François, even if they're swimming in money. Once a piece goes into Barron Sterling's collection, it doesn't come out. And he almost never invites people to his private gallery, so you don't get to see them, either.

I head to Luce's home gym. It's probably rarely used, if ever. Most people love the idea of having a gym, but not using it. The former makes you feel virtuous, while the latter actually requires exertion.

When I step inside, music is playing. I spot Luce on the treadmill in front of a mirrored wall. She isn't doing what many women in my social circle like to do—put on a full makeup, a tight pink tank top and tights, then leisurely move around, occasionally doing a pro forma set but mostly posing and taking selfies to post on Instagram. Luce's long legs move rapidly on the belt, and sweat mists over her flushed face. A quick look at the treadmill panel says she's been at it for half an hour.

"Hi," she pants between rapid breaths.

"Hell," I mutter. Her labored breathing reminds me of the limo ride. My blood heats.

"If you want to run, I have fifteen more minutes."

"I don't." Her ass looks fantastic.

"Okay."

She's a little breathless, which, of course, is normal for someone who's exercising. I shouldn't have a reaction, but my blood starts to flow in the wrong direction: south.

"Why are you up so early?" I say, annoyed that she's in the gym and I'm getting turned on by looking at her.

"It's not early, it's Friday. Have to go to work." She exhales roughly.

"You do?"

"Yeah." She shoots me an *I'm not sure why that's such a shock to you* expression. "Peery Diamonds doesn't run itself."

Of course not, but I expected her to sleep until noon. I assumed she wanted her company for the same reason Preston wants mine—money, prestige and ego.

"I'm just doing some cardio, so everything else"—she waves a hand around—"is yours."

I go to the power rack and warm up for squats. But my mind's not on the sets to come. The mirror in front of me shows her profile. Her butt is round and taut, each cheek flexing and dropping rhythmically. Her calves curve perfectly as they flex, and her breasts jiggle a little with each stride, despite the red sports bra she's wearing.

So she wants some cardio, eh? my cock says. I have an idea—

Shut up.

Tearing my gaze from her reflection, I do my sets. I refuse to get sidetracked, no matter how tempting she is. Today is squat day, and nothing's going to change that.

Once I'm done with the squats, I jump up and grab the pull-up station at the top of the rack for some hanging leg raises. I bring my legs up all the way until they touch the bar, then lower them under control, getting the negative. The treadmill motor dies down from behind me.

Finally, the distracting presence is going to be gone soon.

In my peripheral vision, I see her walk to the ballet barre installed on the wall on the other side of the gym. From this angle, I get a perfect view as she contorts her body like a pretzel. Her flexibility is mesmerizing. One hand on the barre, she effortlessly lifts her unbent leg until it's touching her ear.

I imagine what it's going to be like to push her against the wall and drive into her with that leg raised, leaving her helplessly exposed to me. My cock instantly springs to life. If it could talk, it'd say, "Enough fantasizing. Let's do that now."

Her next pose makes me stop in the middle of a rep.

She pulls one of her legs behind her, the knee straight. The toes are pointed, and she pulls it closer to her back using just one hand to guide it, until the line her legs make resembles a slightly tilted *I*. She exhales, eyes closed, then bends her knee a little, sliding her hand along the curve of her calf until the palm rests on the top of her foot. Her spine is arched, pushing her breasts out. Sweat glistens on her flushed skin, but she looks utterly relaxed in the pose.

My body, on the other hand, is anything but relaxed. I let go of the bar and drop down. You can't do hanging leg raises while sporting a hard-on.

She switches legs. Her lips part, and her wet pink tongue flicks out.

My whole body tightens with the need to loop her ponytail around my fist, bend her over and fuck her from behind. The Toi et Moi ring on her finger winks as she makes small adjustments to her posture. It's like Morse code: *Hey, man, she got your balls along with your name.*

She lowers her leg and smiles. "All yours."

I know she means the gym's all mine, but my libido does its own interpretation. My long strides erase the distance between us. Her eyes widen as shock flares in their blue depths.

"How many men have seen you pose like this?"

She looks at me like I'm being weird for asking. "I've never counted. Why?" As though it's normal for her to stick her tits out or spread her legs in front of other men.

A sharply edged need takes root—to corrupt her, violate her and mark her as mine. I grab her arm and pull her in until the tip of my dick is pushing against the soft spot just above her belly button. A gasp tears from her throat, and I take her mouth. There's no finesse, just raw desire. She smells like clean sweat and female flesh, no soap hiding her scent. Her fingers grip my shoulders, and her tongue invades my mouth. She wraps one leg around my hips, pressing her hot core against my overeager cock.

Fuck the consequences. I want to drive into her right now. But somehow I manage to cling to control. *No condom, remember?*

You can always just pull out. But two of my brothers got their wives pregnant the first time they had sex without protection. There's no way I'm getting Luce pregnant, adding a baby to this mess.

I yank my mouth from her with a supreme effort. The possibility of an unwanted pregnancy can usually cool my libido faster than a thunderstorm dousing a brushfire. But my blood is still running too hot.

"Breakfast," I say, needing to say something to break her spell on me. Her glazed gaze says she'd love to be my breakfast. My hormones demand I take up that offer. "And coffee."

She blinks. The lusty haze dissipates from her eyes. "Matthias should've prepped something by now. Do you want to go to the kitchen?"

I manage to jerk my chin up and down once, commanding my body to cool the hell off.

"Lead the way," I say, then immediately regret it. It's an ingrained habit to let ladies go first, but with that ass...

Desperate, I try to think of all sorts of unsexy things. Like Dad's last birthday party with dick cannons and vagina balloons. Or how he got drunk and shoved his tongue down Mom's throat at that party until he realized it was Mom and not the chick he was hoping to bang.

The former doesn't do much, but the latter is fully effective.

When we reach the kitchen, a man in his late fifties is fiddling with an espresso machine. His hair is gray, but neatly trimmed in a style that flatters his narrow face, high cheekbones and deep-set brown eyes. His lips are set in a neutral line that hints at polished friendliness. A dark navy vest—buttoned to the top—is over a crisp white dress shirt. The creases on his pinstriped navy slacks are so sharp that even Grandma would approve, although she'd probably comment on his lack of tie.

"Good morning," he says.

"Morning." Luce smiles and picks up a toasted bagel. "Sebastian, meet Matthias."

His eyes briefly catalog my ring, then he looks at me, his face unreadable. He'd make a good poker player. "Hello, sir."

I nod, sizing him up. People only show their poker face when they don't like you.

He serves two coffees, one for her and one for me. I take a sip of mine while Luce gets busy dumping sugar into her mug.

"Was your room comfortable?" The question is attentive on the surface, but there's a slight undertone of disapproval. The man doesn't like me. Probably he's upset that Luce brought a stranger home to live with them.

Protective, aren't you? "Very."

Luce doesn't seem to pick anything up from his tone. Maybe she can't imagine her butler being anything but hospitable.

"I was surprised when Ms. Lucienne asked me to prep an extra bedroom." All proper and staid. He could be discussing the weather.

Guess she didn't tell the old man about her underhanded maneuvers. Or the justification we've agreed on to explain our separate bedrooms.

"Well, I—" Luce begins.

"Apparently, I snore," I tell him with a small smile.

Luce shoots me a startled look.

Matthias's eyebrows lift. "You do?" He draws out the words.

"Uh-huh. I guess I keep her up." I give him my blandest smile, then glance at her. Her cheeks are flushed, her gaze fixed on me.

The man considers my response, like he can't decide if I've made a lurid joke or not. "Is there anything in particular you'd prefer for breakfast going forward?" he asks finally.

"Cheese omelets. French toast. Pancakes. Bagels or English muffins, toasted. Not all at once. As long as I have something in my belly before leaving the house, I'm actually *not* too particular."

I down my coffee, filch a bagel from the plate in front and heap a ton of cream cheese on it. I finish the whole thing in a few bites, while Luce nibbles hers, dabbing at her mouth with a napkin like a proper lady. Grandma would definitely approve.

Is that how Luce convinced my family she isn't a mere scandal maker? I love my family, but I'm not blind to their flaws. If they had to choose between substance and polish, it'd be the latter all day long. Appearance and pride are everything to them.

After Luce and I finish breakfast, we head to our separate bedrooms to shower and get ready for another busy day before the weekend. I need to attend an extra meeting this afternoon that was rescheduled from yesterday. Afterward, I'm seeing my brothers for dinner, which should be fun. Despite our busy schedules, we try to get together for a meal at least twice a month.

I check my emails and texts, don't see anything urgent and start heading downstairs. Luce emerges in a deep royal-blue dress with a modest circular neckline. The dress ends an inch above her knees, and she's in a pair of silver stilettos that elongate her already endless legs.

I've never had a leg fetish, but I'm beginning to see the attraction. My mind pictures me throwing her supple legs over my shoulders, those stilettos still on, and...

No, no, no, no, no! I mentally recite the Ten Commandments in Latin. I can't think about Dad and Mom again, because that would be cruel and unusual punishment.

We walk down the stairs together, me once again behind her. Her hair's up in a topknot. I pin my gaze on the elegant line of her neck. It's that or stare at her ass again, although that neck is eminently kissable...

Damn it.

"Is there anything special you want for dinner?" she asks.

"No," I answer, happy for the distraction. "I'm meeting my brothers for dinner tonight."

She looks at me over a shoulder expectantly. "That sounds fun. Am I meeting them, too?"

"No." We reach the foyer.

"Oh." She smooths her hair and turns away.

I don't like the stiff set of her shoulders. Although I promised myself I'd even the scales, this is just petty. "You'll meet them at the wedding reception. Tonight's dinner is a low-key boys' night out. My brothers' wives aren't invited, either."

She relaxes a little. "I see." She smiles at me as a cream Cullinan pulls up. The wall around her seems a little less solid. So a dollop of kindness is all I need to weaken it? That's entirely too easy—suspiciously so.

She presses a quick kiss to my cheek. "Have a productive day."

"You too."

"And take a look at the Sebastian Peery collaboration docs I sent!"

She climbs into the car, then quickly disappears from view. Unless she takes a detour, she'll be in the office before anybody else. I don't know about her abilities as an executive, but I've got to give her full credit for showing up.

I get behind the wheel of my Phantom.

I told myself I'd strip her of what she wanted from this marriage. I read the document she had me sign after we got married. Our union forces Nesovia to recognize her as an independent adult female capable of making her own decisions. But attacking her from that angle is ridiculous. I don't want to manage her money or her affairs. In fact, I empathize with her need to free herself from the legal restrictions.

But that doesn't mean I'm okay with her method.

How about Peery Diamonds...?

She must love that company to have gone to the trouble of marrying me to fully inherit her shares. And she threatened me with losing Sebastian Jewelry.

Well, what goes around comes around.

14

LUCIENNE

—SEBASTIAN: I checked, but never received any docs about the collaboration.

That's weird. I asked Bianca to resend everything to him after our lunch at Gion, and she confirmed that she did. Is he just being difficult? But he has no reason to claim he never got them. This sort of move costs him money, too.

On the other hand, our contract specified I'd be spearheading the collaboration, so this could be a way to undermine me. I swallow a sigh and pull Julio up on the intercompany messenger.

—Me: Would you email all the Sebastian Peery collaboration docs to Sebastian Lasker? slasker@sebastianjewelry.com

—Me: Also can you instruct security to not allow Roderick, Karl or Vonnie into the building under any circumstance? If they are insistent, tell them to contact Jeremiah Huxley at Huxley & Webber. Also, disable Karl's employee badge and access keys.

I set my phone so all calls from Roderick, Karl and Vonnie will go to voicemail. I consider blocking them, but they'd just get other numbers to harass me with. By the time they learn about my marriage, it'll be too late.

That done, I scan my inbox. The most important is an email from my legal team in Nesovia saying that the papers have been filed and acknowledged. Roderick can no longer act as my trustee in any capacity. Nor is he my proxy for the Peery Diamonds shares in the special trust.

Right below that delightful notice is one from Julio with a list of audit teams I could hire to look into my personal finances. I pick a couple, and instruct Julio to set up appointments with them. I need to dig into how my trust fund has been used. Although I'm not certain exactly what I can do about Roderick's generous use of my money—the laws are a warren of loopholes—I need to know the extent of the damage. And a good legal team should be able to come up with some ways to make it hurt for him.

I send instructions to HR to fire Karl for excessive absenteeism and dereliction of duty, then tally up all the days he's been absent and do everything in our power to claw back his salary and benefits for those days.

Afterward, I email Naomi in internal compliance, and ask her to do a thorough audit of expense reports for the last twenty-four months. Every time I tried to use internal compliance to investigate some of the executives' expenses, Roderick did everything in his power to stop it. Even though he isn't a member of our C-suite, he had an enormous say in the way Peery Diamonds is run because he got to vote my shares as he saw fit.

But not anymore. I plan to audit everyone at the VP level and above because I suspect some of them are embezzling. Not that they're doing anything as dramatic as taking a million dollars in one shot out of the company coffers. The most common way to embezzle is padding expenses, and it isn't that difficult for executives to claim additional thousands of dollars a month that haven't been spent if internal control is lax.

I also need to announce my marriage, but after speaking to Sebastian about how we should go about doing that.

My phone pings.

–Bianca: I just saw! I can't believe you got married without me!

–Bianca: Unless it was just fake news and they photoshopped it.

News? Disappointment and resignation settle over me. I guess some paparazzi got us after all. Damn it. I wanted to have our PR team coordinate the announcement with Sebastian's people.

At the same time, I want to pat myself on the back for blocking my family from entering the building this morning.

—Me: Sorry for not letting you know. But there's no mistake.

—Bianca: I wanted to be there for you! You're my best friend!

—Me: I know, but there was Sebastian's schedule, and Jason's as well.

—Bianca: Who's Jason?

—Me: Jason Choi. Remember him from high school? He's a judge now. He agreed to marry us.

—Bianca: Oh. Well that was nice of him, but jeez.

Her texts are brimming with peevishness. I have to smile because I know it's coming from her desire to be there for me at all times.

—Me: I'm really sorry. But I didn't want to bother you while you're dealing with your family crisis. That's more important than this. By the way, how are you holding up?

—Bianca: Okay. Auntie says thanks for the lilies. It was so thoughtful of you.

—Me: It was nothing.

—Bianca: I'll be home soon.

—Me: Don't hurry on my behalf. Do what you need to do.

—Bianca: I don't want to miss anything important in your life. Who's gonna watch your back if I'm not around?

Bianca is the most loyal bestie a woman could ask for. My life would've been so much harder without her on my side.

—Bianca: BTW, how'd you get Gabriella Ricci to make that statement?

My belly burns at the mention of Sebastian's ex. What did she do, and what kind of PR disaster am I in now?

—Me: What statement?

—Bianca: That she dumped him and there was no man-stealing. She was pretty convincing.

That must be Sebastian's doing. I make a mental note to check it out later.

—Bianca: Anyway, I'm happy she said that. I'd hate for people to continue to think badly of you.

—Bianca: Also, just checked the flight schedule. I should be there by Thursday at the latest.

—Me: Then you'll be back in time for the reception! I'll make sure you're on the guest list.

—Bianca: Thank you! Totally forgot about the wedding reception! OMG, it's so exciting. And I already made a guest list. I did it for your wedding with that cheating dickhead, but you can use it for this event, too. Same family and all that. It's on the company intranet. I'll text Julio and let him know.

—Me: You're off the clock. I'll tell him. Just take care of yourself. And if you need more time with your family and relatives, you let me know, okay?

—Bianca: Will do. Love you.

—Me: Same. :heart-emoji:

My calendar app alerts me to a meeting in five minutes. I put the phone down and head out. To make up for yesterday's lost time, I work through lunch. Around four p.m., I ask James to bring the car around. I want to drop by our flagship store in Los Angeles. From time to time, I do an impromptu store visit to make sure all our retail locations have the proper look and feel. Some consultants Darren hired said each place having its own wildly unique flavor is better, but I disagree. Peery Diamonds sells a luxurious experience along with extravagant jewelry, and certain baseline standards must be met. That said, I love seeing the extra touches that the store managers add to make their particular store feel more exclusive and upscale, and figuring out ways to implement the best of them across all our locations.

After I climb into the car, I realize that the unpleasantly familiar paparazzo is still missing.

"Have you seen That Stalker anywhere today?" I ask James.

"No. Haven't seen any of them," he says, his eyes on the road.

"How weird."

He grunts. "I'm glad they're finally leaving you alone."

"I guess..." Although I should be happy, part of me is antsy because something feels off. They've been hounding me since I was a teenager.

Why stop now? Is this also Sebastian's doing? Did he threaten to sue them after they published articles about me, him and Gabriella? Is that why they're stopping?

Should I have tried to sue them when they messed with me before? I've considered it many times, but Bianca convinced me that legal action would draw more attention. She said they might become even more relentless to show that they aren't afraid of lawsuits. "If they were worried about getting sued, they would've never become paparazzi."

She's right, but still...

Spending hundreds of thousands on legal fees would be worth it if it can get them off my back.

As the Cullinan maneuvers through the busy Los Angeles traffic, I stare outside. So many cars, so many people. I let out a long breath.

The world feels so *free* right now. With the international headquarters relocation, internal audits and the Sebastian Peery collaboration starting in earnest, I have more on my plate than ever before—but the endless task list doesn't feel daunting. I'm actually energized, knowing I'm finally in the driver's seat.

A bus roars by on the other side of the street. On its side is a bright eye-shadow advertisement featuring a smiling Gabriella Ricci.

My heart freezes for a moment. Her hair unbound and her smile saucy and carefree, she looks nothing like me, not just in features or coloring, but in demeanor. I don't think I've ever smiled like that. What Ted said yesterday comes back to me.

You're totally not Sebastian's type.

But he wanted me—at least, he wanted my body. I don't know what to feel about the fact that he's in love with Gabriella, but seems to desire me so much. Look at what happened yesterday in the limo and this morning in the gym. I also can't decide if I should be happy or horrified that I crave him back so shamelessly.

Then I realize I haven't checked the statement Bianca mentioned earlier. Gabriella posted a video on her feed, looking as gorgeous as ever.

"I don't know why people are saying that Lucienne Peery 'stole' Sebastian. Do I *look* like a woman who has men stolen from her?" She scoffs, then grins playfully at the audience. "Our relationship wasn't going in the direction I wanted, so it was time to move on, even though

Sebastian's a fabulous guy. It's me, not him." Her tone says it *is* him. "Anyway, I wish them both the best."

So. She dumped him after he told her he needed to marry me. Hardly surprising—I would've done exactly the same in her situation. No wonder he just said he and Gabriella were fine and refused to elaborate. He's probably broken up about it.

My situation feels like emotional adultery. I might have legal claim to him, but it's Gabriella who has his heart.

And although Sebastian was insulted at the notion that I don't expect him to be particularly faithful, the fact that his penis doesn't care whom his heart belongs to makes me sad and feel like a second choice, like I've always been to so many people in my life.

On the other hand, he said he'd be faithful during our marriage, most likely out of some sense of honor or what little respect he has left for me. I can't demand he stays celibate while we're married if he's making an effort to be a decent husband. My own conflicting emotions are my burden for forcing this marriage on him. I'm not going to think about anything except being a good wife until I'm done with the expatriation and we can have an amicable divorce. That's the least I owe him.

The car finally stops in front of the flagship store. James opens the door.

"Thanks," I murmur, and stride into our giant marble and glass monument to luxury.

This location is sentimental. I got my first position at Peery Diamonds as a junior associate here. Grandfather didn't believe that I could be an effective executive if I didn't know how our associates interfaced with—and sold to—the customers.

My heels clack quietly on the shiny champagne-colored stone floor. The crown-shaped mini chandeliers glow softly, and Chopin floats along the air. Every glass case is spotless, the navy velvet pristine. All sorts of gemstones sparkle under the lights, showing off our exceptional cuts and designs.

A couple of Asian women are seated on one of the benches. They're nearly identical in appearance—the same conservative black skirt suit, black pumps and hair pulled back into buns. Their nails are neatly trimmed and without polish, and they aren't wearing any jewelry, except for pearl studs of average quality you might find in any mid-tier department store. The watches on their wrists are functional, with simple round faces and dark brown leather straps, not something you'd find in luxury stores.

In front of them is a table with two velvet trays showcasing cuff links, rings and bracelets. I move closer, curious as to exactly what type of designs they're looking at, since they don't seem to fit the profile of our typical clientele. When I'm three steps from the table, a dark-haired toddler comes running full speed out of nowhere. He's holding a child's sippy cup in one hand, and he runs smack into my leg.

He promptly lands on his butt. The cup flies out of his chubby little hand, half of what proves to be chocolate milkshake landing on me. The icy liquid drenches my dress and drips down onto my shoes. The other half splatters all over the trays, soiling the glittering items.

It happens so fast that the boy just stares up at me like a stunned little angel, his brown eyes wide. He looks down at his empty hand, and at my wet dress. His chin starts to tremble, and tears spike his long eyelashes.

"It's okay," I say.

The Asian women are already on their feet and rushing over. One of them puts a calming hand on the boy's back, making a soothing sound. The other one approaches me, pulling a pack of antibacterial wipes from her huge black purse.

"I am *so* sorry," she says. "I didn't realize he was running." She looks extremely concerned. "He was sitting quietly when we checked just a moment ago."

Rapidly clicking footsteps approach from my left. I turn and see a slim Asian woman running toward us. Unlike the other two, she's in an off-white wide-brimmed hat, purple asymmetrical dress and nude peep-toe stilettos. Her long auburn hair is unbound, and the diamonds on her ears and around her throat are large and of excellent quality—something Peery Diamonds might carry. The watch on her wrist is a limited edition from Sebastian Jewelry's watch launch. She must've been on some sort of VIP list to be able to score one.

"Liam! What are you doing?" Her eyes scan me and the milkshake-soaked trays. Expertly manicured hands fly to her mouth. "Oh my God."

The boy lifts his arms toward her. "Mommy," he says, as more tears flow down his cheeks.

She crouches and picks him up. The boy instantly clutches her like a koala, rubbing his teary face all over her shoulder, but she doesn't seem to care about the mess he's making on a dress that cost well over four thousand dollars. My heart softens at the obvious love she has for the child. It's the kind of interaction I longed for with my own mother—to know I came first.

She turns to the women and says something sharp in a language I don't understand. They respond in the same tongue.

She turns to me. "I'm so sorry about all this. It's my fault."

"It's nobody's fault. Kids are kids," I say with a smile.

"Yes, but regardless, it should not have happened. There's a reason why I have his nanny with us."

My eyes slide to the two women who are looking like they just got caught committing treason.

"Ms. Lim is the nanny. Ms. Kim is my assistant," the boy's mom explains, then turns her attention back to my dress. "I hope the milkshake comes out, but it's so...chocolate."

"It's fine. Don't worry about it."

She doesn't seem to hear me as she makes a distressed sound in her throat. "It just looks awful. And your *shoes*..."

"I have another pair. And this is just a dress." I give them a small shrug and smile.

"Thanks for saying that, but we both know it's not just a dress," she says. "That's a limited edition Avery Parker."

I raise my eyebrows. She's correct; I bought it from Avery Parker, a fairly new designer who's made a huge splash in the last few years.

"There are only fifty in that collection, and they all sold out."

"Okay, now I'm curious. How would you know that?"

"My mother financed Avery when she was new, and I have one of the dresses in my closet. I've been saving it for my anniversary."

Avery Parker was backed by the Hae Min Group... "Are you Yuna Hae Winters?" I ask.

"Yes." She arches an eyebrow. "My turn to ask: how did you know?"

"How could I not?" Anyone who researches the Hae Min Group can find out that it's a multinational conglomerate controlled by the Hae family. The chairman has two children—Eugene and Yuna. Although the latter isn't involved with running the business, the rumor is that if you want a favor from the Hae Min Group, the easiest route is through Yuna because she's the baby of the family and they adore her. "We're in the middle of negotiating a partnership with the Hae Min Group."

Her eyes widen. "Really?"

"Yes! I'm Lucienne Peery. You can call me Lucie or Luce." I extend my hand, while bracing myself for her reaction. People always regard me with cool judgment when they learn who I am, thanks to all the awful headlines out there. Whatever I do afterward doesn't generally change their preconceived opinion of me.

Her smile grows wider, her eyes still warm. "Oh, *that's* why you look so familiar. I love your jewelry! So classy, with modern sensibility." She shifts her boy and shakes hands. "But it isn't always easy to find it. I was consulting with one of your designers because I need something custom-made for my husband. Our anniversary is coming up soon."

Relief floods through me. "Then you're in the right place. I'm sure our designers can do some amazing custom work for you."

"They did! They showed me some preliminary sketches, and everything looks amazing. I'm so excited." She glows beautifully. "The custom matching bracelets they did for me and my soul sister last year were absolutely wonderful, too."

"Soul sister?"

"It's like a soul mate, except your best friend, who feels like your sister, you know? Ivy loves your jewelry, too. Look at this bracelet." She lifts her arm, showing off double strings of platinum charms and diamonds. "We wear them all the time."

"That's pretty." I smile with pride. I reach into my purse, take out my card and hand it to her. "If you need anything, just give me a call."

"Thank you so much. You're the best. Also, here's my card."

One of the Asian ladies instantly produces a card and hands it to me.

Yuna continues, "Call me if the stain doesn't come out. I'll figure something out and make it right for you. I haven't seen Avery in a while anyway." She grins.

"Thanks for the offer," I say, although I have no intention of reaching out to her about the dress. It's really not that big of a deal. I run my hand along the back of Liam's head, feel the smooth silk of his hair. He looks at me worriedly. He knows he made a mess. I smile. "Don't worry, Liam. I know you didn't do it on purpose."

"I'm not in trouble?" he asks in a small voice.

"Nope."

"I'm sorry," he says gravely, while Yuna and I press our lips to not laugh at his heavy sigh, as though the weight of the world rests on his little shoulders.

"Apology accepted."

He looks at the empty milkshake cup, the corners of his soft mouth turning more downward.

"Do you like ice cream? We have some if you'd like that *and* if your mother's okay with it," I add. The flagship store serves refreshments, and ice cream's something we keep in stock.

He lifts his head, his eyes shining with instant happiness. "*Ice cream?*"

"Yes."

He turns to his mother. "Is it okay?"

Yuna laughs. "Uh-huh." She kisses his forehead and turns to me. "Thank you so much. You're so kind."

"My pleasure."

15

SEBASTIAN

INSTEAD OF THE steakhouse where my brothers and I normally have our dinners, I head to Noah's place. Grant is still pissed about the way they treated Aspen, so we aren't going there anymore, even though they have great steak and the best bread in the city. If Noah's sad about that—he's the carb addict of the family—he doesn't show it.

We always watch each other's backs. Screw with one of us, and you just screwed with all of us.

Noah said he hired Jane Pryce, a popular private chef, for our dinner, so it should be good. He asked for something homey and filling, with lots of beef.

It's just the seven of us at dinner, even though three—actually, *four* —of us are married now. Emmett, Griffin and Grant's wives get along well. So when we have our brother-only brunches or dinners, they hang out together, doing facials or whatever women like to do when they're left to their own devices with their husbands' black AmEx cards. Last time, they ordered over a hundred romance novels from Amazon. Although Amy doesn't read much, Sierra and Aspen do, and they read the "good parts" out loud and analyzed the anatomical possibilities of each over chocolate fondue and sparkling white pear cider.

Should I introduce Luce to the trio? Even if she's not somebody I wanted to marry, she is my wife. But will she fit in? Amy, Sierra and Aspen are normal. They don't have dozens of scandalous headlines published about them each year, and they don't do orgies or drugs. Although...Luce might not do orgies or drugs, either—at least, I haven't seen any signs. But she still isn't like them.

Maybe they can be introduced at the wedding reception next Saturday. That way, if they don't like Luce, they won't feel pressured to spend time with her.

Noah's home sits on a beachfront lot in Malibu. All chrome, stone and glass, the place looks out onto the ocean. It's gorgeous when the day changes to evening, the sky turning bronze and purple. The property is fenced with wrought iron that's surprisingly sturdy. Noah reinforced it with an electric fence after Dad's hooker jumped over the wrought-iron barrier to reach him. He says he needs privacy and the beach. I think he just likes to gaze at bikini-clad girls frolicking out on the sand, which you can see from the living room and any of the bedrooms on the upper level.

Nicholas and I arrive at the same time. We park our cars. The other brothers are already here.

Nicholas waves as he climbs out of his Bentley Flying Spur. Although we have different moms, most people can tell we're related. Actually, they can tell all seven of us are related because we all have Dad's coloring and jaw. Joey also says we have Dad's "Promethean" brow, but I prefer not to put much stock into his observations because everything coming out of his mouth is designed to flatter Dad.

There's no nickname for Nicholas because his mom goes by Nikki or Nic, depending on her mood. She's an extremely capricious woman, and I'll never understand how she ended up with a son as steady and stable as Nicholas. He's as sturdy and reliable as a thousand-year-old oak.

Sierra observed that Nicholas would make a great boyfriend. "Just the kind of guy you can depend on. It's so weird he's still single. The women in this city must be blind."

The women aren't blind. He just isn't interested because he's hung up on some girl he refuses to tell us about. And it's been going on since... I can't even remember.

"Nice ring," he says, glancing at my finger. "You always have the best taste in jewelry."

"Luce picked it."

"Luce?"

"Lucienne feels impersonal."

"Ah." Nicholas's smile is entirely too serene and knowing.

"What?"

"Just gathering another data point."

"For...?"

"I think you might like her a little."

"Jesus, stop. This is what happens when you don't drink coffee." He isn't a huge coffee drinker. He drinks it when he joins us for brunches—since the rest of us are coffee addicts—but on his own, he doesn't really seek it out. It's unnatural.

Nicholas and I walk inside. Noah's home is a prototypical bachelor pad with weird postmodern chandeliers that look like handguns and breasts—it's the way the orbs are shaped—and darts, a billiard table, a pinball machine, foosball and a fully stocked bar that's impossible to miss. A gigantic framed black-and-white photo of Marilyn Monroe graces the wall. She's bent forward with her hands on her knees for maximum cleavage exposure. Her signature is scrawled on the right-hand corner, and Noah paid more money than is sensible for it.

Interestingly, there's not a single shot of cheetahs. Noah is a wildlife photographer, although he wants to become a novelist for some reason only he can understand. There's an actual typewriter on the desk in the corner, overlooking the ocean. A huge stack of paper sits next to it, but I'd bet my left nut he still doesn't have the opening line.

On the long cherry dining table is a massive spread of roast beef, poached wild salmon, German potatoes and other side dishes. Since Noah adores carbs, there's a mountain of freshy baked bread in the center.

He's stuffed his mouth with a roll, his cheeks as full as a hamster's. When he notices me, he quickly swallows, then washes it down with Pétrus. "I can't believe you didn't invite us to your wedding!"

"Oh, come on." I scoff as I take an empty seat and help myself to roast beef and mashed potatoes. I'm starving.

"We invited you to ours," Emmett says. Grant nods next to him. He and Emmett founded a venture capital firm together, and they're generally in agreement on everything.

"Do you know that the percentage of people who don't invite their family to their weddings who end up divorced is—"

"I didn't invite you for a good reason," I interrupt before Griffin can launch into the statistics and research papers he's read on marriage failure. He spends way too much time with government records on all sorts of bizarre topics. But then, he's an economist. It's like a fetish.

"You invited Dad," Huxley says. "Noah showed us the pic Joey posted on Dad's Instagram this morning."

"I can't believe it took him that long," I mutter.

Noah says, "Do you want to see the caption?"

"No." I don't need to read what Joey said. I shared the same space with him for far too long yesterday. "I only invited them because the whole thing was a joke."

Grant angles his head, making a big deal out of checking my torso. "Did your new bride stab you for inviting him?"

"Don't see any blood," Nicholas says.

"She probably got disgusted and left," Griffin says.

"Guys," I say, "she *likes* him."

A befuddled silence falls over the room. My brothers stare like I just told them I'd love nothing more than to get butt-fucked with a cactus.

Finally, Emmett gulps down the rest of his Bordeaux. "Say that again, *mais en français*—because I think I lost my ability to understand English."

Since all of us studied in Europe, we speak French, in addition to German, Italian, Portuguese and Spanish—and of course English. So I oblige. "*Elle l'aime.*"

"Fuck. Me," Nicholas says.

"Was she high? Drunk?" Noah asks.

"It'd have to be both," Griffin croaks. He can't imagine any scenario under which anybody could like Dad.

I shake my head. "No."

Huxley gives me a look full of pity. It's a little creepy, because compassion really isn't his forte. "Insanity might be valid grounds for divorce."

I wish. "Can't. We need to stay married for at least five years, unless she decides to dump me earlier."

"If you belch and fart around her all the time, she'll probably divorce you before the month is over," Noah says.

I scrunch my face. "That's disgusting."

"It works. Trust me."

Everyone's head swivels toward Noah, who spreads his hands.

"What? You can't argue with the result. I'm just trying to help," he says.

"Don't. Nothing's going to help. Anyway, all of you are invited to the post-elopement reception at Luce's house next Saturday. Bring your wives and girlfriends."

"Is Dad coming?" Grant asks warily. He'll never let Dad get close to Aspen again after our father offered to make her a soft-core porn star.

"Absolutely not. I've used up my Ted Lasker tolerance quotient for the year."

Emmett relaxes slightly. Dad's been harassing him and Amy about wanting to see his "grandkid." I don't think he knows if it's a girl or a boy. Not because Emmett kept that a secret, but because it's just too much bother for Dad to remember.

"Also, I need your help," I say.

My brothers turn to me, instantly serious.

"I need you to start buying up shares in Peery Diamonds," I say. "I'll fund it."

"Don't be ridiculous." Huxley glares at me, insulted to the core of his soul. "We don't need your money."

The rest of my brothers give me a what-he-said look.

"What is this for?" Grant asks.

"To even the scales. Luce thinks she got what she wants from this marriage by forcing my hand. I'm going to prove her wrong."

Emmett cocks his eyebrow. "And that would be...?"

"I'm going to strip her of her title as CEO of Peery Diamonds."

16

SEBASTIAN

I KEEP quiet as I pad along the hall Saturday morning to avoid disturbing Luce in case she wants to sleep in. I need to grab some coffee before my tennis match with Grant at Tilden Courts, where I play from time to time when I need to decompress. I always ask Grant, Emmett or Huxley to join me.

Other members at the club have expressed interest in being my opponent, but no thank you. They're more interested in socializing than playing. Or talking business while pretending to exercise. It helps them write off the five-figure annual membership fee as a "business expense." They're the kind of guys who bring up their latest merger and acquisition in bed to write off money pay for escorts, too.

Mr. Vaguely Disapproving Butler isn't around, for once. So I make my own cup of coffee and finish it, along with a bagel from the pantry and a fresh tub of whipped cream cheese from the fridge.

My phone rings, and the screen shows it's Grant. I put it on speaker on low volume, while grabbing another bagel.

"You already on your way to Tilden?" he asks.

In my peripheral view, I spot Luce making her way down the stairs. She's dressed casually in a scoop-neck shirt and short pleated skirt that shows off her legs. Damn, they look tasty. My teeth ache with the need to nibble on them. And the rest of her body.

She waves good morning, and I nod oh so casually, then clear the sudden knot in my throat so I can answer Grant. "Not yet. Why?"

Need some privacy? she mouths.

I shake my head.

"I can't go," he says.

"Why not? Did you break something?" Grant's ultra-competitive, and would never back away from a match.

"Aspen's on her period."

I sense Luce moving around in the kitchen, brushing past my back to reach the espresso machine. Heat starts to sizzle, the charge in the air crackling. I focus on the conversation. "And…?"

"She wants me to rub her lower back."

"Jesus. Can't she do that herself?"

Luce chokes on her coffee, then starts coughing quietly. Without thinking, I reach over and gently slap her back.

"That isn't how it works." Grant's tone says, *I'm shocked you aren't a virgin, given your ignorance.*

"Who am I going to play with, then?"

"Emmett? Huxley?"

"They're busy today."

"Noah might be free."

"No. The only time we played together, he pulled a hamstring trying to return my first serve. And that wasn't the lowest point of our time there, either, because it got worse. Much, much worse."

Grant makes a vaguely thoughtful sound. "Yeah, he's pretty awful. I don't know what to say. Aspen needs me."

"I can play with you," Luce says.

"Who's that?" Grant says, at the same time I say, "No."

"Hi. I'm Lucie. Or Luce." She smiles. Not sure why she bothers. Grant can't see it.

"Hi, Lucie. I'm Grant. Nice to meet you. And yes, if you can take my place, that'd be great."

"I don't play with women," I say.

"Don't be sexist," Grant says, then hangs up.

I grit my teeth. Pussy-whipped asshole!

"I'm really not that bad," Luce says, sipping her coffee.

"I'm sure you aren't." At least she has some cardiovascular fitness, and she's flexible, so she won't pull something as soon as we start. But I look at her pretty face and recall the softness of her palms. Does she even know how to hold a racket properly? "But I'm actually *good*, and I want to go all out. Won't be able to do that with you."

"Oh, you can go all out with me," she says, giving me a look over the rim of her coffee mug. "Or is there some other reason you don't want to play with me?"

"It's not you. It's almost everyone. Only three of my brothers can keep up with me, and I'd never ask the other three."

"I promise I won't be like Noah. I won't pull a muscle or whatever was much, much worse."

Does she think I'm stupid? Whenever a woman speaks in that tone of voice, something worse is bound to follow. "No."

"Come on. Besides, it might be a fun couple time."

"A fun couple time?" As far as I'm concerned, the only fun couple time we can have is horizontally in the bedroom. Or vertically in the shower. But not on a tennis court.

"We're married. We should try to get to know each other and get along." She flashes a hopeful smile. "Make the best of the situation."

"I don't think crying and gnashing your teeth because you lost is considered a fun couple time."

I made the mistake of playing with one of my girlfriends once, and it didn't end well. She screamed like a banshee, attracting a lot of embarrassing attention. And then she developed a migraine for two weeks. I finally dumped her because I got tired of her snit. I wasn't going to play another game with her, and no, I wasn't going to lose on purpose, just to make her feel better about herself. It wasn't my fault tennis wasn't her game. Or that her sportsmanship left so much to be desired.

"Couples break up over stuff like that." I wish I could reach into Griffin's mind and pull up relevant stats. I don't need Luce throwing a temper tantrum. If half the stuff I read about her is true, she's going to be a sore loser. And I never throw a game.

"Well. If your ego can't handle it..." Luce shrugs.

I snort. "That's so transparent, you make Noah look like a CIA operative."

"This same Noah who pulled a hamstring?"

"Yes. He could make a wine glass look opaque." I sigh. "All right, fine. But no crying. No bitching. No whining. No screaming."

"I'll try not to embarrass you."

"And no migraines and headaches or whatever women develop when they're mad but don't want to admit they're mad."

"Wow."

"*Wow* isn't an agreement."

She rolls her eyes. "Fine. And the same conditions apply to you."

"I won't lose, so it's a moot point."

Amusement ripples over her. She probably thinks I'm some weekend dabbler. "If you're that confident, you want to up the stakes?"

"What do you have in mind?"

"What are you wagering?"

I narrow my eyes. "If by some miracle you win, I'll get on my knees and go down on you until you come three times."

She flushes, but the sparks in her eyes betray her. "Fine, even though it sounds like a reward—for you."

"Believe me, it'll be a reward for you. *If you're worthy.*"

The slight smile on her pretty face says she's more than worthy, regardless of the outcome of our match. Her confidence is hot.

"All right. And if *you* win," she says, "unlikely as that is, I'll do the same for you. But you only get to come once. Even though you'll be begging for more."

17

LUCIENNE

SEBASTIAN PICKED the wrong girl to make that wager with.

Although I didn't tell him, I was a nationally ranked tennis player when I was in high school and college. I didn't pursue it beyond that because turning pro wasn't the path my mom or grandfather had in mind for me. To be honest, even if they wanted me to see how far I could go, I wouldn't have wanted to. There's not enough time in the day to train to be a world-class athlete and run Peery Diamonds effectively.

Sebastian's probably not too bad, but it's easy to be good playing against people at places like Tilden Courts. Its sole criterion for membership is "Can you afford the annual dues?" If the answer's yes, you're in.

Speaking of which...I should cancel Roderick, Karl and Vonnie's memberships. They joined while Mom was alive, even though they don't play tennis or ride horses. They just want to be able to brag they're members at Tilden. Well, they can start paying for that bragging right with their own money now.

Sebastian and I take his Phantom to the courts. The Rolls isn't flashy, but it's so luxurious, it's like being inside a motorized spa. The buttery leather, the gorgeous line of the dash, and the remarkable colors

—midnight blue, dark wood and a dab of deep purple with a splash of jade. The combination is unusual, but it blends well.

He maneuvers the half-million-dollar vehicle with confident expertise, and the ride is amazingly smooth. Although he looks super-hot in a suit, he's also stunning in his short-sleeve shirt and shorts. His forearms are lean with ropey muscle. He could film himself flexing those forearms and sell it on porn sites for women. It would add another billion to his fortune.

The immaculately verdant grounds of Tilden Courts come into view. The place is always green and lush, but then, members don't pay the fees for brown, dried-up fields.

"Meet you outside the locker rooms?" I say as I climb out.

"Fine with me."

I give him my cocky pre-game you're-going-down smile—*in more ways than one, baby*—and go into the locker room to change into tennis whites. When I come outside, Sebastian's nowhere to be found. Guess he's still changing...? I head to the refreshment area to grab a bottle of Gatorade, then stop in my tracks.

Preston.

I haven't seen him since that infuriating encounter in Barcelona. I assumed he was busy being a scumbag because he never tried to get in touch. Well, not that he could, because I blocked his number. But given that the agreement I have with the Comtois family includes the ownership of Sebastian Jewelry, I thought he'd make some effort and at least write an email to plead his case.

He's dressed to play. His racket looks like it's never been used before. That wouldn't surprise me. If he's anything like the other members here, he's a dabbler.

He stops short as he sees me. "What are you doing here?"

"I'm here for a match." I make myself stand taller. Even without heels, our eyes are almost level.

He gives me a once-over and smirks. "Oh, I get it. Looking for a husband."

I try not to snort. He doesn't watch the news—thinks it's boring—and his family apparently hasn't updated him about my new status. Maybe they disowned him. Wouldn't that be great?

He continues, "I don't know why you waste your time like this. Look, I'm happy to let it go if you'll just see the light and change your mind about our—"

"Don't hold your breath." He's dumber than I thought, bringing up the engagement when I still can't find enough mind bleach to erase seeing him with Vonnie.

"There you are," comes Sebastian's voice from behind me. "Oh, hello, Preston."

When he stops next to me, I put my arm around his waist. "What *perfect* timing." I smile up at him.

He gives me a mildly curious look, but wraps an arm around my shoulders.

See? This is what you get when you're with a smart man. He knows the role you'd like him to play without your having to spell it out. The fact that he's willing to play along without some prior commitment to reciprocate warms my heart. So many people want something first before doing anything for me.

Preston's brow knits as he takes in the tableau. "You guys are together?"

I triple the wattage of my smile. "Preston, have you met my husband, Sebastian Lasker?"

"*What?*" His shout rings in the wide-open space. "You can't marry him!"

"I can't? Oh, that's too bad." I tighten my hold on Sebastian, pressing my side against his. "'Cause I kinda already did." I extend my left hand, so Preston can see my gorgeous Toi et Moi ring and the wedding band.

Sebastian flashes his as well. Man, we make a great team.

Preston blinks rapidly, his eyes fixed on our hardware. Finally, he jerks his head up, his face blotchy. "Why would you want him when you could have *me*?"

"Seriously? Are you blind?" I ask.

"I can see well enough to know those diamonds are tiny compared to the one I was going to give you!" He points at my finger.

I drop my gaze to his crotch for a second before lifting it back up. "His is both *bigger* and *better* than yours."

Preston looks like he just got punched in the face by Mike Tyson. Sebastian shakes against me in silent laughter.

"What's so funny?" Preston snarls.

"You." Sebastian lets the laugh out. "You're third-rate comedy, but at least you're entertaining." He wipes tears from his eyes.

Preston turns to me. "You *bitch*! It's all your fault he's mocking me!"

Sebastian steps forward, pulling away from my arm around his waist, as the mirth melts from his face. "Watch your tone if you want to keep your teeth. Nobody talks to my wife with disrespect."

I pat his back a few times, to let him know it isn't necessary for him to react like this. Part of me is flattered and moved that he's defending me, but another part feels a bit unworthy of his protection because... Well, I did force him to marry me.

Preston slashes the air with his arm. "She's *my* fiancée!"

"She *was*. You call *my wife* your fiancée again, and I'll break your face."

"What happened to bros before hos?"

Sebastian takes another step forward, which puts him right in Preston's face. "What part of 'she's my wife' did you not understand?" Menace radiates from him. Preston's going to get punched for real if he doesn't quit.

"Preston, baby, are you okay? Is my sister being impossible?"

Oh, Lord. He's still with Vonnie?

She comes toward us from the locker room, dressed to play tennis and holding a racket like it's a medieval knight's mace. She's convinced she's too good and too talented for lessons or practice. I can't blame her entirely for that misguided belief, since so many guys lost to her on purpose to get into her panties. But shouldn't she be self-aware enough to know something's off? Because when it comes to matches against girls, she can only beat rank beginners.

Flashing a fake smile, she loops her arm around Preston's and turns her hand so I can't miss the pink diamond still on her finger.

She must really like that foul thing. Or she's just happy she gets to keep something she thinks is mine.

"What are you doing here?" she demands.

"Why *wouldn't* I be here? I pay for the entire family's membership." I let my gaze rake her up and down.

Although her clothing looks simple, she's decked out in ten thousand dollars' worth of outfit, shoes and accessories, not including the diamond. What will she do when she realizes her credit card bills won't be paid out of my account anymore? I already had my accountants cut her off. She probably doesn't know yet, since AmEx hasn't sent her a notice that her bills are overdue.

A petty but satisfying revenge. And still nothing compared to what I've had to put up with.

"Whatever." She tosses her hair over a shoulder. "All you've got is money, anyway." Then her eyes turn to Sebastian and her smile grows even more cloying. "Isn't this your older brother, Preston?"

"Yes!" He points an accusing finger at Sebastian. "And he stole Lucie from me!"

Anger and wounded pride flash in Vonnie's eyes before she shrugs them off. "It's just *Lucie*. No big deal."

Preston raises his racket, pointing it at Sebastian. "I challenge you to a match!" he shouts with all the gravitas of a medieval princeling demanding trial by combat. "Both of you! I'm going to show you that you made a big mistake!"

"You're going to lose," I say.

"No, he won't, because *I* will be playing with him!" Vonnie says.

She's delusional if she thinks she's a net gain for her partner. On the other hand, she's cocking her hips left and right, trying to strike the best pose in front of Sebastian. She probably thinks she can beat him like all the other boys in high school and college.

Sebastian's gaze flicks in my direction. It says, Do you want to go for it or back down and do our match instead?

I give him a look, tilting my head at Preston and Vonnie. I'd rather lick a skunk's butt than back away from this challenge. Wouldn't you?

Sebastian's eyes glow with approval. "You're on," he tells Preston. "Losers get on their knees and shout, 'We are not worthy,' ten times immediately after the match is over. Oh, and you have to genuflect as well."

Preston gives us a superior sneer. "Better get your kneepads ready."

Vonnie laughs. "I'll record it so we can relive the moment forever."

18

SEBASTIAN

WHEN WE'RE on the court and done with some light stretching, I get ready to pull my weight and Luce's as well. The last time I played with Preston he was just average, but Mom says he got some lessons to improve his backhand. And I don't know how good Vonnie is.

Luce sounded self-assured back home, but that doesn't mean anything. Noah was confident too, until he pulled his hamstring. Hopefully, she isn't the type to cry over a broken nail or cracked fingernail polish. If I lose to Preston because she's overwrought about some stupid shit, I'm going to put her over my knee.

Preston put me in a bad situation, and Vonnie was part of the problem. Nothing less than a total annihilation of this duo will satisfy me.

"Let's get going," Preston shouts from the other side of the net, full of self-importance. "I got things to do."

Things. I can only laugh.

"No-ad scoring!" he says impatiently.

I look at Luce, who shrugs and says, "It'll speed up the game."

"That's fine." It doesn't matter what he chooses, because he and his skanky ho are going to lose.

We begin. Preston serves, hitting the ball hard. Luce leaps forward and returns it in a screaming shot that lands about an inch inside the line. *Well, well, well. Look at that.*

She's hyper-focused and moves with an amazing economy of motion. Her long limbs give her a great reach. Her muscles tense, sweat beading on her taut skin.

I have to admit she's good. *Really* good. She must've trained for years to get to that level.

But I can still beat her if we ever play one on one.

Preston and Vonnie try, but they're simply no match for us. Although my half-brother isn't a complete disaster, Luce's half-sister is. Her swings are wild, and she struggles to return even easy shots.

Every time she fails to hit the ball, she lets out a loud shriek. Eventually, other members start gathering around the court to watch us play. A couple recognize me and shoot pitying glances at Preston and Vonnie.

"You're cheating!" Vonnie whines, pointing at Luce. "There's no way you're this good."

Luce merely taps her racket. A confident smirk twists her lips. "Vonnie, the only player you could beat is a half-blind toddler who hasn't been toilet trained."

"You're using an illegal racket!" Preston says.

An illegal racket. "Winners win. Losers blame the equipment," I say.

Fuming, Preston serves. He mishits the ball, which arcs in the air and then falls like a dick going limp without clearing the net.

"That ball went down faster than Vonnie on a first date," Luce calls out.

"Hey, Preston. Having trouble keeping it up?" I say.

Our audience chortles. "Just give up," someone says. "You aren't going to beat Sebastian."

"Shut your pie holes!" Vonnie screams, before turning back to the match.

Luce serves; the ball comes off her racket so fast it looks like a tiny yellow bullet. Preston tries to return it, but ends up tripping and losing his balance instead. He grabs his leg and whines like a melodramatic soccer player.

What an embarrassment. "Get up," I say.

He moans like a wounded hyena.

Luce cups her hand around her ear. "What's that? Did you say you forfeit?"

"What?" he says.

"I think he said he forfeits," Luce says to me with a grin and shrug.

He jumps to his feet instantly. "I never said that!"

"Then let's continue. I got things to do!" Luce says.

I laugh. You gotta love a woman who gives as good as she gets, especially when her swagger comes with competence.

The idiot duo fails to win a single game during the first set.

Luce smiles brightly as she high-fives me. "Wow. That was brutal."

"No mercy," I say with a smile of my own. Victory is always sweet, but for some reason, this one feels sweeter.

"None."

"It's only because this side of the court has too much glare!" Preston says. "The sun's in our eyes."

"Which is why you're wearing sunglasses." I point at the shades wrapped around his eyes.

"It's still distracting!"

I shake my head. Everyone on the court is wearing sunglasses. "Fine. Hope you do better after we switch."

But he and Vonnie don't play any better. I'm treated to textbook examples of what not to do on the court. And how clumsy humans can be.

Luce, on the other hand, is on fire. And more than a little distracting when she leans forward, because her ass is perfection from every angle. I love seeing her muscles flex and power her moves. The earlier set must've been just a warmup, because she plays with even more force and control now. Sweat glistens on her taut skin, and it's all I can do not to stop the match so I can steal a kiss.

When the second massacre of a set is over, Luce drops her racket and raises her hands in the air. "Yes!"

The spectators clap. "Great match," a few of them call out, as the crowd starts to disperse.

"You just got lucky!" Preston shouts.

"Yeah!" Vonnie's shrill voice rises in agreement.

"Then quit pissing off the gods," I say, too pleased to give a shit what they use as an excuse for the spanking they just got.

Flipping them the bird with both hands, Luce turns around and leaps over to me. Her arms wrap around my neck, and she gives me a tight hug. I squeeze her back. She smells like sweat, soap and lavender shampoo. The wall she usually has around her is gone, and she's completely vulnerable, and blindingly beautiful.

"We *won!*" she says, pulling back a little to face me. The smile on her lips hits me like a bolt of lightning, sudden and powerful. The one she bestowed upon Jason in San Francisco that made me seethe was a lightning bug compared to the one she's giving me right now.

My heart races like it's about to burst. A hot jolt crackles along my spine, and pure elation like I've never experienced before swells. I dip my head and kiss her.

Her mouth softens under mine, parting to let me in. Our tongues entwine, and I swear she tastes exactly like triumph. My pulse kicks up as blood roars in my ears like rumbling thunder.

I want her *right now.*

The sound of rapidly slapping feet slips through the thick desire. I go still for a moment, and Luce pulls away and looks around.

Preston and Vonnie are running to the main building. Fuckers.

"Hey, you need to pay up!" I say to their retreating backs.

"Yeah," Luce says. "Get back here and *get on your knees!*"

They don't stop, but they aren't that fast. "You want to drag them back here and make them honor their bet?" I ask Luce.

She grins. "Nah. Vonnie can't run forever. She'll be back soon, begging for money."

"She doesn't have money?" I ask, enjoying her good humor.

"Not anymore. I cut her off. She'll be so sad when she racks up all sorts of charges on her credit cards and can't withdraw any funds out of my accounts anymore to pay them off." Her smile grows diabolical. I love it.

There are men who believe women are best when they're endlessly patient, sweet, kind and understanding. Not me. The best women are the ones who take no bullshit, know what they're worth and fight for what they're due.

Like my wife.

Which makes me wonder... "Why have you been paying for her stuff?"

"It's a long story, but it's tied up with the inheritance laws and property rights in Nesovia. Anyway, I'm going to stop by the admin office and tell them Vonnie's membership fees need to come out of another account, too."

"I need to do the same with Preston's membership."

Luce looks stunned. "You pay for his things, too?"

"Not me. My family. I control everyone's money now, though," I say with deep satisfaction.

"How did you manage that?"

"I married you."

"I thought they only gave you Sebastian Jewelry."

"It wasn't enough. Unlike Preston, I have my own money and don't need the company. I only run it because I enjoy it. They know that, and they didn't want to give you thirty percent of the shares. So now I'm in charge of everyone's trust funds, and Preston's going to have to get a job."

"Well." She gazes in the direction Preston and Vonnie have disappeared into. "I hope he's more competent than my half-brother Karl. I had to let him go for not even bothering to show up."

"Speaking of competence, you didn't tell me you were so good."

She frowns. "At what?"

"Tennis. Were you trying to hustle me? Is that your definition of 'fun couple time'?" I tease.

She laughs. "You were arrogant, so I decided not to disclose that I was nationally ranked when I was younger."

"Were you? Impressive." That explains her skills. I respect the dedication and work that went into it.

"Probably could've gone pro, but I chose Peery Diamonds instead."

She must love that company. Maybe more than I love Sebastian Jewelry. A tiny bit of guilt wriggles its way into my gut at my plan to strip her of her position, but I shove it aside. She started this war. In addition, that's a separate matter from all this...couple stuff.

She gives me a sly smile. "So. What do you want to do about our match?"

"We could go ahead and play it, if that's what you want," I say, pulling her close, determined to enjoy this carefree side of her.

"Or we can say we both won." Her blue eyes are guileless and full of happiness.

She totally forgot what we wagered. But that's okay, because I can remember for the both of us.

19

LUCIENNE

Triumph fizzes in my blood like champagne bubbles. I shiver with excitement as Sebastian drives us home after a shower at the club. I didn't see Vonnie in the locker room or the shower area. She was probably hiding, and she's likely to stay away as long as possible until she realizes she's broke.

I shoot a sidelong glance at Sebastian. He was amazing on the court. Coolly in control. The ball always went where he wanted it to go. That's mad skill. And hot as hell.

Nothing's sexier than a man who's good at what he's doing. Bonus points if he has the body of a Greek god, and an ass that could shame Apollo.

"We make a great team," I say, running a hand through my unbound hair.

"Clearly. Winning teams are the best teams." His voice is warm and rich. And maybe a bit indulgent.

I adore this side of him. It reminds me of our meeting in Paris, when he was so sweet to me.

If I were a little more romantic and idealistic, I might consider us soul mates. Still, what happened today gives me hope that our marriage, despite its rocky start, might progress well. There are relationships that are worse than ours, built on lies and selfish desires without giving anything back. I should know—two of my most significant relationships collapsed because of that. Even when they don't crumble, like Mom and Roderick, they remain toxic, poisoning the couple and those around them. To this date, I wonder if Mom truly didn't know about Roderick's infidelity or if she just wanted to pretend she didn't so she could keep him.

Sebastian speeds up, although not so fast that we get pulled over. We arrive home in no time. He drives past the gates, along the winding road through the lush garden and flowering lavender, and parks in front of the covered rotunda.

I climb out and wait for him to pop the trunk so I can grab my racket, but he takes my hand. I tilt my head, wondering what it's about. Before I can say a word, his mouth is on mine, and his arms are wrapping around me.

He ravages my mouth like a victorious Viking taking what's his. I tunnel my fingers into his silky hair and plunder him, too, the win still sizzling in my veins. Our lips are crushed, tongues reaching aggressively. He tastes so good, like confidence, elation and male.

His hands run along my sides, leaving goosebumps behind. I press into him and feel his erection against my lower belly. Electric shock crackles along my spine, reaching all the way to my clit, which starts to throb.

He picks me up, his mouth fused to mine, and moves us inside. Whenever he carries me so effortlessly, my hormones do cartwheels and I just want to burrow into him. When he has me in his arms and displays his strength, I feel protected...like it's okay if I let my guard down a little, because he's here for me.

"Your room or mine?" he says between uneven breaths.

"Whichever's closest," I rasp, unable to think. I start to pull away, but he only tightens his hold, cupping my ass harder.

My hands still in his hair, I tighten my legs around his waist. His body is hard with muscle, and he smells so good, all hot and masculine with a hint of the eucalyptus juniper body wash and shampoo we used at Tilden. I never thought the scent was sexy until he was wearing it. I bury my nose in the crook of his neck and inhale, shivering as need pulses through me.

He takes me up the stairs. If he means to torture me with barely there touches, he's doing a great job. Every cell in my body is quivering with anticipation as he rubs against me with each step.

He doesn't take us to one of bedrooms, but to a guest room, nearest the staircase. I rock against him, hating every layer of clothing between us. Although I did my best to appear cool and unaffected, I watched him work out in the gym on Friday. He moved effortlessly in ways that require a lot of strength and flexibility, and that can only come from years of consistent effort. And I saw the power and grace of his body again on the court.

I want to experience the muscularity and grandeur of his body without anything covering it.

He presses me against the wall by the door. His palm glides along my hip and thigh, then puts a gentle pressure until I lower the leg. I drop the other one, too, until I'm standing on my feet.

"Take off your clothes," I order him breathlessly, my hand on his shoulder.

A look of light mischief crosses his face as he smiles. "Whatever my winner wants."

Crossing his arms, he pulls his shirt up. The taut muscles along his sides and abs stand out, not an ounce of fat covering them. My mouth dries at the sight. His lats flare out as he pulls the shirt higher and throws it to the side unceremoniously.

"You should never work out with your shirt on," I breathe out softly.

He laughs. The sound dies when I run my fingers along the grooves of his torso. My fingertips tingle as I trace the stunningly proportioned, masculine lines. He's a work of art.

"You make François's statues look...ordinary," I whisper.

"Mmm." His mouth is on the side of my neck, licking and nibbling. The touch is affectionate, although no less heated. He has the power to make me feel desired. The shivers that quiver along my body are just as hot as before, but sweeter now. I reach for the waistband of his shorts, slip my hands underneath and feel his taut butt. Even there, he's perfect.

His lips still trailing kisses along the sensitive tendon on my neck, he gets rid of his shoes and socks, then drags his shorts and underwear down and kicks them off. Finally, he's fully nude.

His cock juts out, the head almost grazing his abs. I extend my hand down to grab it, run the pad of my thumb along the tip, but he wraps his hand around my wrist and pulls me away.

"Later." He slips a hand under my skirt. His fingers loop around the thin string of my thong. "Is this your favorite?" he asks, exerting pressure. If I say no, he's going to rip it off.

"Yes," I say, half honest, half bratty. I don't care if he shreds it.

But he respects my response and pulls the underwear down my legs. "Step out."

I do, then look at him, anticipation pulsing like the sweetest torture. He drops to his knees. He tilts his head, his dark eyes glitter with hot need, a corner of his mouth tipping upward. Pushing my skirt out of the way, he breathes over me.

My knees tremble, and I lock them, leaning against the wall behind me. Excitement sparks through me. He moves closer, raising one of my legs and throwing it over his thick shoulder, exposing me. My heart starts racing, and when he buries his face into me...

My back arches. The air shudders out of me, and I hold his head as his clever tongue and lips lick and suck, sending hot streaks of bliss from my core all the way to the tips of my toes and the top of my head. Every inch of me tingles.

He devours me. There's no other way to describe the way he runs his tongue over me, uses his mouth on me. He laps me up, then growls when I can't contain my moan.

His enthusiasm for the act drives me wild. Pleasure builds fast and hard, and before I even realize what's happening, it crests, overwhelming all my defenses and inhibitions. I grip his hair hard, grinding against him shamelessly. My mouth is open, but nothing comes out, my vocal cords frozen, my lungs empty and paralyzed as an earthquake erupts inside my body.

I quiver with anticipation of a second round, but he pulls back a little and spreads me with his fingers until I'm completely open to his view. My face heats as vulnerability whips through me. I don't know why I'm feeling shy when I just came all over his face moments ago.

He studies me for a moment, then lifts his heated gaze to look into my eyes. "My pretty wife." His whisper rumbles over me like dark thunder. "So hot for me."

My nerve endings crackle at his breath fanning over me, and my own breathing is still uneven. Keeping me completely spread open with his left hand, he kisses my thighs and gently rubs my clit at the same time with his right. I throw my head back and slowly move against his fingers, but every time I try to exert more pressure, he pulls back, leaving me panting at the edge.

I'm so wet, I can feel the slickness on the creases of my thighs. His hand must be a mess, but he doesn't seem to care as he continues to tease.

"Look at your pussy quivering for more." Dark, masculine satisfaction ripples through his words.

I try to rock against his hand, but he stops me by clenching my ass. "Damn it, Sebastian."

"Beg," he orders me, his eyes glittering with control and fire.

Embarrassment fleets over me. I've never begged. But then, I've never felt like I'd die if I didn't feel a man's tongue on me.

As though he can sense my hesitation, he runs his fingers along the fold from the clit all the way to the opening of my pussy, dipping a little inside. Pleasure courses through me, but it's too mild to appease the needy monster inside.

I look down and see the stubbornness in his expression. My God. He's going to do this until I give in. And I *am* going to die if he continues to torment me like this.

"Go down on me," I choke out. "Please. Make me come with your mouth."

"Good girl." And then he's on me again, like my begging has ripped all control and restraint away. Another orgasm swells, rips through me. Before I can come down from the high, he pushes me to a third.

My supporting leg buckles, and one large hand is instantly under my ass, holding me up. I fight for air, struggle for sanity. But he isn't finished, because he's sucking even harder as he pushes two fingers into my dripping, eager flesh.

When the fourth O slams into me, I hear a sharp scream that couldn't have come from my throat. My vision goes black, then white. Fireworks seem to explode in my head, and my heart thunders. He's on me like a man determined to torment and reward me at the same time. Even though he's on his knees with his face buried between my legs, he is the absolute master of my body right now. And I'm responding to his slightest move with shivers and moans.

"Enough," I beg shakily when he gives me a slow lick. "I'm going to pass out if you keep going."

He looks up at me, his eyes hot and steady. "I won't let you fall."

My throat tightens. It feels like he's talking about more than sex for some reason. I take my leg off his shoulder and manage to stand on wobbly feet. Placing my hands on his shoulders, I crouch down until I can look into his eyes without him having to look up. His chin glistens, but it doesn't look messy. It just looks like the most natural display of need.

I take off my shirt and wipe his jaw. "Is this how we're celebrating our victory?"

"Why the hell not? We both won." His smile lances my heart. It doesn't hurt, but it's exciting and scary at the same time.

"We did." I reach down and take his cock in my hand. He lets out a hissing breath, his eyes narrowed. There's so much power leashed inside him, his shaft pulsing in my hand like a beating heart. I let go. "On your feet."

He rises, the movement unhurried and graceful. I'm on my knees, and his cock juts out at eye level, the tip dripping. As a rule I like my sex tidy and neat, but with this man, it doesn't seem to matter. His raw reaction to me—my body, my nearness, my pleasure and need—makes me want to give him the same thing.

I can't quite wrap my hand around the base of his immensely swollen shaft. Veins stand out, pulsing. Holding him, I pull the tip of his cock into my mouth, taste the salt and male, and draw him in deeper. He's so big, it's difficult to take him in. I raise my eyes, watching his reaction, and try to loosen my jaw to take more. His cheeks are flushed, his mouth parted. His gaze is fixed on me. I hollow my cheeks, and a low groan rumbles in his chest.

Emboldened, I grab his butt, digging my nails into the granite-hard muscle as I use my mouth on him. My eyes on his, I run my fingers along his upper thighs, then cup his balls lightly. I glide my tongue along the entire throbbing shaft, tracing the thick veins, before licking the precum off his cockhead. He reacts to every touch like I'm torturing him—and he's enjoying the hell of it.

He was like an unstoppable machine, forcing orgasms on me until I thought my brain would melt. But I tease him, loving the feel of him in my mouth, the slick taste of him on my tongue.

His breathing gets rougher. My hair spills forward, and he gathers it and loops it around his fist. I raise my eyes, and he's looking down at me, all helpless greed. "I'm not missing a second of this," he says between shallow breaths.

His pelvis moves shallowly, thrusting him into my mouth. I increase the pressure of the suction and let him use me for his pleasure. The sight of his slipping control makes the flesh between my legs tingle. Slippery fluid pools in my most sensitive part, and I bring my thighs together to ease the ache. This isn't about me, but him.

But I love what I'm doing to him, how good I'm making him feel—the way he looks at me like I'm a miracle. The sound he makes is louder, and the muscles of his lean abs and legs tighten until they're like marble. Air saws in and out of his lungs, and his hold on my hair gets firmer, making my scalp tingle. I dip my head as much as I can, letting him hit the back of my throat, wanting him to lose himself in a mind-shattering climax like I did.

Abruptly, he pulls out with a harsh groan. Hot white liquid hits my cleavage, splatters onto my cheeks and chin and drips down my chest. The finale leaves me a little stunned, since I've never experienced it before. But he looks at me like he couldn't be more satisfied. His eyes scream, *Mine.* Then he's on me like he hasn't just come, kissing me like he's out of his mind with lust.

I kiss him back. He rips at my bra. I wriggle to help him get rid of it. He runs his hand along the mark the elastic band left around my torso, then cups my breast. I arch into his hot palm. His thumb caresses me around the nipple, and I move restlessly against him, wrapping my legs around his hips.

"Sebastian, please..."

A sound that's somewhere between laugh and groan rolls through him, and his mouth closes over my nipple. The pleasure sears my senses, and a moan catches in my throat.

I clutch him, pressing my breast into his face. He hollows his cheeks, and I shudder as my whole body throbs. He puts his arms under my back and picks me up, his lips still on my nipple.

The change in the position puts me flush against him, and I gasp at the feel of his erection pressing against me. *So soon?* It's like he might have not come at all.

He kicks the door open and carries me down the hall to his room. He lays me on the bed, and I'm enveloped in his scent.

His hands stroke my breasts, his mouth kissing me everywhere. The fact that half my torso is covered in his cum seems to drive him wild. He dips his fingers under my skirt; I close my eyes and let myself enjoy the fire he's stoking again with his touch.

He fumbles around the nightstand, then pulls out a foil packet. He tears it impatiently and rolls the rubber down his already fully erect shaft. I lick my lips, wondering what he's going to feel like.

He wraps his hands around my ankles and pushes my legs up and apart. I'm totally, utterly helpless in this position, but instead of anxiety, my heart pumps with thrill.

"I've been thinking about doing this since I saw you stretching in the gym." His eyes are narrowed. "Maybe before."

"Take what you want."

Those four words ignite a fire in his eyes. He drives into me, his enormous cock stretching me, filling me. I cry out as he rubs against my G-spot. My vision turns hazy, and I grip him hard, digging my fingers into the muscles around his shoulders.

He breathes hard, his eyes glazed. His mouth claims mine, and he pounds into me with enough force to jar my whole body. But I welcome the blatant show of need. It drives me crazy. And I'm so wet, the punishment is simply bliss.

Pleasure spirals out of control. I'm like an animal in heat, and he takes me until I climax again—and again—and again—and I'm a complete mess.

When he finally comes, his groan muffled against my mouth, I hold him like he's the only sane thing left in a world of madness.

20

SEBASTIAN

I LIE ON THE BED, my arms around Luce as my racing heart starts to slow. It takes a while before my breathing evens out. There's something about her that takes my breath away. Is it sexual? Most definitely. I wish I could bury myself inside her over and over again.

But there's something more I can't put my finger on.

"Okay," Luce says, her voice a bit husky. "What are you on? Steroids? Some kind of super-Viagra?"

"What do you mean?" I turn to gaze at her. She's naked except for her skirt and red Converse shoes. I probably should've taken those off, but...

"You were immediately hard again."

"Oh." I laugh. "I just liked seeing my cum on you. And so..." I lift my arm up straight in the air.

She covers her mouth, but I can still hear her laugh.

The sight really did turbocharge my libido. She looked like a goddess who'd been violated and defiled. My dick in her mouth. My mouth on her clit. My fingers in her pussy. It was like there was a war inside me whether to worship or corrupt her, and I finally ended it by pushing my dick inside her hot, tight pussy.

I pull her closer. "We should shower again."

She makes a circle on my breastbone with one finger. The touch is distracting, but in a pleasant way. "I'm going to shower in my room," she says after a moment.

"We should conserve water."

She laughs. "If we try to 'conserve water,' I'll never get clean."

"I'm an excellent washer."

She laughs harder. "You swear we're only going to wash?"

"That's the objective, but you might get ideas and make some other demands. Since I'm an agreeable husband, I'll probably indulge you." To be honest, I feel so good right now that I'd probably say yes to anything she wanted. I used to think that it was stupid as hell when men just gave women whatever they wanted after sex, because I've never, ever felt like saying yes just because I got laid. But sex with Luce is beyond satisfying. It's like getting fed a gourmet seven-course meal.

And I want more.

"I'm starving, though," she says.

"I have an idea for some extra protein…"

"Stop. I'm talking about a real meal. Like tacos."

I smile. "Perfect. That's my middle name."

"What?"

I must've said it too seriously, because she's looking like she can't decide if she should believe me or smack my shoulder for making a joke. "I'm just kidding, although it could've been."

"How?"

"You said you were hungry. So why don't you go get ready, and I'll tell you over some good Mexican food?"

"Deal."

She levers herself up and goes out. I watch her, licking my lips. Does she know how hot she is, walking off while disheveled from sex with me?

I sit up, thinking about how to get her back in bed later. Living under the same roof isn't enough.

I should move into her room. If she's not one hundred percent into it yet, that's fine. I can start sleeping in her bed one night at a time.

21

LUCIENNE

I BARELY RECOGNIZE myself in the mirror. Cum streaks my torso, and my hair is a *mess*. Swollen lips, red marks on my skin... Are they *hickeys*? Oh yes, they are. My face is still flushed from half a dozen orgasms that nearly broke my mind.

I look...*debauched*. It's a word I never thought to associate with myself. Men simply don't do this to me. I don't *let* men do this to me.

But with Sebastian, I not only let him, I begged him for it.

And to be honest, I wouldn't mind if he wanted to do it again after I get some food in my belly, despite a little soreness between my legs. What happened to the nice, staid Lucienne?

Still in shock, I step into the shower and turn on the spray. Hot water drenches me instantly, washing away most of the evidence of our time together.

The thing is, he makes me feel safe. I adore the way he looked at me, like I'm somebody deserving of loving attention. I can't remember the last time a man did that.

Actually, I don't think anybody's *ever* done that. I only mattered when I served a purpose—as the heiress my mom created to placate her father, the would-be CEO who strived to meet my grandfather's standards, the daughter who could give Roderick and his other children what they wanted, the fiancée who could further a man's career and ambitions.

Sebastian was sweet just because. He was playful in the car just because. He gave me orgasms just because. He looked at me with such warmth in his gaze just because.

There was no expectation that I do something to earn any of that from him.

It's exciting and confusing. Scary, even.

Does he have feelings for me? Maybe he actually likes me?

He said he's in love with Gabriella, but maybe she dumped him for good when he said he was marrying me. So he could be on the rebound, but... Is it so bad to savor a little affectionate treatment?

I dry my hair and put on a T-shirt and shorts, then go downstairs. Sebastian is leaning against the kitchen island, checking something on his phone. He's wearing a gray T-shirt and black shorts. The fact that I know how strong and gorgeous his body is underneath the simple clothes heats my blood.

He lifts his head and shoots me a brilliant smile. My mind goes blank, like a girl lost in the presence of her first major crush. *Good Lord, why don't you giggle and blush while you're at it?*

"Ready for tacos?" he asks.

"Yes." I'm glad he gave me a simple yes-no question. I'm beyond forming a complex response that's going to flow logically, not when my emotions are all over the place.

Sebastian drives us. The car's quiet except for some soft rock he puts on. The surface of my skin seems to crackle in the confines of the Rolls-Royce. Normally, I might try to fill the silence with some polite small talk, but not with him. It's so peaceful without any words to break the quiet. I realize it's been a long time since I've been with somebody without feeling a need to *say* something. Even with Bianca, I'm constantly talking.

He pulls into a Manny's Tacos near my place. It's after the lunch rush, so the place is more or less empty. The scent of sizzling meat, veggies and warm tortillas lingers in the air. The speakers fill the place with upbeat Mexican music.

The hostess shows us to a table, and I order a margarita. Manny's has amazing margaritas—cold and strong. Since we're starving, we also order our entrées without looking at the menu—beef burritos and Coke for Sebastian, and fish tacos with extra guacamole for me.

We dig into chips and salsa. "Okay, spill. Tell me how you almost ended up with the name Tacos," I ask after taking my first few bites.

He laughs, then shakes his head. "I don't know if you know this about my dad, but he has seven sons."

"*Seven?* That's a lot."

"Yeah. And we were all born within four months of each other."

"What'd your father have, a harem?" I've heard of some bizarre stories about Hollywood, but this is really out there.

"Not exactly. But a lot of girlfriends and a vasectomy fail. It was ridiculous."

"Wow. I can't imagine. I guess he wasn't ready for children."

"Or anything that didn't fit his lifestyle."

Sebastian's judgmental tone doesn't lessen my empathy for Ted. "But seven kids! I don't know what I would've done in his situation."

Sebastian shrugs. "What could he have done?"

"You're right. He'd already made seven babies. I guess prevention was the key here. Anyway, so...the tacos thing...?"

Our server brings out food and drinks. As soon as he's gone, I look at Sebastian expectantly while biting into my taco.

"My dad isn't the greatest with names, and he couldn't be bothered to remember the names of seven kids, so he named us after our moms. Except me. I'm named after the company my mom's family founded. But to make my case worse, when my mom had me, he stopped by for some reason." Sebastian makes a face, then chomps down on his food with more force than necessary.

"Why was that so bad?"

"Because while his assistant was listening for what name my dad would give me, Dad said, 'Sebastian'...then he saw taco wrappings and said, 'Tacos.' And the assistant, being the idiot that he was, told the nurse who was filling out my birth certificate that my name was to be Sebastian Tacos Lasker."

I cover my mouth with a hand, nearly choking on my margarita. "Oh my God."

"Thankfully, my grandmother caught it and lost her temper. She said no grandson of hers would be named Tacos, and Dad realized what happened. Apparently, he laughed and said, 'Good thing she wasn't having sushi. He could've been Sebastian Unagi Lasker.'" Sebastian rolls his eyes.

"That's kind of cute," I say with a smile.

He looks at me. "Cute? You think that's cute?"

"He was probably just overcome. At least he made an effort." My tone grows wistful.

"An effort to be a nuisance." He sniffs. "I bet your parents didn't try to name you after food wrappings."

"Yeah, because they didn't name me at all." I flash him a pat smile to let him know it isn't a big deal, even though thinking about it stings. "My grandfather had already picked it out. Lucien Francis Caesar Peery."

"That's a boy's name," Sebastian says with a frown.

"Uh-huh. And apparently he was just, like, *despondent* that I was born a girl. And never tried to hide it." I smile to cover my sadness. The emotional wound he inflicted stayed even after his death.

"What a jerk," Sebastian mutters. "Your parents didn't find out if you were a boy or a girl beforehand?"

"They did, but he kept hoping the doctors had made a mistake." I pull my lips in briefly, then shrug. It's one of an endless string of awkward stories of my life. "They wanted me to be certain things. It bothered them—and continues to bother them—that I'm not."

"Like what? A boy?"

I nod. "I would've been a perfect Peery, the ideal heir to my grandfather." I'm slightly uncomfortable that I'm revealing so much. As a rule, I don't talk about my grandfather or parents with others. The only person who knows everything is Bianca, who grew up with me—and probably Matthias, who also watched me grow up. But in the face of Sebastian's tender sympathy, my filter's not working, and the words have poured out.

"That's ridiculous," he says with disgust. "You're fine the way you are."

"But am I? A lot of my friendships failed too. Sometimes I wonder if

Bianca is disappointed with me for not being better." Okay, I need to shut up. I'm not sure exactly why I shared that detail about her because... Well, it's something that has fleeted through my mind from time to time, but I never wanted to voice it in case it was true. There are many times I feel like I could've been a better friend to her, who's done so much to defend me against my family.

"Who's Bianca?"

"My best friend and assistant." I'm glad he isn't asking about the specifics of her possible disappointment with me. "You'll meet her at the party next Saturday."

"If she's a real friend, she won't expect you to change for her. Like I said, you're fine the way you are." His voice is gentle, but firm.

"You sure?" I know I'm fishing for reassurance. He's been so nice to me for no particular reason, and maybe I need him to tell me I'm not too bad.

"You work hard. You're disciplined. You're fun to hang out with."

I laugh, flattered but also a little sad because I feel like they're empty words.

"I'm serious," he says. "You show up. You spent years learning to master the skills on the court, which lazy and undisciplined people can't. I know because *I've* done it. You have a mischievous sense of humor. You don't back down from a challenge, and you understand me without my having to spell everything out." He stops abruptly.

"What?"

He blinks, then looks at me like he almost doesn't recognize me. "Nothing."

"Nothing? Pretty sure there was something."

"It's just...none of the articles about you mentioned any of that."

"Oh." I clear my throat, then take a sip of my margarita. "The tabloids don't like me very much."

He shakes his head. "They're idiots."

Others who know about my situation with the paparazzi have almost always said, "What have you done to get them to hate you?" like it was my fault. Sebastian instantly blaming the media for the unjust treatment I've suffered loosens a knot that's been lodged in my chest for a long time. And, for once, I can breathe easy.

He reaches out and pats my hand. The motion feels like a knock on the gate to my heart. And I can feel it crack open, allowing him to slip inside a little.

That night, when he shows up at my door with a pillow and a tray of magnolia tea to "help me sleep," I laugh and let him in. When he wraps around me in bed like a shield, I clasp him in return, and we do things other than sleep for hours.

On Sunday we have a leisurely brunch and watch *John Wick*—Sebastian's choice—and *True Lies*—mine—in the home theater, sharing a huge tub of caramel popcorn. Our fingers keep brushing as we reach for the snack, and we miss the climax where Arnold Schwarzenegger shoots all the bad guys with his Harrier.

Our time is scarily normal, almost as if there were no contract. Something is shifting between us. And I want to see what happens from here—how far it can go.

22

LUCIENNE

I'M SHOCKED to see Bianca in the office on Tuesday. She said she'd try to get back soon, but I didn't want her to rush. I was actually thinking about texting her to take more time, but it slipped my mind yesterday because I was swamped.

She stands up when she sees me.

"What are you doing here?" I ask, giving her a hug. "How are you feeling?"

"Back at work, obviously," she says, returning my hug listlessly. "And I'm...okay, I guess." The hitch in her voice says she isn't okay.

"You weren't supposed to be back until later." I should've texted her yesterday, no matter how busy I was. She knows about some of the things I wanted to do once I got married—like auditing my finances—and she might've felt pressured to come back to help.

"Plans change. Wanna go into your office?"

"Yeah, sure."

We go inside together. I gesture at the couch by the coffee table and sit down next to her.

She's paler than usual, her eyes slightly bloodshot. But if you aren't close to her, you wouldn't know she's exhausted, emotionally and physically. She's done a good job hiding it with makeup and a sunny yellow blouse and blue skirt. But her smile doesn't have the usual brightness, and her skin's dull underneath the foundation.

I hug her again, harder this time, and feel her sag into me. I wish I could do more, but there's nothing I can do to make things better for her. "When did you get back in the States, anyway?"

"Last night."

Okay, so maybe getting in touch with her yesterday wouldn't have worked because she would've been on a plane. Still... "You should've taken today off."

"I didn't want to. I wanted to make sure you were okay."

"Me?" I put a hand over my chest. "I'm not the one who lost her uncle."

She shrugs helplessly with a forced smile, like she's at a loss for words to describe how she feels, but she'd hate to impose her grief on others.

Empathy stirs. I couldn't figure out what to say when my mom passed away, either. All sorts of feelings come forward, impossible to articulate when so many of them contradict each other, or magnify little things that you know shouldn't matter much anymore.

"I think it's best if I just keep myself busy. And I was concerned about your marriage to Sebastian. I mean, I knew you were going to marry him, but I just didn't like the way he was with me."

"You've interacted with him?" He didn't seem to recognize her name at the Mexican restaurant.

"Well, yeah, of course. When I had to organize things like the lunch or flowers or send him the documents for the Sebastian Peery collaboration. He rarely responded, and when he deigned to bother, he was so abrupt. His assistant wasn't any better, either."

The details about the lunch and flowers feel off. I'm the one who texted him about both. But maybe she got in touch about something related to the lunch dates, and he blew her off. It wouldn't be surprising, because he was so furious with me. But the Sebastian Peery situation doesn't make any sense. "That's weird. He told me he never got the documents."

Bianca's face twists with disgust. "What the hell? He's lying or something. He confirmed that he got them to me."

"He did...?" How odd. Sebastian Jewelry doesn't have a strong foothold in Asia, and this could be the break he's looking for. Sebastian doesn't come across as the type to sabotage his own business project just to spite someone. He could've found some other way to torment me if he wanted to make me suffer.

On the other hand, Bianca has no reason to lie about any of this. She wants me to succeed. She's been my biggest cheerleader all my life.

"There must've been some miscommunication," I say finally. I don't want to take sides, although it makes me feel like a horrible friend to Bianca. But I can't blame Sebastian without more facts when I'm ninety-nine percent sure he wouldn't do something like this.

"We'll see. But I'm not going to be comfortable until he proves himself."

"I don't think you need to worry. It looks like we'll make a good team."

"What makes you say that? Did something happen?" Her eyes sparkle as she sits up straight. "Did he tell you how much he loves you?"

I laugh. "Nothing like that. But we worked so well together." I tell her what happened playing against Preston and Vonnie.

"*Yes!* Oh my God, that's *awesome!*" A huge smile splits her face. "I wish I'd been there. I would've never let those two run away before getting on their knees! I would've recorded it and put it on every site—Facebook, Instagram, Pulse, you name it, I would've put it up! I miss the best things."

"Well...maybe it wasn't the *best* thing." I grin.

She gasps, leaning forward eagerly. "I know that look. You got lucky." She puts her hand on my arm. "Let's hear it."

"I'm not doing a blow-by-blow."

"Aha! So there was blowing!"

"All you have to know is it was amazing. Like...the best I've ever had. He could wear out an Energizer Bunny."

Bianca's eyes grow wide, and she bites into her lip. "I'm so happy for you. Wow. You're right. I don't need to worry about you and Sebastian."

"Told you. Now don't you wish you'd taken today off?"

"Nope," she says, stubborn as ever. "I'm happy to be back so I can help you work through the Sebastian Peery project and plan the wedding reception."

"Sebastian's having his assistant Christoph handle most of the reception. Julio's been helping, but he's not as experienced."

Bianca smiles. "Well, don't worry. I'll make sure everything goes smoothly."

"You're the best. Thank you. But if you need some time off, just take it, okay? Put yourself first for once."

"Thanks, girl." Then she reaches into her leather folio. "This. Back to you." She hands me my black AmEx.

She returns to her desk, and I review the email Julio sent last night regarding the agenda for the day. Two meetings have been moved, and the Hae Min Group's rep promised to send their comments on the contract this week.

Finally.

I look at the new campaign idea from the marketing team. It's slick, but it's missing something. It brims with luxury, but it doesn't scream, "Buy me." I send them my feedback, requesting updates by the end of the week, since they may have to start over.

There are a couple of brisk knocks at the door, then Julio brings a bouquet of white and pink calla lilies. It's so big, it almost eclipses him from the waist up.

Are they from Sebastian? My heart does a little samba.

"This just came for you," Julio says.

I take it from him with a broad smile. "Thanks."

He leaves, and a girly giggle bubbles inside. I pluck the card in the middle of the gorgeous blossoms and open it quickly.

And as soon as my eyes scan the card, my shoulders droop a little.

Dear Lucie,

Congratulations on your marriage! Wishing you all the love and joy!

—Yuna H Winters

Maybe I should've realized Sebastian couldn't be the one behind the bouquet. He's never sent me flowers, and just because we had great sex and some nice couple time, and have started to sleep in the same bed, it doesn't mean he's going to become romantic overnight, especially to a woman he doesn't even love.

Come on. Stop being so morose. It's sweet that Yuna made the gesture. She didn't have to.

I find her number and text her.

–Me: Thank you so much for the flowers and warm wishes! They're lovely!

I don't have to wait long before I get a response.

–Yuna: My pleasure! It's so romantic to elope like that. Loved the setting, too.

–Yuna: By the way, do you know where your L.A. store gets its ice cream? Liam's been driving me and my husband crazy asking for it, and we bought him a bunch of different brands, but he says they aren't the same. :eyeroll-emoji:

–Yuna: So far the only person who's enjoying this is his twin sister, who's been eating all the ice cream he's rejected.

I laugh, shaking my head with sympathy.

–Me: Liam's an absolute epicure for a toddler.

–Yuna: Really? He's not just being difficult?

–Me: Nope. Our L.A. store sources their ice cream from a local organic gelato place that makes specialty batches just for us. I can ask the store manager to set some aside for Liam if you'd like—or have it delivered to your place, whichever is easier.

–Yuna: Oh my God, you're amazing. Where have you been all my life?

I laugh harder.

–Yuna: Thank you so much! I don't want to impose any more than I already have. I'll send one of my assistants to pick it up today. I owe you a favor now!

I hesitate for a little. Most of the people who are invited to the wedding reception on my side are business associates. I don't really have any close friends other than Bianca. But Yuna seems so nice, and I'd love to get to know her better.

—Me: By the way, if you're free, I'd love to invite you to the wedding reception. Since Sebastian and I eloped, we decided to have a party instead.

—Yuna: Really? I love love LOVE parties!

—Yuna: Also it's nice to have an excuse to dress up and hang out with other adults I like. :wink-emoji:

—Me: Great! I'll send you the invite and add you to the guest list.

I send the guest QR code to her phone and smile. Maybe this can be the start of a beautiful friendship.

23

LUCIENNE

I'M ABSOLUTELY EXHAUSTED by Thursday. The Hae Min Group's lawyers sent a bunch of notes and questions, and our lawyers responded. But they also need me to review some of the main points to make sure I'm okay with the proposed changes.

I'm learning more about Korean luxury retail and wedding customs than I ever imagined. It's fascinating, but tiring because everyone's squabbling about every minute detail. What's worse is that the Korean counterpart is very slow to respond. The contract was sent over eight weeks ago, and it didn't come back to us until yesterday. It's almost like this project isn't really a priority for them.

Which is absurd. When I visited the Hae Min Group's headquarters in Gangnam, Vice-Chairman Eugene Hae indicated he was very interested in the exclusive luxury custom designs Sebastian Peery can do for their ultra-ritzy department stores. They want something new to offer their clientele, and some of their top spenders are looking for unique high-ticket items as status symbols. He explained their top customers are in a special loyalty program, and they need to spend at least a million dollars a year at the Hae Min Group-owned department stores to qualify and maintain their status.

And yet...things are dragging...and sapping my energy.

Since I'm tired of coming home around midnight, I leave the office early enough that I can be home before ten. Not that I can go to bed anytime soon. There are still at least five more reports and documents to review.

The kitchen is empty—I told Matthias I was grabbing dinner at work—and Sebastian's probably doing whatever he likes to do in the evening. I have no clue what he does after work because I haven't been around enough. A sliver of guilt lodges in my gut. I told him I wanted us to make the best of the situation, and I've been a neglectful wife.

But there's nothing to be done until things ease up a bit. If I'd known Sebastian would end up being my husband rather than Preston, I might've specified in the contract to request more involvement from Sebastian Jewelry for the collaboration. But given Preston's lack of experience and ability, I made myself the person in charge for handling the Hae Min Group. Nothing can go wrong with this project because I have to prove myself to the board.

Once the distribution deal with the Hae Min Group is finalized, I'll have some breathing room. Maybe Sebastian and I can find some hobbies to try together. Not just tennis, but maybe going out and doing things that he'd like, although...

Probably not. That Stalker's back. So are his privacy-violating buddies. So far they haven't been able to generate any embarrassing headlines, but that's only because all I've done since they reappeared in my life is go back and forth to work.

Hopefully, they won't bother Sebastian. I don't understand why they're so obsessed with me. I'm a minor celebrity of sorts due to my inheritance, but there are far more interesting and famous people in Los Angeles.

I go to my bedroom and kick off my shoes. My stilettos are generally comfortable, but nothing beats bare feet. I get out of my clothes, and let out a sigh as soon as my bra's gone. So much better.

Next to come off is the jewelry, except for the Toi et Moi ring and wedding band. The island in the center of the walk-in closet has six huge compartments for my jewelry and accessories.

Sebastian's watch sits among mine, so he must've gotten home and changed already. Although he could just keep all his things in his bedroom down the hall, he's started to leave some of his stuff in my closet, like a guy who's spending more and more time at his girlfriend's place. It's sort of cute.

I stick my hand into the home wear section of the closet and pull out the first thing I grab. A lacy silk nightie in amethyst purple. Bianca gave it to me when she learned I was engaged to Preston. Well, that cheater's out of my life, but the gift is still nice. It's pretty and has never been worn, so I'm going to pretend it has nothing to do with my asshole ex-fiancé and enjoy it.

I put it on. The fabric glides coolly over me, like a cloud against my bare skin. It hangs low, and the lace strategically covers my chest. But then, it's supposed to be sexy and powerful. And I need to feel like that right now.

I wipe off my makeup in the bathroom. As the eye shadow, mascara and foundation vanish, my dark circles and fatigue become more obvious. The nightie is sexy, but the woman wearing it is just tired. And hungry.

What I told Matthias notwithstanding, I haven't had anything since lunch. I sort of lost track of time, and Bianca, who would normally get me to eat something, had to leave early to pick up her aunt at the airport.

I'm going to grab a bowl of cereal, since I can't cook and don't want to bother Matthias. I take my bag and go downstairs so I can eat and review the docs at the same time. Marketing sent their revised campaign, and they're waiting for my final approval.

But this time the kitchen isn't empty. I smell the aroma of coffee filling the area and see Sebastian standing in front of the espresso machine. He's in a white T-shirt and boxers, his feet bare. His hair is slightly mussed, like he's run his fingers through it a few times. And, surprisingly, he's wearing wire-rimmed glasses, which make him look like a hottie professor.

My hormones go shivery. I'm tired, but not dead.

He turns around and stops abruptly. His eyes are on my face, then they drop to my chest.

And my nipples get pointed like...tiny little hos with minds of their own.

Now I wish I hadn't lost my bra so soon. But it's too late.

He tears his eyes from my breasts and looks at me. But from the dark gleam in their depths, it's obvious he thinks I dressed like this to seduce him.

Clearing my throat, I place the black leather bag stuffed with printed copies of the documents—and my laptop—on the counter. His eyebrows pinch.

"What are you doing here?" I ask, then sigh. It's obvious what he's doing. "What I mean is...I thought you were watching TV or something."

"I had some stuff to look at. I thought you were working late again."

"I still have things to go over, but I wanted to come home early." I go to the pantry and grab a box of cereal. "*Early* being a relative term."

Sebastian takes the milk out of the fridge for me.

"Thanks. Can you get me a bottle of water, too?"

He places it on the counter.

"Thanks." I grab a bowl and dump the cereal and milk in it.

He stays out of my way—and the kitchen is large enough that we aren't brushing against each other or anything—but my whole body is aware of where he is at all times.

Sebastian isn't the type of man you can ignore, even if he gives you space. He's like a lion lazing in the sun, watching gazelles in the field before him.

I should act like one of the gazelles and mind my own business. After parking myself on a stool by the kitchen island, I gulp everything down fast.

He takes the stool next to me. "Didn't you have dinner?"

"No time. I need to wrap this up soon."

"Want something more substantial?" He jerks his chin at my bowl.

"Don't feel like ordering something and waiting, and I can't cook."

"I can't, either," he says, making a face. "For everyone's health and safety."

His mild irritation over the fact that he can do anything he sets his mind to—except cook—makes me laugh.

"When do you find the time to party and have fun if you're working all the time?" he asks.

"I don't. Contrary to what people think, I never partied much. Most of the events I was photographed at were work-related." I try to keep my tone unironic. "Photographed" is a euphemism for paparazzi harassment, but that isn't Sebastian's fault. "Besides, I'm trying to lie low. I can't seem to avoid scandals no matter what I do, and I don't want anything to embarrass you or your family."

"You don't have to do anything on my behalf. Or my family's."

His terse tone makes it sound like he's saying there's a line between us and I shouldn't cross it. And it annoys me after the weekend. "It's the least I can do for your family," I say, trying to not sound hostile. I don't want to fight, but I don't want him to be unfair, either.

"They aren't worth it. You should do whatever makes you happy."

I bite my lip. *I totally misjudged him.* I must be more tired than I thought. Usually, whatever men do just rolls off me. Some of my boyfriends got fed up with what they called my aloof and distant attitude and broke up with me. But it's impossible to keep Sebastian at arm's length. Everything he does and says elicits a visceral reaction.

"What are you working on?" Sebastian glances at my bag.

"The marketing campaign. And I need to look at some of the Sebastian Peery launch items. Probably sometime next month or the month after, we should be able to sign off on the deal. I want to move fast and aggressively."

He takes a thoughtful sip of his coffee. "You continuously surprise me."

"How so?"

"You just seem...so dedicated. Much more so than I imagined. I saw you work hard, but I didn't expect you to put in this many hours."

"It's important. To be honest, I wasn't super interested in Peery Diamonds when I was younger. It just seemed like something I shouldn't care too much about, especially when my grandfather was so disappointed that I wasn't a boy."

"He was wrong." Sebastian's response is quiet and sympathetic, not pitying or judging. If I want to say more and maybe even lean on him, he'll respect that. If I want to retreat into my shell, he'll respect that just as much.

His consideration breaks another section of the dam inside me.

"Well." I shrug to hide the old pain—and the embarrassment that my grandfather held archaic, sexist beliefs. "He had a set way of looking at the world. And to him, girls were pretty and vulnerable things who required the protection of men. Too weak-willed and capricious to be in charge. So I wasn't sure if I'd ever be deemed good enough for Peery Diamonds, and I didn't want to get attached to it. And I was pretty successful at that." I take a long swallow of my water.

"So how come you ended up in charge?"

I lower my glass. Is Sebastian going to remember if I tell him? Or is the event in Paris so inconsequential that he doesn't remember any of it? Watching him closely, I start. "When I was fourteen, my family and I went to Paris. I was so upset, I thought about running away."

"Did you?"

"For an hour or two, maybe?" It felt like an eternity on that snowy night in the City of Light, but I doubt I was gone for too long. "I don't know what I was thinking, since I didn't have money or a phone with me. I hadn't thought things through. Then I met this guy, who told me I should fight for what was mine." I turn so I'm facing Sebastian fully.

He's nodding, but there's no recognition in his eyes. So. He doesn't remember.

Figures. I don't know why it disappoints me. How many rich guys in their twenties would remember a gangly girl without the good sense to dress properly for the weather, who was nonetheless shameless enough to demand that he buy her hot chocolate?

I continue, "And he was right. Peery Diamonds *is* mine. I'm the only Peery left. Roderick and his two kids aren't Peerys. If I'd walked away, Grandfather would've had no choice but to leave his fortune to them. Once I decided it was mine, I wanted not only to keep it, but to make it amazing. I want the company to flourish under my leadership. I want everyone in the world to know what Peery Diamonds is."

Sebastian merely gives me a steady look. I can't read his eyes behind the lenses. Suddenly, I wonder if I've spoken too grandly, and he's thinking I'm delusional. Bianca didn't think so, but she's always on my side. Darren said the idea was "unrealistic"—another mark against him —and Roderick said I should focus on squeezing out as much profit as possible. Karl doesn't care.

I start to reach for the water, trying to hide my discomfort. Maybe I'm just doomed to be with men who disappoint me in some way.

"I think that's fabulous," Sebastian says finally.

My hand stills in midair. "What?"

"You heard me." A small smile curves his gorgeous lips. "Your vision's perfect."

"You think so?" I search his face, looking for signs that he's just humoring me.

"Yes. An executive needs to have ambition for the company they're leading."

A large chunk of the bitterness dripping inside me dissolves. It's incredible what this man can do with a few words. I grin, suddenly energized. "*Thank* you! I think so too."

"Want me to take a look at some of the launch plans for Sebastian Peery with you?" he asks.

"I thought you had something to do..."

"I don't mind. And it's supposed to be a collaboration between us, anyway."

I beam at him. "I'd love that."

Sebastian

I'm glad Luce took my offer to be more involved with such easy grace. Some people might have argued or rejected the idea, thinking I was trying to stick my nose where it didn't belong or take over the project altogether.

I looked into the details of the collaboration after our marriage. It wasn't part of the original offer she sent my family. She'd been working on a deal with the Hae Min Group for a while before she targeted the Comtois to get herself a husband. But my grandfather saw a chance to carve himself a slice of the Korean wedding jewelry business—Sebastian Jewelry isn't strong in Asia—and Luce gave in.

She must've really wanted a husband. Desperately, in fact, to marry someone as shitty as Preston. I wouldn't wish him on anyone, except maybe that horrible Vonnie.

I go over the documents she brought and make notes in the margins. Luce is studying something on her computer, her eyebrows pulled together in concentration. She hasn't fidgeted or shown any indication she's tired or bored. She works like she's waging a war—life or death. I've never felt that way about my work, but it's oddly endearing that she takes her job so seriously.

Finally, when she closes her laptop, I put down the documents. "What's the rush, by the way?" I ask, curious about the timeline she specified in the collaboration chart.

"I want a big chunk of it done before the next shareholders' meeting. They weren't too thrilled about the launch in Korea, especially after Roderick told them how fickle the Asian market is." Her mouth purses, annoyance and determination rolling through her flashing eyes. "With him no longer able to vote as my proxy, I need to show the shareholders and the board that I have what it takes to be the CEO on my own."

"Don't they already feel that way about you to keep you as the CEO?"

"Half the board are men from Nesovia, and they have sexist ideas about where women belong. They only tolerated me because they thought Roderick was 'controlling' me." She makes a disgusted sound. "And he had a vested interest in keeping me as the head of the company because he needed the money I could bring in."

I shake my head. "Your family picked the wrong country to found the company. They're going to lose all the female talent with that attitude."

"Which is why I'm moving the company to the U.S."

"The shareholders agreed to it already?"

"It's in our governance charter to allow us to move to a country with a better human rights record, so long as there isn't an increase in tax liability. And it would be difficult to argue that America is somehow more sexist than Nesovia." She places her fists on the counter. "I don't want to treat our female employees differently, or have them feel discouraged that they may not be able to climb the corporate ladder like the men. And pulling the company away from a country that doesn't respect women is a good starting point."

Her chin juts out stubbornly; her shoulders are tense. She's a warrior fighting a good battle she believes in. It's admirable.

I get up and go over, then rub her tight neck and shoulders. She melts into the touch. "Let me know how I can help."

She tilts her head. "Thank you."

The smile she gives me makes me feel a hundred feet tall. And I have an inexplicable desire to never disappoint her.

24

LUCIENNE

I CAST a critical eye on my reflection for the thousandth time. If people knew just how obsessively I've been checking my appearance, there'd be another scandal-rag headline saying Lucienne Peery is an absolute narcissist.

But I can't worry about that right now. Today's D-day...or R-day. The reception is the first event Sebastian and I are holding as a couple, and I want everything to go smoothly. I'm especially focused on making a good impression on his brothers, whom I still haven't met.

Although he hasn't said much about them, I know they're all very close. He has to be, to have dinner with them—he's insanely busy with all the work he has at Sebastian Jewelry. I also noticed he frequently texts with them, and is generally in a good mood when he interacts with them.

My hair is curled and arranged so it falls over my shoulders and back in soft waves. A couple of topaz butterfly pins keep it in place, and I'm wearing chandelier diamond earrings and a matching necklace and bracelet. My off-white dress with a thigh-high side slit fits perfectly, and the lace trim adds a lovely bridal touch to the look.

I turn my face left, then right. Should I have gone for darker and more dramatic eye shadow? I have an hour before the caterers and quartet arrive. I can redo my makeup.

On the other hand, I'm not the friendliest-looking person in general. Bianca once said smoky eye makeup can make me look unapproachable, and that isn't what I want.

Friendly. Sweet. Approachable. That's the goal this evening.

"What are you worried about?" Sebastian says, approaching from the kitchen.

I pull my gaze from the reflective surface on the dark glass wall in the living room and look at him over a shoulder. "I just—"

A bespoke tux from Italy fits his broad shoulders and narrow waist perfectly, hiding his raw power underneath a layer of civilized fashion. Cool confidence rolls off him in waves, and the arrogant tilt of his head says the world goes around the way he wills it. There's not even a smidgeon of nerves. He either believes everyone's going to like him or doesn't give a damn what people think. Probably both.

"I just want to make a good impression with your brothers." Then I remember another thing. "And their wives."

Anxiety rachets up.

He comes over and kisses my left-hand knuckles, right above our "engagement" ring. "You're fine."

"Are you sure?"

"My brothers aren't that difficult."

"That isn't what I read."

He arches an eyebrow. "Did you look them up?"

I nod. "Bianca made a profile for each. Your brothers are intelligent and particular, and they care about you deeply."

He scoffs. "You wasted Bianca's time, because I would've told you that if you'd asked. And I'm telling you now: there's no reason to be nervous."

I don't know about that. The information Bianca dug up indicated they're incredibly protective of each other. She wrung her hands when she whispered, "What if they hate you for forcing Sebastian to marry you? Should we try to have a dinner or something before the party? To clear things up?"

"Maybe they don't know," I told her, but that's just wishful thinking and my wanting to delay what could be an ugly encounter. There's absolutely no reason for Sebastian to hide how our marriage came about. Even if he never said a word, they had to know something was up when we got married so quickly and didn't invite them to the wedding. But at least his father attended the ceremony. That should make our union look less weird.

"I wish your father was coming," I say.

Sebastian gives me a strained smile. "He says he's *very* sorry about that."

Closing my eyes, I breathe out, hoping to settle my nerves. "Maybe we can invite him over for dinner instead."

"I'll ask, but he's generally pretty busy with movie stuff." Something about his tone says he'd rather not dine with his dad. Not sure why—Ted is such a sweet, well-meaning man. I would've been overjoyed if my father was anything like him.

"I just need a friendly face." I expel a breath.

"I'm not enough?" His tone is half insulted, half teasing.

"I mean, obviously we're going to play a nice, happy couple, so—"

Sebastian puts a hand on my waist and spins me around. I gasp, and his mouth fits over mine, his tongue gliding in. I melt into the kiss, the pulsing pleasure of his touch. His large hand supports my back, the warmth seeping in like heated honey.

He presses his mouth on my cheeks, forehead, over my brows and along my jaw line. "You worry too much," he says between kisses. "And you're way too tense."

"I just want people to like me. Us." I don't want them to look at us and think you're wasted on me, like your grandparents and mother do.

"What they like or don't like is irrelevant. The only thing that matters is you're my wife."

"But..."

"If they have a problem with *us*, they can go fuck themselves."

I blink, but somehow the crude words fit. He honestly doesn't care what our guests think.

"And don't forget, I'll be right beside you the whole time."

He squeezes my hand. The anxiety that's been plaguing me since I got up this morning retreats. My belly's still tight, but my nerves settle a bit. He raises my hand and kisses the back of it.

I go up on tiptoes and kiss his cheek. "Thank you."

"And I brought this for you." He reaches into his pocket and pulls out a small velvet box with a discreet Sebastian Jewelry logo on it.

I open it and gasp at a pair of stunning butterfly pins. Beautifully cut blue stones glitter in the shining platinum setting.

"Sapphires and diamonds," he says.

"Thank you. These are gorgeous," I whisper, then look up at his handsome face, at his eyes gazing at me like my reaction means everything to him.

"I happened to be in our L.A. flagship store. These caught my eye and made me think of you." He plucks them out of the box and places them over my hair. "See? Perfect."

My heart pounds as pleasure warms my body. I look at my reflection. "They are."

"*You* are perfect, wife," he corrects me, then places a sweet kiss on my temple.

I can feel my cheeks heat with delight. I pull the topaz pins out, then stick Sebastian's gifts into my hair. The butterflies sparkle, like good-luck talismans.

My confidence skyrockets. I roll my shoulders and exhale deeply and slowly. Facing the crowd no longer feels so daunting.

I'm Sebastian's wife.

Everything will be fine.

THE QUARTET PLAYS Pachelbel in our converted garage, now a completely decked-out ballroom. The guests arrive, showing their invitations to the security personnel. This reception isn't the kind people are dying to crash, but I can't let my guard down with That Stalker and his buddies around.

Sebastian had the Aylster Hotel come to our place and cater the event, which was a smart move. Their team did an excellent job setting up a huge spread of gourmet food and two bars that seem to have every liquor known to man.

Although Matthias wanted to help host the event, I told him to take the weekend off like he's supposed to. His granddaughter just had a baby, and I didn't want him hanging around when Sebastian and I already have enough people to make things go smoothly.

There's no special toast or first dance, since it's a post-wedding reception. I want this to be more like a high-society party. It isn't as if Sebastian and I married in the most conventional way, and he might feel weird about toasts and all the rest of it. *I* would feel weird, since people would probably toast to everlasting love, and that isn't what we have between us.

Sure, we share the same bed, have great sex and work well together. But that isn't love. He's never hinted he feels anything but mild affection for me, and I know better than to expect more. Men just don't fall in love with me.

Bianca gives me a tight hug. "Relax, girl. This is going to be amazing. I just know it."

"I hope so. But people always think they already know me. It's like a preexisting condition or something." Most of the time I don't get a chance to show who I really am because people just can't see beyond the headlines. I know people like that aren't worthy of my affection or friendship, but it still stings.

"Well, that just makes them dumb." Bianca pats my arm. "Don't let them bring you down on a day when you're supposed to be happy."

I put on a smile. "You're right."

"I know." She winks.

Laughing softly, I watch her go check some details with the staff. Although she's here as my guest, she was part of the planning team for the event. It's just like her to reconfirm every detail. She wants this to be perfect as much as I do.

More and more guests start to arrive. Yuna comes over with an absolutely gorgeous man on her arm. I recognize him. Declan Winters— a former underwear model and now an actor. He's considered one of the most handsome men in Hollywood, and has a lot of fans for his engaging personality, too. His devotion to his wife is legendary.

Yuna is perfectly dressed in a bright emerald dress and cute stilettos. The pearls on her are lustrous and huge, and she glows like the happiest woman. It's like *she's* the newlywed.

"Lucie!" She hugs me. "Thank you so much! You saved me!"

I laugh. "I guess Liam likes the ice cream?"

"He adores it. Now he wants to know when he can meet and thank his ice cream fairy." She smiles.

"Awww. He can drop by anytime."

"We might. And can I bring his twin, too? She wants to have a bracelet designed especially for her tiny little forearm." Yuna rolls her eyes a little.

"Of course. I'd love it." I put a hand on Sebastian's quite sizeable forearm. "By the way, have you met my husband?"

"I don't believe so," she says.

"This is Yuna Hae Winters. She's the daughter of the Hae Min Group's chairman."

Sebastian gives her his most brilliant smile. "Very pleased to meet you."

"Likewise. You run Sebastian Jewelry, right?"

"I do."

"That's so cool. Look at you, the most perfect merger of two jewelry empires. Mom was just gushing when I told her about meeting you." She then turns to her partner. "This is my husband. Declan Winters."

We say hello and exchange pleasantries. I start to relax under Yuna's easy smile and friendly chatter. As more guests come in, she lets us go to greet them.

As another heiress, London Bickham, is telling me about her latest trip—she's convinced we need to take time off and visit Mallorca—Sebastian dips his head and whispers, "Your family's here."

I straighten and turn. Roderick and Karl swagger in together. They're in bespoke tuxedos, again paid for with my money. Roderick isn't wearing any jewelry except for the wedding band from his marriage to Mom. He never takes it off, and some think it's because he still hasn't forgotten her. But I know better. He just wants to remind everyone who his wife was.

Karl doesn't have the brain to consider things like that, so he generally wears a lot of rings and a necklace. Sometimes he goes overboard and looks like he's auditioning for a music video. But today, he doesn't have anything on him. It's almost like he's having...money problems.

Which he might, since I cut him off. HR and legal must be after him to claw back the salary the company paid him while he didn't bother to report to work. Instead of his usual I'm-the-hottest-thing-on-the-block smirk, he's wearing a slightly strained smile.

There's no sign of Vonnie, but that isn't surprising. She still owes me and Sebastian for losing the tennis match. She might assume she could bat her eyelashes at Sebastian, but she knows I'm immune.

Anger swells hotly in my chest. Security should have never let those two through. I made sure to keep my family *off* the guest list, and they shouldn't have even received invitations.

Bianca glides over. "Excuse us, Sebastian." Without waiting for a response, she pulls me aside. "Oh my God. What are they doing here?"

"I don't know, but I'm having them thrown out," I say under my breath, and reach for my phone to get in touch with security.

"Wait," she says, placing a hand on my wrist.

"What?"

"If you do that, everyone's going to notice. They didn't crash the party to be dragged away meekly. They're going to make a scene, and it could make you look bad."

Damn it. It isn't just me who's going to look bad. It could make Sebastian look like a jerk for evicting his wife's father and half-brother from the party. I don't want anything to mar the first event we're hosting as a couple.

"Argh. So frustrating!"

"It's just one time," Bianca whispers. "And there's no way they're here for you. They're probably here to 'network' or something, so just ignore them."

I exhale, counting to five. It doesn't do much to calm my temper, but I need to do what's best, given the circumstances. "You're right."

"I'll try to keep them away from you."

"Thanks."

She squeezes my hand in support, and I nod. Roderick and Karl are coming straight for me and Sebastian. They're going to insist on an introduction.

Instead of looking at them, Sebastian picks up two flutes of champagne and hands me one. I take it, almost out of reflex, and manage a smile. I don't really want champagne right now, but it may be useful when Roderick and Karl annoy me too much. I can accidentally slip, and—*oops*—spill it all over their fancy tuxedos. I'll have to apologize profusely, but it'll be worth it.

"Lucie, my girl!" Roderick spreads his arms open, ready to hug me.

I'd rather be covered with centipedes. I step out of reach and stand closer to Sebastian. "Hello, Roderick."

The overt gesture of aversion doesn't deter Roderick. On the other hand, if he were the type to care about things like that, he wouldn't have been able to marry Mom. Grandfather never hid how little regard he had for Roderick. If Mom hadn't been his only child, Grandfather might've disowned her.

"I can't believe you're married," Roderick gushes.

"Guess it's time to get your believer fixed. Because I did."

Roderick's mask freezes for a second. The tips of his lips quiver as he maintains his smile.

God, it feels so good. I laugh like I just made a joke.

Roderick joins in, although his eyes are feverish with calculation. He's dying to know the exact nature of my marriage. He can't believe I managed to find my own mate.

"This is my husband, Sebastian Lasker."

Sebastian nods. "How do you do."

"Nice to meet you, son." Roderick manages to widen his smile, while Karl purses his lips like he has a lot to say about the situation and is trying to sort his thoughts.

"I'm not your son." Sebastian's tone is cold enough to frost the flute he's holding.

"Well, in a manner of speaking, of course." Roderick lets out an affable laugh. "You became like a son to me when you married my daughter."

If he thinks he's going to be able to squeeze anything out of Sebastian, he has another think coming.

Roderick turns to me, probably to give himself some time to regroup. "We've been trying to see you—"

Karl scowls. "I don't know why my employee badge quit working—"

Roderick elbows him. "—but you've been difficult to get a hold of." His smile reminds me of a sewer rat.

"I've been busy," I answer him in my best dutiful-daughter tone.

Karl's complexion grows blotchier. Why is he so upset about the employee badge not working? Didn't he realize that revoking headquarters access is one of the first things Peery Diamonds would do when I fired him? Or is he honestly so arrogantly stupid that he thought he'd still have unfettered access to everything?

"It's such a bitchy thing to do to block me like that. I know you're greedy, but this is low, even for you." Roderick takes his arm, but it doesn't have much effect.

I stiffen my spine. Karl has always treated me like dirt, but he tries to be subtle about it in front of other people. It's embarrassing that he's being obnoxious in front of Sebastian. I start to open my mouth to put Karl in his place, but stop when Sebastian wraps an arm around my shoulders.

"Talk to my wife like that again, and I'll make sure you never talk at all."

I cock my head to look up at him. If he feels my gaze, he doesn't show it. His cold eyes are on Karl.

My half-brother's lips twist. "What did you say?"

"Deaf as well as stupid, I see," Sebastian says.

"Did you just threaten me? You're gonna what?" Karl sticks his chest out like an angry rooster and spreads his hands. "Kill me or something?"

What's up with him? He's acting like a kid with something to prove. He generally controls himself better, and takes pains to project the indolent playboy in public.

"Killing isn't the only way to ensure somebody won't talk." Sebastian sounds almost bored.

Karl's knuckles turn white, but he hesitates. Sebastian's half a head taller, and broader too. And you'd have to be blind to miss the fact that underneath the fancy tuxedo is a ruthless strength. Even without the wealth and power of the Sebastian Jewelry fortune, Sebastian could easily take Karl.

Still, I wonder if Karl's going to throw a punch, because he looks that furious. My mouth dries at the thought of violence between the two of them.

"Hey, bro," comes a light voice.

Sebastian keeps his eyes on Karl. "Noah."

Recalling Bianca's cheat sheet, I shift my focus to Sebastian's brother. Noah's a photographer, an aspiring novelist who's working on his first book and a social media addict. Still, he's a billionaire from numerous wise investments, so he can't be as vapid as his resumé makes him sound. If he were really that silly, he would've squandered his money by now.

Disapproval flashes in his eyes as he glances at Karl and Roderick, although it disappears fast, replaced by a mild curiosity and amusement.

"Are we having an Instagrammable family moment?" Noah says, lifting his phone like he's about to snap a photo.

Roderick flinches, while Karl looks like a cat that just had a bucket of water dumped on him. He doesn't like to be on social media unless he's in charge of the content.

Sebastian just smiles, although there's no humor in his eyes. "It's possible."

"Stay out of this," Karl snarls, sizing Noah up. He doesn't like what he sees. Noah's also tall and broad, albeit trimmer than Sebastian. But that still makes Noah the kind of guy you don't want to pick a fight with. "This is a family thing."

"Then I should stay." Noah smiles. "By the way, Lucie, I just wanted to tell you you're gorgeous, and my brother was lucky to marry you. I still haven't forgiven *him* for not inviting me to the wedding"—Sebastian sighs—"but *you're* all good. I could never get upset with my sister-in-law." His eyes sparkle with good humor.

"Thank you." I'm grateful he's here, because Karl's backing down, at least for the moment. He's still burning with unresolved anger at Sebastian for standing between me and him.

I make a mental note to instruct security at our headquarters to blacklist him and Vonnie not only in our offices but from all our retail locations. I don't trust him to behave. He'll escalate, whether he does it himself or through Vonnie. Roderick will stay out of it, since he considers himself above his "children's conflicts."

"I can't believe you only have one photographer for this event," Noah says to Sebastian.

"I didn't think it was that important." I'd prefer to have *no* photographer. Every time somebody points a camera at me, my chest clenches with dread. If it wasn't for the publicity angle for the Sebastian Peery collaboration, I wouldn't have bothered. But our marketing team thought it'd be great to release some of the photos from the event to the Korean media to publicize our marriage—and talk up the wedding jewelry we're going to be launching in the country.

"We only had a couple of lousy shots from Joey for the main ceremony, so we should have a few good ones from today," Noah says. "I'm a wildlife photographer, but don't worry. I'm pretty decent with people, too." He grins.

"You didn't bring your camera," Sebastian says dryly.

"But I have my phone." Holding it in front of him, Noah crouches down. "Say cheese."

I step closer to Sebastian and smile. He pulls me close and presses his lips to my temple, surprising me. But I remember to keep on smiling because that's one thing I'm good at.

"See? Wasn't that hard." He flips the screen and shows me the picture he just took. Sebastian's the definition of an adoring husband, and I'm the happy new wife who's just a tad shy about the public display of affection. We look like a regular, normal couple who fell in love and got married.

Relief sweeps through me.

"Hey, there's Huxley. And Nicholas and Griffin," Noah says suddenly, pointing at a trio of men coming toward us. "Is Griff shielding his wife? My God, we're at a party, not a war zone."

Sure enough, one of the men has a woman mostly hidden from view. Wonder why he's doing that? Did Noah or Sebastian warn them about a possible scene?

I flick my eyes in Karl's direction. Roderick is whispering something to him, one hand on his shoulder. Karl is listening, but his blazing eyes say, *Fuck you, this isn't over,* before he casually walks to the buffet table.

I hope that whatever they put in their mouths is contaminated and they get epic cases of diarrhea that force them to leave early. But of course I won't be that lucky.

Soon Emmett and Grant arrive with their wives. I'm glad I already looked everyone up, because I would've been overwhelmed otherwise. They're all tall and large, and it isn't every day I'm surrounded by men who make me feel...almost dainty and girlish. On top of that, their presence is formidable. They know they're intelligent, wealthy and powerful, and they wield their influence like spears.

Although those spears aren't pointed at me, they aren't exactly pointed away, either. Unlike Noah's, their greetings are restrained. They treat me with a neutral politeness reserved for strangers they don't plan to associate with in the future. Grant and Griffin seem a bit surprised when Sebastian keeps his arm around me. I can't decide if their attitude is due to my awful reputation or their knowing the story behind our marriage. He never told me he shared the true situation, but that doesn't mean he hasn't. Also, they seem close, so they probably suspect something's off even if Sebastian's kept quiet.

At least the wives aren't aloof. Amy is a pretty blonde with even features. She smiles easily, but her sharp eyes miss nothing. She gives me a hug. "Welcome to the family."

The redhead who came in with Grant wraps her arms around me and hugs me hard. "Yes. Welcome to the family. I'm Aspen."

Sierra is next. "I'm so glad we have another woman for our girl time." Mischief sparks in her voice. "Please tell me you like romance novels!"

"You haven't even read the ones we bought last time," Amy says.

"Doesn't mean we shouldn't buy more," Sierra says.

"You can never have enough romance novels on your shelves," Aspen says. "Don't you agree, Lucie?"

I look for signs of judgment. But the women just smile like they've never seen a headline about me. Just like Yuna, they're open to getting to know me and forming their own opinions. My insides stop twisting into knots and relax. I haven't been lucky with making new friends or creating the best first impressions, and I'm grateful I'm getting an opportunity with these ladies.

"Absolutely," I say. "And I'll be honored to be part of girl time *and* buy all the romance novels we need for it. And Sierra, I *love* your company's products." She's the CEO of Silicone Dream, a popular sex toy company.

She smiles. "Thank you! Clearly you have excellent taste and a fun personality." Everyone laughs, and the ice is broken.

More and more guests arrive to congratulate us on our marriage. Sebastian's family on the Comtois side is late. Still, the party is in full swing and everyone's having a great time. Roderick and Karl seem to have disappeared. Maybe they left, since they aren't going to get what they came here for—to get me to cough up money—without making a scene.

And for once there isn't going to be anything embarrassing happening or leaking to the press. Although Roderick and Karl were able to sneak past security, I haven't spotted a single paparazzo. The guests aren't just friends, but business associates. They wouldn't upload anything on social media that could damage their relationship with me or Sebastian.

I should be relieved. Grateful, even. But my head throbs from hours of tension squeezing my skull, and my cheeks feel like rubber from smiling for so long.

I put a hand on Sebastian's sleeve. "I'm going to grab some Tylenol from the pantry. Want anything?"

He cradles my cheek in his warm palm, the gesture protective and husbandly. "Are you all right?"

"Just a headache, nothing serious. I'll be back soon."

"Okay." He kisses my cheek.

I sense some women around us sigh with envy. I maintain a smile full of warm hospitality as I make my way to the pantry.

Bianca trots over. "Hey, everything's going fabulously." She grins. "I'm so relieved."

"Me too."

"I can't believe the number of people who came. By the way, do you know if the Comtoises plan to be here? I haven't seen them anywhere, and I thought they RSVP'd yes. I'm going to have to check the list."

"I haven't seen them," I tell her. "Sebastian should've invited them." He's taking care of his side of the family and friends.

"The party's already halfway over. Maybe they aren't coming." She purses her lips. "They could've at least *called*."

Or maybe they couldn't bring themselves to congratulate us when they believe I don't deserve Sebastian. Marie hinted rather strongly that I should just let Preston's indiscretion go and proceed with the wedding. She didn't hide her displeasure when I refused.

Pearls and swine. Just recalling the Comtoises' contempt intensifies my headache, until I feel like somebody is sticking a chisel into the top of my skull.

"Let me go check with catering. I heard some grumbling about the champagne," Bianca says.

"Thanks." I give her a smile, hoping she doesn't notice there's anything wrong. She'll fret.

A coolly smooth voice says, "Such a *fabu*lous party."

My mouth goes dry as I turn and see Gabriella Ricci. *How did she get in?* She wasn't invited.

The woman is even more gorgeous in person. She stands, hipshot and haughty, chin raised high and an arrogant smile on her full lips. She knows she's beautiful and loves to flaunt it.

Now my head pounds harder. But long-ingrained manners dictate I say something polite in response. "Thank you," I manage, my temples pulsing.

"I know you want to make sure everyone knows you won Sebastian from me, but this is pretty low, even for you."

"Well, if you didn't crash the party..." My tone is sharper than I'd prefer. But right now I don't have a lot of patience, especially when she's being unfair. I haven't done anything to counter what she said in the video.

"'Crash.'" She laughs. "As if."

"Isn't that what you call it?"

Her face twists. "You invited me."

"What?"

"Look, I know you're jealous, but just leave me out of your marriage, okay? I have lucrative deals with Sebastian Jewelry and his brother's ad agency. I don't want to ruin those because of your insecurities." Her red lips curve slowly into a cynical smile. "Just enjoy what you have while you can. Sebastian's great in bed."

Am I supposed to respond to this? I don't know why or how she's here, or what she's hoping to achieve. My head hurts too much to come up with a suitable response, much less decide how I should feel about this. My stomach churns. Is this nausea from seeing her—or the image of Sebastian and her rolling around in bed together?

I turn away and proceed to go to the kitchen pantry. In my experience, it's best not to engage.

Fortunately, no one else stops me. I exit the ballroom and let the door shut behind me. The noise dies down abruptly, plunging me into blessed silence.

I sigh softly, letting my shoulders droop a little as I roll my neck. The encounters with Karl, Roderick and Gabriella should be as bad as this party's going to get. But I can't shake off a feeling that it's going to get worse. I've never been to an event where everything went perfectly. Is this some instinctive dread over the fact that Sebastian's family hates me enough that they won't bother to even feign they're happy about the marriage?

I walk past the arched doorway into the pantry. A bottle of Tylenol is on one shelf. I toss a couple of pills into my mouth, then pull out a bottle from a case of water and wash them down. The water's lukewarm, but it's nice after being inside the chilly ballroom.

"There you are." Karl's gravelly voice comes from behind me.

Tension returns in full. The muscles at the base of my neck bunch, and my shoulders rise until they almost hit my ears. I turn around and stare at him. "What are you doing here?" I demand. "This area's off-limits."

"What? I can't visit my sister's home?"

"Half-sister. And you aren't visiting. You're trespassing."

"Oh, come on. Don't be such a bitch. Jeez, no wonder nobody likes you."

"Get out of the way!" Irritation drips into me like poison. This pantry has only one entry point, and Karl's blocking it.

"Make me."

The taunt is juvenile, but the expression on his face is serious. The amused air of entitlement is gone. In its place is an anger that's been simmering for a while, edged with desperation.

Dread wraps its little tendrils around my pounding heart. But I do my best to hide my fear. He's a bully who loves to bluster and intimidate, but he can't do anything to me. I won. And this is my home.

"Ah, but you can't," he says, smirking. "You're nothing without your husband and your money. You little whore. Why'd you have to cut me off and sic your fucking lawyers on me? Wilhelm made me an executive at Peery for good reason, but you pulled me away and now you're trying to fucking ruin me!"

"You couldn't bother to come to work, so of course I fired you and asked my lawyers to get back all the money we paid you!"

"Shut your fucking mouth! I need my fair share."

"What 'fair share'?"

"Half a million." He shakes his head. "Actually, twenty."

The nerve! "Are you asking *me* for money?"

"I'm not *asking* for anything! I'm taking what's rightfully mine! I'm Wilhelm's grandson, too! Why should I be left with nothing?"

"What have you done to be a good grandson to him? Drinking? Gambling? Womanizing? Should he have been grateful you managed to not spawn any babies?" Then I stop as another possibility occurs. "You owe the casino."

His face is so red, it's almost purple. "It wouldn't have happened if you weren't such a greedy cunt!"

I'm sick of this—and him. "Get a job and pay it off!"

He steps forward. "*You fucking bitch!*"

Pain explodes in my face. Stars burst in my dimming vision. A metallic taste floods my mouth, and I lose my balance and hit the shelves hard enough to make things behind me rattle.

"I'm gonna teach you a lesson."

25

SEBASTIAN

THE PARTY BECOMES lackluster without Luce pressed against my side. It isn't exactly my idea of good time to smile and nod while people congratulate me on a forced marriage.

Roderick comes over. "Have you seen Lucie? I can't seem to find her."

"She stepped out for a moment. Do you want me to tell her you need to see her when she's back?"

"No, no." He smiles. "That won't be necessary. I wanted to talk to you, actually."

I cock an eyebrow. He and I don't travel in the same circles. I met him once at his wife's funeral. Luce made an impression. He didn't. If somebody had asked me about him afterward, I wouldn't have had a single thing to say.

"I'm sorry about Karl being a little obnoxious earlier. He thought she was making a mistake." He gestures at the wedding band on my hand.

"Are you saying her marrying me is a mistake?" Does he know the truth behind our marriage?

"No, but I don't think you meant to marry her." His tone says he's on my side.

I don't trust people being on my side without a good reason. "I don't make commitments without knowing what I'm doing."

"Of course, of course. But she's only doing this because she's upset over the lack of control she has at Peery Diamonds. She thinks being married is going to change people's perception of her, but that isn't right. I don't know why she specifically dragged *you* into this, though. She could've picked anybody."

"What's the point of this conversation?" I ask, out of patience.

"I'm just saying I could help you be free of her."

"She's my wife."

"Yes, but you might not want her by your side for long."

I don't like his smile. "Why are you working against your daughter?" Does he only like Karl because he's a boy? Luce's grandfather was a sexist, and Roderick could be just as bad.

"I hate seeing her get worked up about the company and marrying a man who isn't right for her." The sneaky glitter in his eyes says he's going to keep poking until he gets the desired response.

Who the hell does he think he is to judge my marriage to Luce?

He flashes me a friendly smile. "Not that I don't think you're a good man, of course. But that doesn't mean you and she are suited for each other. Anyway, she's too young and better off letting others manage the company while she collects her dividends. She can still be fabulously wealthy and comfortable."

As obsequiously sly as Roderick is, I have to give him credit for being persuasive. If I hadn't seen Luce working hard, I might've bought into his view. Hell, even I thought she was just playing around at first. But he's her father. He should know better and not belittle his youngest to a man he just met. "She seems competent. And often what moves us isn't money, but a passion for what we do."

"Everyone wants money," Roderick says, spreading his hands.

"Not when you have the kind of money we do."

"Are you telling me you aren't doing what you're doing to make money?"

"Money is the icing on the cake. I do what I do for the sense of accomplishment and because I love Sebastian Jewelry and its people. I suspect Luce runs Peery Diamonds for the same reason."

"I see. Well, I'm happy she found a husband who understands her so well." He's smiling and saying all the right things. But my bullshit radar says, *Don't trust a word out of his mouth.*

"I'm glad you approve." *Not that I need your approval.*

I dismiss him with a nod. He gets the hint and goes to chat with somebody else. He reminds me too much of the Comtoises' disappointing behavior and attitude in the last few weeks, which is why I didn't invite any of them to the reception. Also, I really dislike the way he chalks up everything Luce does to greed and ego. What the hell kind of a father is he? No wonder she was unhappy when he showed up.

Still... His devotion to his late wife is well known. Maybe he's just bad at expressing himself. I'm going to give him the benefit of the doubt for the moment.

Speaking of which... Is Luce okay?

She hasn't been gone that long, but it shouldn't take ten minutes to grab some Tylenol. The pantry isn't that far away.

I remember the pallor beneath her makeup. She's been anxious and stressed about the party for some reason. She behaved like she expected something to go wrong, which I don't understand. A good event can be pulled off if you have at least two out of the big three—money, time and expertise.

We spared no expense, and money can buy expertise.

Maybe she's feeling worse than I thought. I start toward the pantry to check up on her and walk past my brothers, who are talking animatedly.

Noah grabs my elbow. "Come and tell Nicholas my plan is genius!"

Griffin groans. "Oh my God, you're going to get him killed."

"What plan?" I ask. Noah's grip is firm enough to signal he isn't letting go until he gets my take on it.

"I told Nicholas to hire an escort to seduce the boyfriend of the girl he likes."

"Terrible idea," I say.

"Don't be so judgmental!" Noah protests, at the same time the rest of my brothers say, "*Seeeeeeee?*"

"If she finds out, she'll murder Nicholas," I say.

"That's what I said," Griffin says.

"But if the boyfriend's the one for her, he won't have sex with the escort. It's just a test to see if he's worthy!" Noah explains.

Nicholas shakes his head. "That's low."

Noah opens his mouth.

Nicholas raises a hand. "Nope, nope, nope. It's six to one. And you're going to shut up about this, just like you promised."

Amy walks up with a glass of white wine, wraps an arm around Emmett and smiles at me. "Did I tell you how much I'm enjoying myself? Adult time is so nice." She's a new mom. Although she loves Monique, she probably wants to be around people who don't require cooing as a part of communication.

"I bet. Anyway, let me go," I say to Noah. "I need to see if Luce is okay."

"I'm sure she's fine," Amy says. "Her brother was just going to check up on her. He seems a little tense, but—"

Shit. I rush to the pantry. He called her a bitch right in front of me. If he treats her like that in front of her husband, what kind of abuse is he capable of when she's alone?

My heart races. I need to see with my own eyes that she's okay.

My brothers' rapid footsteps follow. They know from my reaction that something is wrong and are ready to provide backup if needed.

Raised voices. I round the corner and spot Karl standing in the doorway, trapping Luce inside the pantry.

"You fucking bitch!" he shouts.

He backhands her, his knuckles striking her face. She staggers backward, crashes against the shelves and falls down. Blood trickles from her nose, dripping down her mouth and chin, falling on her pristine white dress.

A scarlet bomb seems to go off in my head.

"I'm gonna teach you a lesson!" He raises his hand again.

I take a quick step up behind him and grab the wrist, twisting it painfully backward and kicking him in the side at the same time. He stumbles and goes down, rolling a couple of times to get away from me. He tries to regain his footing, but I get between him and Luce and literally punt his ass, propelling him three or four feet forward. He drops to his hands and knees.

"What the hell," he gasps.

I circle and kick him in the side again. He wheezes, going down on his back in a feeble attempt to escape. I do it again, and he grabs his side and folds up. A rib or two must've cracked. Maybe even broken. I stomp the hand holding the ribcage, then again until I can feel the bones going. His scream pisses me off. Luce was so traumatized, she couldn't even whimper.

Fucking asshole. I'm going to murder him.

I smash a heel into his crotch, and his screams go up an octave. My brothers inhale sharply, but they don't try to intervene.

I kick Karl's kidneys a couple of times, then stomp on him until he's a bloody mess. Nicholas comes over and puts a hand on my shoulder. "You don't want to kill him. He isn't worth going to jail for."

"Mom can get him off," Huxley says casually.

"Hux. Not helping," Nicholas says.

"Nicholas is right," Grant says. "That piece of shit's taken enough of your time. Your wife needs you right now."

My wife. I turn around. "Where is she?"

"Amy took her upstairs," Emmett says. "She probably doesn't need to see this."

"No, she doesn't," I manage, purposely slowing my breathing to settle my temper. I don't want to look like a raging lunatic when I face my wife, when she must be traumatized. But *fuck.* It's impossible to calm down. I exhale hard.

I flick Karl a look full of contempt. But some of the contempt is directed at myself. I should've checked up on her sooner, instead of letting Roderick take up my time with his bullshit. Did he keep me occupied on purpose? If so, I'll put him in the hospital. "Stay away from my wife, if you value your life."

Karl moans, struggling to get to his knees. "What the...? She's my sister!" He tries to shout, but it comes out as a half whine, half wheeze.

"*She's my wife.* Nobody touches what's mine."

"Fuckin' sue yer ass," he slurs.

For fuck's sake. The negative publicity is going to stress Luce out. Maybe I should keep kicking him.

"Good luck finding a witness," Huxley says, scratching his ear.

"You saw," Karl says.

"I was checking the news." Noah waves his phone.

"Saw what?" Grant says, looking around.

"I saw somebody trying to exterminate a pest. Not exactly a crime," Emmett says.

Nicholas sighs, like the unthinkable has happened. "It's too bad the cockroach lived. But then, they can live through nuclear explosions."

"When people fall in a kitchen, they often suffer catastrophic damage," Griffin says. "There are studies."

I smile at my brothers' unified front against Karl. I should've known better than to worry about publicity.

"You can't—do this to me!" he wheezes.

"We just did." Finally having my temper under control, I start toward Luce's bedroom, then stop and turn back. "Listen, you piece of shit. I don't care what happened in the past. Actually, that's not true. I *do* care—a lot—about what you did to Luce."

Karl tries to look defiant, but it's hard to do when you're lying bloodied on the floor.

I exhale harshly. "Next time you see my wife, you won't even meet her eye. You're going to keep your head down and you're going to apologize."

"Wh-why?"

"Because if you don't, you're going to spend the rest of your life being fed through a straw."

26

LUCIENNE

I'M in a daze as Amy leads me away from the kitchen. I'm larger and taller, and my legs are shaky, but she supports me just fine while making soothing noises. I'm not sure why she's being so nice. This is going above and beyond, isn't it?

Maybe it's a good thing Bianca didn't witness the attack. She would've tried to fight Karl, and it wouldn't have been pretty. She's my best friend, so there shouldn't be any secrets between us. But I wish I could hide what my family is like from everyone, forever.

What are Sebastian's brothers going to think? And Amy... Does she pity me? Is this incident going to leak? Get twisted somehow and bring on negative publicity we don't need?

Some asshole tabloid writer might even claim I tried to attack Karl first and he was only trying to defend himself. That's happened before. Somebody's leash broke and her dog came at me. I had to jump back and try to get the dog to go away—because it was baring its teeth and acting weird—but the media twisted that into my kicking the animal.

But I never touched that dog. And the owner never tried to set the record straight.

Amy takes me upstairs and gives me a questioning look. I point to the left, and she takes me to my bedroom.

The blood has stopped dripping from my nose, but it's crusted over my mouth and chin. There are spots of rust on my dress, which is ruined. I think vaguely that the stain's unlikely to come out and that Karl won't care. Then I wonder what's wrong with me that I'm worried about a dress.

But that seems preferable to thinking about the state I'm in. My cheek throbs horribly, and my lips sting. He probably broke the skin. Did I get blood on my necklace, too? That, at least, will come out. It isn't that difficult to clean jewelry.

Amy leads me to the bench at the foot of the bed and has me sit down. I move like a robot.

"Let's get the blood off your face," she says. "And get you some ice, too."

I look at her. What's going through her head right now?

She goes to the en suite bathroom and returns with a warm, damp washcloth. The door to my room opens, and immediately there is a charge in the air.

I don't have to check to know. *Sebastian.*

I look down at my lap, keeping my eyes focused on a tiny red spot near my right knee. I can hear Amy move and murmur some words to him. My mind tries to fill in the blanks.

Are they wondering if I'm okay? Are they pitying me right now? Do they think my family's out of control? Or are they curious about what I must've done to provoke Karl?

Do you think she deserved it? I imagine Amy's question and squeeze my eyes shut for a moment. I'm being unfair—she's been nothing but kind. But my past has proven that the truth isn't important. The only thing that matters is what people *presume* is the truth. And Karl has a far better public image than I do.

Amy leaves, shutting the door behind her. Sebastian crouches in front of me. "Look at me," he says, his voice steady. "Let me see your face."

I glance at his hands. Amy led me away after he kicked Karl a couple of times. His hands are pristine. So maybe the fight ended soon after we left. I hope so, anyway.

"Lucienne. Show me your face." Sebastian's order is gentle but firm.

I tilt my chin up, although I don't meet his eyes. I didn't do anything wrong, and I'm the one who was abused, but an inexplicable shame blankets me like a sheet of frost. I shiver, rounding my shoulders. My face throbs, but somehow the pain feels deserved. I probably should've realized Karl wasn't going to leave without making a scene. Or I should've realized he wouldn't give up his gravy train without escalating the situation. I keep wondering what people are going to say about the altercation. Did Sebastian call the police?

He uses the washcloth Amy prepared and cleans the blood off my face. His touch is careful and tender, like he's cleaning a treasure that might shatter. I steal a glance and see an impassive mask on his face. I wish I could read his mind. *Does he regret marrying me?* But of course he regrets it. I forced him.

"You shouldn't have hit him," I say finally.

"A man's entitled to protect what's his."

The starkly possessive way he says "his" makes my heart race, but I know better than to give it any weight. I'm still reeling, and I can't think straight. "He'll sue."

"Let him try."

"He needs money to pay off gambling debts."

"Good. But he's not getting it from me. I'll have my attorneys drag him through every court in the state until he has nothing left to his name."

I give up. He isn't listening, and will do whatever he wants in any case.

"You don't have to worry about Karl anymore," Sebastian says. "He'll never touch you again." When the washcloth brushes against my mouth, I inhale sharply. Dark fury erupts in his eyes. "I should've broken every bone in his body."

Tears spring to my eyes so fast, I don't get a chance to blink them away. They fall down my cheeks. Suddenly I feel as vulnerable as a snail with a broken shell. I look away quickly, hoping he doesn't notice as a dull ache starts in my chest.

I don't know why I'm crying. Sebastian isn't being mean. As a matter of fact, he's being entirely too kind. I'm used to people being cruel, and I never shed a single tear when they fling nasty comments or judgmental glances in my direction.

"I'm not upset with you, Luce," he says softly.

"I know," I whisper, my breath hitching.

He reaches out as though to cup my face, then drops his hand. "Look at me."

I stubbornly keep my gaze on the foundation brush I left on the vanity after getting ready for the party.

"Luce."

"You should probably go back downstairs." I can't return to the party looking like this, but our guests expect us to be there until the end.

"Don't worry about it. My brothers are handling it."

"We can't both be absent," I insist.

In my peripheral vision, I can see his jaw tighten. "Who cares about the damn party? It's not important. You are."

I finally turn to look at him. His face is twisted with pain and recrimination.

"I'm sorry," I whisper, unhappy I ruined our first event together as a couple.

"No." He lightly dabs the tears with the cloth. "Never say you're sorry for what happened."

I blink, and more tears stream down my face. "Why aren't you upset with me?"

He looks at me like I just slapped him. "Upset with *you*?"

"I ruined the party. I should've known Karl would crash it, and I should've done a better job to make sure he couldn't. And if I couldn't do that, I should've had security drag him away as soon as I realized he was there."

His mouth parts, and he just stares at me like I unloaded all that in a foreign language. "You did nothing wrong."

"But—"

"Listen to me. You didn't do anything wrong, Luce. Karl's the bad guy, not you."

"But I could've done *something*—"

"No. You didn't have to do anything. If he were a decent human being, he wouldn't have crashed the party. If he were a decent human being, he wouldn't have cornered you in the pantry. If he were a decent human being, he certainly wouldn't have hit you. It was never about *you*. It's all about him and what a subhuman piece of garbage he is."

Sebastian's saying all this like he means it. His defense of me is absolute, I realize. And he's being so kind and understanding, like he was all those years ago. The ache in my chest swells, and I can't breathe. I put a hand over my breastbone, feeling my heart pulsing erratically.

I clench my teeth as the air in my lungs shudders. Something crumbles in my heart. Tears fall endlessly, and I can't stop them.

Sebastian pulls me to him until I'm in his lap. His arms wrap around me protectively, shielding me from the world.

I cry until I'm out of tears. Even then, he doesn't let go.

27

SEBASTIAN

WHEN LUCE'S tears finally dry, I reach over and pluck some additional Kleenex for her. She blows her nose carefully, and seeing that makes me want to both hold her tighter and break Karl's nose.

She gives me a wan smile. "Thanks."

Her face is blotchy, her nose red. Her previously impeccable makeup is smeared with tears, the mascara smudged around her bloodshot eyes. The butterfly pins I gave her hang limply in her messed-up hair. The sight of them makes my blood boil again. Death is too good for Karl. She was nervous, but somewhat optimistic about the party. She relaxed some more after meeting my sisters-in-law. She should've shone at the event, enjoyed herself.

Instead, she can't even go back to it. I don't know if she can go to work on Monday. It looks like her cheek's going to bruise. Her lip is busted, and I don't know how long that will take to heal.

If it were me, I could claim Griffin hit me too hard by mistake when we were sparring. But Luce doesn't have such a convenient excuse. People are going to stare and wonder, and she'll hate that. Although she acts like whispers don't bother her, the slight tensing of her jaw and shoulders says otherwise.

"Guess the party's over," she says quietly.

"We'll throw another one." I keep my tone light.

"Yeah."

"And I'll make sure Karl never attends it." I still don't know how the asshole crashed the party, but I'm going to find out. And fire the security team hired for the event. Actually, that isn't enough. I'm going to sue them into oblivion.

"Thanks." She gives me another smile, a better one this time. "Can you help me get up? I want to change, but my legs are asleep."

I adjust my hold on her and help her stand. She teeters slightly. I crouch down, untie the stiletto straps around her ankles and pull the heels off her feet. "Better?"

"Much. Thank you."

I find myself hovering. Maybe I should give her some space, but everything inside me rebels at the idea of leaving her alone when she's vulnerable. She's safe in our home—or should be—but damn it, I thought she was safe earlier too.

She grabs a nightshirt out of the closet and goes into the bathroom. I park myself on the bench and watch the door, fantasizing about inventive ways I can destroy Karl.

Something clatters inside, followed by a sharp inhale.

"Are you okay?" I move toward the door. She might've tripped. *Shit. I should've been—*

"I'm fine!" She doesn't sound like she's in pain. "I'm just...a mess."

Guess she saw her reflection. I want to soothe her, but I'm not sure if more tenderness is what she needs right now, especially after all that crying.

"You should see the other guy," I say, overly casual.

There's a beat of silence, then a small giggle. "What happened to Karl?"

"He, uh, fell down some stairs. And then ran into a couple of doorknobs."

"Gosh, that's too bad."

"Hey, shit happens when you don't exercise good judgment."

She makes a little *go on* noise, but she doesn't need to know the details. Hell, I probably don't remember everything myself. I was too furious to care about anything except kicking his ass.

She comes out of the bathroom, still fully dressed. Her hair's down completely, the pins gone. "Um. I need your help. I can't reach the top of my zipper. My back's a little too sore." Then she turns around, pulling her hair to one side.

The top half of her outfit is made of sheer white material. As I tug at the zipper and pull it down, the dress parts. What I see puts a red haze over my vision again.

Purplish bars mar her otherwise smooth and flawless skin. She must've really slammed into the shelves when Karl hit her.

The damage I've dealt him isn't even close to evening the scales. But they'll be even—and more—by the time I'm done with him.

She slips into the bathroom when the zipper's undone. I pace as rage roils through me.

My phone buzzes in my pocket, and I pull it out.

–Emmett: All good and taken care of.

–Grant: If anybody noticed you weren't around, they didn't say. They probably assumed you were doing newlywed things.

Good. Even if anybody wanted to probe, Grant would make sure they kept their curiosity to themselves. He's affable and friendly because he knows people want him to be a good guy, but he unleashes his inner asshole when necessary.

–Me: Thanks.

–Nicholas: How's Lucie holding up?

–Me: Better than expected, considering. But I still feel like I haven't done enough.

My brothers will know exactly what I mean.

–Griffin: I just want you to know that after you left, I kind of tripped over him.

–Huxley: I've never heard a man hit a note that high.

I smile at the text. Griffin is an excellent kickboxer.

–Noah: Take photos of her bruises. In case Mister Shoulda-been-worm-food tries to do something. Like sue, or get the police involved.

Noah's probably right, but I'm not going to ask Luce. She's been traumatized enough. So let Karl try. I wasn't kidding about destroying him if he doesn't stay away. Actually, I'm going to go ahead and do that anyway, since it's the least he deserves. He should have every bone in his body pulverized.

When I recall how Luce blamed herself, I wish I could grab that asshole now and throw him from the roof of a skyscraper. I don't think Karl actually hit her before. She wouldn't have been in shock for so long if it was a common occurrence. But that doesn't mean he treated her with dignity and respect, either.

I read somewhere that victims sometimes blame themselves because they want to believe the world is logical and they need to cling to the belief that bad situations can be avoided if they themselves do better. But I loathed the way she took that whole weight on to her shoulders. Her tears ripped at my heart.

It was all I could do to maintain control—she needs me to be her rock, not some raving maniac.

–Me: Thanks. That won't be necessary. I'll do it my way. She's my wife.

–Nicholas: I thought you're still upset about her forcing you to marry her? You want us to quit buying up the Peery Diamonds shares?

I scowl.

–Me: That's a separate issue.

–Nicholas: Got it.

Despite his response, I wonder if he really does get it. He isn't the most relationship-savvy guy. Otherwise, he wouldn't be pining over some girl to the point that he's getting advice from *Noah* on what to do.

–Emmett: Need help avenging your wife?

–Huxley: I can come up with something creative.

–Me: Thanks, but I've got this one. Believe me.

–Noah: FYI, he gambles a lot. And loses. He owes a ton of money to one of the casinos he frequents, and unless I'm mistaken, the place is connected to the mob. If he doesn't cough up the cash, it won't end well for him.

That's a lot of information he's gathered about Karl.

–Emmett: How do you know so much already?

–Noah: Research. God created social media for a reason.

–Griffin: God most definitely did NOT create social media.

–Noah: You could win the Nobel Prize if you spent more time on social media for research, Griff. Anyway, what I'm saying is that even if you do nothing, he might disappear all on his own.

–Me: They collect their debts, and I'll collect mine.

Luce comes out of the bathroom. She's in a night T-shirt that ends a few inches above her knees. Her hair's a little damp, but the makeup's gone, and she doesn't look as blotchy as before, although her eyes are still bloodshot.

I put my phone away. Is she the type to lick her wounds alone? I don't want to leave her side. "Do you need anything?"

She hesitates. Then she finally nods, wrapping her hand over her other elbow awkwardly. "Can you just hold me tonight?"

"Of course," I say, the tension easing. "Let me change. I'll be right back."

THE NEXT MORNING, I open my eyes then blink a little. The bedroom smells like flowers and lavender...like Luce. I turn my head and watch her sleep. She must have been exhausted. She hasn't stirred even once.

Probably needs the sleep to recover from the trauma. Fucking Karl.

I stay in bed for a while, listening to her breathing. It's even and slow, and she clings to me like she knows she'll be safe. The fact that she trusts me to protect her sends an indescribable sense of tenderness through me.

When my stomach starts to growl, I get up carefully and pad down to the kitchen. Matthias is off, so it's just me and Luce for the day. I start some coffee and head to the pantry to grab English muffins. The area has been cleaned and tidied up. Most likely Nicholas's doing. My brothers are great, but they aren't the neatest, except for him. And Amy definitely wouldn't have done it—cleaning isn't her thing.

I toast the muffins, pull out some jam and butter and check my phone for messages. There are multiple texts from my brothers.

–Noah: Did you see this?

He includes a link to some article by *The Hollywood News*. It's a notorious gossip site, most of it crap.

Love Gone Wrong? the headline reads.

I can feel my brow knitting as I scroll down. A photo of me and Luce last night. And...*Gabriella*? Why was she here? I didn't invite her, and Luce had no reason to either.

Crashing a party simply isn't Gabriella's style. She's too proud to go to an event where she isn't going to be adored and fêted.

Did some asshole at *The Hollywood News* Photoshop this? I look carefully, but it's impossible to tell. These days, you can fake anything, including videos.

The text that accompanies the pictures claims that after Luce stole me from Gabriella—the "reporter" doesn't believe what the latter said about there being no man stealing—I apparently realized that I didn't want to give up Gabriella and invited her to the party for a "rendezvous." According to a "source close to the couple," the reason Luce disappeared for the rest of the party is because she caught me and Gabriella together. The writer's certain we're going to have an ugly divorce, and Gabriella has to decide if she wants to take back the man who left her for another woman.

This is malicious, even for *The Hollywood News*. But what's disturbing is that nobody with any connection to media was at the party. The staff who catered and took care of security were all vetted and clean.

So. That leaves the guests.

Who would hate Luce enough to do this?

Karl.

Damn it. I should've broken his phone last night.

–Nicholas: So easy to be a "journalist" these days.

–Huxley: That's why we have defamation lawsuits.

–Noah: Careful. The Streisand effect and all.

–Huxley: You may not have to sue. Just mention Bollea v. Gawker, and they'll cave.

–Griffin: Isn't that the lawsuit that bankrupted Gawker?

–Huxley: Yup. Fuck around and find out. It isn't that expensive to bankroll a lawsuit like that.

It's tempting. Luce could see the article and stress. She was so anxious about the party. She doesn't need this.

The doorbell rings. I glance at the grandfather clock in the living room—9:48 a.m. *Who's visiting this early?* Did Luce hear the chime, too? It was pretty loud.

It rings again. Better not be some "journalists" wanting comments.

I check the security panel screen, then scowl when I see Mom's chauffeur by the gates.

What does she want?

I let the car through, then wait by the main door so they don't hit the bell again and disturb Luce.

Mom's Phantom pulls into the driveway. The chauffeur jumps out and opens her door. She climbs out, gorgeously attired in a sleeveless black-and-white dress that shows off the body she spends hours in the gym to maintain. Her ears glitter with four diamonds each, and clusters of sapphires and diamonds sparkle on her throat. Her hands are covered with thin black gloves that come all the way to her elbows.

What's gotten into her now? This is her *I'm here to complain about the injustice of the world* mode. The only "injustice" I can think of is the fact that she can't control her funds, and I've made some adjustments to how the Comtois family trusts distribute money. But that's what she gets for trying to backstab me.

Travis climbs out after her. He's in a neutral beige sports jacket, white button-down shirt and buck-hide-colored slacks. There's a medium-thick gold chain around his neck and a thick ring with the Comtois family insignia on his finger, like he's desperate to show the world he's one of us.

He's here to lend her his support. Not sure why he's bothering, since he's never been able to influence my decisions. Perhaps in his mind he's a father figure to me, which couldn't be further from the truth. Just because he married my mom doesn't make him my dad, and I only tolerate him because it would upset her if I didn't.

Still, he's trying. Somebody give him pompoms.

"Mother," I say impassively.

"Sebastian." She smiles and runs her gaze over my white T-shirt and gray sweatpants. "Don't you look at home?"

I don't bother to feign a smile. "I *am* at home."

"Aren't you going to invite us in?"

"If you promise to be quiet."

"You know your mother. She doesn't raise her voice," Travis says.

He's either deaf or a liar. Probably both. Mom tries to act calm and placid in public, but she has a temper that rivals an active volcano—loud, fiery and destructive.

"I didn't ask you, Travis," I say.

"Of course I'll be quiet. What kind of unmannered barbarian do you think I am?" Mom says stiffly.

Since she wouldn't have put on her battle gear just to leave meekly, I let her and Travis in. I pour myself some coffee, but don't offer them any.

"I'd like some tea," Mom calls out, taking the armchair in the living room. She crosses her leg, right over left. She's feeling justified about her issues and confident they'll be resolved to her satisfaction.

Travis sits to her right, the view of the garden behind him. He pats Mom's hand. *There, there. It's going to be okay, love. I'm here for you.*

I gag inwardly.

"We don't drink tea," I say as I sit with my back to the kitchen. I saw various types in the pantry.

Her expression cools. "Then coffee?"

"I didn't make enough for guests. No advance notice." Get the hint and tell me why you're here. Or better yet, leave.

"It's rude for you to have coffee without offering me any."

"Believe me, it's better than my talking to you *without* coffee."

That shuts her up. She knows I don't do well without my morning brew. "Fine," she says, taking a composing breath. "This is about you."

"Me." I let the word sit there and sip my coffee.

"I know you're upset, and I can see why you didn't invite any of us to your wedding. Although it was quite unfair, considering you invited Ted!"

"He *is* the father of the groom," I say dryly.

"You don't even like him."

"I don't, but he's not a formal enemy." I give her a meaningful look.

She blanches, then catches herself. But it's too late. Her unintended reaction seems to fuel her rage over the injustice she suffered at my hand. "You made us sign papers! You could've at least invited us to the party last night! It was so embarrassing."

Of course, this is about her all-important public image. "Don't worry. No one knew that none of you were invited. People probably assumed you couldn't come."

"Which makes us look ungracious!"

"Then tell them the truth. And keep your voice down, Mother. You sound like a banshee with an air horn." I don't want her waking Luce up over this stupid stuff.

"I do *not* sound like a banshee!" Mom hisses. "And what you suggested would also make us look ungracious!"

"What do you want me to do about it?" I drain the last bit of coffee from my mug. There isn't enough coffee in the world for this inanity. "I'm not going to decide the particular way that you should look ungracious."

"You never used to be like this, Sebastian." Her lower lip trembles. Her gaze is fixed on my reflection in the glass-top coffee table.

Travis reaches over and squeezes her hand. "She's been distraught for weeks." His tone is halfway between chiding and pleading, which only serves to irritate me. Mom and I don't need a sycophantic middleman to communicate.

I lean forward, pointedly excluding Travis, and say in a low voice, "You backstabbed me, and you expected nothing to change?"

"But you don't have to be so mean." She pouts. It used to work well, but that was before.

"And you didn't have to betray me. Now, if you're done wasting my time—"

"I'm not finished," Mom interjects quickly. "We need to talk about Preston."

"What did he do now?" I pause for a second. "Did he run to you and ask you to intervene on his behalf so he doesn't have to honor the wager?"

"What wager?" Her confusion seems genuine, but she's a pretty decent actress.

"He and his 'girlfriend' challenged Luce and me to a tennis match. The losers were supposed to get on their knees and say, 'We are not worthy,' ten times. While genuflecting."

Mom's jaw slackens. She knows how well I play.

Travis's expression remains blank. But then, he knows very little. His only saving grace is he has good instincts, and right now he's doing a fine job of blending into the background.

"He and his girlfriend didn't get a single point," I say.

She squeezes her eyes shut.

"And both ran like their pants were on fire after the match."

Her chest heaves as she blinks and tries to think of something to say. Finally, she flicks her hand dismissively. "It isn't about that."

"Then what is it about?" Preston always has issues.

"You can't cut him off."

"Why not?"

"He's your brother, Sebastian."

"*Half*-brother." I resent that we're related at all. Brothers are supposed to be fun, smart and cool—somebody you can count on. Like my Lasker half-brothers. Not somebody whose messes you have to clean up over and over again.

"He looks up to you," Mom says.

"Well, I am taller."

"You know what I mean."

"We can agree to disagree." Amicable, that's me.

"What you did hurt him." She's in *I'm going to say my piece no matter what* mode.

"Why? Did he have to get a job?"

"Sebastian. Have a little sympathy. He just wants to have a carefree life."

"What he wants is an *irresponsible* life with no purpose or benefit to society. I won't be an enabler."

"I never asked you to! But you won't even let *us* help him!" She clutches her chest dramatically.

"Because you coddle and enable him. Why do you think I wanted to control the family funds?"

Mom gasps. "You're such a cruel child!"

"Finally! A point we can agree on!" *Now* is she going to go away? And take Travis while she's at it?

"I raised you better than this!"

"I'm the best I can be, Mother."

"I am not 'Mother.' I'm Mom!" She knows the distinction I place on the words. Mom is someone I like. Mother is the woman who gave birth to me.

"Right now, I don't like you very much."

Her chest starts heaving again. "Because I want you to share a tiny percentage of your money with your brother?"

"He didn't earn it."

Suddenly her eyes light up. What the... I turn around and see Luce coming down the stairs. She's changed into a loose spring dress in yellow.

When she turns, revealing her bruised face, Mom gasps. I grip my mug hard, anger and sympathy surging equally. Luce's cheek looks much worse in the light. Like a semi ran over half her face.

"Oh my goodness! What happened to you?" Mom's words come out in a soft breath.

"Well..." Luce smiles awkwardly. "Hello, Marie."

"Your face," Mom says again, pointing with a shaking finger.

"It looks worse than it is," Luce says, then clears her throat.

Mom turns toward me. She stares like she doesn't recognize me. Travis's thumb twitches over his phone, like he's debating if he should call 911.

Are they serious? "It wasn't me!"

Mom seems shaken, but Travis is skeptical. Bet that asshole wishes I *was* a woman beater, so he could blackmail me with it on Mom's behalf.

"There was an accident at the party," Luce says. "But Sebastian took good care of me."

"Well. If... Um... All right. That's good. That's very good," Mom says. "But if you ever need anything, anyone to talk to, you know my number."

"Thank you." Luce comes over to me and places a hand on my shoulder.

The gesture seems to reassure Mom a little, and disappoint Travis. God save me from my "family."

"So. To what do we owe the honor? I didn't realize you were coming over," Luce says.

"It's about Preston," Mom answers quickly. "Sebastian has cut him off, quite cruelly, I might add. Families don't do that to each other." She spreads her arms beseechingly. "Maybe you can make him understand."

"I heard some of what you were saying earlier," Luce says.

I knew it! Mom was too loud.

"Marie, I happen to agree with Sebastian. I don't know why you would think I'd side with Preston. In case you've forgotten, seeing him in bed with my half-sister is permanently etched into my brain." Luce reaches over and threads her fingers with mine. I squeeze gently, enjoying the united front we're creating.

Mom and Travis have the decency to blush.

"If you're here to insist that Sebastian give Preston money he doesn't deserve," Luce says, "I'll have to ask you to leave."

"I've never..." Mom jumps to her feet and huffs, but she's smart enough to retreat when she knows she isn't going to win.

Travis stands and puts a hand on her elbow. "Let's go, Marie. Maybe we can come back when they've had time to think things over."

"Come back when Preston can part the Red Sea!" I call out at their retreating backs.

Once we're alone, Luce and I go to the kitchen. I make more coffee. "Sorry about that," I say as the aroma of the well-roasted beans fills the air.

"It's okay. I'm surprised your mom is so unfair about you and Preston."

"He's her favorite. Everyone in the family loves him because he's the fun one."

"He is...?" Her eyebrows pull together in confusion. "Then why did your family refuse to let me marry you?"

"They wanted him to have Sebastian Jewelry. If he didn't marry you, he wouldn't have had anything." My fury with my family surges again. The idea of Luce with Preston is profane. I'll break his face if he dares to touch her.

"But that isn't what they said. They told me you were 'too good' for me, and offered Preston. If they wanted to justify giving Preston Sebastian Jewelry, they didn't have to put it that way. Same thing if they cared about him more than you."

"That's true, they didn't." *Hmm.* My family acknowledges I'm an excellent executive, and they love the money I make. But they never think I'm "too good." They didn't think it was a big deal to throw me to Luce when Preston screwed up. "There must've been some kind of misunderstanding." I shake my head. "Nobody's 'too good.' Everyone gets what they deserve." I serve her coffee.

"Thanks." She takes a few sips. "Regardless, it isn't right they don't treat you fairly. Even if Preston hadn't cheated on me, I wouldn't have wanted him to be anywhere near the Sebastian Peery collaboration."

"You would've married him if he hadn't cheated on you." The idea immediately roots itself in my head, a mental worm impossible to dislodge.

She gives me a look. "That isn't even close to what I just said. But yes. I might've gone ahead even if he'd cheated, so long as he wasn't caught with my half-sister."

"You want him that much?" Searing acid eats away at my belly. I shouldn't have settled for just cutting Preston off. I should've wrung his neck for being an idiot and a generally irritating presence in my life.

"*Wanted* him? No. What I needed was a husband who'd sign the paper you did after the wedding. My so-called 'family' has been living well off my trust fund, and I wanted to put a stop to it. Surely you can understand that."

Karl and her half-sister are both pieces of work, but that doesn't lessen the burning sensation in my gut. "I do, but I don't have to like it that you were engaged to my half-brother."

She runs a soothing hand down my arm. "Then let's thank God that I married you instead. To be honest, I like you better." She smiles, then sips the coffee.

As I mull over her motivation for this marriage, something else strikes me. "What about your father?" From what I can gather, Roderick seems somewhat decent.

Her expression cools. "He's a sperm donor. If I could, I'd give back the genetic material I got from him."

"Why do you hate him so much? His devotion to your mother is legendary. He won't even remarry because he can't forget her."

She laughs humorlessly. "People don't know what he's really like. He cheated on my mom ever since I was a little kid. Probably even before. She just looked the other way because she wanted to feel loved."

Jesus. "I'm sorry." My initial distrust of him was warranted. I hate him for his unfaithfulness and hurting not only his wife but Luce throughout the years. At least my father never married. It's sad when somebody can make Ted Lasker look like a decent human being by comparison.

Luce shrugs. "I'm never going to let myself be blind to a man's disrespect because of love. When I give my love to someone, it'll be a man who deserves it."

"Like who?" She must have someone in mind.

"I don't know." Her wedding band winks under the light. I remember when we exchanged vows...and how brilliantly and openly she smiled...

Jason the Judge. She claimed he was just a friend, but friends don't smile at friends the way she did.

"But you were thinking about marrying Preston anyway," I say, although what I really want to know is why she didn't marry Jason Choi in the first place. Was he not rich enough? Too much history?

The question lodges in my throat. It's like I'm apprehensive about her response.

Me? Fearful of a few words? Ridiculous!

"I would've divorced him as soon as I got what I wanted," Luce says. "The marriage was just a means to an end."

So she was planning to divorce Preston. It should make me happy, but my mood sinks lower. To her, this marriage is just a convenient way to get something. A legal necessity.

I don't know why the idea bothers me so much when I already understood that. You'd have to be a fool to think this union was meant to last forever.

But it disturbs me anyway, and I hate it that I'm bothered at all.

28

SEBASTIAN

ALL THROUGH SUNDAY, I keep Luce distracted. It isn't difficult. We watch movies and have pizza and Chinese delivered for lunch and dinner. She avoids looking at her phone. Not because she doesn't have anybody pinging her, but because I told her we should take a day to unplug from the world.

Later, I get some ointment Grandmother swears by and spread it on Luce's back. Her bruises have bloomed like deathly flowers.

I should've kicked Karl until he peed blood for a week.

I hold her that night, too. Her cheek is mottled purple, although it looks better than her back. The swelling has mostly gone down, and she rubbed some of the ointment on her face. But she can't go to work tomorrow like this, and I hate it that she has to change her routine because of Karl.

On Monday, I get up at my normal time, check her face—still bruised, although looking better—and slip out of bed. After a quick run in the gym, I shower and get dressed in my room, then send a quick text to Christoph to arrange for a chat with John Highsmith. Noah hasn't sent more links, so that means *The Hollywood News* is the only one that has published a trashy story about us.

I put on my suit for the day, but I can't seem to manage my tie. The

Windsor knot should be simple—I've done it thousands of times—but I'm too distracted and annoyed. I leave the unknotted tie around my neck and head down for coffee. Maybe that will help.

As I approach the kitchen, the scent of coffee washes over me. Matthias must be back on duty. It ratchets up my concern for Luce—does she want him to see her with bruises on her face? Although the swelling's gone down, you can't miss the signs of abuse, and I don't want her upset or crying.

Should I speak with Luce before she comes down and give him another day off?

When I round the corner to the kitchen, both Matthias and Luce are there. I almost do a double take. Why is she in a royal-purple dress with a jacket, like she's ready to go into the office?

"You should work from home today," I say.

"I have a few meetings I can't miss. I'm going in."

Matthias's lips are so thin, they've almost disappeared. He shakes his head fractionally. Guess he tried to persuade her, too.

"Use Zoom," I tell her. Matthias nods, then discreetly withdraws so we can talk this out in peace.

"Can't, really. It's a design meeting."

"So? Tell them to send you the docs ahead of time."

"I'm not staying home until bruises fade." The angle of her chin is firm, the same stubborn tilt that made me think of a Valkyrie when she marched into my office. "Besides, you can't really tell."

"I can still see the purple under the makeup." It's a bit of an exaggeration. Whatever she did hides the bruises well. Unless you looked really hard, you wouldn't notice anything.

Uncertainty fleets through her eyes for a moment, then she shrugs. "I'll get foundation with better coverage."

"Whatever you put on your face, I don't want you out there." *To be the topic of more speculation and hateful gossip?* No. She's suffered enough.

She sighs. "I've given this a lot of thought, and you were right. It happened because Karl is an awful human being."

Good. She got that straight.

"But hiding here isn't going to solve anything. I'm not going to let Karl stop me from doing my job. Some of the designers from Sebastian

Jewelry are coming to discuss the joint venture at nine. I can't miss the first meeting."

"You're the CEO. Delegate it." It's what I'd do. "Using your people effectively is part of being a good executive."

"Sebastian, I can't. This project is too important."

She's going to stay on her path, even if it bothers her that people might notice the damage Karl has done. But I don't want my wife out there alone, defenseless and vulnerable. I've seen enough to know that, other than her assistant, she doesn't have a lot of allies. And since Roderick and Karl held influence within Peery Diamonds, those who are loyal to them might try to mess with her.

"Fine," I concede. "I'll join the meeting."

"But you aren't scheduled for it."

"Christoph will make the necessary adjustments." I brush my thumb over her uninjured cheek, then tuck a loose tendril behind her ear. "There's nothing more urgent than making sure you're going to be okay today."

I could be overreacting, but I'd rather be safe than sorry. Roderick and Karl don't respect her, but they're wary of me. I have no problem doing whatever is needed to lend her support.

A smile appears on her face, slow but bright. "Thank you."

"My pleasure."

She tilts her chin at my undone tie. "Want some help with that?"

"What? This?"

She nods.

"Do you know how to tie it?"

"I can't do a Windsor, but I can do an Eldredge," she says.

"An Eldredge knot? That's unusual."

"I learned it because a friend wanted to wear it, but couldn't master it."

"Fine." My tone is casual to hide the acid burning in my gut. Who did she learn the knot for? Jason? Or somebody else?

She leans toward me and starts to loop the tie into a complex asymmetrical knot. She's so close, her warm breaths fan my chin and neck. Silk whispers, and her entire focus is on my neck—what she's doing to me. I never realized how intimate having a woman knot my tie could be.

And some other man was treated to this. The need to find out who and kick his ass is inexplicably overwhelming. I draw in a deep breath.

It doesn't matter who she learned to tie the Eldredge for. I'm the last man she'll be doing it for. The surging possessiveness is so intense, it stuns me.

"It can look a little weird on a guy who doesn't have the confidence to pull it off, but I think you can do it." She smiles and pats me on the chest, all finished.

"One must have enough panache to dominate one's wardrobe." I'm disappointed it didn't take her much time. "Thanks."

"You're welcome."

After breakfast, I follow her Cullinan in my Phantom. Siri reads my new texts out loud.

—Christoph: All rescheduled.

—Christoph: Also, I moved your call with John Highsmith to eleven a.m. Is that okay?

I reply "Yes" to the text and pull into the Peery Diamonds lot.

I hold the door open and follow Luce into the headquarters. Peery Diamonds is three generations old. Although it's housed in a modern building with chrome and tinted glass, the music in the lobby is a Chopin nocturne and the overall ambiance is elegant old money. Orchids in red clay pots dot the walls. Photos of some of Peery Diamonds' most popular and talked-about pieces hang from the walls. And there are others featuring celebrities. Grace Kelly. Sophia Loren. Princess Di.

A lanky man in his mid-thirties approaches, eyes glued to his phone.

"Good morning, Darren." Luce's tone indicates she's more interested in warning him that she's in his path than greeting him.

He glances up, then gives her a superior smirk I immediately want to wipe off his face. "Jeez. I didn't realize you were coming in today."

"Why wouldn't I come in?"

"Shame, maybe? After you provoked your husband into violence? What's wrong with you? I mean, I kind of knew there was something off, but..."

I put a hand on Luce's shoulder and step around her. "Are you calling me a wife beater?"

Darren's eyes widen. Guess he didn't realize I was right behind her. "Uh... What are you doing here?"

"Answer the question."

"I'm just saying..." he mumbles, glancing at Luce for help.

Luce folds her arms. *You're on your own.*

Just what kind of assholes work in her company? She should fire him right now. I would, if any of my people dared to disrespect me.

"How about this?" I say, looking down at the man. "Shut your mouth unless you know what you're talking about. Defamation lawsuits are expensive to defend. And I'd love nothing more than to make you an example."

He jumps. "But I wasn't talking about you! I was talking about her!"

"You implied I hit her."

"I just meant whatever you did is her fault."

Somebody take away his shovel. Luce puts a hand to her forehead, closing her eyes. "You want to repeat that to my attorney?" I say.

His jaw hangs loose. I wait a beat so Luce can have her say. But she merely shakes her head.

I put a hand on her elbow. "Let's go."

Bianca stands up behind her desk. I gesture for her to sit down and follow Luce into the meeting room. We're the only ones in the huge space with a long table and numerous chairs.

"Who was that?" I demand as she settles down at the head of the table. I take the seat to her left.

"Our CFO." She doesn't quite meet my eyes.

"And you let him talk to you like that?"

She sighs, tapping the edge of the table. "He and I have some history."

"History?"

29

LUCIENNE

At Sebastian's tone, I realize "history" isn't quite the right word. But—too late now. *Stupid Darren.* Why couldn't he have just looked up from his phone, said, "Good morning," and walked away?

"We were engaged," I say finally. "Obviously, it didn't work out."

"You were engaged to a man who can't bother to treat you with respect?"

He's right about Darren's attitude toward me. And I should've done something about it sooner, before it came back to haunt me.

But I don't want to get into the embarrassing details of my ill-fated engagement to Darren and my grandfather's and Roderick's reaction to the way it ended. "It's complicated." *Let's not talk about it.*

"How many men did you try to marry?"

Is he judging me? My hackles rise. "I don't know why that's relevant."

"Are there more in the building?" He looks around like he's ready to confront every man in the right age bracket. Then he waves his hand dismissively. "Never mind. Fire him."

"What?"

"Fire. Him." He pulls a finger across his neck.

"I can't do that without just cause." My response is swift and automatic. "It's going to look like I'm being vindictive over an engagement that went bad."

"He's being insubordinate, talking to you like that. You're entitled to get rid of him for creating a hostile work environment. This is your kingdom, Luce. Defend it."

I stare, processing what he's telling me. I didn't realize I was allowing Darren to create a bad environment for me because he's been impossible since he got caught with his assistant. But my grandfather let it go, and back then, whatever Grandfather wanted was the law. And I didn't have the courage to demand that he fire Darren.

But Grandfather isn't in the picture anymore. Sebastian's right. Peery Diamonds is my kingdom. I have to defend it.

His advice from eleven years ago flashes through my head. *Fight for what's yours.*

I should fight. No. I should fight *harder*. I did all the work to be independent, but that isn't enough if I let others treat me rudely. "You're right," I say calmly. "I'll look into our employment contract with him and see what I need to do to get rid of him."

Sebastian looks slightly taken aback.

"Why are you so shocked?"

"You agreed so readily."

I have to laugh. "You sound suspicious."

"Well, you have to admit—"

"Look, I'm not dumb enough to stay on the wrong path when somebody points out a better one. Pride matters, but it isn't *that* important."

He relaxes and reaches out to squeeze my hand. "I'm proud of you."

I grin. "Thank you. I'm proud of myself, too."

Three knocks come from the door. It's exactly nine. The design people from Peery Diamonds and Sebastian Jewelry come in, followed by Bianca. She's taking notes so we can distribute them to all attendees once the meeting's over.

"I didn't know you were going to be here," Selena, one of the leads from Peery Diamonds, says, glancing at Sebastian.

"I wanted to see for myself how it's going," he responds, smoothing his tie.

The leads from Peery Diamonds get to the point quickly. It's an old corporate habit from my grandfather's era. "I'm not paying them to say hello. I'm paying them to do their job," he would always say.

The new designs are gorgeous and romantic. Although I'm not personally a fan of pink, they've included a lot of pink gold and pink gemstones, including pink diamonds. The supply is limited, though. Selena's certain we can charge a premium for some of the colored diamonds.

"And for our launch year, we're going to try a Korean Flower Language Collection," Mo says. She's the design lead from Sebastian Jewelry.

Sebastian cocks his head. "Korean flower language?"

"It's something Eugene mentioned as being popular," I say. "Many flowers and trees have secondary meanings, which can be used to convey unspoken messages."

"Interesting," he says.

"I'll send you some literature on it," Mo says. "Anyway, the launch is going to feature purple hydrangeas, which mean 'a sincere heart' or 'earnest emotion.' Like that. Here are some of the preliminary designs." She puts them up.

The design is fairly complex, but the flower will look gorgeous once the proper stones are set. The facets will reflect the light perfectly. I can see it in my mind.

"They need to be cut and set very carefully. But they can be turned into lots of different things, like brooches, hairpins, pendants and so on. It'll be too big for rings and bracelets, though."

"I love it," I say with a smile. Sebastian nods.

"Everything for the launch is going to be customizable," Selena adds. "We did it that way on purpose."

Patrick from Sebastian Jewelry points at a set of stunning bracelets. "And these bracelets, for couples who are dating but aren't thinking marriage quite yet, are pretty cute."

"What about these 'couple rings'?" Sebastian asks.

"We have those, but these are extra. Apparently, bracelets are popular, too," Patrick says.

The diamond and platinum bracelets come with locks instead of the usual clasps. You have to have the matching diamond and platinum key to put it on and take it off. And the key is a pendant that goes around your neck. So the girl puts the bracelet on the guy and keeps the key, and vice versa.

I can see how young couples might enjoy that. Excitement fills me as some preliminary ideas to market the products start to stir. I'm going to have to schedule a marketing meeting soon, too.

"What if you lose the key?" Sebastian asks, ever practical.

"Then you bring the bracelet to the store, and we can make another key based on the serial number," Patrick answers.

"Perfect." I smile, then turn to Sebastian. "What do you think?"

The corners of his eyes crinkle. "Very interesting. I see the potential."

"What's the feedback from the Hae Min Group?" I ask.

"I haven't heard back," Bianca says. "I emailed them last Wednesday and marked it urgent. I requested their feedback by Monday their time."

Korea's sixteen hours ahead. Somebody from Hae Min should've sent their feedback. "Follow up with them again then," I say.

"Got it." She types away furiously on her laptop.

After the design people and Bianca leave, Sebastian turns to me. "Is it common for Hae Min to be late?"

"Sadly, yes. This is the third time they missed a deadline," I say. It's like they've lost all their enthusiasm for some reason.

He frowns. "Was there a change in the management?"

"No. I was careful to pick a stable company with excellent executives." For a second, I wonder if I should contact Yuna and ask if anything's going on at the Hae Min Group...but no. If it's some family issue, she's not going to tell me. And I don't want this deal to color our friendship. I'm loath to taint it when I've finally made my first new friend in ages.

"How long have you been working with them to finalize the deal?" Sebastian asks.

"Over six months. But it's been one mix-up and mishap after another since my visit to Korea."

His eyebrows pinch. "Are they jerking you around?"

"I never got that feeling. It's just...they seem unable to make up their minds at times. On top of that, some of their people talk in circles, so it can get a bit confusing. I learned recently that if they say something is 'difficult,' what they're really saying is that's impossible. So—maybe something cultural? But even then, I feel like it's taking longer than it needs to."

He considers for a moment. "Do you want me to handle it?"

"Thanks for the offer, but you don't have to. My bringing this deal to the table is part of the contract I signed with your family. I can't let you do what's essentially my job. But I swear, it's all going to be fine."

"Why don't you send me all the documents for the collaboration? I want to take a closer look and see what I can do to hurry it along."

30

SEBASTIAN

JOHN HIGHSMITH SAYS it won't be a problem to get *The Hollywood News* to cough up the source for the photos they got. They're a bunch of spineless weasels who'll cave at the first threat of losing everything.

"If they don't cooperate, proceed with the lawsuit," I say.

I end the call and return to the documents on the Sebastian Peery collaboration, which are spread out on my desk. The initial projections and timeline are aggressive but reasonable. But the execution is off. Delays. Delays. More delays. Bad communication. Mishaps.

At least Luce's team did a decent job of logging all the issues in chronological order, so it's easy to see what's gone wrong so far. A lot of them are problems that could have been avoided if Luce had more experience and a better team. Like that jackass who talked to her with utter disrespect. He can't be the only one in the organization with an attitude. He might have started out as the sole asshole, but one bad apple tends to ruin the whole barrel. It's especially true when the person in charge is soft. Which Luce seems to be.

Perhaps it would be better if she stepped down as the CEO, got away from the pressure to perform and got some experience under her belt before taking up the position again. I want her to succeed, but she won't if she keeps going this way. She'll get pushed out for failure or burnout.

The key is how to tell her without pissing her off. Preston blew up when I told him he needed to learn the business by working at one of Sebastian Jewelry's retail locations. His ego couldn't handle it—he was *better than that.* I don't think Luce has an impossible ego, but she might be hurt or come to resent me.

I make a mental note to come up with a diplomatic way to approach this, then get up from my desk for my lunch meeting with the central regional retail manager for Sebastian Jewelry. He's in town on business and wants to catch up in person.

As I head out, I notice a finger painting pinned to one of the cubicles. Underneath the painting is a framed photo of a couple and a baby. I sweep my eyes along the other cubicles. Small stuffed animals. Some plants. And lot of photos featuring families or significant others.

My desk doesn't have anything like that. But then, I never had a reason to put anything on it except for a small clock and calendar.

I pull out my phone.

—Me: Noah, can you send me the pic you took of me and Luce?

—Noah: Sure. By the way, you can thank me. I take great photos, even if the subject isn't cheetahs in heat.

I roll my eyes. Noah often says cheetahs wait for no one. He's obsessed with them.

—Me: You should write a book about them. You'd finish it in no time.

—Noah: I'm not writing cheetah porn. They deserve dignity.

Like getting photographed while they're doing it in the wild is dignified...?

Noah sends the pic. Luce is adorable in it, her eyes a little wide with shock, but her smile is gorgeous. It's perfect for my desk.

Now that I think about it, Luce probably doesn't have any photos of us, either.

I Google for a frame and find a crystal and silver one that's perfect. I forward the picture to Christoph.

—Me: Print this in high resolution. Two copies.

—Christoph: Any particular size in mind?

—Me: 4x6.

Wait, that's too small. I want to be able to see Luce's smile clearly.

—Me: Actually make that 5x7. Frame both. Use this frame.

I insert the link to the frame.

—Me: One's for me. The other's for Luce. Send it to her office.

THE LUNCH MEETING, held at an Italian restaurant inside the Aylster, is productive. But that isn't the sole or even main point. If somebody asked me to define consistency, I'd point at Sabato. He isn't a showy man, and his work style isn't showy, either. He's six-one, medium frame with a moderate amount of muscle from a daily morning exercise that he adheres to religiously. He has intelligent brown eyes over a thin mustache. He speaks in a surprisingly deep, modulated tone, and his clothes are expensive but staid. His only jewelry is a wedding band of simple platinum.

Nobody would realize he's one of the most successful regional managers at a luxury jewelry brand. The man is diligent to a fault and doesn't believe in shortcuts.

I value those qualities more than any other. Prima donnas and attention whores don't grow a company. I make sure he understands that honest work is rewarded at Sebastian Jewelry, and he's shown his appreciation by staying with us for over fifteen years.

"Your youngest is graduating from high school this year, isn't she?" I ask over cheesecake drizzled with a raspberry reduction.

"Yes." He smiles fondly. "You remember." He doesn't sound surprised. He knows I keep track of the people on my radar.

"Talk to your wife and see if you'd prefer L.A. or McLean," I say, naming our two headquarters. "Your choice."

"How much time do I have?" His gaze is somber, but there's a hint of excitement. There is the seriousness of taking on bigger responsibilities, but he likes a challenge.

"At the end of this fiscal year."

"That's this summer."

"Right. Should give you and your wife enough time to discuss things and come to a decision. If you want to stay in Chicago we can arrange something, but opportunities are better at the headquarters." I plan to groom him for the COO position eventually. Our current COO, Abner Cox, wants to retire in the next five years. He and I agree that Sabato would be a perfect replacement.

As we head out of the restaurant, I spot Gabriella leaving Nieve with her agent. Our eyes meet, and she whispers something to her agent and starts toward me.

"I'll get going now. Another meeting to get to," Sabato says diplomatically.

"Great. Talk with you later."

Gabriella's smile widens as we approach each other. Her skin's glowing—probably had another spa treatment or something—and she's in a gorgeous red dress that flatters her dramatic coloring. Her makeup is a bit dark, but she pulls it off.

But then, she can pull off anything. That's why Sebastian Jewelry's marketing team decided to make her the brand spokesperson two years ago.

"Why did you come to the party on Saturday?" I ask, half hoping she denies it. *The Hollywood News* could've Photoshopped everything, and I want to believe my ex isn't totally indiscreet and tactless.

"I'm doing very well. Thanks for asking." She finger-walks my shoulder playfully.

I shrug off her touch. "This isn't funny, Gabriella."

She lets out a soft sound of irritation. "Why are you acting like *I* did something wrong, when your wife's the one who sent the invitation?"

"What are you talking about?" Luce had no reason to invite Gabriella. She stresses about causing negative publicity for me, and having my ex-girlfriend at the party would definitely cause a stir. "She didn't send you anything."

"Then it was you, I guess."

That makes even less sense. It's my motto never to think about or bring my exes into my current relationship, and Christoph knows it.

She shrugs. "It isn't important who sent it. What's important is that I got it."

I'm going to see who I need to fire for the screwup. "You still didn't have to come."

"I was curious. Did Sebastian Lasker really fall in love with Lucienne Peery at first sight? The Sebastian I know isn't capable of that."

Curious, my ass. "You could've asked. I haven't blocked you on my phone."

"I know, but you wouldn't have told me the truth."

My temper starts to fray. I open my mouth to give her a piece of my mind, but she raises her hand.

"I'm not calling you a liar, but sometimes we deceive ourselves, believing what we want to believe."

"So?"

"So I wanted to see for myself. I can't say I like Lucienne because I was—well, still am—fond of you. You're one of the best boyfriends I ever had. But you do seem to like her."

"Of course." I try not to get too irritated with Gabriella for coming to the party to check on something that obvious. "She's my wife."

She chuckles and pats my shoulder. "That isn't why, but you just keep right on thinking it is."

31

LUCIENNE

I WORK through lunch at my desk with Karen. There are so many tasks that have to be completed before the launch can happen, and other than me, she's the biggest champion for this collaboration within Peery Diamonds,.

"The timeline's too tight now," she says. "Hae Min is taking too long to make decisions, and we can't do this."

"I know." I try to speak calmly, but my voice is too tight with frustration.

She taps her chin with her index finger. "Can we select another partner?"

"That might delay us more."

"But it's a sunk cost. Maybe the realization that they aren't the only ones we can work with might get them off their butts."

She's right, but I hesitate. I don't want to go through the pain of vetting another conglomerate.

"I'm not just saying this to make you uncomfortable, but you need to realize there are people who question your leadership. So this project's progress is even more important."

"I'm...aware of that."

"It isn't just people within the company. Some of our shareholders are becoming concerned. You being a young woman doesn't help matters, either." She sighs. "It's the same kind of misogynistic attitude everyone had when Wilhelm was in charge."

Karen would know. It must've been much worse over thirty years ago when she started her career at the company.

"But people like that will always find fault with me for my age and gender." I say it mainly to reassure myself. The fact that the collaboration isn't going as well as I hoped is an acidic knot that's permanently occupying my gut at this point. It was supposed to be my chance to prove to the board that I have what it takes.

"They do, and they'll undermine your efforts. They assume the accomplishments from the last two years are due to Roderick's oversight. Even now I hear whispers—where is Roderick? Why isn't he doing more to help?" Karen bites off the last sentence. She doesn't get along with Roderick. She blames him for the division within management.

I grind my teeth, since I agree with her assessment. The only thing he's good at is submitting expense reports. But somehow people at the company act like he was the engine that ran Peery Diamonds.

He sure knows how to manage his image.

"Anyway, we should keep pushing ahead but not limit our options," Karen adds. "Plus, we need to think of some ways to highlight our wins, so you can defend yourself if some shareholder expresses doubts about your ability. The shareholder meeting is next month."

That's true. It's happening earlier than usual this year, which is worrisome, given the lack of significant progress on the project. "Since there isn't much to say about the collaboration, why don't we create a list of other accomplishments we can take to the meeting? Our stock price has gone up a fair amount in the past few weeks. That's a good sign." I wish the audit team was done going over executive expenses, but they told me it's going to take a while, so I can't even bring that up as something I'm doing to clean up our less-than-ideal corporate culture and control costs.

"I'll get on it," she says.

After Karen's gone, Bianca hands me a sandwich from the deli next to the office. "Grabbed you a turkey and cheese."

"You're the best." I smile. She made sure the sandwich has nothing but turkey, Swiss cheese, tomato and basil mayo. I don't like anything else on my sandwiches.

"Karen should've let you have a lunch break," Bianca says.

"She didn't have anything either. Can you see if she needs anything?"

"Already sent her a grilled cheese." She grins.

"Thanks." Bianca thinks Karen works too hard, but she also gives our COO credit for her support. I take a bite of my sandwich.

"By the way, this came for you from Sebastian Jewelry." Bianca hands me a small brown box she's been holding, then starts walking toward the door. "I'll let you enjoy your lunch. Just yell if you need anything."

"Will do."

I put my sandwich down and rip the cardboard box open. Inside is another box, silver and beautifully wrapped. It doesn't feel like jewelry. Sebastian would've used a special courier for that. Or better yet, he would've given it to me at home.

I tug on the ribbon and lift the lid. Under the white tissue papers is a beautifully framed photo of us from the party. It's the one Noah took.

Suddenly the stress and mental fatigue melt away. I smile at the framed photo. Sebastian and I look good together. I adore the way he looks at me in the picture, like he has real feelings for me.

I pull out my phone and text.

–Me: Thank you! Love the photo!

–Sebastian: You're welcome.

He attaches a picture of his desk, which has the same photo on it. I press my lips together so I don't squeal like an overly excited teenager. But this makes me feel like we're a real couple. Like we could be a true family.

He could be getting over the breakup with Gabriella. I study our picture again. He's been so attentive and kind since the tennis match that hope stirs within me.

I put the frame on my desk, then take a snapshot and send it to him. He doesn't respond, but he's probably in a meeting by now.

I start to put my phone down until I see a notification from the Google Alert I set for Sebastian. Most are photos. Maybe Google found a good one? It occasionally finds some old shots of him at a fancy gala or something.

I click on the first link. The pictures that fill my screen are from the party, and many of them feature me and Sebastian. Some of the guests probably uploaded them on their social media accounts.

I scroll down. Maybe there are some shots here that I can save. My thumb hovers over a couple of photos of me and Gabriella. Somebody must've taken them when she came by to talk. She looks so gorgeous and radiant, and I appear... Well, I appear tense. It was from that headache, but my mind is already conjuring up what people will say.

Gabriella Ricci said she chose to end things with Sebastian Lasker. But would she have if it hadn't been for Lucienne Peery?

Lucienne Peery stole Gabriella Ricci's boyfriend and married him, and now L's acting jealous and petty too?

Shouldn't Lucienne Peery apologize to Gabriella?

I feel sorry for Sebastian Lasker. He could've done far better.

My hands grow clammy, but I try to ignore the unpleasant sensation. People always talk trash about me. So what else is new?

I scroll past the photos of me and Gabriella, then almost drop my sandwich when I see the last one. Sebastian and Gabriella, standing close, his head dipped low. They're in the lobby of the Aylster, and there are other people around. But the angles of Sebastian and Gabriella's bodies display the kind of intimacy that can only come from a couple who've been together for a while.

My good mood vanishes. I stare at the picture of Sebastian and Gabriella, studying it for clues that it was taken months ago. But no. There's that Eldredge knot.

There must be another explanation. The paparazzi always take photos that will create the most stir. They crop and frame their subjects so that people will come to the most lurid conclusions.

It could be that Sebastian and Gabriella had a chance, innocent meeting. She could've just said hi, and he said hi back.

But a small voice in my heart says that if that were the case, they shouldn't be standing so close. They shouldn't be at a hotel, and their heads shouldn't be together like they're planning something clandestine.

I put my phone on the desk, screen down. My eyes fall on the framed photo Sebastian sent. Instead of soothing my jagged nerves, it only serves to stick a knife into the hot, writhing mess in my chest.

Roderick often sent Mom presents after he screwed Gwen. Or when he thought that he might get caught. Presents were his way of managing Mom. And she let the flowers and pretty little things blind her because that was easier than confronting the painful truth.

I realize I never asked Sebastian if he invited Gabriella to the party. Or if he still wants to be with her. Although I told him early on I was okay with his being with other women if he was discreet, I'm anything but okay now.

I should try to give him the benefit of the doubt. Jumping to conclusions would be unfair, especially when I know how things can be, even with photos. Unless tabloids plaster the Internet with Sebastian and Gabriella rolling around naked, I need to calm down and talk with him.

Knocks come at the door. Bianca slips through. "Got a minute?"

"Yeah," I say, happy for the distraction. "What is it?"

Her steps are unusually heavy. She takes the seat in front of my desk that Karen occupied earlier. She can't quite meet my eyes.

"You're making me nervous. What happened?"

"I got an email from Chul-Su Park." I frown, and she adds, "You know, one of our liaisons at the Hae Min Group."

"Okay," I say calmly, doing my best to pretend there isn't a giant hole in my stomach. "What did he say?"

"He said they reviewed our launch proposal, and they love it."

"Oh." The burning sensation eases. "Well, that's great."

"Um... Yeah." She licks her lips.

I brace myself. "Tell me the bad news." It couldn't be that terrible if they loved the proposal.

"I don't want to upset you or anything because... God, you don't need this, but..."

"Just tell me, Bianca," I say, trying to get her going. When she gets nervous, she drags her feet before getting to the point. Even though she means well, it drives me crazy because it draws out the apprehension. It's currently balled up in my throat. If she doesn't spit it out soon, I'll probably pass out.

"They want Gabriella Ricci as the brand ambassador for the Sebastian Peery collaboration."

I stare at her for a moment. Nothing computes, and finally my brain gives up. "What?"

"That was my reaction, too." She slides a hand across her chin. "But they're serious. Apparently she's really popular in Korea."

Agitation churns in my gut. Now I wish I hadn't had anything for lunch. "There are other models. And they must've seen all the love-triangle stuff gossip sites are saying about me, Sebastian and her. Having her could damage the brand."

"I know."

"And I was thinking about using local celebrities."

"I told them that, but they seemed pretty set on Gabriella Ricci. Although he never said anything really, you know, explicitly."

"They never do." Leaning back in my chair, I put a hand over my throbbing forehead. Maybe Karen's right. I need to find a new partner, one that's more sensible.

"But I got a sense that maybe there's some kind of external pressure for them to do this."

I straighten, dropping my hand. "What do you mean?"

"It's just the way he phrased it."

"So Eugene Hae wants to use Gabriella?" I ask, trying to get a clear picture of what's going on. When he and I spoke, he seemed fine with selecting Korean celebrities to promote the brand.

"No, I don't think so. It's hard to say for sure, but it's like the decision came from somewhere outside the group. Chul-Su kind of hinted that that's why it took so long for them to get back to us."

"Pressure from outside the group."

"Yeah."

"And enough pressure that they won't go through with it without Gabriella."

"Well... It's hard to say for sure. But Chul-Su said it would be 'difficult to proceed' if Gabriella Ricci isn't the launch ambassador."

32

LUCIENNE

BY THE TIME I'm home late evening, my head is about to explode. From the way pressure squeezes my skull and my temples are throbbing, it's the beginning of a nasty tension migraine. The bombshell demand from the Hae Min Group has been on my mind all afternoon. As well as that damn picture of Sebastian and Gabriella.

Gabriella's agency doesn't have enough influence to force a Korean conglomerate like Hae Min to do anything. That leaves two other possible outside forces with any say in the project: Peery Diamonds and Sebastian Jewelry. And I certainly don't want her.

So that leaves Sebastian.

It's perfectly understandable that he'd want to keep her close. She's the face of Sebastian Jewelry, and she's the one he loves. The former is public knowledge, and he told me the latter before we got married.

There's no reason for me to feel this sick.

But hot fury and betrayal have been clawing at me for hours. I could barely get through my meetings. Thank God none of them required me to make any big decisions.

James stops the car and steps out to open my door. I take a moment, my eyes closed.

This is just an arranged marriage. I have *fond* feelings that might border on a girlish crush for Sebastian. But the intensity of the pain that's been plaguing me says "fond feelings" is insufficient to describe what's in my heart.

Still, I re-create the mask I need to face my husband. It's the smooth one I put on every time I see a nasty headline about myself. Carefree. Proud. Impervious.

Only when I'm certain of my composure do I step out of the car. "Thank you, James. Good night."

I step inside the house. I pray Sebastian's working in his home office, but he's at the kitchen counter with his laptop. He looks relaxed and at home in nothing but shorts.

If I hadn't seen the photo of them at the hotel or if I hadn't heard the Hae Min Group's demand, I might be admiring the gorgeous, lean muscles of his chest and abs. But right now, toxic thoughts bubble in my heart.

Did he do more than just *see* Gabriella at the hotel? Is that why he changed into another outfit?

Stop being ridiculous. Why would he stay in a suit after his day was over?

But logic doesn't want to be in charge. It's already ceded the driver's seat to emotion. I tighten my grip on my control.

"How was your day?" he says with a smile.

I search his expression, looking for any hint he is hiding something or wants to tell me what he's done. But no. It's just a smile.

"Tiring," I say, giving him the same smile.

He makes a small sympathetic noise. "Sorry to hear that."

His response feels mocking. He's the reason my day was tiring.

"How are your face and back?"

"Fine." My response is like marble—smooth and cold. The bruise on my cheek is the least of my worries. I heal fast. You can hardly see it now. My back's a little sore, but nothing more.

I wish I could conceal my churning emotions as easily as I can cover up the bruises.

I place my purse on the counter and get a glass of cold water. The iciness gliding down my throat pulls me out of the fatigue fog. The fluid sloshes in my empty stomach. I haven't had dinner. Bianca brought me some soup and salad, but I couldn't choke them down.

"There's something I wanted to tell you, though." Concern and bemusement twine on his handsome face.

"Okay." Is he about to come clean about how he went behind my back to make Gabriella the face of the Sebastian Peery launch?

"I looked into who leaked photos from the party to *The Hollywood News.*"

Shock slaps me. "That wasn't necessary," I say sharply. "They always do what they want, and going after them only comes back to haunt me."

His stunned expression says I'm being unreasonable more eloquently than any words. "*I'm* the one who's going after them. They won't bug you about it," he says. "You can't just leave these guys alone. Not when they violate your privacy like this."

"They've always violated it," I say, fighting to keep my voice calm. There's no point to having an impervious façade if I'm going to start shouting.

He doesn't care about my struggle, though. "Well, in this case they couldn't have done it without somebody feeding them the photos."

"Any guest could've done that." Gabriella could've done it. And now that he's brought it up, I'm sure it was her.

He must sense my silent accusation. His face starts to turn red. "Not one of mine."

Is he kidding? "Of course it was yours! Who else would want to leak photos making me look like a complete bitch except Gabriella?" Staying above this drama is impossible now. I want to bury my face in a pillow and scream into it to vent my frustration.

"Gabriella—? What? She has nothing to do with this."

I raise a hand, palm out. I can't do this right now. "Stop defending her. You're making this worse."

"And you stop jumping to conclusions before I can even tell you what I found."

The pain in my head is getting worse. The nerve behind my forehead is pulsing. Am I going to pop a vein in my skull?

He continues, "It was sent through an anonymous Gmail account, and whoever did it used your home Wi-Fi."

It takes a moment before the meaning sinks in. "My home Wi-Fi?"

"Yes. So it couldn't have been Gabriella. Obviously. She doesn't have the password, and she isn't savvy enough to crack the network's security."

"All right. That leaves you, me, Bianca and Matthias, but Matthias was off. And there's no way Bianca did anything like that."

"Regardless, somebody was on the network."

For the briefest moment, I wonder if he did it to put Gabriella in a sympathetic light, then dismiss the idea. Not even Roderick would sink to that level, and I can't imagine Sebastian doing it.

But he might've gone to the Hae Min Group behind my back for her, not caring about the effect on me or the milestones I've set. He took all the Sebastian Peery collaboration docs to review, so he has to have seen the marketing plans and launch timeline.

"Did you contact people at Hae Min and ask them to use Gabriella for the launch?" The question slips from my lips before I can catch myself. *Damn it!* I shouldn't talk about this with a splitting headache and emotions running high.

He jerks back and stares at me like I took a swing at him. "What are you talking about?"

"They don't think proceeding with the collaboration is possible if she isn't part of the marketing campaign. Which makes no sense, because they were initially okay with using Korean celebrities to promote the products. They implied there was some outside pressure, and I didn't do it. That leaves you."

"I don't give a damn what model they pick as long as it's the right person for the job."

Is he just explaining his position or over-protesting to hide the fact that he's the one who did this? But he has to know the liaison from Korea would tell me everything, so why would he be lying? I can't sort my thoughts out, and I hate it that I can't trust him. "Maybe you think she's the right person for the job."

"How did you get that from what I just said?" he demands.

"By using my brain," I shoot back, then put the empty glass I've been holding into the sink. I need to leave before I say or do something I'll regret.

He takes my arm and stops me. "What's wrong with you? Do you want to fight? Is that it?"

"No. I don't want to talk to you right now about how important Gabriella still is." *For you.*

He looks at me like I've sprouted mushrooms from my head. "What the hell does that even mean? You're the one who brought her up."

"And you're the one who's in love with her and keeps throwing her in my face." A vague voice in my head whispers that the accusation is unfair—he couldn't have done anything about the photos, including the one from earlier today at the Aylster. But the stubborn and pissed-off part of me says that it's his fault for letting her get close to him.

"What?" He couldn't look more horrified if I'd told him I like to snack on roadkill to add a little variety to my diet. "I'm *not* in love with her."

My heart pumps harder, pulsing blood through my veins painfully, like poison. *Lies, lies, lies.* "Stop treating me like a fool, Sebastian. You told me you were in love with her before we got married."

"What..." He stops. "Damn it."

"If you want to lie, you need to remember what you've been saying."

"I'm not lying. I'm not in love with her."

"But you said you were in love... Oh my God. So you're in love with *someone else*, but were dating Gabriella? That's..." I struggle for a suitable word, but give up. It isn't worth it, not with the headache. "Wow. You're just as bad as all the other guys I've known. Actually worse, because you wouldn't stay faithful to the woman you love, even before you were forced to marry me."

Sebastian growls in frustration. "There was no one to stay faithful *to.*"

Contempt curls my lip. I try to tug my arm free, but his hold is impossible to shake off.

"Okay, look. I lied about being in love with someone when we talked about it," he says. "I was upset and wanted to be a dick. I'm not in love with anybody, especially not Gabriella."

Am I supposed to just nod and say, "I believe you about your previous lie"?

"I would never have married you if I were in love with another woman."

That's the least convincing part of what he said. My life taught me better. "But you love Sebastian Jewelry. You'd do anything to avoid handing over thirty percent of the company. Besides, the contract says you can end the marriage after five years, so all the love of your life has to do is stick around for that long."

"My family is the one who can't afford to give up the shares, not me. I'd never choose Sebastian Jewelry over a woman I loved."

Would he really, though? The words coming out of his mouth sound romantic. Something I might hear in a movie. But this is real life.

"You don't have to explain anything." All the fight drains out of me, and my whole body goes limp. I'm too mentally drained to stay here and have this talk. I just want to take a hot shower and sleep.

But he's still holding on to my arm. Guess he won't let go until he hears what he wants to hear. But I don't want to lie to him and say I believe him or that I understand. I'm not my mom, who always looked the other way.

So instead, I say, "You can see her if you want. Stop twisting around trying to justify your lies. I've had enough of that in my life."

He looks at me like I've just slapped him in front of everyone in the city. What is he so upset about? There's nothing unfair about what I said. Then I realize I also lied to him just now—because I'm not okay with his seeing other women, even if he's in love with them.

I need to go to my room before I say anything else that I don't mean.

He lets go of my arm. Before I can make my exit, he loops his hand around my long hair, threading his fingers along my skull. His mouth crashes against mine. I keep my lips closed, but his teeth scrape the tender flesh, and his tongue probes. The air in my lungs grows thin and fire blazes through me, more anger than lust. I bite his lower lip, but some sanity within me pulls me back before I cut him deep enough to make him bleed.

The bite doesn't make him pull away. A deep growl vibrates in his chest, and he clenches my hair tighter. He ravages me, moving his tongue in like he's trying to fuck me with it. The heat unfurling in my chest becomes more lust than anger. And it pisses me off.

I slap at his hard shoulders, but it just hurts my hands. That only fuels my frustrated wrath. I grip his hair and try to pull him away, but he's too strong. He wraps his arm around my waist and pulls me close, until his erection is pushing against my belly.

Fuck you, fuck you, fuck you, I rage as embarrassingly hot slickness pools between my legs.

Since I can't stop him, I pour all my fury into the kiss, tightening my hand in his hair until it has to hurt. But he doesn't retreat. His cock grows harder and thicker, and I realize he welcomes the pain I'm doling out.

He grinds against me through the clothes. "Do you think I'd be this hard if I were fucking somebody behind your back?"

His eyes are steely and dark. They warn me to choose my words wisely.

But I'm beyond being wise. Caught in the vise of his grip, I can still shrug. "You're a man in his prime."

"You little bitch."

I bare my teeth in an ugly smile at his bald words. I like them better than polished lies.

"You know I'm constantly hard around you."

My mouth dries as the tension of the day drains away. The pulse in my neck flutters. A desire for the sexual oblivion I know he can give seeps through me. If he sticks his hand under my skirt, he's going to feel how wet I am. The raw lust twisting his face is honest. And I can't resist it. "Congratulations. What do you want me to do about it?" It's intended as a taunt, but the words are breathless.

"I want you to realize there's no one else." He places me on the kitchen island, then pushes down his shorts and underwear in one jerky motion. His cock springs out, the veins on the thick shaft pulsing. "This cock is yours." He pushes my skirt up and rips my panties. "And this pussy is mine. My exclusive property."

"Screw you," I shoot back.

"Say what you like, but your body doesn't lie." He runs a finger down my folds and shows me the glistening liquid.

The triumph blazing his eyes doesn't do anything to help rebuild my filter. Everything spills out, uncensored. "So what if my body's slutty? Do you think that means anything?"

"It means you're *my* slut. *My* wife." He lifts me off the island, wrapping his arms around my torso, and slams into me.

All the breath gets knocked out of me. Pleasure pours over me; my legs wrap around his waist of their own volition, and I cling to him. He handles me like I weigh nothing, and he thrusts into me like he has every right to, plunders my mouth like he can't stop. His rough movements drive me crazy. When we're both frenzied like this, I feel reassured of his need for me—he can't be faking it.

Whether he loves somebody or not, whether he means to be faithful or not, I have no space for any of that in my head. Lust is the most honest mutual emotion we share.

A searing climax spins all my senses. I hold him, like he's the only anchor I have left in my life. When he comes inside me, I shudder again, digging my fingers into him.

I should be comforted—maybe even relieved—that he insists he's faithful and demands the same in return. But the emptiness in my heart continues to gnaw at me, and I don't know if I can ever fill it up.

33

LUCIENNE

When I open my eyes the next morning, I realize I'm alone in bed. Sebastian brought me upstairs and held me until I fell asleep.

Maybe he went back to his room later.

I roll out of bed and change into workout clothes. A good run should help me organize my thoughts. Clear my head.

The door opens. "You're up," Sebastian says, coming in with a cup of water. "Here." He hands me Plan B. "I just grabbed it. Thought you might want it."

I look at the box for a moment. And think about how sensible and considerate he's being. We didn't use a condom last night, and I'm not on birth control. I was planning to stop by the pharmacy to grab one on my way to work.

The conversation Sebastian and I had at Manny's Tacos flashes through my mind. Neither of us wants a pregnancy.

At some point, I'd love to have children. But right now, a baby would only complicate things. I'd rather not bring a child into the world when I'm not ready. "Thanks."

I swallow the pill, then look down at the floor for a second to gather my thoughts.

He takes the empty glass back. "About last night..."

"I was pretty melodramatic and not myself." The frustration of the delays with the Hae Min Group and the drama with Gabriella have completely derailed me. "It won't happen again." I smile like everything's fine.

He looks at me like he has a lot to say, but I don't think I can listen to him right now.

"I want to go run now. You're welcome to work out with me if you like."

I put AirPods into my ears, turn the music on as loud as I can tolerate it and head to the gym. He follows, but he doesn't try to talk. He just gazes at me thoughtfully, which is almost as bad as our talking about what happened, because it keeps poking at my raw emotions. And I have no idea what he's thinking.

We go to work, and Bianca informs me Chul-Su hasn't responded yet. Later that afternoon, Sebastian sends me stunning scarlet dahlias.

"They're gorgeous," Bianca says dreamily, staring at the flowers on my desk. "He sure knows how to treat you right."

I smile wordlessly. She didn't grow up like me. To her, gifts are just gifts, not ulterior motives or pretty blankets to lay over lies.

She tilts her head. "What's wrong?"

"What do you mean?"

"You have that look. Come on. You can tell your bestie."

"It's nothing."

She shoots me a you're-full-of-shit look.

"Fine. Take a seat."

She promptly complies, and I sigh and tell her what happened yesterday, skipping the explicit details. I can't decide if I'm making any sense. To be honest, I'm not sure if I can put logic to my emotions. They're so contradictory and volatile.

"You have feelings for him," she says when I'm done.

"Of course I do. He's my husband."

"No, I mean *real* feelings. At the very least, you like him, and you want him to like you back. You're frustrated because you don't think that's going to happen."

I let out a laugh. "I've never... That's ridiculous."

"Don't kid yourself. You wouldn't have reacted like that if you didn't have any expectations."

"But you know why I married him—the circumstances of our marriage."

"So? He was your first choice all along." She raises a hand. "We aren't going to talk about Darren because that piece of shit was your grandfather's pick, not yours. And Preston was pushed on you by the Comtois family. The fact that you hand-picked Sebastian tells me you felt something for him from the beginning. On top of that, he acted in ways that would mess with anybody's mind." She leans closer. "He's kind to you. I've seen the way he looks at you."

"Okay, so...?"

She rolls her eyes. "He looks at you like you're the center of his universe."

Something warm and happy shivers through me, but I shake it off. I don't want to hope only to be let down again. "He's acting."

"He's a hell of an actor, then, because I bought the whole thing, even though I know exactly what's going on." She stands and pats my shoulder. "The man's gorgeous and treats you well. You could do *much* worse. Don't be so hard on him."

"Hey! You're supposed to be *my* friend."

"Which is why I'm telling you all this. If I wasn't your best friend, I would've told you to dump him and get yourself a new boy toy." She starts to leave with a playful smile. Before closing the door, she says, "You have a meeting in ten minutes with the finance team."

I nod and plunge into the rest of the day, which is jam-packed with meetings. Just as I end the final one, my stomach cramps in that familiar but unpleasant way. My period has started.

For once, I actually welcome it. *No unintended consequences.*

After I wrap up a few last-minute items on my agenda, I pick up beef burritos with extra cheese from Manny's Tacos and head home. Sebastian texted he was going to be home late.

I eat my dinner alone in the huge, silent house. For some reason, the place feels even bigger and quieter today. He doesn't come home until I've been tossing and turning in bed for a while. The cramps are making it impossible to get comfortable.

He changes and slips under the covers. I ball up on my side, my back to him.

"I'm on my period," I tell him before he can touch me. "So you can sleep in your room if you want. I'm going to be tossing and turning a lot."

He says nothing, but I can feel the weight of his gaze. I hold my breath, waiting for him to leave.

"Sometimes I just like to hold you at night without wanting sex," he says quietly, his breath on the back of my neck.

I bite my lip.

He pulls me close, lays a large warm hand on my belly and rubs gently. The heat and the massage seem to alleviate the cramps.

Placebo, I tell myself. No matter how protective his arms feel around me, the gnawing emptiness is still in my heart. Bianca's words that I want him to like me back float in my head, and it's a struggle to fall asleep.

He continues to hold me every night, and I keep being silent, mulling over what Bianca said. By the time my period ends, I've given up and admitted she's right. But that doesn't provide me with a guideline for future action. How do you demand that someone like you just because you like him? There's a reason words like "unrequited" exist.

We also don't discuss what *The Hollywood News* claimed about the origin of the photos, although I ask Bianca to hire a security team to look into my home's IT infrastructure. She turns horrified when I tell her what Sebastian discovered, but recovers and promises to get on it as soon as possible. We'll find the real culprit behind the photo leaks. Unlike him, I'm not going to assume anything.

Sebastian and I also don't discuss what the Hae Min Group said about Gabriella. The peace between us is as fragile as a butterfly's wing. You breathe wrong—it's going to break. And I don't want to be the one to breathe wrong.

So instead, I instruct Karen to look into getting another partner in Korea, since the Hae Min Group seems to have become unreliable. I also ask her to look into ending the venture altogether.

"That would be catastrophic for you," she says, deep lines between her eyebrows.

"I know, but the Hae Min Group might not work out after all." If everyone's dragging their feet and going behind each other's backs, the venture's doomed. We should end it before we spend more money and energy.

"There's a penalty for pulling out," she says. "Sebastian Jewelry's legal team wasn't stupid."

"I'm not saying I'm going to do it." I press my lips together tightly, trying to hide the frustration welling. This project should have never been this complicated to execute. I don't know where it derailed so badly. "I just want you to look into minimizing the loss. Just in case."

She stares at me for a long time. "Okay."

After she leaves my office, I sigh. The shareholders are going to be infuriated if I end the collaboration. I spoke highly of it before, and many of them were excited over a new market and bigger profits. I need something to distract them, something shinier, but can't think of anything. It doesn't help that I have less than forty-eight hours to come up with a new idea for the shareholders' meeting. But is that what they really want? I've had so many great ideas that eventually flopped for some reason. They aren't going to be pleased about the latest.

My phone rings. It's Yuna.

"Hi, Yuna," I say, with a warm smile in my voice.

"Hi. Am I interrupting anything?" She sounds...taut.

"No. Is everything okay?"

"Not really. But I wanted to talk to you first. Knowing what I know, I just can't accept their side of things."

Dread slowly wraps its fingers around my heart. "What happened?" Tabloid gossip? Did someone say something to her?

"My dad is furious that Peery Diamonds is refusing to create a custom-designed diamond set for my mom for their anniversary."

"What?"

"He thinks you aren't taking the deal seriously, and this is your way of expressing how little regard you have for the business relationship."

"Wait, wait, wait," I say. "Hold on. I never heard about this."

"How is that possible? His assistant called and spoke directly with yours. Mr. Park does not make mistakes. He wouldn't have been at Hae Min for so long as my dad's right-hand man."

"What did he say was my assistant's response?" There has to be some kind of miscommunication. Maybe Julio mishandled it while Bianca was out of the country.

"She told him it's not happening. Without any explanation." Yuna sounds insulted.

She? "Maybe he misunderstood," I say woodenly as my thoughts spiral out of control, trying to piece together what must've happened.

"He doesn't misunderstand. He speaks four languages, and his English is excellent."

My whole body starts shaking. I prop my elbows on the desk and press the heels of my hands against my pulsing temples. She's right about Mr. Park. I met him, along with Eugene and a few others, when I visited their headquarters. The Hae Min employees take their work more seriously than a heart attack.

Yuna isn't finished. "Dad is fuming, and Eugene isn't thrilled, either. They think you're jerking them around, because you don't respond to the group's emails in a timely fashion. And when you do, it's often with ambiguous wording or not what was agreed upon. Like insisting on using Gabriella Ricci."

I jerk my head up.

"Wouldn't it be awkward to work with your husband's previous girlfriend? Especially when the gossip sites claimed you stole him from her? I can't imagine a situation like that. And it isn't like she's the only acceptable model out there."

Blood roars in my head. This is the exact opposite of what Bianca told me.

Yuna continues, "It wasn't a big topic in Korea because there was a juicier scandal at the time. But if this collaboration launches with Gabriella Ricci as the brand ambassador, the media there *will* talk about the three-way relationship involving you, her and your husband, and it *will* create a negative brand image."

Nausea wells. A bitter-sour tang coats my mouth.

"Eugene is ready to cut ties and sue both Peery and Sebastian Jewelry."

Holy mother of God... Dread pours over me. The shareholders' meeting is two days away. A lawsuit from our overseas partner would be the final nail in my coffin.

"But I told him I needed to talk to you before he did anything. Because what he said doesn't jibe with what I know."

I squeeze my eyes shut, struggle to breathe...and think. "Okay, I... That isn't how I understood the situation." My voice is shaking, and I stop and inhale. I can't afford to get emotional. *Project calm leadership—and see what can be done to salvage all this.* "First of all, my assistant should never have said that, assuming there was no miscommunication or misunderstanding. We're always happy to do custom work, and I already told my design team to come up with special gifts to celebrate the partnership. Maybe she didn't articulate the situation well. As for Gabriella Ricci, my understanding was that *Hae Min* wanted to use her." Bianca said Chul-Su wanted Gabriella, but would he have said that knowing Eugene would have the same concern that Yuna just voiced? "But like we discussed before, I'd prefer that we use a local celebrity with the right image and fanbase."

A silence. "What's going on, Lucie?" Yuna asks. Her tone's softer now, concerned.

"I don't know," I say, although my churning gut says I do. But I simply can't imagine my best friend doing all this when she knew how much her actions would hurt. She has nothing to gain by lying like this between me and the Hae Min Group. There has to be another explanation. "I'm going to have to look into this. I want to understand how so many mistakes were made."

"If your assistant isn't doing her job, you're going to have to let her go," Yuna says quietly. "She's cost you and Hae Min a lot of trouble and time."

"She's my best friend. She'd never do anything that could harm the company. Or my reputation."

"Lucie. I think she already has." Yuna isn't unkind, but that makes me feel more like a failure. The worst judge of character.

I clench my trembling hands.

"I hope you can safeguard your company. I'll speak to my brother, and see what we can do. But if this issue isn't resolved immediately, he won't work with you."

"I understand." I choke out the words, then clear my throat. "Thank you for letting me know, Yuna."

"It's not a problem. And Lucie...good luck."

We hang up. I bury my face in my hands. If it hadn't been for Yuna, the Hae Min Group would've terminated everything and sued. What a disaster that would've been.

But now that I know what the problems are with the collaboration, I have to address them as soon as possible. Everything points to Bianca, but it doesn't make any sense. We've been friends even before we started preschool. *There has to be another explanation for this.*

I hit the intercom to ask her to come in, but I can't say the words. My throat is scratchy and raw, like it's full of little splinters. If Bianca sees me like this, she's going to know something's wrong. I don't want her to think I suspect her.

I don't. I can't.

I pull up the intercompany messenger instead.

34

LUCIENNE

I DRUM my fingers on the desk and look around the office. The sky's an immaculate blue. My friendship with Bianca should've been just as absolute and beautiful. But...

Doubts drip into my heart, like acid. It burns, and I put my hand over it to soothe it without success. There has to be some mix-up. Some kind of miscommunication that can be cleared up easily.

Gathering myself, I type up my message for my best friend.

–Me: Hey, do you know what happened to the request from the Hae Min Group's chairman asking us to design a special diamond set for his wife? Eugene sent me an email. Apparently he's upset over our lack of response.

One heartbeat. Then two...three...four...

I count up to thirteen. The messenger beeps.

–Bianca: Oh my God! I'm so sorry. I just found the email in my spam folder! I don't know how it got there.

I put a hand over my burning belly, the air frozen in my lungs. Yuna said Mr. Park *called*. Regardless of cultural and language barriers, nobody mixes up a call with an email.

–Me: Nobody called to follow up or discuss it personally?

—Bianca: Nope. I wish somebody had. Then I would've realized their email landed in my spam folder sooner.

But did it...? The skin around my eyes stings, and I blink away the tears. My head feels like a tornado has ripped through it. I can't decide what to feel—what to do.

Finally, I muster a response.

—Me: Okay, I see. Can you please reply to them?

—Bianca: Drafting an email right now. I am SO sorry! I'll make sure to check the spam folder more carefully from now on!

—Me: Are there other emails too?

What about phone calls? But I can't type the question.

—Bianca: Just this one, thank God. But it's an important one. We don't want to upset them.

No, we certainly don't. She knows how hard I've worked on this deal. How much I need it to go well so I can prove to everyone I have what it takes to lead the company. If this venture fails, I'll look like an inexperienced fool.

I think I'm going to throw up.

—Me: I don't feel well, so I'm going to head home. Can you reschedule my appointments and meetings, and let me know the new times?

—Bianca: Of course. I'll let James know you're leaving. Is there anything I can get you before you go? Tylenol?

See? Look how concerned she is for me. How can somebody like this be the one sabotaging my work?

This doesn't add up. Something's fishy. Maybe this perfect Mr. Park lied because he let the request slip through cracks.

Except that doesn't explain the Gabriella Ricci matter.

I close my laptop, shove it into my purse and walk out of the building without saying goodbye to anyone. James is waiting, and I get in and have him pull out.

The cityscape flows by, and I just stare out the window. My brain refuses to process anything. It can't think of a good scenario to explain what Yuna told me without laying the blame on Bianca, so I won't even try.

I prefer that to attacking my best friend. Or so I tell myself, even though my stomach is twisted into a knot that's growing more painful with each passing moment.

Finally, I step inside my home. Matthias looks up from wiping down the kitchen counter, then frowns. "Are you all right?"

"What?" I shake my head, realizing I can't tell him anything. "Yeah, sure. I'm fine."

"You're pale," he says, peering at my face.

"It's just the heat."

He raises a skeptical eyebrow. I was in an air-conditioned office, then in an air-conditioned car—and now I'm in an air-conditioned mansion.

"Heat as in pressure from the new Korean venture. Business heat." I force a smile. "Don't worry."

I go straight to my home office on the upper level, dump my purse on the desk and start pacing. Bianca's always done everything I asked her to. There's no way she's been deliberately obstructing me.

Miscommunications happen when you're working through email. I should talk with Sebastian and see if we can fly to Korea and do a face-to-face meeting to resolve all the remaining issues so we can move forward.

My phone pings. I fish it out of my purse.

–Bianca: All rescheduled. I sent you an email with updates. Review it in case you need to change something. Hope you're feeling better XOXO.

See? She did what I asked. If I call Karen right now, she'll tell me she'll see me tomorrow at eleven. And HR and legal are still looking for a way to fire Darren without giving him a golden parachute, and the audit team she hired on my behalf to look into my trust fund is busy at work.

Nothing's wrong. Not. A. Thing.

But I can't settle down. Anxiety burns through me, and I continue to pace. Bianca and I are best friends. My childhood would've been bleak without her. When Grandfather belittled me, it was Bianca who hugged me. When Karl and Vonnie made their asshole moves, it was Bianca who sat with me and came up with a billion ways to get them back, to cheer me up. She almost got suspended from high school once for trying to punch Vonnie in the face...

Knocks on the door startle me out of my endless pacing. "Yes?"

Sebastian walks in. He must've come up right after he arrived. He's still in his suit.

"What are you doing here?" I ask. "Don't you have meetings to attend?"

"Meetings? It's six."

Six? I've totally lost track of time, stressing about the situation with Bianca.

He takes my wrists gently and peers at me. "What's wrong?"

"What do you mean?"

"Matthias said you holed yourself away in your office as soon as you came home and wouldn't answer his questions about dinner or snacks."

I don't remember any of that. But then, I was distracted. Maybe... just maybe that's what happened with Bianca and Mr. Park. She's overworked and needs another assistant in addition to Julio. You can only juggle so many balls before you start dropping some.

Then why didn't she ask?

Maybe she overestimated her bandwidth...

And Gabriella Ricci?

It's an unanswerable question. And there's nobody I can talk to about this. I really don't want to discuss the situation with Sebastian, especially because it feels disloyal to Bianca.

But he has a right to know what's going on with the collaboration.

I sigh. "I got a call from Yuna."

"Okay." He leans against my desk.

Hugging myself, I tell him what she said about the multiple miscommunications.

He runs his hand along his jaw, his eyes narrowed. "That's...wild."

"I know, right?" I say, desperate to have somebody confirm Bianca is my true best friend. "It's more than wild. It's outlandish." I resume pacing.

"But serious." He straightens and takes my arms gently, forcing me to be still. He lifts my chin so I can look him in the eye. "You need to investigate this."

"I *know*. But she's my best friend." My voice cracks.

Sympathy softens his gaze. "She might not feel the same way about you."

"How can you say that?" I demand, furious he thinks so little of my friendship with her.

He remains calm. "I've been wondering why so many things aren't as they should be. Your family shouldn't have been at the party. There shouldn't have been paparazzi taking our picture when we first 'fake dated.' Why would that have happened?"

"I'm famous, that's why!" My voice grows shrill, almost hysterical.

"So am I. I grew up with famous people, and none of them have issues like you."

"Maybe they're just nicer people."

"Nicer than Lucienne Peery?" He smiles sadly. "Nah."

I close my eyes for a moment. I wish he were an asshole. Then he wouldn't be saying things that force me to consider the most horrible, unimaginable possibility.

"Yuna told you the secretary spoke to Bianca," he says. "Does she come across as the type to get confused about something like that?"

"But it's *Bianca*."

"Only the people who are close enough to stick a knife in your back can betray you."

I shiver uncontrollably as my blood chills.

"Do you know why I lost my temper when my family told me I had to marry you or lose the company? It's because I was backstabbed by people I thought I could count on." He runs his thumb over my cool cheek, the gesture tender. "If you don't look into her, you'll never be sure." He sighs heavily. "I've seen how hard you work. I'd hate to see you undermined from within. That just...wouldn't be fair."

"I don't want to be disloyal," I whisper. "Doubting her feels like I'm betraying her."

"But if you never find out for sure, you'll always be second-guessing her motives, and your friendship will be ruined anyway. Plus, you might be right that she's innocent. In which case, you need to find out who's really misrepresenting Peery Diamonds and framing Bianca to take the fall."

That pulls me up short. I hadn't considered the possibility that somebody could be framing Bianca. But she might have enemies, too. Julio? Darren, maybe? "You're right. Somebody could be setting her up."

I'm going to find out who, and when I do, oh boy are they going to pay. I pull out my phone and text the head of IT and cybersecurity. He's a night owl and doesn't come to work until at least noon.

–Me: Is it possible for you to pull all emails, texts and phone logs for Bianca Martin? I don't want you to hack into her phone or anything. Nothing illegal.

I add the last part because Dex is a reformed hacker. But some of the employees whisper he still breaks into other people's phones and whatnot for fun.

–Dex: Nothing illegal. Got it.

A few moments later, there's another text.

–Dex: Turns out I don't need to do anything illegal. I just checked and see she's using a company phone. All the company stuff comes with a release allowing us to look into activity on the devices. They come with monitoring apps, which will make things simple.

–Me: When can you have the info?

–Dex: Twenty-four hours at the most. I'll email you everything direct. Guess you don't want Bianca to know about this.

–Me: No, I don't. Not her, not anyone. Thanks.

The phone slips from my nerveless hand. It's done. Dex will be thorough. He's going to clear Bianca.

He has to.

"Let's get you fed." Sebastian takes my chilled hand and rubs it.

I eat but immediately forget what I put in my mouth. I can't follow anything, from him or the TV show he turns on. I'm trapped in my thoughts, the accusation against my best friend rolling around in my head.

Dex texts me at quarter till eleven with an attachment just as I'm about to climb into bed. I exhale shakily.

"It can wait until tomorrow," Sebastian says, placing a hand on my shoulder.

"No, it can't. I'm not going to be able to sleep otherwise." I look at him with a smile. "Dex just said, 'Here you go.' If there was anything damning, he would've texted, 'I'm sorry.' Right? I mean, he knows Bianca and I are tight."

Sebastian doesn't smile back. "Maybe. But it's not good to look at something that could upset you before going to bed."

He doesn't hope Bianca is innocent as much as I do. The realization shouldn't shock me—she isn't his friend—but it still stings. It feels like it's just me and her, and I've gotta do what I can to protect her, just like she's done for me all my life.

"But I'm not going to *be* upset," I say. "Not when this email is going to clear my bestie."

I open the attachment. Read the emails Bianca's been writing back and forth with the Hae Min Group.

Then I read them again.

My chin trembles. I clench my teeth. My heartbeat thunders in my head. *Fool, fool, fool...*

Yuna was right about Bianca's interaction with the liaisons from Hae Min...

But there's more...

Texts she had with That Stalker, telling him where to find me, the sort of headlines he should aim for...

Pictures from the party that she sent to *The Hollywood News*...

Google Alerts for me and everyone associated with me...

Multiple anonymous user IDs for gossip sites so she could be the first to leave the nastiest comment or egg others on...

All the things a best friend would never do. But she did them. Using a phone my company paid for.

I don't have the fortitude to go back further, but the interactions between her and That Stalker make it clear she's been working with him for years.

Were we ever friends...?

My eyes burn as tears fall. I drop the phone and cover my face with my hands. I start to collapse, and Sebastian catches me. His palm is on the back of my head, his arm around my back.

He doesn't try to comfort me with words. But then, there's nothing that could soothe the pain blooming in my heart.

The truth will set you free.

That's a lie.

The truth is jagged shards of glass you breathe in, shards that shred you until you think you'll never recover.

35

LUCIENNE

THE NEXT MORNING I get up early, run like always, then put on a red dress and my favorite diamonds. Sebastian watches, his concerned eyes following my every move.

"You can have Jeremiah handle this," he says.

I curl my lashes and apply mascara. "Bianca's my problem." I'm surprised at how calm I sound. But it's as though the emotional explosion last night wrung me of pain, leaving nothing but numbness. "I want to deal with her myself first."

"You want to know why she did it."

I pause for a moment. That wasn't the conscious why, but I realize he's right. I deserve to know the reason she betrayed me. "Yes."

"You'll never understand her. People who do things like this to their best friends don't think or feel like we do."

"But I'm not going to get closure if I don't talk to her." I run red lipstick over my mouth, then put it down on the vanity. "This is for me, so I can close this chapter."

"She may give you a sob story to get you to forgive her."

He believes in evening the scales. And fighting. He'd never let somebody screw with him and get away with it. He even forced his family to hand over control over their trusts.

"I won't. I promise." Even if Bianca has a really good reason—although I can't imagine what that would be—we can never go back to how it used to be. She didn't just burn that bridge. She nuked it.

"If you need anything, call me." He regards me like a small child about to dip her toes into an adult pool for the first time.

"I'll be fine." I'll have to be.

After giving Sebastian a kiss and wishing him a good day, I say good morning to James and climb into the Cullinan. I check my texts and agenda like there's nothing wrong.

But I struggle to focus and finally put my phone down. As James drives to Peery Diamonds, I recall how shocked I was that That Stalker didn't chase me when I was eloping. Or follow all of us to the steakhouse after the ceremony. Sebastian's right about me not being *that* famous. His father is a far more significant celebrity, but he didn't have paparazzi harassing him.

I didn't look at all the emails and texts extracted from Bianca's laptop and phone, but she might've been behind the video that made me look like a dog kicker. It was one of the worst periods of my life with so many people attacking me online. Some even cussed me out in person.

Bianca always told me it would be best to ignore them because nothing good would come of it. Lawsuits draw attention. She said that's what my lawyers said, too. I wonder if she asked them at all.

But then she overplayed her hand. Eventually I got fed up with lawyers who always said no and hired Jeremiah Huxley myself. And Jeremiah has always contacted me directly, bypassing Bianca. She said she didn't like going through an assistant on legal matters, in case of miscommunication or misinterpretation.

Thank God.

When I step onto my floor, Bianca's at her desk. She's in a pretty blue Dior dress I bought for her birthday last year. Her necklace is a stunning platinum and sapphire pendant I commissioned to celebrate our friendship when we graduated from college.

Did she feel any guilt accepting them? Or did she laugh at how stupid and gullible I was?

"Hey, good morning," she says, flashing a smile. "You feeling better?"

No. "Much." I force a smile. It's amazing what humans can achieve. The air still feels like it's full of broken glass, but I can will myself to behave like I'm just fine. "By the way, can you have security send a couple of guards up to my office? And I also need you in there, too."

"Yeah, sure." She gives me a quick, curious look, then picks up the phone.

Even now, she doesn't suspect I know. The possibility has probably never entered her mind. Is she laughing inwardly?

My stomach burns. I enter my office and put my purse on the desk. I grab a bottle of icy water from the mini-fridge, twist the cap open and guzzle it down.

By the time I've managed to suck down about half the bottle, she walks in. "So. What's this about?"

"Close the door and have a seat." I gesture at the chair she likes to take.

She sits casually, crossing her legs. Her pink lips curve into a smile. All innocent. All friendly.

Why did you do it? Did you ever feel guilty? Are you sorry? Did our friendship mean anything to you?

So many questions spin around in my head, but I don't voice any of them. I remain standing and finish the rest of the water, then drop the empty bottle into the trash bin. It makes a clattering noise.

She finally notices something's off. "Is everything okay?"

I look down at her, my hands hanging loose by my sides. "Dex from IT and cybersecurity audited your laptop and phone."

There's a moment when she sits absolutely still. Only her eyes go slightly wide. Then she jumps to her feet. "What? He can't do that!"

"Actually, he can." I'm shocked I can speak so evenly. I thought I might lose control and start yelling at her. "You're using a company laptop and phone."

"So?" Half defensive. Half defiant.

"So they belong to Peery Diamonds, and Dex can review what's on them as he sees fit. All totally legal."

"Still!" She runs a hand through her hair. "That's a gross violation of my privacy!"

I just look at her. Tell me you're sorry. Give me some excuse.

"I have some personal stuff on them," she mumbles. "I just didn't want him to see my, you know, private photos. That's all."

Disappointment crushes me. But I remain standing tall. "Private meaning a little risqué?"

"Well...yeah."

"You mean the *risqué* emails you sent to the Hae Min Group? Or the *risqué* text exchanges with That Stalker and other paparazzi? Or all the *risqué* photos of me you took and distributed to the tabloids?" My tone's flat. I was worried I'd rage—cry, even—but nothing comes. It was probably good that I read what Dex sent last night. Imagine how embarrassing it would be if I burst into tears now, while Bianca glares at me like everything is my fault.

"You're so fucking stupid," she says finally with a small laugh. "Took you long enough to figure it out."

Her cruel words hit me, a wave pounding against a sandcastle. My heart crumbles. I don't know exactly what I expected, but her calling me "fucking stupid" wasn't it. "We're—we *were*—friends, Bianca."

She rests her hands on her hips. "Oh my God. I was never your friend. I was a charity case to make you feel good about yourself. To make you feel superior! It's disgusting how you fooled my parents. They always told me I should be grateful to you! And your mom! For what? Paying for my fucking tuition?"

I almost take a step back at the raw vitriol. Her eyes glitter with something unholy as she clenches her hands, an ugly dark flush streaking her cheeks. "I *never* asked you or your mom! I *never* wanted to go to those fancy schools with the rich kids! I *never* wanted to try to fit in, or be told that I was lucky to be going there, or that I should be *grateful!*" She shakes her fists. "I fucking *hate* that word! *Grateful!* I earned *every*thing. I fought for *every*thing! I despised you for paying for all those school trips and activities so you could drag me along. I never wanted to go to. *Never!* But everyone knew you were a loser who couldn't make any friends. You could only *buy* friendship. And you continued to buy me even after I graduated from college, and I couldn't do what I wanted! No! I had to work for you, so you could shine *by using me!*"

I grit my teeth at the pain. All my life, I thought she was my best friend. I asked Mom to pay for those trips and activities because Bianca's family couldn't afford them, and it wasn't a big deal for mine. I never imagined she'd hate me for trying to help.

I only offered her a job at Peery Diamonds because when she graduated, the job market was awful and she couldn't get any callbacks. "I told you that you could go elsewhere any time you wanted," I say finally, my voice trembling.

She shakes her finger. "Oh no. You made sure I could never leave by showering me with perks."

"I wanted to treat you well! I thought you were my friend!"

"Stop with your sanctimonious bullshit! You only gave me nice things when you wanted to be sure I'd stay loyal and be your friend." She gestures at her chest.

"This pendant and this dress! You only gave them to me because you wanted to remind me I'm not as good as you—that I'll *never* be as good as you."

Absolutely nothing I've ever done for her was taken at face value— my wanting to be nice, show my appreciation and love for her. "What should I have done to make you feel respected, then, Bianca?" I ask, needing to know where I've gone wrong.

"There's nothing you could've done! Nothing! *Your very existence pisses me off.* You got everything handed to you because you were born rich! If it weren't for your inherited money, you'd be nothing because you're such an idiot! Do you know how much I loved messing with you without your suspecting I could be behind any of it? It's hilarious how you took everything I said as gospel. You know what? Your husband's family never said no to you asking for Sebastian, because I didn't even ask. I just told them you'd like to marry Preston. They were surprised— probably because they knew that Preston was a crappy choice—but they said okay. Why the hell not? They could offload him for a good price. And you didn't suspect. You thought I asked them like you told me to and they said no. Same goes for your stupid lawyers. I never told them what you wanted, and I told you they said what you wanted was impossible.

"But you never doubted me because you're just—that—dumb. When you hired Jeremiah Huxley behind my back, it was annoying. But all I had to do was get furious that your previous lawyers were too lazy and incompetent to do their job and fawn over what a brilliant attorney Jeremiah is, and you didn't suspect a thing." She smirks. "It was *easier* than taking candy from a baby."

If I thought my head was like the aftermath of a nasty tornado before...it's total devastation. I try to hold on to what control I can, but every hateful word out of her mouth claws at me, leaving trails of blood. "And the video of me supposedly kicking a dog... Was that you, too?"

"Well, yeah. You don't have what it takes to abuse an animal, but it isn't like the public knows that. Or cares. I thought it was hilarious." She laughs.

"I cried on your shoulder." My voice cracks.

Nasty glee twists her face. "And I let you. You know why? Because *that's what you pay me for.*"

Tears spring to my eyes. How can I still have more left to shed for her?

Someone clears his throat. I blink rapidly to clear the tears. The security team I asked for is standing in the doorway. Both men look like they warm up for a workout by crushing skulls—their arms and legs bulging, chests thick underneath the black uniforms. They glare at Bianca.

"What?" she says defiantly, tossing her hair over her shoulder.

"You're a piece of work," one of them mutters.

"This person doesn't work here anymore. Please make sure to confiscate her laptop and phone and escort her out," I say, refusing to look at her.

"You can't take my phone!"

"It's the *company* phone," I tell her. "You have to turn it in the second you're terminated from the company."

"You can't fire me!" she screams.

"I already did." My throat feels raw. "If I speak to Jeremiah, she'll advise me to sue you as well."

That shuts her up. Guess she didn't think that far ahead. "You'll never do that! If you do, I'll tell everyone what a shitty human being you are."

"You mean you'll continue with your past behavior?" I ask, pain ripping up and down my chest. I turn to security. "I think I'll survive. Gentlemen? Please."

"Wait!" she shouts, but the men loop their arms around hers and drag her out. She screams an endless string of cuss words, all directed at me. Everyone on the floor stares. Julio's eyes are so wide, they seem to take up half his face.

"Julio, I'll need you to brief me on the day's agenda, please."

He swallows, then blinks. "Uh. Yeah. Sure. Can you give me, like, a minute?"

"Of course. You'll be taking over all of Bianca's duties, auditing all the tasks she's *supposedly* done and making sure they're completed properly. You can select an assistant to help you. Oh, and you'll be getting a raise, effective immediately."

"Yes, *ma'am*."

I throw myself into my work. I need to figure out how to salvage the collaboration Bianca has damaged, and come up with a way to convince the shareholders to give me another chance at tomorrow's meeting.

AROUND ELEVEN, Julio comes in with a huge bouquet of purple freesia, white lisianthus and roses.

"This came for you." He hands it to me.

"Thank you." A few lavender sprigs add to the gorgeous scent. The tension headache eases, and I can breathe better.

A corner of Julio's lips turns up. "Glad the flowers made you smile."

Did I just smile? I guess I did. "I'm all right, Julio."

"I just... I'm sorry about..." He jerks his thumb in the direction of Bianca's now-empty desk.

"I know." I keep the smile on my face. It isn't his fault that I made a huge mistake with my friendship.

He clears his throat, then leaves.

I pluck the card buried in the large blossoms.

Been thinking about you. Hope you stay strong. Remember, you did nothing wrong.

—Sebastian

I sigh, and a gooey feeling pulses in my heart. This is sweet. I might've screwed up in the friendship department, but maybe I didn't totally mess up in husband selection. Suddenly, I no longer feel so alone.

I pull out my phone.

—Me: Thank you for the flowers and making me smile. I needed that.

—Sebastian: I'm glad. Is it done?

—Me: Yeah.

—Sebastian: Wish I could've been there for moral support.

—Me: I'll settle for a shoulder to lean on tonight.

—Sebastian: My shoulders are yours, anytime. By the way, do you want to go get some lunch?

—Me: Can't.

—Sebastian: Surely you need to eat.

I laugh at him throwing my own words back at me.

—Me: Yes, but there's too much to do. I'm working through lunch to figure out exactly what Bianca's done to the collaboration. Karen—our COO—is having her team go through Bianca's email to see if there are any other projects she's sabotaged.

—Sebastian: Okay. I hope you find out exactly what she's done and destroy her.

I go still. Although I mentioned Jeremiah and a lawsuit, I haven't decided if I should sue Bianca. She doesn't have enough money to pay for the damage she's caused, and she's obviously never going to apologize or be truly sorry for what she's done.

Jeremiah might also advise me to avoid a lawsuit because it'll be an expensive endeavor with very little reward at the end. And to be honest,

I feel the same way. At the same time, I'm still in shock. I might develop a different perspective on the matter.

–Me: Haven't decided yet. The whole thing with Bianca's been such a blow. I'm still sorting through my feelings and what to do.

–Sebastian: If Jeremiah says the lawsuit's going to cost too much, tell her to shove it. I'll make it my wedding gift.

I laugh a little. It's just like him to want to even the scales. But then, that was what he told me to do eleven years ago, and he hasn't changed. The fact that he's consistent is actually kind of soothing. I could use some consistency.

–Me: Most men give jewelry.

–Sebastian: Justice is better. But I'll send you something pretty, too.

–Me: I was just joking! I don't need a bracelet or anything.

–Sebastian: I was thinking about an anklet. It'd look hot on you.

Have I worn one around him before? Oh wait... I did that one time. I'm surprised he remembers.

–Sebastian: Since you have a diamond anklet, I'll send you rubies.

–Me: Bring it home so you can put it on yourself. :wink-emoji: Anyway, I need to get back to work. See you tonight.

The buoyant feeling his flowers and texts have given me dissipates as the day goes on. Bianca's screwups with the Hae Min Group that are documented on email are fairly straightforward to undo. The problem is the damage she's done with phone calls, since we have no way of knowing precisely what was said. So many people's feelings are hurt, and I don't know how to make up for that.

I get an email from Eugene later in the day.

I heard about what happened. It's terrible what your assistant did. However, if you're still committed to this project, I'm willing to renew my commitment as well. I can speak to my people, and they'll cooperate. Ms. Hong will continue to be my main point of contact. She will work directly with you until you find a replacement for Ms. Martin.

I let out a sigh of relief. He's being more than reasonable. Ms. Hong is a great one to liaise with. She's the most senior of the four executive assistants Eugene has. The woman isn't exactly warm, but she's courteous and highly efficient.

Plus, I envy his absolute confidence that a talk from him is all it will take to get his people to perform as he wishes. I've never been able to develop that kind of self-assurance, but then, Bianca's been interfering since forever. For a brief moment, I wonder if I struggled to make friends because of her, too. Her resentment is old, and I doubt she held back when we were in school.

I type up a reply.

Thank you for your kind and very generous response. Please be assured that I am completely committed to the project, and look forward to working together smoothly to ensure its success going forward.

I hit send, then work with Karen to redo the timeline of the project but also to figure out what I'm going to say to the shareholders at tomorrow's meeting.

"Honesty is going to be your best course," Karen says. "Nobody can dispute you got screwed."

"I know." I hold my head between my hands. "But it also makes me look like an idiot for not realizing sooner."

"She was very close to you." Her tone is patient. Kind, even. "Sometimes we're blind to our friends' and family's flaws. We have expectations, hopes and dreams about them, and we only see them the way we'd like them to be."

"But all this time?"

"She's been with you since you were a child. Of course you didn't see it. Blame her for betraying your trust. Actually, the entire company's trust. And remember, no one else suspected anything either."

That's true. "Do you think Grandfather suspected something?" He was never particularly warm to Bianca.

"I doubt it. If he'd suspected she was interfering with the company's goals, he would've fired her on the spot. But what she did to sabotage the projects you spearheaded probably contributed to his reluctance to put you fully in charge of the company."

I straighten, my eyes on hers. "I thought it was because I was a girl." He often lamented that I was too much like my mom. Or that I was too soft.

She shrugs. "I'm a woman, and he appointed me as his COO."

I blink slowly. I never considered that.

"He had some really old-fashioned ideas, but he also loved growing this company. He wasn't going to give up on a talented employee because of gender. Trust me, your performance mattered more. The fiasco with the Milan project three years ago was the last straw."

I wince. That one didn't even get started. "But he kept me on as the CEO. Why?"

"Because you had good instincts and ideas. You had good plans. You just couldn't seem to execute them. He thought I'd be able to assist and get them going. Just remember, it's best to work with people who *aren't* your friends. That way, personal feelings don't get in the way."

36

SEBASTIAN

WHEN I RETURN from my one o'clock meeting, a document with the revised timeline and budget for the collaboration from Luce is waiting in my inbox. I open it to see what she's done. The new timeline is aggressive, but not unreasonable. Besides, why do a project at all if you're going to be lackadaisical about it?

The only thing I don't like about all this is the pain Luce had to suffer. Her tears just about killed me. I've witnessed a lot of women crying. Mom will wail at the drop of a hat, and Grandma likes to shed just enough tears that she can dab at her eyes without ruining her makeup. Some of my ex-girlfriends preferred to make a lot of sound without shedding tears—and some simply liked to scream.

But Luce just sits with her jaw tight, her eyes glazed with pain. The tears fall silently and endlessly. Her breathing is even too. It's like she knows nobody's going to comfort her—she's alone in her grief.

I wish she hadn't cried like that after the confrontation with Bianca. Some people in my office apparently heard about the scene through friends at Peery Diamonds, and Christoph brought me the gossip.

I immediately sent flowers because my showing up to comfort her in person could have undermined her. She needs to look stronger than ever before in front of her people, and that means standing on her own.

When we're alone tonight, I can hold her and give her whatever she needs.

While I plot my revenge.

Luce sounded reluctant to sue the shit out of Bianca. But I'm going to destroy that bitch. I have the standing to sue. Her interference in the collaboration cost Sebastian Jewelry money too. But more importantly, I hate her for hurting Luce. And if a lawsuit turns out to be insufficient, there are other means. There are a million ways to destroy someone.

"By the way, are you attending the shareholders' meeting for Peery Diamonds tomorrow?" Christoph asks.

I check my calendar. "Isn't that next month?"

"Normally, yes, but they changed it this year."

What the hell? "Why?"

"Not sure." He fidgets. "Do you need me to find out?"

"No." Shit. The damn proxy votes!

The initial meeting agenda had something about Luce's performance. Given the colossal clusterfuck with the Sebastian Peery collaboration at the moment, the discussion won't be pro forma. But she deserves a chance to prove herself without Bianca getting in the way. She shouldn't lose what she's worked so hard for—

I stop as an abrupt realization punches me in the heart, sending a shock wave reverberating through my entire body. *I don't want her to get kicked out of the company.*

It doesn't matter that she forced me to marry her. If she told me she didn't need me anymore, I'd refuse to leave her.

Idiot.

The jealousy that spread through me like poison because of that smile she gave Jason...

My uncontrollable spike of libido every time I see her...

The fury that spiraled out of control when Karl backhanded her...

The ragged lacerations each of her tears created in my heart...

The overwhelming need to make everyone who hurt her suffer...

And the profound desire to shield her from the ugly world...

I've been kidding myself. None of that is because she's my wife and I'm feeling what a proper husband should. I care about her.

No. *Care* is too diluted.

I think about my brothers—Emmett, Griffin and Grant. Rational men who became completely *irrational* after meeting their wives.

Holy *shit*. I run a hand over my jaw.

I'm in love with her. Maybe I fell for her the day she strutted into my office like some Nordic warrior princess. I just never wanted to admit it because I had this idea that I wasn't supposed to fall in love with a woman who had scandals attached to her name or who was devious enough to back me into an untenable situation.

But really? I could've walked away. I've never allowed anybody to exert this much control over me, and I didn't have to begin with her.

I pick up my phone and start typing.

—Me: Hey, change of plans. Luce needs to stay as the CEO.

—Noah: What?

—Grant: You're saying this now?

—Me: Obviously, she can't go.

—Nicholas: I knew it! You have feelings for her. But sorry, it's too late. I already sent my votes against her.

What a dick!

—Me: You sent them when you noticed I had feelings for her?

—Nicholas: I noticed at the party, but you said it was a "separate issue."

Crap. I don't have to scroll up to see. I remember what I texted. Somebody invent a time machine, so I can go back in time and kick my own ass!

—Emmett: I already sent mine in, too.

—Me: Okay, so only Emmett and Nicholas sent theirs?

I can salvage this if it's just them. I have enough shares.

—Grant: No. I did too.

I hang my head. Of course they did it together. Grant and Emmett work in the same office.

—Noah: I sent mine too. Didn't want to let you down. Sorry, bro.

—Griffin: Yeah. Sorry.

—Huxley: Same.

—Me: Did anybody forget?

No response. Of course not. My brothers would never forget. I can't even get angry with them because they did what I asked.

—Grant: There might be enough people supporting her. Her family's been in charge for so long. But if that fails, try to appoint an interim CEO who's friendly to her. It can be an extended vacation, so she can recharge and come back even stronger.

—Griffin: Precisely. Think about Steve Jobs. He was ousted from Apple once, but when he came back, he was unstoppable.

—Huxley: It's all about framing and perspective.

Spoken like a true ad executive. On the other hand, they're right. If I can't save her CEO seat, I can at least help her make the best of the situation.

Still, I can't just sit on my ass.

"Christoph, get me a list of every major shareholder at Peery Diamonds. And their contact info. *Now*."

⌖

I CANCEL ALL my meetings and tasks for the day. I look over the list Christoph brings and sort people into three categories—pro-Luce, anti-Luce and unknown.

Christoph and I spend our time calling and texting people in the unknown category. Many don't have any particular feelings for Luce as the CEO one way or the other. Those people generally agree she might deserve another chance when I explain the cause of her difficulties. But there are others who are less tractable.

"A bit unusual, to have a CEO's husband campaign for her," Miles Wellington observes. He's an assistant to Barron Sterling, who is one of the top shareholders. "Not terribly 'corporate.' But sweet in its own way, I suppose."

This isn't good. There's been talk of Barron turning into a bit of a romantic himself in the past several years, but he didn't build his multibillion-dollar empire by mixing personal matters with business. He would think badly of me if I tried to appeal to his new reputation. "I'm not contacting you as her husband, but as a fellow shareholder and a business partner. Sebastian Jewelry and Peery Diamonds are doing a joint venture together, and I'm afraid it won't succeed without her involvement."

"I see." His voice softens a little. "I'll let Mr. Sterling know."

But not everyone's like Miles. Some openly say they agree with what Roderick has told them. "She's too young. It's too bad about her assistant, but if she were more experienced, maybe she would've realized her assistant was suspect."

Fucking Roderick. He makes it sound like he cares about his daughter's wellbeing, but in reality, he just wants her out. Probably just petty revenge—he must be pissed that she cut him off, along with his worthless children. How many in the unknown category secretly side with him? Do I have enough firepower to counter them?

If only I had my brothers' votes... Then Roderick wouldn't matter.

Focus. I can't undo what's already been done. I can only try to mitigate the damage. Christoph and I manage to get through all the unknowns. By the time we're done, it's after eight. I tell him he can take some comp time in the morning. After he's gone, I text my family.

—Me: You will support Luce at tomorrow's shareholder meeting.

—Mom: Why?

—Me: Because I want you to.

—Travis: What's in it for us?

How about I don't choke off all funds so you won't experience what it's like to have to balance your checkbook?

I bite my tongue. That isn't going to get them to act.

—Me: Would you like to be able to control your money again?

—Mom: Really?

—Grandmother: How do we know you're going to keep your promise?

—Me: Sue me. You have the text.

—Travis: I need a contract!

—Me: Offer, consideration and acceptance is sufficiently binding. Ask your lawyer.

—Grandfather: Sebastian's correct, Travis. Is that all you need? Our support for Lucienne Peery tomorrow?

—Me: Not just tomorrow, but as long as she needs.

—Mom: And the trust funds will be back under our control.

Mom's eyes are always on what's most important to her, but that makes her easy to manage.

–Me: Yes. But you won't be able to direct anything to Preston. That I cannot allow.

–Mom: Why do you hate him so much?

–Me: It'll be better for him to learn how the real world works. Otherwise, he'll squander all his money and be left destitute. Remember —you needed me to run Sebastian Jewelry regardless of who owned it. You know Preston doesn't have what it takes, and it's mainly because he was never personally accountable for anything.

I wait a beat. Mom loves Preston, but she loves herself more. She won't hesitate for long when I've provided the perfect excuse.

–Mom: Very well. I accept.

–Grandmother: I suppose it's time Preston grew up.

–Grandfather: He's a smart boy. He'll learn.

Good. But there's still one holdout.

–Me: Travis?

–Travis: Sometimes fathers have to make difficult choices for their children.

I snort. He's just happy he doesn't have to beg me for money. He knows I'm not a fan.

I drive through the brightly lit streets, drumming my fingers on the steering wheel. *Should I tell Luce what I've done, so she can be prepared?* But I can't be sure if she's really going to lose her CEO seat. I ran some simulations. If at least sixty-two percent of the unknowns side with her —or abstain—she can stay as the CEO, especially with me and my Comtois family voting to support her.

But sixty-two percent is a lot. Roderick's already done his work, turning many against her. Just because they didn't overtly say anything doesn't mean they're going to be on her side.

Anxiety winds around my heart like poison ivy. The hold only tightens as I park my car and step inside the huge mansion. The light's on in the living room. It was supposed to be a temporary residence until our marriage ended. But now, it feels like home.

Luce is sitting cross-legged on a couch, reviewing something on her tablet. She looks impossibly young and cute in a white T-shirt and yellow shorts, her feet bare and her hair twisted into a topknot skewered by a pen. In front of her on the coffee table is the purple and white bouquet I sent to her office. She put it in a vase.

"Hey," she says with a smile.

"Hi." I bend and kiss her. I search her face for signs of tears or grief. There's nothing except a smile, but that doesn't mean anything. I've seen her mask before. I wish she would trust me enough to let her shields down.

She might never do that after tomorrow.

No. I did everything I could to fix it. It will go fine. It has to.

"Everything go okay at work?" I ask.

"As okay as could be expected. Bianca's gone." She sighs. "Apparently, I was only being nice to her to make myself feel good."

"That's absurd."

"Everything I did made her feel small, and there's nothing I can do about her feelings. So." A corner of her lips quirks up in a lopsided smile. "Guess that's how things go."

"She never deserved you."

"Thank you. I suppose I'll have to be more careful about who I associate with." She shrugs. "Lesson learned. And better now than later, I guess." She gestures at the tablet. "Anyway, that's why I'm going over the presentation for tomorrow's meeting. I'm going to make my case and ask for another year of their confidence. That's why the new collaboration timeline is so tight. I *have* to have a win for next fiscal year." She looks apologetic. "I hope you're okay with some all-nighters."

I sit next to her, wrap my arm around her shoulders and pull her close to me. I place a kiss on her temple. "Valkyrie, it'll be my honor."

She laughs. "Seriously?"

"For real."

I look down at her, see the glowing light in her blue eyes. They were arctic when I first saw her. I chalked it up to her being cold, but she kept them frozen and still so they'd betray nothing. Now I see so many things glittering underneath—anxiety, relief, grief, regret, apology and gratitude. It's the last one that twists my gut, because I'm not worthy of it.

37

LUCIENNE

I ROLL my shoulders as I make my way to the company auditorium. Shareholder meetings are always nerve-racking. Although I'm the CEO, the shareholders are the owners. They've always been a difficult bunch to deal with. Even Grandfather struggled from time to time.

I'm in my absolute best outfit—a conservative black Dior and nude stilettos. Sapphires and diamonds on my ears, neck and wrist. My hair's up in a French twist, and I maintain my most confident posture—shoulders back, spine straight, feet even and chin up.

Grandfather always said a Peery does not bow his—or her—head.

I've gone over my remarks twenty times with Karen's assistance. Sebastian listened to it after he came home and helped me tweak it some more. I've never been more ready.

Still, when I'm in front of everyone, my legs grow nerveless. My suitability as CEO is the last item on the agenda, immediately after welcoming Sebastian as a new member of the board, so my nerves are stretched taut.

I lock my knees and paste a neutral friendliness on my face. Thankfully, I say all the right words confidently, without a single stumble. From the approving smile on Sebastian's face, I know I'm doing well.

A short Q&A later, I'm back in my seat. I look down at my phone.

–Sebastian: Amazing job!

–Karen: You did well.

I smile with relief. If they're saying this, I didn't just do the best that I could. I objectively did well, on par with other executives.

I maintain my calm. It's going to be fine. The talk about my suitability started to become more serious in the last few weeks because I kicked Roderick out of the company, and he's stirred it up to fever pitch because he has to make a case in order to continue leeching off Peery Diamonds. He's probably dying to come back as a "consultant." He needs money more than ever before, and I wouldn't be shocked to find some backdoor dealings between him and Darren. Or even somebody on our BOD.

But as the board and everyone present have their discussions and the votes are tallied, the numbers are very, very tight. How can Roderick have so many behind him?

Karen whispers something to Darren, and he looks at me with a smirk. My stomach tight, I ignore him and look at Sebastian. He's tapping away on his phone with a frown. Maybe he hasn't seen the tally yet. Some emergency could've happened at Sebastian Jewelry.

Or maybe he knows the final tally will come out in my favor. I don't need a convincing victory. Just enough to hang in there so I can prove myself.

My fingers grow cold, my palms clammy. I clench my hands together, then realize what I'm doing and force myself to hold them loosely on my lap.

But my composure is crumbling inside as the seconds tick by. My gut says something's not right. It's the weird charge in the atmosphere, like the eerie silence before a terrible storm hits.

The announcement is made:

I'm out.

By less than one percent of the vote.

The number doesn't change after a recount.

I sit, dazed and trying to process. Just because I'm a Peery doesn't mean I'm guaranteed a leadership position, but...this...

This will be the first time somebody other than a Peery will be the

CEO. Shivers run through me, and I realize I'm cold. I doubt I'll continue to sit on the board. They appoint Karen as the interim CEO.

That's good, at least, I think numbly. She's a great executive. Peery Diamonds is in good hands. I should be relieved, I tell myself through the emotional fog.

Darren shoots me a quick, condescending grin. "Ah well." He walks past me. He knows it would make him look like a dick to rub it in. He'll want to do that in private.

"I'm sorry," Karen says somberly.

I manage to thank her and stand shakily, looking for Sebastian. He's talking with some of the board members. Roderick approaches him with a broad grin. Sebastian's expression darkens. He tilts his head as though he can sense me watching him.

I start toward him.

"We couldn't have done it without your brothers' help." Roderick is exuberant.

"Shut up," Sebastian responds.

Roderick is too drunk with victory to listen. "I knew they'd vote wisely."

I look at Sebastian. Guilt flashes across his face.

And I know.

He has six brothers. All wealthy, all capable of grabbing enough shares to challenge my leadership. He made it clear that he hated my maneuvering to get him to marry me. Obviously, this was his way of balancing those scales he so loves to even.

But if that's what he wanted, why did he have to be kind? Why did he have to make me think he cared? Why did he have to make me want more?

I look at the broad shoulders I laid my head on. The gorgeous eyes that shone when he looked at me. The beautiful mouth that kissed me like I was everything he ever dreamed of.

Of all the betrayals of my life, his is the hatchet that cleaves my soul. The pain robs my lungs of air, my mind of words.

I glance down at myself. I'm not bleeding. I don't know how I can look fine, my clothes perfect, my posture erect, when the most unbearable agony is tearing at me. If my physical self could reflect what's happening inside, I'd be lying, burnt and flayed, on a bed of razor blades.

I look around. The ambient chatter grows muffled. Faces blur. Nobody seems horrified. Nobody is shocked. I should be grateful the damage is invisible to their eyes.

People will never discover the devastation Sebastian has wrought. No archeologist will unearth it a century from now. And I can pretend I'm untouched by it all. I still hold a great deal of shares. And I have money of my own, independent of Peery Diamonds.

I'll be fine. I have to be fine.

But I feel something draining from me, like sand flowing out of a broken hourglass. I can't remember why I struggled so hard, why I even bothered to come to this meeting.

The lights above hit my Toi et Moi ring and fracture into gorgeous slivers all the colors of creation. Why did I marry Sebastian again?

Suddenly, everything feels like too much. It's all I can do to remain upright.

Someone starts moving toward me—Sebastian, maybe. But some people get in the way. They're saying something to him.

I turn around. I have no feeling in my limbs, but they move, allow me to leave without stumbling. The auditorium is freezing, but the hall is even colder. I walk right past everyone, my strides growing longer and longer.

I rush out of the lobby. The bright blade of the sun slices into my eyes.

"Ma'am," comes James's voice. He touches my hand. "You're freezing."

"No, you're feverish," I say numbly, then climb into the car.

"Let's turn the heater on," he says.

"Don't." I don't want to be thawed.

38

SEBASTIAN

FUCKING RODERICK.

We couldn't have done it without your brothers' help.

The bastard is so loud, Luce hears it. The light in her eyes dies and the smile goes frozen, then slowly vanishes. A deathly pallor leaches all color from her, and she glances down, then around, like she's lost in the dark. Her eyes slide right past me, and remain unfocused as she stiffly turns away.

Roderick's spewing more bullshit. I shove him out of the way. More people stop me to say something, but I ignore them.

"Luce!" I call out.

She doesn't hear me. Or maybe she does, and doesn't want to deal with me. She exits the auditorium, her phone clenched in her hand. She doesn't stop to take her purse. I double back to grab it from her seat and then push my way through the shareholders to go after her, but she's in her Cullinan already.

Fuck.

I rush to my car and drive home. I have to talk to her. Make her understand.

So many words swirl in my head, but none of them feel adequate. Will anything make an impact?

By the time I pull into the driveway, James is about to get into the Cullinan.

He stops. "There you are. Now I don't feel so bad about leaving her home alone."

"What happened?" I ask, panic skittering down my spine.

"She's not feeling well. You might want to get her something."

"Where's Matthias?"

"I believe he has a doctor's appointment this afternoon, but he should be back shortly."

I nod an acknowledgment and step inside. It's as silent as a tomb, the air cool. The only sound is the pounding of my heart.

Luce is sitting on an off-white leather bench. Her hands are curled around the edge of the seat and her shoulders are stooped. It's as though the world has finally crushed her.

But I know better. It wasn't the world. It was me.

Her face is colorless, but dry. I thought it was the worst when she cried silently, but I was wrong. It's worse when she can't even muster tears. The warriorlike mask she puts on to face the world has fractured, the shield and armor gone. A glimpse of unbearable agony flashes between the cracks. It's like she's in such pain she can't even cry.

"Luce," I say softly.

"Congratulations."

Her tone is flat and inflectionless. It's more damning than her screaming. Fear leaves a sharp tang in my drying mouth.

She keeps her gaze on the floor. "You got exactly what you wanted."

I move so we can talk face to face and crouch in front of her. "I *didn't* want this for you." I reach out and lay my hands over hers. They're icy. I squeeze, trying to warm them. Cling to hope because she doesn't pull away.

Something bright flares in her eyes as she looks at me. "Your brothers *didn't* vote against me?"

I'd give anything to be able to say no, but I can't lie. And my hesitation is response enough. The light dims. She removes her hands from mine and lays them in her lap. "I see."

The pain of having her withdraw slips into my heart like a knife. I had no idea how much it would hurt to be shut out. "In the beginning,

I planned this because I was angry with you. But then later, I thought maybe you should step down from your position and learn the business as a junior executive or something because I thought the difficulties you've had were due to your lack of experience. A lot of your projects failed because of miscommunication and minor mismanagements."

"I understand why you didn't tell me you wanted to kick me out at first. But why didn't you talk to me about your concerns over my experience later, after we got closer?" she asks quietly, her eyes glassy.

"It's my fault. I should've said something sooner." I should've done everything in my power to ensure I wasn't the cause of her pain.

Two unbearable heartbeats. "Did you want me to succeed when you listened to my presentation for today and tried to help tweak it?"

"I did—"

"But evening the scales mattered more."

Her words are like acid pumping in my veins. "I tried to talk to my brothers and stop it, but it was too late. They had already sent in their votes."

"Okay."

Her response is entirely too calm. But the suffering I've seen is still twirling underneath the surface. I don't know how to begin to console her when she's so remote.

I want to ask if there's a way I can make it up to her. Or if that "okay" was the okay women use when they really want to say, "Go fuck yourself." But I can't. I'm terrified she's going to cut me out of her life.

"I'd like you to leave now," she says.

"What?"

"This is my home. I don't want you here." Her tone says, *You understand that, don't you?*

"But we're married," I say, desperation surging. "You said you wanted us to look like a real couple. How will it look if I leave?"

"Like we aren't doing well. But I don't think we can continue to pretend after what happened today."

Grief and shattered dreams lurk in her eyes. The glowing confidence and swagger that shielded her lie at her feet in pieces. All her affection for me has turned to ashes, lodged in my throat and choking me.

She isn't crying because she's too much in pain. She isn't crying because she believes she's truly alone.

"Can I have the ring back?" She tilts her chin at my left hand.

Instinctively, I pull my arm back. It feels too final to give up our wedding band.

Her expression grows even more distant. "Fine. Whatever. Keep it. I don't know why I'm acting like it ever meant anything."

"We both need some time to recover, Luce."

"No, Sebastian. I just need you gone."

I COULDN'T EVEN ARGUE my case to her. Nothing I said would penetrate. I've squandered all my credit. I'm a deadbeat, unwanted garbage in her world.

Although her resolute expression makes it clear she wants me to move out permanently, I don't take my things. If I leave my stuff, I can drop by later to get it. I can figure out some way to make it up to her.

I go to the Aylster Residence. It's always been a hotel, but it couldn't have felt more transient. It's nicely appointed, but sterile.

It has everything but Luce.

My phone pings. I whip it out, praying it's my wife—

—Nicholas: I heard about what happened. Are you okay?

I close my eyes for a moment. Of course it isn't Luce.

—Me: She knows everything.

—Emmett: Define "everything."

—Me: She knows I wanted to take the company from her, and I asked you to vote against her.

—Grant: Ouch. But didn't you vote in support of her?

—Me: Of course.

Maybe I should bring that up next time I see her...?

—Noah: I doubt that's going to matter. Women only remember the results.

Shit. He's probably right.

—Me: We tried to make the best case we could to the shareholders who came.

—Huxley: But I'm not sure if I can really blame them. She wasn't the best CEO.

—Me: There was a reason for that.

I text a brief summary of what Bianca did to her.

—Griffin: And you let her live? What's happened to you?

—Nicholas: Did Lucie let the board and the shareholders know?

—Me: Yes, but not all of them seemed to buy it. Or at least, some seemed to think it wasn't as serious as it sounded.

—Huxley: Did you sue her?

—Me: Not yet. But her time is coming.

Dealing with her backstabbing friend was the last thing on my mind when Luce was hurting and trying to regroup from Bianca's betrayal, especially with the shareholders' meeting to manage.

—Grant: There's your mistake. Her time should be NOW.

—Huxley: If you don't sue her, of course people are going to assume it wasn't that big of a deal. They probably think Lucie is throwing her best friend under the bus to save her own ass.

What...?

—Grant: Just imagine, if somebody did this to you, would you let it go?

—Me: Never.

—Emmett: Exactly.

Ah, *shit.* I should've thought of it from that angle.

—Nicholas: Sue the bitch. She hurt your woman, and she shouldn't get away with it.

My brothers are right. Bianca needs to be punished—publicly—in order for Luce to have a chance at getting her job back. It may not earn me Luce's forgiveness, but I'm going to do it anyway. If she's going to hate me, she can do it while she has what she wants the most.

And I'm going to clean up Peery Diamonds. Get rid of Roderick and everyone who sided with him, so that when Luce comes back, the house is in tiptop shape. A sleazy creep like Roderick will have a lot of dirt. It shouldn't be that difficult to destroy him and his associates. I text Christoph with instructions.

A couple of hours later, the concierge notifies me that six boxes have been delivered. They're from Luce. She sent my things back.

My hands shake as the bellhop brings them up. This feels so final. Permanently rejected. Like the wedding band she said she didn't want back because it didn't mean anything.

I rip open the boxes, hoping she included something that isn't mine by mistake, so I can take it back to her. But, box after box, everything's mine.

Finally I get to the last box and pull out a coat from the bottom. I stare at it for a moment. It's a winter coat, warm enough for snowy weather. I don't keep clothes like this in L.A. But it isn't hers, either. The cut indicates it's a man's.

But whose?

Even now, jealousy flares—which is ridiculous. I can't even look at another man's coat without feeling like I want to punch something, and I thought I'd be fine taking revenge against her.

What an idiot I've been.

I feel through the pockets for a clue as to whom it belongs. My fingers brush something crinkly. I pull out an old receipt and smooth it flat and take a look—

Is that my signature? The date's from eleven years ago...

This is the credit card slip for a dinner I had in December in Paris. I cast my mind back. *The American girl I met there—Miss Hot Chocolate.*

The world seems to stop turning for a moment. *That was Luce?*

She was sad and lost, and I told her to fight. To even the scales. She must've taken that advice to heart. And she fought hard and valiantly. Did everything to defend her kingdom.

And then I destroyed all her effort. Left her kingdom in ruins.

No.

Without thinking, I run out of the residence and have the valet bring out my Phantom. When the car stops at the curb, I pause before climbing inside. What am I going to do when I get to her place? Beg her to take me back? Throw my things back inside the house?

I haven't done anything to earn her forgiveness. She's never going to trust anything I say after what's happened.

So many men have failed her. Her grandfather, who didn't have faith in her because she's a girl. Her father, who was unfaithful to her mother and undermined her. Fiancés who cheated on her and thought nothing of it. I'm sure they all had something pretty to say to justify what they've done. People like that always do.

I don't want to be the latest in a long string of losers who betrayed her and tried to excuse their behavior with empty words. I have to *prove* myself, and that requires concrete action. Action that doesn't include me showing up at her doorstep to make a verbal nuisance of myself.

"Never mind," I say, tossing the fob back to the valet.

The valet, a tatted-up headbanger with dreadlocks, looks at me. "You sure?"

"Yeah." I hand him a hundred. "Sorry for the inconvenience."

His face splits into a grin. "Yo, bro, inconvenience me all day long."

I watch the valet take the Phantom back. Next time I see Luce...

It'll be *after* I've made myself worthy of her time.

39

LUCIENNE

THE HOUSE IS IMMERSED in silence without Sebastian. Matthias sent his things as well, so now my place is my own again.

So why doesn't it feel like home anymore?

I go to the kitchen. Look at the gleaming counter. The sparkling espresso and coffee machine. The spotless fridge. I can smell fresh coffee, the mouth-watering aroma of muffins and bagels being toasted.

Why am I smelling these things?

Then I realize—they're what Sebastian used to have when he was living here.

The spot behind my breastbone flares with pain, like somebody's scraping it with an ice pick.

Matthias pauses in prepping dinner. "Is there something I can—?"

"No. I'm fine."

I move away from the kitchen island. My thighs tremble at the memory of the wild, raw sex we had there. The first time he came inside me without a rubber. How he went out to grab Plan B afterward, so I wouldn't have to. We both lost our heads, and he didn't want me to have a baby neither of us was ready for.

My strides grow longer and faster. The staircase...and the hall—his room on the other side, my room on the opposite end. I refuse to go to his bedroom, and head into mine instead. Matthias must've changed the sheets, but I swear I can still smell Sebastian on the bed, his body wash in the shower.

A black razor sits on a shelf in the stall. It isn't mine—Matthias must have overlooked it. I throw it in the trash. But my nerves remain singed. I ball up a bunch of toilet paper and dump it on top of the razor so I can't see it.

But it doesn't matter. A phantom warmth brushes over the cheek that Karl backhanded. Sebastian held me and made sure I was okay. Pressed a careful, featherlight kiss on the throbbing spot, like he could take away the pain. I grip the edge of the vanity in the bathroom and stare at my reflection. I can see him brushing his lips on my temple, wrapping his strong arm around my shoulders, silently communicating that he's got my back.

I shiver at the memories of an affection and love that weren't real. Tears prickle my eyes. It's unfair that this haunts me when I know the truth.

How could he have acted like he cared? Why did he touch me like I mattered to him?

Why, oh why, did he come after me once he'd gotten what he wanted? Why did he crouch down and look up at me, his whole body tense, imploring me for a chance?

Doesn't he know that some betrayals can't be righted? That some lines, once crossed, can never be retreated from?

Sometimes there can't be another chance.

I see my phone plugged into the charger by the bed. Must've been Matthias's doing. I don't remember bringing it from the office.

I have to put a stop to the awful memories. There's simply no living like this.

I pick up the phone and text Jeremiah.

–Me: Can you file for divorce?

Several moments pass. It suddenly hits me that she might veto the idea because the relocation of our headquarters hasn't been fully completed yet.

But I have to do this. For my own sanity.

—Jeremiah: Yes. Perfect timing, too. Congratulations. Now Peery Diamonds is officially an American company. It has no ties to Nesovia.

I gasp, my hand over my face. *I did it.* Elation sweeps through me, followed by swift bitterness. How ironic that what I did to be free of that godawful country led me to getting kicked out of management and having my heart trampled in the process.

I shake my head. I shouldn't be negative about this. It's a huge milestone. I lost my CEO position, and my heart throbs mercilessly, but I should be proud of what I've accomplished. Hopefully my action showed those suited Neanderthals that they need to treat their women better if they want to keep talent and businesses in their country.

—Me: Thank you.

—Jeremiah: My pleasure. As for the divorce, it'll take a while, but we'll have everything going smoothly. I presume we're going to abide by the contract you signed with the Comtois family?

—Me: Yes.

—Jeremiah: Got it. Although it's too bad I can't flex my legal muscles to get you more.

I almost smile at that. Maybe if I hated Sebastian, I'd ask her to go for the jugular. But I don't hate him. I'm not even bitter.

I'm disappointed and heartbroken. The ache that's been plaguing me might never ease.

But it isn't the first time that someone close has hurt me. I just have to keep my chin up and continue with my life.

40

SEBASTIAN

CHRISTOPH'S VOICE comes from the intercom. "Sebastian, somebody is here to see you. A Yuna Winters? She doesn't have an appointment, though."

She must be here for my wife. "Send her in."

"Okay. But you have a meeting in ten."

"Reschedule it." This is more important.

Yuna walks in. She's of average height, but her presence is anything but average. She walks with an overweening confidence, like she expects people to fall to their knees and welcome her wherever she goes. Her dress is made of scarlet silk and flares out dramatically around her legs. She's slim, and a small Birkin bag hangs off her pale wrist. A wide-brimmed hat sits on her head, and she looks at me straight, her haughty eyes slightly narrowed, her mouth flat and disapproving.

She doesn't wait for an invitation before sitting and crossing her legs. She steeples hands that have exceptionally long fingers. Interestingly, the nails are trimmed short, and only a diamond ring and a wedding band adorn her fingers, although her ears and throat are practically dripping with gems.

Seconds tick by as she studies me. I meet her gaze directly. I don't know exactly why she's here, but I assume it has something to do with the Sebastian Peery collaboration and the lack of progress. The dossier on the Hae Min Group indicates Yuna has an enormous influence within the conglomerate. How difficult is she going to be?

"Is it true you were instrumental in removing Lucie from Peery Diamonds?" she finally asks.

A little warmth uncurls in my belly at the realization she's here for Luce. "Yes."

Her face turns redder than her dress. Her hands tighten into fists. "You...jerk!" She adds something under her breath in Korean. From her tone, it's nothing flattering.

"I'm planning to rectify that." I don't want her working against me. We're on the same team.

She regards me for a long moment. "How?" The syllable brims with skepticism.

"I have plans." And I *will* execute them all in rapid succession.

"Plans." More skepticism.

"Yes. I ousted her. I can bring her back."

"I'm supposed to just take your word for it and wait like an obedient puppy?" She glares at me. "I'm going to have a chat with my father. Hae Min will not deal with a replacement. We want Lucie. And *you*"—she points at me—"can consider yourself persona non grata until you fix the mess you've made."

"It won't take long."

"It better not. A woman who doesn't lose her temper with a child ruining a one-of-a-kind dress and soothes him with ice cream is a lot nicer than anybody says. I hope you didn't hurt her because of some silly tabloid gossip?" The glare is now a death laser.

If I answer *yes*, it won't matter that I'm at least a head taller and outweigh her by a hundred pounds of muscle. She'll murder me with her bare hands. "Of course not."

"Good. Otherwise you'll never be worthy of her."

That drags a reluctant smile out of me.

Her eyes flash. "You think this is funny?"

"No. I'm just happy that you're here to defend her."

"Of course I'm here to defend her! I like her. She's a friend. She's just...so sweet." Her expression says, *How could you hurt somebody that lovely?*

"I know. And it's good that she has a new friend." I have a feeling Yuna isn't the type to get insulted over a gift or thoughtful gesture. "And I swear to you, I'm going to fix everything, no matter what it takes. We're on the same page, Yuna. And the same team."

She gives me a long, assessing look. "Fine. I'll give you this one chance." She stands up. "And if you actually manage to fix what you've broken, I'll consider forgiving you."

"Forgiving me?" I repeat half in confusion, half in amusement.

Her tone turns dry, like she's talking to somebody who's too intellectually challenged to know better. "Obviously things can't be the same when you hurt someone I regard as a friend, can they? You'll have a lot of convincing to do."

41

LUCIENNE

THE NEW HOUSE is much better. It's in Malibu, so I get the beach. And the place is gated, so I get my privacy.

But most importantly, this place isn't haunted with memories of Sebastian. Sometimes I think of him—my head is slow to update my marital and relationship status. But every time something triggers me to remember him, I meditate or do yoga. Or just wrap a blanket around myself and go to sleep.

I can't remember how to undo the Google Alert, so I've turned off my phone. It was weird to be unplugged at first, but now that it's been a few weeks, I enjoy the peace. Besides, who's going to text me? I have no friends or family. I don't even have a job. And Jeremiah has Matthias's number. She can get in touch with him if she wants to talk to me.

I lie on the yoga mat and stare at the ceiling. When was the last time I had absolutely nothing to do? I worked through all my vacations for years, always checking emails and texts.

Somewhere in the back of my mind is the thought that this kind of lazy, purposeless lifestyle isn't like me, but I push it aside. People are entitled to relax after life deals them a horrible defeat. When it lands three powerful punches back to back, it's a sign you should stay down until you figure out what you want to do.

Somebody pounds at the door. I can hear Matthias going to the foyer. Loud voices, both of them familiar. I tense and sit up.

Bianca pushes past Matthias and rushes in. She looks nothing like the confident best friend I used to have—or the arrogantly defiant traitor who slung insults at me. Her hair is frizzy and wild—when was the last time it saw a brush?—and her eyes are wide. Her lipstick is smeared, and her silver dress is wrinkled. Her yellow sandals clash with the dress.

"You have to stop him!" she shouts.

Matthias tries to catch her arm and drag her out. But she eludes him.

"It's okay, Matthias," I say, not wanting him to get injured trying to remove her. She won't care who she hurts as long as she gets what she wants.

"He's gonna sue!" she shrieks.

I stare blankly. "Who?"

"Sebastian! He's suing me!"

"Oh." Still seated on the mat, I rest an elbow on my knee and prop my chin in my hand.

"Oh? *Oh?*" Her breathing roughens. "Is that all you're going to say?"

"What do you want me to say?" I ask in genuine confusion.

"You're supposed to be my friend!"

"You threw our friendship away, Bianca." It's so strange I'm not experiencing any strong feelings that would bring tears to my eyes at the sight of her. It's like I'm looking at a lump of cancerous cells that were excised.

"Fine. Then make him stop. Do it as your final act as my friend."

I just look at her. Does she honestly expect me to lift a finger for her after she backstabbed me?

She must be reading my thoughts. After all, we were together for a long time. "You have everything! This is the least you can do!

"I owe you nothing, Bianca. Leave before I join Sebastian in the suit."

"I can't! Nobody will hire me after this."

"Call Roderick." He's been looking for a new young assistant since he broke up with Gwen. Bianca meets his requirements.

"He's getting prosecuted! He'll be in jail by the time this is over!"

Prosecuted? "For what?"

"What the *fuck*?" She's so loud, it's making my ears hurt. "Check your fucking phone once in a while!"

"Mathias?" I say. "Could you please call 911?"

"Certainly." The answer comes with cheerful alacrity.

Tears spring to her red-rimmed eyes. "This just hurts," she chokes out. "Bitch! I was right to be wary! You're miserable—like always—and you want everyone else to be miserable, too! You *suck!*" She spins around and stalks out, her heels pounding into the marble. Not sure why she's doing that, because she's only going to hurt her feet and ruin her shoes. Those sandals weren't designed to cushion her feet.

After the door's closed behind her, I slowly get up and stretch my arms over my head. I guess I should see what's going on if Bianca's freaking out like this. I still can't believe Sebastian is suing her. For what? For being a shitty friend to his soon-to-be-ex-wife? That's not a crime.

I pad to the table where I left my phone. The second I turn it on, a bazillion messages pop up. Almost all of them are from Bianca and Roderick, with several from Darren.

I skim them to get the gist of the information. Sebastian is suing Bianca for negligence, malice, malfeasance, embezzlement and unjust enrichment, among other things. He says she's hurt the Sebastian Peery collaboration, which cost Sebastian Jewelry *incalculable* damages, submitted false expense reports regarding the project and so on. I almost laugh at the overdramatic language his lawyer used. Karen and I already priced it out. It isn't *incalculable*. And if such a miserly sum could put Sebastian Jewelry under, I wouldn't have wanted to partner with them.

Roderick is in a more serious situation, though. The audit team I had Julio hire finally completed its work. They found over seven hundred irregularities. When they couldn't reach me, they reached out to Sebastian, who obviously took matters into his own hands. He's having the federal prosecutor go after Roderick. Sebastian wants Roderick in jail.

Darren... He's been fired and arrested for embezzlement. Also getting prosecuted. He sent me over one hundred texts. The latest one reads: *Please! You have to save me from your crazy husband! For the sake of our old memories!*

He shouldn't have added that last part. The only old memory I can really recall is him pounding into Frankie.

I let out a long sigh. What's Sebastian trying to accomplish? Does he think punishing people who screwed me over is what I want?

How does he plan to punish himself on my behalf? Is he going to sue himself? Lock himself in a jail cell?

There are a few texts from Roman Wellendorff, the deputy minister of finance from Nesovia.

—Roman Wellendorff: I don't understand why the hasty corporate move was necessary.

—Roman Wellendorff: I thought we had an understanding.

In whose mind? The condescending and sexist "For your own good. Women are to be protected and taken care of" voicemail he sent me wasn't an understanding.

I block him. He's in the past. I don't want to deal with him or anybody like him anymore.

Then I finally notice a few texts from Sebastian. My heart skips a few beats.

—Sebastian: I hope you're doing better. I'd like to talk whenever you're ready.

—Sebastian: I want to make things right for you.

Chest tight with something between pain and disillusionment, I tap the edge of the phone. I don't see the purpose of another talk. On the other hand, he apparently won't stop siccing prosecutors on people until I do. I don't know what else he could mean by "make things right" for me.

Maybe he just needs better closure. His talking while I was in a total state of shock probably wasn't sufficient, even if I said everything that needed to be said. I don't want anyone else disrupting my peace because he won't quit going after people in my past.

—Me: Meet me at Z tonight at 11.

His response is immediate.

—Sebastian: See you tonight. VIP lounge.

42

LUCIENNE

Z WAS THE LEAST ROMANTIC, most impersonal place I could think of when I texted Sebastian. It's one of the most popular clubs in the city.

The air inside always throbs with pounding music. Expensive liquor flows freely. Drugs not as much, because the owner doesn't tolerate people doing stupid things at his establishment.

But tonight, the speakers are silent, the bars and the dance floor dark. I almost stop and turn back, wondering if the club is closed and the bouncer let me in by mistake. I pull out my phone to see if there's a message from Sebastian, but before I can check, a tall man in a black suit and shirt walks over. "Are you here for Sebastian Lasker?"

"Yes," I say.

"This way." He leads me to the upper level and down a darkish corridor, where the VIP lounges are. He takes me to the one in the middle and opens the door with a flourish.

Sebastian is inside with a half-full whiskey glass.

My heart picks up speed with a hint of apprehension that this might not unfold the way I envisioned. He must've rented out the entire club for the night. I don't know how he managed to pull that off, but it's not entirely surprising. He's thorough and exacting about what he wants.

My keeping him at arm's length must've conflicted with his desires, even if he agreed to the impersonal venue.

I turn to the man in black. "Can I get a dirty martini, please?"

"Of course." He disappears back into the shadowed corridor.

I walk inside and sit on the couch opposite Sebastian, then study him in the dim light. He's in a white dress shirt, no tie, and dark slacks. His jaw line seems sharper, his cheekbones more prominent. Are there circles under his eyes? It's hard to tell.

He takes the moment to scrutinize me too. His eyes roam over my long, curled hair, my face, then down my body in its off-shoulder teal dress and golden heels. When his eyes stop at the diamond anklet on my left ankle, I go still as a mixture of dismay and annoyance cuts through me.

I dressed for him. The outfit, the shoes, the anklet... I was thinking of him, hoping he would regret betraying me.

It was foolish to think I was over him. I'm nowhere near over him. But that doesn't mean I'm willing to pretend he didn't hurt me and go back to the way we were before the shareholders' meeting.

When my drink arrives, I down it quickly, then eat the olive from the bottom of the glass. His face twists with something that vaguely looks like pain. What did I do? I follow his gaze and see that he's realized my ring finger is barren.

But why should I wear those rings? They're meaningless.

"You look good," he says finally.

"I've been resting." My response is stiff. Awkward.

"Good."

"I've had a lot of free time recently." Catty.

He shuts up.

Pain pulses through my heart. I don't want to be here. I don't want to rehash how we've wronged each other. All I want to do is close the awful chapter in my life and move on. Take stock of what I do have and try to muster some gratitude. "What are you doing, Sebastian? Bianca nearly broke into my place to confront me about your lawsuit."

His eyes darken ominously. "She's supposed to call Highsmith if she has a problem with me."

"Like John's going to tolerate her behavior?" He's a notorious dick in court, and old-fashioned about manners outside of it. He would never put up with her shrieking or temper tantrums.

Sebastian's jaw tightens. "She should've thought of all that before backstabbing you."

"You're going after Roderick and Darren too. Is this your apology?"

He nods and takes a healthy swallow of whiskey.

"Are you going to sue yourself, too?" *How far does he plan to go?*

He chokes, then laughs dryly. "Obviously not. But I want to do what I can to clean up Peery Diamonds."

"The company does not concern you."

"Doesn't it?" He sips his whiskey. "It's my partner for the Sebastian Peery launch in Korea. I don't want anyone who can undermine you there."

"I'm not *there*," I point out. "Thanks to you."

He closes his eyes briefly. "Believe me, I'm fully aware of that. But things will change soon. I'm going to bring you back. Peery Diamonds is your kingdom."

"Is that all?" I ask, trying to wrap up the conversation so I can leave. Seeing him is re-damaging the wall around my heart, whose cracks I've done my best to seal.

"No. I want to call in the favor you promised after I agreed to the post-wedding reception," he says.

"But you refused my offer."

"And you didn't accept my refusal. So I have a right to collect."

I don't know what he's going for. He swirls the ice in his glass, and the wedding band on his finger twinkles dully under the light. "If you're trying to fight the divorce—"

"I'm not. I'll sign whatever papers you want."

I should be glad he's going to cooperate. But I'm inexplicably sad. *Do I secretly want him to fight the dissolution of our marriage?*

Maybe I do. I want to see that I wasn't alone in my feelings, although his maneuvers against me clearly proved he felt nothing for me. "If you want to pretend you didn't hurt me—"

"I just want a little bit of your time," he says.

"I don't have any time to spare, not for you."

He smiles. "You need to eat."

"Stop throwing my words back at me!" It's an effort to contain rising frustration.

"It's difficult when the words were so wise. And I'm only asking for three dates."

I open my mouth to say no. What will three dates prove? That I haven't gotten over him? That he's trying hard to make up for what happened so he can assuage his guilty conscience?

Then I notice the tight set of his shoulders. The white knuckles around his glass. Under the smile is a hint of strain, the desperate intensity in his gaze. He looks at me like the fate of the universe is riding on my answer.

And the *no* gets stuck in my throat.

"Fine." My response is curt and ungracious.

However, the tension in his shoulders and hands eases. His smile becomes more relaxed. "Thanks. You won't regret it."

"Oh, I don't plan to spend any more time on regret. And what are three dinners? I do need to eat. I might as well make you feed me something expensive."

43

LUCIENNE

A WEEK LATER, Sebastian sends a car for our first date. He hasn't told me where we're going, and when I pressed him for a dress code, he said to wear whatever I wanted.

I try on four different outfits before the limo's arrival, finally settling on a blue asymmetrical dress that brings out my eyes. Then I put my hair in a topknot and secure it with a topaz pin. Aquamarine drop earrings on my earlobes and a silver-and-larimar necklace around my throat. Casual enough, I tell myself as nerves flutter in my belly.

I stare at my reflection in the mirror by the foyer. My cheeks are overly flushed, and there's a sparkle in my eyes.

It's a familiar expression—the girls in high school wore it when they finally scored a date with a major crush.

I turn away in embarrassment. *Sebastian Lasker is not a crush.* Not anymore. He's just...

This is actually our first real *date.* I had to arrange the "date" we had before the wedding and send him flowers to bring so everything would look proper to the world.

At five sharp, a white limo pulls up. A chauffeur in a snowy uniform comes out and opens the door for me.

I murmur my thanks and climb inside, then freeze at the sight of Sebastian. "I thought you were sending me a car."

"And I did. With me in it. A combo deal." He smiles. "You look gorgeous."

"You don't look too bad yourself." That's such an understatement. He's hot as hell in his black bespoke suit.

He laughs softly, like he knows I'm full of it.

He smells of fresh soap, and I realize he showered and re-groomed himself before coming over. Were we both nervous about this "date"? "So. Where are we going?"

"You'll see," he says mysteriously.

At least I'm not overdressed. The only jewelry on him is the wedding band.

"You don't have to wear that ring anymore," I tell him.

"I know, but I want to." His voice is soft, but firm.

"It won't change my mind."

"I'm not wearing it for you. I'm wearing it for me, so everyone knows I'm taken."

When he says things like that, my heart reacts badly. Irrationally. Dangerously. *I can't afford to be foolish.* "Sebastian—"

"You didn't want it back, so it's mine to do with as I wish."

I say nothing. He's so, so stubborn.

"By the way, I saw the coat you sent me."

It was an impulse that made me put it into the things I sent to the Aylster. I regretted giving it back for a moment, since it was doubtful he remembered the frozen ice block of a girl.

"It's amazing that you kept it for so long," he says. "I never thought I'd see Miss Hot Chocolate again."

The memory of the hot chocolate surfaces—how soothing it was to hold something warm and take comfort from a stranger who showed more kindness than my own family. Something cold and hard in my heart shivers, giving a little, like a glacier shifting under a relentless sun. "You remember."

"Of course."

I smile a little. "You made an impression. Mr. Cashmere Coat. You were the only one who actually listened. Mom was busy feeling loved by

Roderick. He was busy playing the loving partner to Mom and carrying on an affair with his assistant. Grandfather was too important and disapproving to encourage me to speak. If I hadn't met you in Paris, I might've run away for real."

"I wish I'd recognized you when we met in my office. I thought about you—how you'd turned out."

"Well, what do you think?" I spread my arms, trying to keep our conversation as light and meaningless as possible.

He looks at me with an odd pride. "I could not have imagined better."

My heart misses a beat. *What am I doing?* I raise my shield higher, refusing to let him affect me again.

The limo stops, and the driver opens the door. Sebastian steps out and extends a hand. I take it, feeling his fingers wrap around me securely. The gesture's sweetly protective—and possessive.

Ignore the sensation. I look at a tall block of a building in front of us. It's one of the most boring I've ever seen. No windows. A high, sloped roof and a drab beige exterior. The parking lot is empty except for the limo.

"This isn't a restaurant. And even if it were, it's definitely not open," I say.

"It better not be open."

"Did you rent the whole place again?"

"Not exactly." He ushers me toward the building. He pulls out his phone and runs the screen over the security panel, then presses his thumb over the smooth screen.

The light on the panel turns green, and the door opens with a soft click.

"Sebastian, what's going on?" I ask.

"You'll see."

"If I trusted you less, I might think you were trying to kidnap me or something."

He laughs.

"I'm serious—"

The words die as the interior brightens. Bronze statues dot the huge, open space. On the wall are a few paintings, but my focus returns to the statues.

"Are these *François's works?*" I can't keep the awe out of my voice.

"Yes."

"But didn't Barron Sterling buy them all? He doesn't let anybody see them."

"That isn't why he put them into this windowless gallery," Sebastian says. "He doesn't want any sun damage."

I laugh. "I know that, silly. I was just wondering about the voodoo spell you must've cast to get him to open this gallery for us."

"I asked his girlfriend."

"You know her?" I recall reading that she's in her sixties or something like that. I thought it was very sweet that he was dating a woman close to his age rather than somebody who could be his granddaughter.

"Sebastian Jewelry did some custom work for her. I remembered how happy you were about your François, and I thought you'd like to see more."

I'm surprised he noticed. That was when our relationship was still new—and he was upset with me for forcing him into marriage. "Thank you. I thought you were taking me to three different restaurants."

"I told you I'd feed you, but didn't promise to limit myself to restaurants."

Of course not. Sebastian isn't the type to limit himself. Even when others try to place restrictions on him, he finds a way around them.

He is by far the most dynamic and intriguing man I've ever met. And I can't afford to let myself be seduced...again.

I stare at the latest piece, which I was dying to get but couldn't. *Absolute Love.* Unlike most of François's work, this one was titled in English. It caused quite a stir when Barron Sterling paid forty million for it, then promptly hid it after releasing a few photos of the piece.

I can't tear my gaze away.

"Is this your favorite?" Sebastian asks.

"I just think it's brilliant. Do you know anything about it?"

He shakes his head. "I'm not really big into art like you."

"He said he created it in a couple of months after he had a dream of his childhood." I gesture at the statue. A man and a woman are hugging tightly, their arms entwined. At first, you can't see it, but if you look closely, you can see a child between them, his face upturned and smiling.

"Nice," Sebastian says.

"He said in an interview there's no love like the love a man and a woman have for each other and the life they've created together—civilizations rose and fell for that love."

"That's a grand statement."

"He's an artist. Of course he's going to make grand statements about his work. When I first read the interview, I thought good for him for having that kind of childhood and experiencing that kind of love." My voice grows wistful.

"I'm sorry," Sebastian says quietly, taking my hand.

"Even though I didn't grow up knowing that kind of love...maybe I secretly wished I'd get to have it when I grew up—when I met somebody special." I realize I've said too much and pull away, disengaging our hands. Seeing my favorite artist's works up close somehow brought my defenses down.

Thankfully, Sebastian doesn't try to take my hand again or continue with the topic. I look at the rest of the collection. Admire the immense spectrum of themes and expressions. Some of the works appear more realistic, while others are abstract.

"I've never understood this one," I say, as we stand in front of the last piece. "*La Tranquillité.* There's nothing tranquil or peaceful about the work."

The piece looks like a representation of dark water being agitated in a huge container—minus the container. The lines are jagged and rough as the almost-black bronze soars to the sky.

"I think it's about what's to come. There's a peculiar kind of relief that you get after a violent storm," Sebastian says.

I shoot him a quick look. "I thought you said you didn't know much about art."

He shrugs. "I know something about life."

"Wouldn't a violent storm leave destruction behind?"

"Probably. But the air is clearer. And whoever is still alive has gained a little bit of confidence that they can survive something else like it in the future."

"So if another one comes..."

"They ride it out." He takes my hand again and kisses the back of it, the gesture full of tender affection.

And inside me, little cherry-blossom petals seem to flutter.

"I want to be there for you—ride it out with you."

"It's too late," I say, although I don't pull my hand away this time. And I easily could—he's not holding me hard. But it's like he's leaving the decision up to me.

"Nothing is ever too late."

I look at him levelly. "What will you do to even the scales for me, then?"

"Anything," he says, holding my eyes.

His response is too easy. I've heard so many men glibly say whatever they need to say to get what they want.

I pull my hand out of his and take five long steps back. He watches, his eyes dark. "If I tell you to crawl on your knees for me, will you?"

"For you?" A corner of his mouth lifts, as though he's saying, *That's all?* "Over the proverbial mile of broken glass."

Skepticism lingers. *Words.* Such easy words.

He drops to his knees. My lips part as a stunned breath leaves me.

He crawls toward me. He should look small—servile, even. But instead, he seems oddly powerful and resolute—like a man who knows what he wants and is going to do anything to get it. His eyes ensnare mine, and I can't move as he closes the distance between us.

He stops when he's only an inch away from the tip of my shoes. He looks up with a smile. "How did I do?"

I remain speechless. I'm not worth him throwing away his pride and doing this... I don't have anything left for him to take.

His face grows taut, like he can read what's flashing through my head. He wraps his arms around my waist and pulls me flush against him. "*You* are worth it, Lucienne Peery. *You* are the prize. I can do this over and over again until you believe that."

Tears prickle my eyes. I lay my left hand on his hair. "This is unfair.

You weren't supposed to fight this dirty. You were just supposed to ply me with pretty words over dinner."

He takes my hand from his head and threads his fingers through mine, his wedding band warm against my skin. He presses his cheek to the back of my hand and looks up at me like a man who has his prize in sight. "All's fair in love and war. And *this* is love."

44

LUCIENNE

Sebastian buys me dinner afterward and drops me off. He doesn't try to pressure me to have sex with him, and I certainly don't offer.

Would an overt refusal to sleep together deter him? Pretty much any woman has had the experience of men getting annoyed—and losing interest—if she didn't want to sleep with them.

But a man who dropped to his knees and crawled to prove himself to you doesn't sound like the type to give up over sex—or a lack thereof, my female vanity says gleefully.

I toss and turn all night. I can't deny I felt excitement—and was overwhelmed by his gesture when he tossed away his pride. But is that enough? Am I just going to forgive him after that one gesture, when I've lost so much?

What about his saying it was love? Do I really buy that? He said he'd sign the divorce papers, so he doesn't want me as his wife anymore. Maybe he just wants a girlfriend? No, that doesn't make sense. He could have any woman he wanted.

Then... Maybe he just feels guilty?

Of course. This has to be him overreacting to that sense of guilt. It can't be about love. He's going to think he's done enough by the third "date."

I get up around nine and exercise. Unlike my old place, this one doesn't have a fully equipped gym. A treadmill and a very basic bench and some dumbbells. No barre. Still, I get a decent run and stretch.

Matthias hands me some coffee when I exit the gym. I drink it gratefully. I'll do some yoga in the afternoon because... Well, I need something to do. It's just so weird not to have my day scheduled down to the second—no pressing meetings, no urgent emails or texts that require my immediate attention. My life has been one crisis after another—most of them due to Bianca.

It's nice just to be able to breathe and focus on myself.

I hold the mug and look out at the tranquil ocean. Is this what Sebastian meant when he said the sculpture was about the calm to come after the storm? I'm still unhappy about losing my position as CEO, but now that I've had some time to sort out my thoughts, I think I'm more upset over never getting a fair chance to prove myself than the actual ouster. I'm not egotistical enough to believe that I should be CEO regardless of leadership ability. Peery Diamonds isn't my personal toy. It's a company responsible for thousands of employees and countless customers and partners.

At least Karen is the interim CEO. I hope the board makes her permanent—she deserves it—rather than bringing in an outsider. She's one of the most capable executives I've ever worked with. I know she'll maintain good stewardship of the company.

I swallow the last bit of coffee and then shower. When I come down for breakfast, Matthias shows me an enormous bouquet of gorgeous purple hydrangeas.

"These just came for you."

My heart races. "Thanks." I take the card. I don't need to read it to know who sent it, but I'm dying to know what he wrote.

Hope the flowers make you smile. And no, this doesn't count as a date.

I laugh and pick up my phone.

—Me: Do you know that in Korean flower language, hydrangeas mean heartlessness and cruelty?

—Sebastian: Ah, but that's BLUE hydrangeas. PURPLE hydrangeas indicate sincerity and a true heart.

I grin.

—Me: Guess you did some research.

—Sebastian: Of course. When you left, the venture fell upon me. Hae Min wanted to kick my ass for what happened to you, and told me they didn't want to proceed.

Well, there's your answer as to why he went that far yesterday. Money and a foothold in Korea, which is a new market for Sebastian Jewelry.

I don't know why I suddenly feel so dejected. I knew it wasn't because he loved me or anything outlandish like that.

—Sebastian: Before you think I want the dates to salvage the project, I don't. They agreed to continue. But I have to liaise directly with them.

My emotions shoot right back up. This simple text exchange is like a rollercoaster for my heart.

—Sebastian: By the way, keep next Saturday free for our second date.

—Me: What are we doing? Another special gallery?

—Sebastian: Nope.

—Me: What am I supposed to wear?

—Sebastian: Anything you want.

—Me: You're unhelpful.

—Sebastian: I'm indulgent. :wink-emoji:

I shake my head with a laugh. *Indulgent...?* Is that what he calls his clue-deprived response?

Although I teased him about another gallery, I doubt he'll do the same thing twice. That wouldn't be like him.

My heart is doing cartwheels as I imagine what he's going to do on the second date. I mentally go through what I have in my closet and decide I don't like anything.

I'm going shopping.

I put on a bright red top, boot-cut jeans and a pair of cowboy boots I picked up in Texas on a business trip a couple of years ago. I've never worn them. They aren't the kind of thing a jewelry CEO would wear to the office, and most of my time has been dedicated to Peery Diamonds.

I put simple solitaires on my ears and head out.

"James hasn't brought the car around," Matthias says. "Let me just call him."

"Don't. I want to drive myself."

"Are you quite sure?" He's been anxious ever since the ouster.

"Yeah. I'll be okay." I smile, putting on my sunglasses. "Just want to have some fun outside the house."

He smiles. "Very good. I was a bit worried when you stayed in for so long."

"Did I?" Then I realize he's right. I didn't leave the house until Sebastian asked to see me. "Sorry I worried you. I'll try to do better."

"No need to apologize." His eyes are kind as he regards me. "You've always done your best."

An urge to hug him pumps through me, and I give in. As I wrap my arms around him, he stiffens in shock. "Thank you," I say.

I leave Matthias looking cutely nonplussed and head to the garage. Today seems like a bright red Ferrari kind of day. As I speed past the gates, my phone pings with a call from Yuna.

"Hi, Lucie! Do you have some free time?" she asks.

"Today? Sure. But if it's about your daughter's bracelet, you're better off contacting the L.A. store directly. I'm not at Peery Diamonds anymore." I try to sound bright and cheery.

"Oh, this isn't about that. I heard about what happened. I'm so sorry. It's partly my fault."

Her fault? "How?" The question comes out more sharply than I intend.

"I should've told Eugene to buy some shares in Peery Diamonds. We sometimes do that with our venture partners. But this time, with so many miscommunications, that just fell through the cracks."

The tension eases. Yuna didn't betray me. She's just upset she couldn't do a better job of protecting me.

"Thanks for that, but I'm fine." I consider for a second...then decide, *why not?* "You know what? I'm going shopping right now. You want to join me?"

She squeals a little. "Of course! Shopping is my number one hobby! Where are you going?"

"I honestly have no clue. It's for a date."

"With Sebastian?"

"How did you know?"

"I told my father and brother there was no way in hell we were going to do the project without you. But Sebastian said if that were a condition, he wouldn't be able to convince you of what you meant to him."

"Which was what, exactly?" It comes out before I can catch myself.

"He'll just have to show you," she says slyly. "I'm not going to make his work any easier. The man needs to grovel until you're satisfied. Anyway, he doesn't want you to think he needs you back to continue the project. He said he'd rather cancel it altogether."

I gasp. Sebastian never told me, even though he could have while we were texting earlier. "There's a steep penalty for pulling out without just cause."

"I guess winning you back was more important. Besides, 'a *steep* penalty'? It's just money. He can afford it." Yuna lets out a diabolical laugh. "He can't afford to lose *you*, though."

I bite my lip as uncertainty and hope go to war. What would he lose by losing *me*? I don't understand what I bring to the table for him.

Yuna adds, "He should pay for hurting *my friend*."

"You're going to make me cry." My voice cracks a little.

"Why?" She sounds genuinely confused. "I'm telling the truth, Lucie."

"But you hardly know me."

"I know you're smart, patient, honest, sweet and generous. You've never faked anything with me or my family, especially my kids."

"But I know who you are. Don't you ever think I'm using you?" Bianca's toxic accusation that I used her to make myself feel better rings in my head.

"No. You didn't yell at Liam when he spilled the milkshake on your dress, and you had no clue who his mom was. Trust me, I know when people want to use me. Most people who approach me want something. Not you. If I don't become friends with people like you, who *can* I be friends with? I'm going to cry if you tell me we can't be friends." She adds the last part with a sad sigh.

"We can be friends," I choke out, half laughing and half crying.

"Awesome! As for shopping, if you can't think of a store, let's go to my favorite. Is that cool?"

"Yeah."

"I'm sending you the address right now."

45

LUCIENNE

SEBASTIAN TAKES me on a gorgeous picnic in Napa for our second date. I tilt my head to feel the warm sun and the cool breeze. The silky green backless halter top and pale blue jeans Yuna and I picked out during our shopping spree are perfect for the outing.

"That feels so good," I whisper, then lie back on the blanket.

"I'm still shocked you've never been up here."

"Never had any time."

He pops a small piece of camembert into my mouth. It pairs well with the dry Riesling. Out of the ten different vintages, I think this one's my favorite. He seems to notice, because he pours me more of it. Then he lifts my head and slips his knee underneath so I can prop myself up enough to sip the cool wine.

It puts my head on his lap, and my heart does another weird cartwheel, but I decide what the hell. It feels too good and comfortable, and I don't want to move, especially when he's massaging my scalp. He has a surprisingly gentle touch that melts away all the tension and helps me relax.

"This is the first time I've really had time to just do what I want," I say. "I struggled for so long, like one of those salmon swimming upriver. Except at the end, I had nothing to show for it."

"That's Bianca's fault."

"Yeah, but that doesn't mean I wasn't getting tired. You're going to go all the way with her lawsuit, aren't you?"

"Yes." He hesitates. "Do you want me to call it off?"

"No. You should do what you want. I'm not going to worry about what happens to her. Life's too short."

"I'm making examples of the three—her, Roderick and Darren. After this, nobody'll screw with you at Peery Diamonds."

"Why do you want me back there? You don't need me to get Hae Min's cooperation."

"This isn't about them. It's about you." He picks up my hand and kisses the fingertips. The soft brush of his lips sends shivers all over my body. "I like seeing you relaxed and happy, but I also like seeing you fulfilled through your work. I want you to be in charge of Peery Diamonds if that's what you want. I want you to have a chance to do everything you want to do there without someone getting in your way."

He just knows, I realize, my belly fluttering. I never said a word, but he knows.

"If you decide that being the CEO isn't what you want after all, then of course you should pursue something else. And I'll be behind you one hundred percent. But you shouldn't have been forced out like that. Everyone deserves a fair shot. I want you to have yours."

"What if I tell you that I don't want to be the CEO at all? Then what?"

He shrugs. "Then nothing. I'll work with Karen and Hae Min myself. You can do"—he waves a hand in the air—"whatever."

"And Bianca? And Roderick and Darren?"

"I imagine they'll end up in jail. They need to pay for what they did."

Then I realize something else. "What happened to Karl and Vonnie?" They should've been the first to pound on my door, not Bianca.

Sebastian smiles. "Karl doesn't have the bandwidth to bother you, since the casino he owes money to is anything but happy. Apparently, the owner is furious, especially since Karl tried to hit on his baby sister. As for Vonnie, I'm guessing it's a combination of not wanting to honor the bet she lost and seeing what I'm doing to her father. If she so much as looks at you wrong, I'm going to destroy her, and she knows it."

His tone contains a firm finality—all the drama involving those two is permanently over.

"All those people are trash in your life, Luce," he adds. "Let me take them out for you."

"What if you throw out all my trash and tidy up my life, but I don't invite you back in?" I say, curious precisely what he's expecting in return. I just can't believe he's doing all this just to get me back.

"Then I'll have to try harder. But I'm doing this for you, so you can be happy."

"And if I see other men?" I say, looking up at him.

"That would be terrible."

"Terrible how?"

"Well, you know. Young men, in their prime. Dying so early." His tone is light, but his eyes blaze.

"You're jealous."

"Yep."

"And possessive."

"Only an idiot wouldn't be possessive of the only woman he wants."

Well, there it is. "The only one, huh? You sure about that?"

"Very."

I sit up. "Then show me."

He takes a sip of the dry Riesling he's poured for me, then gently but firmly takes my hair in his hand, the other arm going around me, and claims my mouth. His tongue glides over my lips, then slips inside. There's an aroma of the wine I've been enjoying so much, but it's the taste of him that's making my heart pound.

I miss him—the heat, the need, the sheer honesty of his reaction. He shocked me before with the raw, uncivilized plundering of my body. But right now, he's kissing me like a man granted a sip of cool water after a long travel in the desert.

Pleasure spreads, then coils around me. I wrap around him, lost in the kiss. My fingers dig into the soft silk of his hair, drawing him close.

He pulls back. Our rough breaths mingle. I blink up at him, the flush in his cheeks, the undisguised desire lurking in his gold-green gaze.

"Don't stop," I whisper, licking my lips.

He looks at me like he's pained, but doesn't close the distance between our mouths. "I love you."

I blink. "What?"

"I love you," he says again. "Do you believe me?"

A knot forms in my throat. Every cell in my body chills, then overheats. I don't...*can't* make sense of this sudden declaration. I'm not ready... I didn't think...

How can he love *me*?

"Do you want to take me back?" he asks.

I can't speak.

A sad, dry smile twists his lips. "This is why." He dips his head until his forehead touches mine. "I have to stop because you don't believe I love you."

"It never mattered before," I rasp.

"Because I was too slow to realize I was in love with you."

"But...I don't have anything to give you." My words come out in a thin, lost cry.

"I don't want something you have. I want *you*."

"What happens if I never believe you love me?" I whisper. Even now this feels like a dream.

"Never say never, Valkyrie."

46

LUCIENNE

DOES HE REALLY LOVE ME?

The question continues to swirl in my head. I sometimes find myself staring at nothing for hours, pondering it. Good thing I'm not working. I can only imagine how embarrassing it would be to get caught wondering if my soon-to-be-ex-husband was in love with me.

He's sent another bouquet. White asters. I look up the meaning in the Korean flower language reference book.

Have faith in me.

He should've sent flowers that meant "take a leap of faith." The emotional wave that rises every time I think of him saying "I love you" in that gorgeous green field isn't composed entirely of anticipation and joy. There's fear, too. Lots of it—that I could be believing him too easily. That I'm ignoring all the evidence of how simple it is for men to make empty promises. That I'd better heed all the warnings or I'm going to end up like Mom, who tried so, so hard to pretend everything was fine in her world, even as people, including her own child, pitied her for being blind.

But if he does mean it...

My heart knocks so hard, I put a hand over my chest. If he means it, I could have what I saw in *Absolute Love*.

He has only one date left to make his case. What's he going to do?

Am I going to be convinced?

But he still hasn't said he's going to contest the divorce. Jeremiah told me he was cooperating.

This is too confusing. And it doesn't help that he says he just wants me.

As if I, alone, am enough.

I stare at myself in the mirror in my bedroom, note the cool, guarded blue eyes, the stubborn set of my chin. What am I if I don't have anything to give back? What do I mean to people who don't want something...external?

Sebastian says *I'm* enough. By myself. And it's scary. What if I don't measure up? What if I'm *not* enough?

I look in the mirror again. Drop the shield I've been holding up for so long. See the uncertain blue eyes. And the bravado I'm putting up so nobody can ever see that I don't feel worthy the way I am.

If I could just be a better friend...

If I could just be the kind of heir my grandfather wanted...

If I could just be the kind of girlfriend men like...

I look at the asters again. *Have faith in me.*

I have to have faith in myself before I can have faith in Sebastian. And it's scary as hell. I grip the edge of the vanity, face the terror clawing at my gut.

"I am worthy."

I wait a beat, and my head whispers, *As long as you can—*

"No," I say. "Just the way I am."

But are you, though? It's a voice that sounds like Bianca, Grandfather and Roderick rolled into one.

Chills run through me. My knuckles turn white as I tighten my hold on the vanity. No way in hell am I letting those jerks mess with my head now. "Yes. I *am* worthy. Just the way I am."

You sure...? the voice questions again.

"Yes. I'm so damn fucking sure." It's unnerving to say it out loud. "I'm worthy of everything. I'm worthy of love. I am *enough.* And I'm going to say that out loud every time you try to mess with me."

Three heartbeats pass in silence.

I blink, stare at myself in the mirror. My cheeks are flushed, my eyes bright. I feel a little drunk—a little high. As nerve-racking as that was, it also felt liberating. I don't have to be anything I don't want. I don't have to meet any expectations except my own.

People will just have to take me as I am. I cover my face with my hands, then spin away from the mirror and walk out, wishing I could talk to somebody. I pick up my phone to text Sebastian, but stop. What am I going to tell him? That I've argued with my internal voice? That sounds pretty crazy, although my head couldn't be clearer and my heart is the lightest it's ever been.

For our final date, Sebastian again refuses to tell me where we're going. Instead of getting a limo, he picks me up in his Phantom. I climb inside, feeling the leather seat mold around my tense body. Anxiety, expectations and trepidation mix together into an intoxicating and scary cocktail.

"You look beautiful," he says, pulling the Rolls into traffic.

"Thanks." I smile. The golden dress I have on is an Avery Parker original that Yuna sent two days ago. Apparently, the dress "screamed my name" and she had to get it for me. I never told her that Liam's milkshake wouldn't come out, but she knew anyway.

The new dress fits perfectly, as though Avery had my exact measurements. Since the color is on the lighter side, I slipped on my favorite white stilettos with thin, delicate heels that I almost never find a good occasion to wear.

Sebastian looks amazing in his dark suit. I note his tie. "I thought the Eldredge knot was too complicated to bother with."

"I thought of it—and you—this morning."

I smile, amused at how much he must have cursed trying to master the new knot. "Are you trying to convince me?"

"Am I succeeding?"

"Not quite yet," I say primly.

"I didn't think a tie knot would do it."

"But...?"

"But every little detail adds up. Show the woman I love what's always in my heart, no matter how small the gesture."

I have to smile. "Does this mean I'm not getting a *grand* gesture?"

"Do you want one?"

"No," I say, shuddering. I grew up with grand gestures. Whenever Mom felt particularly unloved, Roderick had to do something big. "I'll take the little daily stuff any time."

We drive into the city. Eventually, Sebastian stops his car in front of Sebastian Jewelry's flagship L.A. store. "What are we doing here?" I ask.

"We're going to have our third date."

"Are you giving me diamonds?" If so, I'll be disappointed.

"No." He takes my hand. There's a sign outside stating the store's closed for the day.

"You closed it for our visit?" I ask in shock. This is one of the biggest and most profitable Sebastian Jewelry retail locations in North America.

"Yes."

He leads me inside the empty store, to a private room in the back. I've visited the store before—to check out the competition—but I've never been in this area. It's a beautiful space with lots of reflective surfaces and lights. There are three huge display cases, a couple of plush black leather couches and a glass-top table.

"This is used for the VIPs who need privacy and discretion," he explains. "Most of them are celebrities or foreign dignitaries."

He takes me to the center display.

I look down and see designs familiar from the collaboration meeting. Earrings and necklaces with hydrangea motifs made with amethyst, iolite, sapphire and tourmaline in the most gorgeous purple sparkle under the lights. They couldn't look more stunning. I close my eyes for a moment, picturing how a bride-to-be would look in our jewelry. She'd glow, like all women in love. And our jewelry would sparkle with her. Excitement bubbles. This launch in Korea is going to be amazing. I can feel it in my gut.

I open my eyes and smile at him. "They're perfect. People are going to go crazy for them."

His thumb brushes over my cheek. "You miss your work."

"I do. I miss making people look and feel beautiful."

"You should come back, then."

"But I'm out."

He shakes his head. "If you feel uncomfortable about that, you can come back as a consultant, rather than CEO. See how you like it. See if you want to take over the company's management again." He reaches inside the case, plucks a stunning violet iolite hydrangea pin and sticks it in my hair. "Made it just for you because this was your favorite design."

And he picks up something else from a different display case behind him and crouches down at my feet. I feel a cool weight around my ankle. I look down when he stands—and see a string of rubies.

The ruby anklet he told me about. The bright red stones glitter like hearts pulsing with hope and anticipation.

"I would've brought it sooner, but it took a while to reset the stones from bracelets into the anklet. I didn't like the stones on the ones we had on hand."

I'm touched he remembered, but I'm also confused. Does he plan to give me pretty things to prove himself now? The one thing I've never lacked in my life is beautiful baubles.

"What are we doing?" *What are* you *doing?*

"I'm giving the woman I love something nice that I made while thinking of her." He takes a moment to look at me. "You're the moon in my night sky. I'm just putting a few stars around you so you can shine even brighter."

"But why? We're getting divorced. You aren't even going to contest it. So why are we here?" *Do you really love me?* The most important question gets lodged in my throat.

"Not contesting the divorce doesn't mean I don't love you or don't want to be with you," he says quietly. "Our marriage didn't start out right. You deserve to be courted, made to feel special. I should've proposed to you properly, and I should've put my ring on your finger."

This time, he reaches into his pocket and pulls out a dark, square velvet box. He drops to a knee and pops the lid open. "I designed this ring for you. So I can beg for another chance from the woman I love."

It's a stunning Toi et Moi ring made with a sapphire and a diamond. But unlike the one I got, it has a constellation of smaller diamonds that sparkle around the bigger stones.

"You and me," he says. "Plus all the people in our orbit. You think you don't have anybody, but you do. Matthias. Yuna. And you have my brothers and their wives on your side as well. Regardless of your answer, you are the owner of all our shares. I'm having them transferred to you. I don't ever want to see you lose your dream. And I convinced the board to bring you back."

"How?" I manage as shock shoots through me like a bolt of lightning.

"By guaranteeing you'd hit all the milestones you said you'd hit during the shareholder meeting."

"That couldn't have been enough." I grip his forearm. "What else did you do?"

He shrugs. "If it doesn't work out, I'm on the hook for a few hundred million, payable to Peery Diamonds."

"No!" I gasp.

"I have to put my money where my mouth is, Valkyrie."

"But Sebastian—!"

He smiles up at me. "I have faith in you. You should, too."

Tears sting my eyes, and my cheeks get hot. Never in my life did I dream that someone would do this for me. "You're crazy," I say between sniffles.

"Crazy in love with you."

"Ask me," I demand, doing my best not to burst into tears.

"Will you marry me?" He takes my left hand and kisses the spot where the rings used to be. "I'll devote every moment of my life to making you happy."

"Yes."

He gives me a smile more brilliant than the gemstones on the ring. He slides it on my finger, where it sparkles perfectly.

As he stands, I wrap my arms around his neck and kiss him. He kisses me back, and heat rises between us. I clench my hand in his hair, pulling him close.

I can't get close enough.

I can't get enough of this man.

I miss him so much.

All my inhibitions and walls are crumbling. He loves me...really loves *me*... And I can't keep him out.

He carries me to one of the couches and lays me on the thick cushions. Impatience rising, I rip at his tie, his clothes. The fancy knot comes undone with a slithery whisper of silk. The suit that costs tens of thousands of dollars falls on the floor in an unceremonious heap. I tug at his buttons. My hands shake so hard, I can't unbutton his dress shirt fast enough.

He pushes my clumsy fingers out of the way, grips the sides of his shirt and pulls hard. Buttons fly, pinging as they hit the marble tiles. He undoes and drops the cuff links on the table.

His hands land on each side of my head, and he begins to lower his mouth to mine. But I put my hand on his shoulder to stop him when I notice something on his chest.

"What is that?" My voice trembles as incredulity works its way through my heart.

There is black writing over his heart that wasn't there before. It reads:

EXCLUSIVE PROPERTY OF LUCIENNE PEERY
TRESPASSERS WILL BE REMOVED WITH EXTREME PREJUDICE

I lick my finger and wipe it over the writing to see if it comes off. It stays.

He laughs. "It's a tattoo."

"Oh my *God*. When did you get this?"

"The day you served me with the divorce papers."

Shock slackens my jaw. *"Are you insane?"*

"If it makes you feel better, I'd planned to get it done earlier. I just didn't have a chance until that day."

"But you went ahead and did it anyway?"

He nods. He's looking at me tenderly, but now I'm beginning to wonder if our contract said I was supposed to get custody of his sanity upon divorce. "What if we never made up? What if I never took you back?" My voice shakes as his overwhelming love wraps around me like a cocoon.

"What does that matter? Our marital status doesn't change the fact that my heart"—he takes my hand and places it over his thudding chest—"belongs to you."

My eyes grow teary. "I thought you didn't do grand gestures."

"I don't think putting your name on what's yours can be considered grand." He brushes his lips over my forehead and eyebrows.

"You crazy man," I choke out. "I love you too."

His smile is brilliant.

"Just kiss me, okay?" My voice is thick with emotion as I pull him down.

Laughing, he does as I ask. Runs his warm, reverent hands along my face, then my neck and the rest of my body like he's holding something infinitely precious in his arms. My dress falls off my body, and I cling to him in nothing but my heels, jewelry and his gorgeous ring on my finger.

As he gives me everything I ever dreamed of and more, the emptiness that's been gnawing my heart for so long vanishes, replaced by love and joy.

I'm finally home.

47

SEBASTIAN

—ONE YEAR later

It takes exactly one year to have our proper wedding. Not because I didn't want to make her mine sooner. But because I wanted our initial marriage to dissolve first. I didn't want any part of the old union to stand in our way.

Some of the gossip sites speculate about our wedding-divorce-wedding, but Luce and I ignore them. We have bigger things—our lives, our future—on our minds.

In addition, I wanted to give her the space and time she needed to accomplish something concrete as CEO. We hired three wedding planners, but anything less than a year of wedding prep would've been too much on her plate.

As it is, she showed the board she's the boss. She not only met all the milestones and financial targets, but she exceeded some of the metrics by ten percent or more. She credits her COO for her success, saying nobody executes like Karen, who was happy to have Luce back.

Not only that, the Sebastian Peery collaboration in Korea is a smashing hit. We actually sold out our initial inventory within the first seventy hours and had to ship more immediately. Eugene said Sebastian Peery is one of the most sought-after *yae-mul* in Korea, and Hae Min's department store in Gangnam can't keep up with the demand.

Luce tried to give the shares back to me and my brothers afterward, saying she's secure in her position, but we declined.

"We can't take back what we gave you! Don't you know that if you take a gift back you get warts?" Noah said.

"That's the most ridiculous thing I've ever heard," Luce said.

"Give him a few minutes," Griffin muttered. "He'll say something more ridiculous."

"No, I heard it while traveling," Noah insisted. "I've seen evidence."

"He's probably right," Nicholas said.

Luce gave me an *are-they-serious?* look, and I shrugged. "I want to be on your side, but I'm in a difficult position here," I said. When her expression changed to *Et tu, Sebastian?* I finally caved a little. "It's possible he misunderstood, but let's not risk it. Don't you want me to stay handsome for you?"

She finally laughed. And didn't bring up the shares again.

But there have been times—when she's having a particularly rough day—she stands in front of a mirror and says, "I'm worthy, just the way I am."

At those times I hold her quietly, to let her know I'm proud of her—and that I've got her back. She won't suffer alone when her old doubts resurface.

Our ceremony is lavish, no expense spared. We invite everyone—my brothers and their wives, all our friends and everyone else who want the best for us. The château in Southern France is perfect for the wedding. The green field is strewn with purple hydrangea petals. They actually look a little bit like lavender Japanese cherry blossoms in the gentle breeze.

"Gorgeous weather," Grant says, squinting at the immaculate blue sky. "You'd never believe it was storming just yesterday."

"The ground isn't too bad, either," Emmett notes. "I thought it'd be muddy and gross."

My phone buzzes. I check it, to make sure there isn't anything off with today's ceremony.

—Dad: What the hell? You're really getting married again? In France?

I roll my eyes. It's Joey. He always texts using Dad's phone, pretending to be the all-important Ted Lasker.

—Me: Hi, Joey. Yes. We're getting married for real.

—Dad: What about that other one????!!!!!

—Me: The one you were invited to?

—Dad: Yes!

—Me: You were the only one invited. Do the math.

—Dad: You asshole!

"Everything okay?" Griffin asks.

"Yes. Joey's pissed because he realized I'm getting married for real today, and Dad wasn't invited."

"Why did he think Dad was going to get invited?" Nicholas asks.

"Because he's insane. Dad promised to introduce Luce to a plastic surgeon for a boob job."

My brothers make a face.

"God only knows what he would've promised this time if I'd been dumb enough to invite him."

"A ride on a cock cannon," Huxley says. "He told me the next son of his to invite him to the wedding will get to ride a cock cannon."

"A *what*?" Aspen says.

I shake my head. "You really don't want to know."

Griffin checks his phone. "It's time."

Yuna walks toward the piano with a wink. She's in a pale lavender dress and matching shoes. An iolite earring and necklace set from the Sebastian Peery launch sparkles on her ears and throat. I didn't know until we were trying to decide on music that she went to the Curtis Institute of Music, and she's volunteered to play at our ceremony.

Yuna hits the familiar notes from "Here Comes the Bride." Since Roderick's in jail—not that he would've been asked to attend under any circumstances—Matthias walks Luce down the aisle.

Holy shit. My heart nearly bursts at the sight of my bride. Little diamonds twinkle like countless stars on her ivory chiffon and silk dress as she approaches. Under the thin veil she's smiling, her blue eyes on me.

As she closes the gap between us with each step, my heart pounds faster, anticipation building unbearably.

When she's finally within arm's reach, I extend a hand. She lays hers on it, and I close my fingers.

Mine. My future. My wife.

TITLES BY NADIA LEE

Standalone Titles

Contractually Yours

The Ex I'd Love to Hate

My Grumpy Billionaire

Baby for the Bosshole

Beauty and the Assassin

Oops, I Married a Rock Star

The Billionaire and the Runaway Bride

Flirting with the Rock Star Next Door

Mister Fake Fiancé

Marrying My Billionaire Hookup

Faking It with the Frenemy

Marrying My Billionaire Boss

Stealing the Bride

The Sins Trilogy

Sins

Secrets

Mercy

The Billionaire's Claim Duet

Obsession

Redemption

~

Sweet Darlings Inc.

That Man Next Door

That Sexy Stranger

That Wild Player

~

Billionaires' Brides of Convenience

A Hollywood Deal

A Hollywood Bride

An Improper Deal

An Improper Bride

An Improper Ever After

An Unlikely Deal

An Unlikely Bride

A Final Deal

~

The Pryce Family

The Billionaire's Counterfeit Girlfriend

The Billionaire's Inconvenient Obsession

The Billionaire's Secret Wife

The Billionaire's Forgotten Fiancée

The Billionaire's Forbidden Desire

The Billionaire's Holiday Bride

~

Seduced by the Billionaire

Taken by Her Unforgiving Billionaire Boss

Pursued by Her Billionaire Hook-Up

Pregnant with Her Billionaire Ex's Baby

Romanced by Her Illicit Millionaire Crush

Wanted by Her Scandalous Billionaire

Loving Her Best Friend's Billionaire Brother

ABOUT NADIA LEE

New York Times and *USA Today* bestselling author Nadia Lee writes sexy contemporary romance. Born with a love for excellent food, travel and adventure, she has lived in four different countries, kissed stingrays, been bitten by a shark, fed an elephant and petted tigers.

Currently, she shares a condo overlooking a small river and sakura trees in Japan with her husband and son. When she's not writing, she can be found reading books by her favorite authors or planning another trip.

To learn more about Nadia and her projects, please visit http://www.nadialee.net. To receive updates about upcoming works, sneak peeks and bonus epilogues featuring some of your favorite couples from Nadia, please visit http://www.nadialee.net/vip to join her VIP List.

Printed in Great Britain
by Amazon

41701855R00199